AMONG THE WILLOWS

I0564275

JUNE LARK

Copyright © 2025 by June Lark

All rights reserved.

This is a work of fiction. All names, characters, businesses, places, and incidents portrayed in this book are products of the author's imagination or are used fictitiously and are not to be construed as real. Any resemblance to actual events, organizations, places, or persons, living or dead, is entirely coincidental.

No part of this book may be used or reproduced in any manner whatsoever without written permission from the publisher or author, except as permitted by US copyright law.

ISBN: 979-8-9904659-9-2

Published by: June Lark Books

CONTENT WARNING

Explicit language, incarceration, abandonment, loss of a parent (off page), narcissistic parent, domestic abuse (off page), assault, suicide attempt (off page), mental health representation.

I hope you enjoy the world of Thornbrush Ranch, but first and foremost, take care of yourself.

Everyone deserves relationships free from domestic violence. If you or someone you know is experiencing abuse, help is available.

National Domestic Violence Hotline offers free, confidential support 24/7.

Visit: **thehotline.org**.

Or call 800-799-7233 or text START at 88788.

You are not alone.

To those who feel like running is the only answer, there's a cowboy out there ready to chase you, fight with you, and fight for you.
Until then, honey, there will always be
Jude "The Bull" Larsen.
And to my hubby, thank you for always fighting for us and believing in me.
This one's for you, babe.

Playlist

"Goodbye Earl" by The Chicks

"She Thinks My Tractor's Sexy" by Kenny Chesney

"Streetlight" by Sam Barber

"Watermelon Moonshine" by Lainey Wilson

"Cowgirls" by Morgan Wallen (feat. Earnest)

"Body Like a Back Road" by Sam Hunt

"Heart Like a Truck" by Lainey Wilson

"Ends of the Earth" by Ty Myers

"Wind Up Missin' You" by Tucker Wetmore

"The Git Up" by Blanco Brown

"Miles on It" by Marshmello, Kane Brown

"Cover Me Up" by Morgan Wallen

"Gunpowder & Lead" by Miranda Lambert

"Last Night" by Morgan Wallen

"Worst Way" by Riley Green

"horses" by BRIM

"Hooked on an 8 Second Ride" by Chris LeDoux

"Last of My Kind" by Shaboozey (feat. Paul Cauthen)

"Wild as Her" by Corey Kent

"A Lot More Free" by Max McNown

CHAPTER 1
Romy

I needed a big glass of wine.

Scratch that!

A whole damn bottle of cab.

Once again, I was getting laid off from another teaching job because of budget cuts.

I heaved a big sigh, unlocking the front door of my San Jose apartment. This was my fourth school in four years. How they expected any new teachers to make a career out of this was beyond me. Putting up with the behavior of thirteen-year-olds, trying to teach them about history and literature to meet the standards, without any support from administrators, only to end up on the cutting block. As Principal Wayland said, "We'll have to let you go." He said it as if I was held against my will and he's doing me a favor now by setting me free. I can't say I'm disappointed, but I am frustrated I haven't even been given a chance to get my feet underneath me.

I dropped my keys and purse off at our entry table, kicking off my high top Converse and letting my tired feet sink into the plush carpet. All I wanted was my quiet apartment, my "girl dinner" of cheese and crackers, and to watch a bunch of hot singles on a beach be forced to abstain from hooking up.

The lights were already on, and I could hear the shower running in the en suite.

Hmm, he's already home?

He was never home before nine during the week. Now that was something I was actually disappointed about.

A year together, and I'd already gotten used to Travis's late work nights. I'd often be in bed by the time he came home, usually reading until I fell asleep. The last thing I would hear as I drifted off would be the microwave running as he warmed up leftovers. At some point, he'd slip into bed. In the morning, I'd find him beside me, sound asleep on his stomach.

It was starting to feel like we were two roommates who slept in the same bed and occasionally fucked. But now, even the sex felt as if we were just doing it to get off. If I was being honest with myself, the connection had died a long time ago, and we were just staying together because we couldn't break our lease.

I walked into our bedroom and headed to the walk-in closet. Shedding my jeans and T-shirt and pulling on my favorite gray sweatpants and oversize tee, I noticed Travis's phone had slipped out of his discarded work slacks and was just lying there.

Casting a glow every so often, as it lit up with messages.

@CATARINAXOXO *CAN'T STOP THINKING ABOUT YOU.*

My breath froze in my chest.

Instagram notifications blinked on his lockscreen.

@CATARINAXOXO *THAT THING YOU DID WITH YOUR TONGUE.* 😊

@CATARINAXOXO *WHAT WILL I DO WITH MYSELF UNTIL NEXT TIME?*

What the actual fuck was I seeing?

Travis was cheating on me?

I grabbed the phone off the floor and marched into the bathroom. Steam hit me in the face and filled the room. The shower must be on scalding. *Good.* I hoped he scorched his balls off or killed whatever germs he contracted from Catarina XOXO. I did not take the time to think. His shower was no more searing than my rage. *Fuck him!* I chucked his cell phone over the shower curtain and heard it hit Travis with a soft *thunk* before crashing to the shower floor.

"What the hell was that?" he called out.

"Your cell phone, asshole!" I yelled. My chest heaved, my body vibrating with rage.

"Romy, what the fuck? It's getting soaked."

"Put it in rice! Then you can catch up on all your DMs."

"You were looking at my phone?" asked the cheater.

"You left it in your pants on the floor, and Catarina XOXO was lighting up our closet!"

Soap bottles slipped from their shelves, hitting the shower floor as Travis fumbled to turn off the shower.

The shower curtain flung open with a metal slide of the rings. Grabbing his towel from the rack, he wiped off his phone, then hurriedly wrapped the towel around his waist—his annoyingly trim waist because the man was a nutrition freak. He ran a hand through his dripping-wet, dark hair before

3

setting his cell phone on top of the toilet.

He scrambled out of the shower, careful not to slip, his body tense, as if preparing himself for my onslaught of emotions. *Fuck him!* Fuck this.

"I was waiting to tell you until our lease was up in August, but I met someone," he said evenly. His voice was calm. Too calm, like a doctor telling a patient their fatal prognosis.

"Are you serious right now? Fuck our lease, Travis! What were you going to do? Sneak around, sleep with me because you felt obligated while you fucked Christina or whatever her name is?"

"It's Cat."

"Excuse-fucking-me, Travis. Are you for real?" I shrieked.

"You and I barely see each other anymore. We've been drifting apart for months now."

"And whose decision was that? You didn't have to take those hours."

"The sales are better in the evening. You know that was the best decision for us. You agreed to it."

I threw up my hands, rolling my eyes toward the ceiling. "Keep telling yourself that. Whatever lets you fucking sleep at night because officially, there is no *us*."

"Romy, please."

"*Please* what?"

I waited for him to finish. His mouth opened as if to speak. "What, huh?"

He shut his trap with a click of his teeth.

"That's what I thought." I shook my head, running my tongue across my teeth. "I'm going to Brit's house." Brit was my one friend. Since college at San Jose State, we've helped each other through many breakups.

"Wha-what about the apartment?" he stammered.

"Fuck the apartment! If you're so concerned about keeping your deposit, you can ask your sidepiece, '*Cat*,' to move in with you."

I marched out of the bathroom, charging to the closet to find an overnight bag. I snatched a tote from the shelf and started shoving clothes into it.

"Don't dismiss our relationship as if it was nothing!" His voice rose as he followed me around the bedroom.

"No, you did that all by yourself," I said, opening my underwear drawer.

"I care about you. I've stuck around."

"Not enough if you're banging someone else!" I grabbed a handful of lacy underwear and bras, jamming them into the side pocket of the tote.

"You never want me anymore," he excused. "You're always tired."

"Because the only time *you* want me is in the middle of the fucking night, and I have to get up at five thirty in the morning!" I snapped. "It has always been on *your* schedule."

I turned, heading toward my nightstand, but Travis moved to step in front of it.

"Get out of my way, Travis. I'm leaving."

"Can we at least talk?" He reached out to touch my arm, but I quickly drew it back. He raised his hands in surrender.

I didn't like to be touched when I was angry.

"I'm not ready to hear anything you have to say."

"Romy, please, let's just cool down, take some breaths, and talk about this?" his big, brown eyes pleaded. Eyes that made me fall for him from the beginning. Now, they were only fucking infuriating.

He was always trying to talk to me when I was angry, instead of giving me the space I needed to process and regulate my emotions. All it did was make me feel as though my feelings were invalid and pissed me off even more.

It made me want to punch him in the face.

"Move!" I blurted out.

Travis stood his ground for a minute, searching my eyes.

"Ugh! Fine!" I pushed him out of my way to get to the nightstand to grab my book, lotion, and vibrator.

"Yeah, don't forget to take your precious lovebug."

I shoved the mini ladybug vibrator into my bag, burying it beneath the layers of clothes and hair products.

"Pretty fucking sure you gave that thing way more attention than you ever gave me."

"So it's my fault you cheated? Fuck you, Travis!"

It was at that moment a truth dawned on me.

Travis was never home before nine.

"Wait." My eyes narrowed on him. "Why are you home right now?"

"I—I … what do you mean?" He stammered as if he knew he was caught.

"You don't get off work till eight thirty." Like I had to explain his schedule to him.

"I—I—I …"

The stammering son of a bitch!

I closed my eyes for a moment, taking a deep breath to center myself. "How long has this been going on?"

"Wha-what?"

"How *long* have you been cheating on me, Travis?" I could feel the red-hot lump of rage growing in my throat.

Travis's body crumpled, folding in on itself as he sat down on the side of the bed. Defeated. His hands drooped between his legs.

"For four months," he relented.

"Four fucking months! You took me to your sister's wedding in March! I met your family! And you were fooling around with someone else this whole time? Are you for real? I bet you don't even work till eight thirty, do you?"

"I'm off at four." He confessed so quietly, it barely registered.

"Unbelievable!" I threw up my hands.

I was so done with his bullshit.

"Don't call me, don't text me, don't you dare show up at Brit's. We're fucking over."

Then I walked out of there with my shoulders squared and a stiff upper lip, just like my mama taught me.

It wasn't until I was in the safety of my white Honda Civic before I could yell "FUCK!" at the top of my lungs. Tears of hot anger coursed down my cheeks.

CHAPTER 2
Jude

"What! What the fuck happened?" Heat washed over me, and my jaw went slack.

"I don't know exactly." Uncle Chuck's voice sounded raspy over the phone, as if he'd been yelling all day. "But Jesse was shot in the head, and Hazel was found driving her truck down Highway 20 like a bat out of hell. She had the gun on her, Jude. There's still crime tape around the bunkhouse, and the ranch has been crawling with cops. It's like nothing I've ever seen. Nothing like this has ever happened in Willows."

Shit! I pushed my cap back, scratching my forehead, before turning it backward. Was I hearing him right? I checked the clock on the waiting room wall. I wasn't going to find out very much five minutes before my appointment.

"Have you been able to talk to Hazel? What about Romy?" Just her name coming out of my mouth was like a gut punch, yet it felt *damn* good. It had been too long since I said it aloud. I bit my lip just to keep myself from repeating it. *Fuck! Get it together.* "Has anyone gotten ahold of her?" Romy had a complicated relationship with her sister, Hazel, but she needed to know.

"Frank spoke to Hazel. She called from jail, but she's not talking. He said he's been trying to get ahold of Romy all day, but she hasn't answered his calls. I texted her to call me, but she hasn't replied yet."

"Wait. What? You have her number? How did you—" All these years, and my uncle had it. Of course he'd have it. Romy and Hazel practically lived at the ranch. Uncle Chuck loved those girls as though they were his own.

"Romy and I text from time to time. Just to check in. Mostly around the holidays, we—"

"Can you give me her number?" I cut him off in a hurry. All I was concerned about was Romy and how she was going to take the news that her sister was in jail for murder. I didn't know if she would speak to me, but I felt that I should try.

I heard a loud sigh. "Sorry, bud. She asked me years ago not to share it with anyone."

"What the hell?"

"I'll tell you what. If I can get ahold of her and she's okay with it, I'll give you her number."

But I knew she would not be okay with it. Not with the way we ended our friendship.

The office door opened, and Dr. Deborah stepped out with her last patient. I turned in my seat, quickly flipping my cap back around and pulling it low to hide my face.

"Hey, I gotta go. Can I call you back later?" I asked quietly.

"Sure thing, bud. I'll keep you posted."

"So how long has it been since you went home?" Dr. Deborah asked, looking up from her notepad.

"Twelve years. I haven't been back since …" I remembered the last day I was in Willows, Oregon. Uncle Chuck's call made it all rush to the forefront of my mind. It felt as if I got bucked off a horse or thrown in a fight. The air rushing out, my lungs frozen in my chest.

"Since when?" she prompted.

"About twelve years ago, right before I left for college. I had a full-ride wrestling scholarship to Ohio State." It started out as one of the best days of my life, then ended in one of the worst. It was the day Romy and I finally gave in to our childhood crush … or maybe it was just *my* childhood crush. Fuck if I know. Romy never said shit to me after that. She did the only thing she knew how to do—run.

"That's a long time to be away from home. You haven't wanted to go back?"

"No. No, I haven't wanted to go back." I released a heavy breath, leaning back into the couch. "My heart was fucking left shattered there."

Her brows pinched, studying me over the rims of her glasses. "Should we visit that today?"

No, I didn't want to fucking visit that today. Or any day, really. I had bigger things to worry about now. More pressing matters. More fucked-up matters. Like a murder on my family ranch.

"Another time?" I offered, grimacing. "My uncle Chuck is dealing with a lot of shit at home, and I'm not there."

"How do you feel about that?"

I should be used to the therapist's "how do you feel" questions, but they still bothered me, even after four months of therapy. It always made me uncomfortable, as if I had an itch I couldn't scratch. I had to release a big breath before reminding myself to check in with my emotions, identify them, then communicate how the fuck I felt. No one ever taught me how to do that.

Growing up, I was surrounded by good ol' boys. Grandpa and my uncle Chuck raised me after my mother took off when I was a tot. They were always saying "just rub some dirt in it," or "quit your blubberin'," or "I'll give you something to cry over." Larsen men did not *do* feelings. We were men of action, showing we cared through the dedication of time and effort.

Huh, maybe that's why the women in our lives never seemed to stick around? They probably needed more than just a kitchen remodel.

Good for me. That had to be growth right there!

Yet I still hit rock bottom. It was my third knee surgery in five years. My MMA career was essentially over. At least, that's what the doctor said. Time to set down the gloves.

It was Jessica, my girlfriend, now my ex, who said, "It's been a good run, sweetie."

I still didn't know if she was talking about our relationship or the fact that she could no longer sit cageside for a four-time light-heavyweight champion. Perhaps the relationship expired long before it ended. We wanted different things. More than anything, I wanted a family—someone waiting for me when I stepped out of the cage, someone to make me a dad, to be the mother of my children.

She didn't want that, though. Her career came first. But even if she had, she wasn't who I wanted. It was better if she just remained my publicist and not my girlfriend. So, while she managed her other clients, she suggested it was time to get some help with my depression. I knew she was right. I wasn't happy. I hadn't been happy for a long time. Now the one thing that had ever made it manageable was being stripped from me too soon.

MMA was my life. It was my career. It was all I ever knew once I lost my scholarship to failing grades and had to find something to pay the bills. Uncle Chuck told me that if I came home, he'd put me to work. But I hadn't wanted to. I didn't want to be a failure and have to go home.

I was young, wanting to make my own mark on the world, and even if my uncle was there, there was no way in fucking hell I'd return to the place where my heart was ripped from my chest.

Fighting was in my blood. I loved the adrenaline rush, the strategy of facing off against an opponent, the blood and sweat. Every time, it felt like a total release. A purge of the angry parts of my soul. I reveled in the feeling of complete exhaustion after going three rounds, the high of victory. The cash reward and sponsor payouts were the cherries on top.

The cash was still there, nice and fluffy in my bank account, in mutual funds, in the Vegas house, or in whatever Uncle Chuck was willing to take for the ranch. If anything rubbed off on me from my country-boy roots, it was frugality. Money was not the issue. I could live comfortably for years. No, the real issue was that my passion was being stripped from me before I was ready, and now I had no choice but to go home.

Dr. Deborah stared at me silently, her pen poised over the notepad.

How did I feel?

"Like shit, that's how I feel. I've done nothing to pay my uncle back for all the years he took care of me." I stretched out my right leg. Sitting for long periods of time still made it lock up. I needed to remind myself to do my physical therapy exercises when I got home. "Now, with this fucked-up situation at home, I feel as though it's all out of my control, as if I'm helpless." I shook my head, still in shock.

Dr. Deborah scratched some words on her notebook and clicked her pen closed, bringing me back to the present. "You're going from one disappointment to another; what you're feeling is totally valid. You're still living in the trauma and grief of a possible career end. It will be a big lifestyle change … a change in how you see your value. A lot of this is out of your control. Is there anything you can do right now that *is* in your control?"

I nodded, leaning over my knees and clasping my hands to keep them from balling into fists. "I need to go home."

CHAPTER 3
Romy

I sat in the school parking lot after work, checking my phone. There were two texts from Travis, apologizing for how things ended and asking when I'd like to get the rest of my stuff, a text from Brit, telling me she'd grab a pizza on the way home from work, four missed calls from a 541 number, and a random collect caller.

The 541 number had to be Frank. I told my father years ago to lose my number, but he'd always convince my older sister, Hazel, to give it to him. It was always because he needed money or to gloat about some rodeo star he was working with. The phone call would always end with him calling me a "fucking bitch." I've changed my number three times now because of him. It usually resulted in me having to chew my sister out for betraying my trust and ignoring my boundaries. Then I'd block her until I started to feel homesick.

The phone buzzed in my hand. It was the collect caller again. Who in the world calls collect anymore?

Curious and stalling—I needed to grab a few things from the apartment and did not want to run into Travis—I answered it. "Hello?"

An automated voice came over the phone, "This is a collect call from—*Hazel Miller*—from Arnold County Jail," my sister's soft voice announced through the recording, and my stomach clenched.

Oh God! Hazel, what happened?

"This is a recorded line. Do you accept the charges?"

I gulped and barely released the word, "Yes."

My heart pounded in my chest. I fumbled for my credit card in my wallet while I listened to the automated voice give instructions. My hand trembled as I dialed in the card number.

Please, don't hang up, Hazel!

"Romy?" came my sister's voice over the line.

She sounded so small and far away.

"Hazel, what happened?" I clenched my jaw, shielding myself from the answer. I was scared to know.

"Oh my God, Romy." She burst into tears. "I'm so glad I got ahold of you. I gave Dad your number in case I couldn't reach you."

My eyes shuddered, a bitter taste in my mouth. Of course she did. I wanted to snap at her, but I bit my tongue.

"I only have five minutes, and they listen to the line. There's something I need you to do for me."

Never in my life did I ever think I'd have to answer someone's jail call. Never would I have imagined it would be Hazel calling. She was the golden girl of Willows, hardworking and passionate about horses, outgoing and bubbly, although a bit bossy. She was their rodeo *queen*.

"I need you to go to Thornbrush Ranch. You know, the

Larsens' place?"

The Larsens' ranch? I didn't want to step foot in Willows, much less Thornbrush. I hadn't been back since that day. The day I fucked up. The day I decided to hook up with my best friend and ruined the only true friendship I had. The day Jude and I acted on our lust. Embarrassed, confused, and hating myself, I ran and never looked back.

"Yeah, but Hazel, what can I possibly do?"

"I need you to pack my stuff that's in the bunkhouse. There's something there for you, too."

"Okay …" She was being rather vague, but I was worried that if I asked her too many questions, she may say something that could get her into trouble.

"Could you maybe rent a storage unit and store my things there until I get out?"

Get out? *Get out* sounded hopeful.

"I just don't know about … well, is Jude there?"

"Jude?" She sounded confused.

I suppose it was a random question, all things considered. She didn't know Jude and I hooked up before I left twelve years ago. Or that I ignored his calls and all my friends—friends who were never really my friends, but hers—before getting a new phone. Because, truthfully, I was never good at making friends. I wasn't as likable as Hazel. I always felt like the default to them when she wasn't around. The only one who never made me feel that way was *him*.

"Is Jude at home?"

"Fuck no," she scoffed. "He hasn't been home since he left for college. Chuck's been rather upset about it since he's had to take care of Lloyd without any help. I think he sends them money, but he never comes home. You know he's a big shot cage fighter now?"

Yeah, unfortunately, the guy I dated before Travis was a sports fanatic, and our dates were often in sports bars. He'd always make sure he got the seat facing the TV over the bar. I saw a few of Jude's fights from over my shoulder.

And, wow, he looked good. Better than I remembered. Ripped. Older. Sweaty. Tatted up. *Hot.* I'd end up thinking about him the whole date, flashbacks of his fit body hovering over mine while he gripped my hands above my head.

Dates with "sports bar guy" didn't last long after that.

"Yeah, I heard something about that." I sighed in relief. "Okay, I'll buy a plane ticket tonight for this weekend. I'm not sure how long I can stay, though. There are two weeks left of the school year."

"The school year? Are you still in college?"

Hazel and I barely spoke now. Between our separate lives, and my own bitterness that she continued to choose our father over me, our communication had dwindled. My nose stung. My big sister was in jail for who knows what, and I hadn't spoken to her in months. Pretty sure our last text was "Happy New Year."

We had drifted apart. I let all that time pass without her knowing me and me knowing her.

There was a time when I'd do anything for her—especially if it meant getting her undivided attention. I worshipped the ground she walked on when we were younger. I wanted to do everything she did. She put on makeup; I wanted to put on makeup. She got blonde highlights; I wanted blonde highlights. She learned to barrel race; I wanted to learn to barrel race. She did everything perfectly. We were only a year apart, as close as two sisters could be, and I idolized her. I followed her everywhere.

When I was younger, I didn't mind, but when we became teenagers, constantly being compared to her, or ignored if she wasn't with me, made me feel like I never truly belonged. Even my high school boyfriend told me during our breakup that he would have asked Hazel out instead of me if she had been available. It hurt knowing everyone preferred Hazel over me. I was the least desirable of the Miller girls. Not only did the town make it clear, but so did our father.

When Mom died of breast cancer, Hazel took the reins. She made sure I got to school. She helped our father with the chores. He saw her as an extension of himself, while I was the fuck up. According to Frank Miller, I was ungrateful, rude, and disappointing. The sun rose and fell with Hazel, and my father couldn't wait for me to get out of the house.

An automated voice came over the line, reminding us this was a timed call.

I sat up straighter. "No, I'm a teacher."

"A teacher! That's amazing, Rom. Mrs. Lin would be so proud. I knew you'd get out of our Podunk town and be somebody."

Somebody who keeps getting laid off.

"Thirty seconds," the recorded voice interrupted.

"I'll be there as soon as I can. Don't worry."

"Thanks, sis."

"Do you need anything else?"

"Five seconds."

"Just to tell you I love you."

And the dial tone whined in my ear.

Chapter 4
Romy

It was midnight by the time the winding mountain pass turned into Willows's two-lane Main Street, shaded by ponderosa pines. And my bladder was killing me!

I didn't let my father know I was coming, nor did I want to stay with him. Traveling on short notice, I hadn't had time to search for a place to stay.

The nearest motel was thirty miles down the road, and I was too tired to make that drive. Most tourists either stayed in the cabin rentals at The Butte on the outskirts of town or camped down by the Deschutes River, both of which you had to book months in advance to find a vacancy.

Willows was one of those small towns most people drove through on their way to the mountains, destination hiking trails, or resort towns. Main Street was lined with specialty shops, galleries, a grocery store with a butcher and smokehouse, two cliché western restaurants, the burger and shake stop—I vowed I'd get one of their cookies-and-cream shakes before I left—Willows Coffee Company, which roasted their own beans and served breakfast, and, of course, the Rooster. Not much had changed in the past decade outside of a fresh coat of paint here or there and an updated sign above the coffee shop to look country chic, appealing to the tourists who traipsed through.

The Rooster, the only bar in town, blazed its red, neon rooster above the shake roof. It was the brightest beacon on Main. The Open sign flashed in the window. Thank goodness it was dark out, and so was the bar. No one should recognize me if I just dipped in to use the restroom.

I pulled my rented, red Hyundai into the small parking lot, the wheels crunching on the gravel. Every F-150 and their mom appeared to be here, and I reminded myself it was Saturday night in Willows. There was nothing else to do but get drunk at the Rooster.

A man and woman pushed open the front door, Kenny Chesney's "She Thinks My Tractor's Sexy" flowing out with them. The woman in a jean skirt and paisley print top clung to the man in denim and canvas coat, giggling. I glanced at them, wondering if I knew either of them as I parked the car.

Nope. Strangers. Thank God!

Hopefully, I'd be just another stranger, too.

Stepping out of the car, I flung my purse across my shoulder and went inside.

Just keep your head down.

The bar was packed. Patrons on barstools chatted with two bartenders pouring beer on tap and stirring vodka cranberries. Every table was full, and there was a cacophony that only came from a full, drunk bar—laughter, talking, hollering, classic country playing over jukebox speakers, billiards breaking in the back. It was warm with all the body heat and smelled like stale beer and fried food. Neon beer-and-cowboy signs decorated the walls. A large, hand-painted, red rooster was posed in midcrow over the full bar.

The restroom sign hung over the lone hallway to the left of the front door, and I hurried down the hall to the women's restroom, pushing open a vacant stall.

I breathed a sigh of relief. I hadn't even realized I was holding it.

A couple women came in, chatting while they used the toilets. I vaguely recognized one of their voices. Flashbacks of hiding in the girls' bathroom in high school, overhearing classmates talk shit about me, made me question whether or not this was a good decision.

The women took their time washing their hands, primping in the mirror, while they laughed about some cowboy hitting on their friend. I held my breath, expecting them to say my name, to have noticed me come in. But they didn't. I puffed out a big breath of relief. I waited until they left before I stepped out.

This was going to be a long night, and I needed to figure out where I was going to stay. I washed my hands and decided I could ask for a glass of water before I got back in my car to figure this shit out.

My head ducked, I headed toward the bar. A single barstool was vacant at the end. I slid on and waved a hand at one of the bartenders. Her curly, dark hair was thrown into a messy bun, and freckles dusting the bridge of her nose contrasted against her bronze skin. She had made an excellent choice in red lipstick, brightening her white smile.

"What are you having, darlin'?" she inquired, setting a napkin down in front of me.

"Can I get an ice water, please?" I asked.

Her dark brows rose. "Just an ice water? On a Saturday night? I make a mean margarita. You're looking like you need some tequila in your life tonight."

She wasn't wrong, but I didn't think tequila would solve my problem. Tequila and I were not always simpatico. Not since college. But tequila did make the worries seem to fade, and I did have a lot of them. Most of which I would not be able to solve tonight.

"You know what? Fuck it. Why not." I had made worse choices in Willows.

Messy Bun's bartender smile widened, and her brown eyes brightened. "Atta girl! One margarita coming right up. I'll still bring you that water, though." She finished with a wink.

I shrugged off my purse and hung it on the hook beneath the bar. I always loved it when bars had purse hooks. Maybe the Rooster wasn't as much of a dive bar as I thought. Being that I was eighteen the last time I was in town, I'd never stepped foot inside the Rooster. Like most teenagers, I did all my minor age drinking by the river or in a friend's basement.

"Salt on the rim?" Messy Bun called from where she was fixing the drinks.

"Please!" I called back.

She nodded, pouring water from the fountain into a glass of ice before spinning a second tumbler in a saucer of salt.

Turning in my seat, I risked a glance at the people in

the bar. Most of them were older, except for a group of guys shooting pool in the back. A shallow lamp illuminated the pool table, and I gulped because I recognized a few of them from high school. I quickly turned back to the bar.

"Here you go," she said, setting the water and margarita-on-the-rocks on napkins.

"Thanks, girl …" I began, hoping to get her name.

"Sage." She smiled. The name didn't sound familiar, so I figured she was someone who just came into town for work. She looked like she was about my age.

"Romy. Thank you, Sage."

"Do you wanna open a tab?" she asked.

"No, we can close it."

She nodded before heading to the register to print the receipt.

I took a sip of the margarita, and happy endorphins immediately shot through me. It was like summer in a glass. I exhaled. This was exactly what I needed. I'll just finish my drinks, maybe use the restroom one more time, and head back to the car. Maybe I could park by the river and get a few hours of rest before heading to Thornbrush in the morning.

"Holy shit!" one of the billiard boys yelled, disrupting the whole bar. Everyone turned to look his way. He set down his cue, his disheveled, chestnut hair swooping his forehead, his eyes crinkling with his beaming smile as he looked toward the door.

Shit! It was Christian, one of Jude's old wrestling buddies. Pretty sure he was with another friend from high school. I ducked my head and turned back to my drink, hoping he wouldn't see me.

Maybe being here was a bad idea.

Then he bellowed, "Jude 'The Mood'!" He prolonged the *oohs*. The energy of the bar ratcheted up with the announcement. My stomach dropped.

"It's 'The Bull' now," a deep voice boomed back, cutting through the jukebox music and inebriated chatter.

I froze, clutching my ice-cold drink. My breath hitched, and heat washed over my body.

No, no, no, no, no. It can't be.

This margarita was about to become my lifeline. I stared into the lime-green liquid.

My stomach did a flip into my throat.

Don't look. Don't look.

I took another gulp of the margarita, hoping to settle my stomach and steel my nerves.

The guys abandoned their pool game, breaking through the crowd toward the door. The air shifted as they collided behind me.

"So good to see you, bro!" the other guy greeted. I heard them slap hands in what one could only describe as a who-can-grip-harder man handshake.

Don't turn around.

Don't. Turn. Around.

Then he laughed. His booming, raspy chuckle that seemed to be sexier than I remembered.

And my damn body betrayed me.

I involuntarily turned around toward the rowdy reunion. Even after twelve years apart, I could not deny the pull that was uniquely Jude and me. Just like the rest of the bar ... just like everyone always had been ... I was drawn to him. After all these years, his presence still did something to me. *Shit!*

He was a contradiction. He always had been. It's where he got his nickname, Jude "The Mood," in high school. He was your typical, angsty teenager. Moody and brooding. Maybe a little bit mysterious since he mostly kept to himself or his close-knit circle. All the girls in high school were gaga over him—probably another reason to hate me because he had no interest in any of them. But even on his grumpiest days, he exuded chill, cool, and collected. That was probably why he was a state wrestling champion his junior and senior year. He never cracked under pressure. Something I always appreciated about him. Something everyone liked about him.

Jude never seemed to care. He was the one who always sought me out, annoying Chase. I did my best to keep him, and the little flutter in my chest, in the *friend* zone. But he made it challenging whenever Jude "The Mood" gave me a flirty smirk or refused to let me walk to class alone—even if it meant he was perpetually tardy to his own classes. It was the kind of flutter that scared me, that would only end in heartbreak when we inevitably went our separate ways. But it was this flutter that even after twelve years, I still craved.

I also ended up dating Chase way longer than I should have, just to try to keep Jude at a distance. That is, until I was truly leaving, and Hazel insisted I come to Thornbrush. She wanted me to watch her last barrel practice since I was going to miss her parade as rodeo queen.

And just like it was then when he walked up behind me in

the riding arena, drawing my attention directly into his fierce, blue eyes, I couldn't help but turn now.

As soon as I glanced up, his eyes went from his friend to catching mine like a fish to a lure.

Was it hot in here? It felt *really* fucking hot in here.

He looked better than I remembered. Better than he did on TV. Jude Larsen stood two steps away from me. He was taller than most people in the bar, his six-foot-plus frame thick with muscles. Even the arms of his black hoodie seemed to advertise "this body could treat you real good." I gritted my teeth just as I squeezed my knees together.

Get it fuckin' together, Romy.

His dark hair was longer now, curling beneath his baseball cap. As he turned it backward—that had been a nervous tick of his—my pussy clenched. I always thought it was so damn sexy. And it was still *damn* sexy.

His bright blues pierced into my soul. I could feel them even in the dim light of the bar.

I gulped.

It wasn't fair that he only grew hotter in the last twelve years. A shadow of scruff accentuated his square jaw. A little crook in the bridge of his nose from a break made him look rugged. He must have taken care of himself, too, because he didn't have cauliflower ears like most fighters. My eyes went to his throat, where his Adam's apple bobbed as he swallowed. He had a black-and-gray tattoo along the right side of his neck, and I yearned to get closer to see what it was, to run my tongue up it and make him shudder.

Ugh! Don't be a moron.

It was like he could read my thoughts. One side of his mouth tipped in that lopsided grin of his.

"Romy." He said my name on a long exhale. It came out in a deep rumble, and it went straight to my core.

A flush burned up my chest and face.

Damn tequila.

CHAPTER 5
Jude

"*Romy.*" I said her name as if I'd been holding my breath for the last twelve years and I could finally breathe again. Relief washed over me.

I thought it would take days to track Romy down, to convince Uncle Chuck to give me her number. Yet here she was. It was as if the universe heard my plea.

My heart hurt to know I'd missed all those years watching her become more beautiful.

I couldn't help but check her out. From her white high-tops to her shocked and vulnerable eyes.

Even in that formless, army-green bomber jacket she wore, I could see her curves. Faded black jeans frayed above her shoes. And was that a tattoo? Rips in her jeans from her knees to her thigh gave me peeks of her creamy skin. One of her legs was decorated with what appeared to be blue, orange, and red feathers. The last time I'd seen those thighs bare, they were wrapped around my waist, absent of decoration other than my fingerprints. A ribbed, white tank clung to her, and I couldn't help but imagine my hands sliding up the flare of her hips, along the curve of her waist, until they skimmed the fullness of her breasts. She had a woman's body now, and all I could do was swallow down the lump in my throat.

Feeling my eyes on her, she brushed her blonde hair over her shoulder. It was darker now, with brighter sections woven through, and hung to her waist in waves.

Her dark lashes fringed her gray eyes, blinking as if to clear her vision.

Pink stained her cheeks underneath minimal makeup. A gasp left her mouth, her lips opening in a small O shape.

Fuck.

And it went straight to my cock.

"What are you doing here?" she asked.

At the same time, Christian wrapped his arm around my shoulder and said, "Wait! Romy Miller? No fuckin' way! I knew this drama would bring out the cockroaches, but I never guessed you'd show up."

I broke my eyes away from Romy and gave him a withering glare.

Romy fidgeted on her stool, tucking her hair behind her ears. She had a couple of stud earrings, and a small, silver hoop pierced her right cartilage. A vision flashed in my mind of my teeth skimming her earlobe before sucking it into my mouth.

"Yeah, well …" she started. She was uncomfortable.

I tamped down the vision.

"This is like a high school reunion," Rob chimed in, glancing between Romy and me.

Christian was looking at me with a knowing smirk.

They were old wrestling buddies from high school. They

both knew we had hooked up. I'd told them when I'd been in the depths of heartbreak, but it was in this moment I wish I hadn't. High school was not kind to her, and I had done everything in my power to protect her from it. Until I gave in to what I thought we both wanted. Ruining the best friendship I'd ever had.

God, I missed her.

The last thing I wanted was to make Romy uncomfortable and cause her to run again.

"Sage! Pour us some shots!" Christian called.

The bartender with bright-red lipstick glared at him. "Four tequilas?" she asked, while placing a receipt in front of Romy.

Romy turned her back to us. "None for me, thanks." She pushed her half-drunk margarita away and took a big gulp of water before reaching into her purse to slide her credit card across the bartop.

The bartender, Sage, nodded before looking back at us.

Christian shrugged. "Make that three then."

"Just two," I corrected.

She was about to bolt, and hell if I'd let her walk away from me this time.

Sage poured two shots of tequila before swiping up Romy's card from the bar and heading to the register.

The boys stretched over the bar, causing Romy to lean away from them. My hands twitched at my sides, ready to catch her if she tipped off her stool.

"How long are you in town?" I asked, wanting her gaze back on me.

"Just the weekend." Her eyes flitted to mine before shifting back to the purse in her hands. "I have work on Monday."

I wondered what she did for a living, and my brain flipped through everything I could say—if only it meant keeping her here. But every question sounded stupidly shallow or too intrusive. I'd never been good at small talk.

Sage returned with her receipt and card, and Romy scribbled her signature. I couldn't help but peek over her shoulder, noticing she still signed it Miller and her left hand was absent of a ring.

Good. Not married.

"It was good seeing you guys," she said, shrugging her bag over her head. She didn't look back at any of us as she slid off the barstool.

"Great seeing ya, Romy!" Rob called after her.

"See ya," Christian said dismissively.

She waved over her shoulder as she walked out of the bar. I couldn't help but appreciate how incredible her ass looked in those jeans, round, pert, and begging me to grab a hand full.

Hot damn! My cock twitched at the same time my heart squeezed.

I was watching her leave again.

A firm hand hit me in the chest.

"What the fuck, bro?" I turned to see Christian looking dumbfounded at me. "Aren't you supposed to be 'The Bull' now? Go get her!"

Shocked and dazed, I hesitated.

"Don't be an idiot." Rob gave me a shove in the direction of the parking lot.

I nodded absentmindedly. Romy was *here.*

Christian and Rob stared at me wide-eyed, expectantly.

"Okay, I'll be right back," I told them, hurrying after her.

"Forget it. We'll catch you tomorrow." Christian waved me off.

Saluting goodbye, I pushed through the door.

A cold drizzle fell, hitting my face, and I turned my baseball cap back around. Romy stood beside a red Hyundai, shuffling through her purse, almost frantically.

"Romy, wait."

She looked up. Her eyes were downcast, and her cheeks appeared paler in the single streetlamp illuminating the parking lot. Twelve years, and I could still read her. Heartbreak was written all over her face. Her response—*run*.

"I gotta go, Jude. Can we do this another time?" She sounded exhausted.

Do this, as if talking to me was a chore?

Growing up, we never ran out of things to talk about. It never felt stilted or forced. It was a natural banter that grew into something more. A connection between two souls that recognized each other.

Had I imagined the tectonic-shifting chemistry we had when we were eighteen? Granted, we were *only* eighteen. Horny teenagers with little sexual experience. But had I imagined how good it was? Had I convinced myself that it was the best sex I ever had simply because it was with Romy?

I mean, I've learned some things since then. I had my fair share of relationships over the years, but I was always comparing them to Romy. The chemistry and connection were never there. Not even with Jessica, though at the time, I had wanted it to be. Had I built it all up in my head?

I cleared my throat. "I know this has to be a lot for you, with Hazel and all, but I'm here to help in any way I can."

Romy's shoulders sagged in relief.

"Thanks. Do you know what happened?"

Had no one told her?

"Has Frank not said anything?" I asked. I didn't know if I should be the one to tell her, but the last thing I wanted was for the Willows's rumor mill to do it for me.

She shook her head. "Hazel called me from jail asking to put her things in storage, but it was a recorded line so she couldn't say more."

I nodded, turning my cap backward. The rain pelted me in the face, and I realized Romy didn't have a hood.

"It's raining." *Great, Captain Obvious.* "Do you want to sit in the car?"

She studied me for a beat while she considered before shoving her hand back in her purse in search of her keys.

"My truck's right over there." I threw a thumb over my right shoulder, and Romy followed my gesture to Uncle Chuck's old Chevy pickup. I'd borrowed it when Rob texted to meet at the Rooster.

I watched the gears turn in her pretty head while the rain still fell, leaving dark spots on her jacket. She was taking too long to decide. She had always been indecisive. It would take her an hour just to pick a movie from our DVD collection, and it would be eleven o'clock before we decided just to hang out and talk instead.

Stuffing my hand in my pockets, I grabbed the keys and

walked a few steps to unlock the passenger-side door. The door opened with a creak, and I made a mental note to grease the hinges for Uncle Chuck tomorrow.

"Get in the truck, Romy."

Her head fell, watching her feet as she approached the truck.

I always had to get bossy with her, but back then, she had fought back with all her sass. It got my blood boiling, and I loved it.

Now, though, it appeared that her fight was gone, and I hated it. I clenched my jaw.

Her arm brushed mine while she passed, sending a shiver up my spine. Reaching for the door handle, she vaulted herself into the cab. I took a deep breath because Romy Miller was about to be inches away from me. In a closed vehicle. I shut the door. The hinges whined closed, and I hustled around the front to jump in the driver's side before she changed her mind.

Now in the pickup with her, I felt the air thicken. I ran my hands along the cracked leather steering wheel. I was nervous. Women didn't make me nervous. But this one did. She always had.

The leather squeaked while Romy settled in the seat, and I turned to look at her. She was devastatingly beautiful. Her dark lashes fluttered as she looked everywhere but at me. She lightly bit her bottom lip. Was this as nerve-racking for her as it was for me? I gripped the wheel, keeping myself from reaching out to touch her to make sure she was real. Seeing her again had only ever been a dream, never a reality. I had hoped, but I never thought it would happen. And not like this.

"Tell me," she demanded, waiting expectantly.

I sucked in a deep breath, held it for a count of ten, then exhaled. Just like I learned in therapy. I'd be doing a lot of mindful breathing while Romy was in town.

Best to rip off the Band-Aid. I'd tell her everything Uncle Chuck told me earlier, but I'd leave out the assumptions. Only Hazel really knew the full story, and Romy would need to hear it from her sister.

"Earlier this week," I began, "Uncle Chuck heard gunshots go off at the bunkhouse. It was late, and he was worried wolves were on the property again. So he grabbed his rifle and ran out to see if one of the ranch hands needed help."

Romy's eyes were as big as saucers, and I watched her swallow slowly. I could almost hear the pounding of her heart.

"When he got out there, he saw your sister jump in her truck and peel off down the road. He immediately knew something was wrong. When he went to see Jesse, one of the ranch hands, he found him crumpled on the floor with a bullet in his head. Uncle Chuck was the one who called the cops. They found her going down highway with the gun on her, and she was arrested."

"Oh my God!" Romy's hand flew to her mouth. "Hazel." Unshed tears glistened in her eyes, and I hated that I put them there. "Was she hurt?"

I thought for a moment. Uncle Chuck hadn't said anything about her being injured, so I shook my head. "She was pretty upset, but no, she wasn't hurt."

She didn't respond, only squeezed her eyes shut.

"I'm sorry, Romy."

I couldn't help myself. I shifted, hitching my right knee in the seat just enough to take the ache away, and rested my arm along the back. My fingers were inches away from the hair over her shoulder. I wanted so badly to touch her, to comfort her.

"What is she being charged with?" she asked, her voice barely a whisper.

My nose stung hearing the emotion in her words. I swallowed before I spoke. "Illegal carry of a firearm, evading arrest, and murder in the first degree."

"Oh my God!" she repeated. "This can't be real. Hazel is so … responsible. A pain in my ass sometimes, but she'd never kill anyone." Tears slowly cascaded down her cheeks, and I curled my fingers into a fist to keep myself from wiping them away. "How did this happen?"

She said it rhetorically, and I didn't have the answer, but God, did I crave her words. "I don't know."

"What am I going to do?" she asked.

I knew that helpless feeling all too well.

"I don't know," I answered again, but this time I added, "but we can figure it out together."

Her wet eyes blinked, and the look on her face changed as if she was seeing me for the first time. As if she was also realizing this was real and not a dream.

The rain pinged off the truck, and the streetlight glowed through the fogging windows. Her scent had already invaded the cab, floral and sweet with a hint of coconut. If only we were seeing each other under different circumstances, as I'd imagined so many times in my head. I'd thread my fingers through her hair, drawing out every breath and moan as though we were eighteen again and our only problems were the jackasses at school.

My fingers twitched. Damn it, I couldn't help myself. My fingers relaxed behind her on the seat, and I reached out to brush a lock of hair from her shoulder.

If I didn't know her, I wouldn't have noticed a reaction, but I felt her eyes flare like silver flames as they met mine. She didn't shrug off my touch, giving me permission enough to rub the silky strands between my thumb and forefinger.

"I'm so sorry, Romy. I know this is upsetting. Where you staying? Let me follow you there, make sure you get there safely."

She pulled away then, brushing her own fingers through her hair so I'd release her. It stung to feel her walls go back up.

"No, I'll be fine." Romy messed with the fringe from a rip in her jeans. I was trying so hard to avoid staring at the ink on her soft skin. "I'm just going to Frank's, and then I'll be at Thornbrush early. Are they letting people into the bunkhouse?"

I nodded. "They took down the police tape this afternoon. I think they got everything they needed."

She nodded, too, in understanding. Her eyes left mine to peer out the windshield. She gathered her purse and reached for the door handle.

My hand landed on her thigh to stop her. It definitely stopped her. She flinched. *Fucking idiot.* I quickly drew back my hand, my fingers curling in on themselves as if to savor the heat caused by the warm firmness of her thigh.

"At least find your keys before you head out into the rain."

But without another word, she was already gone

CHAPTER 6
Romy

I dozed in and out most of the night while I slept with the front seat reclined. At some point during the night, I climbed into the back seat to huddle beneath my jacket. It helped hearing the rush of the Deschutes River over the cool mountain breeze through the cracked window, but I couldn't get Jude out of my head.

His damn crooked grin, those bright-blue eyes that seemed to look more piercing against his tan skin, that scruff along his jaw ... what would it feel like to have it scrape along the inside of my thigh? And that peek of a tattoo on his neck. I knew he had more; I'd seen them when he was on TV. There was a large, black-and-gray bull skull across his back, and he had intricate details covering his arms. A full sleeve had never looked so sexy. I thought about what it would be like to gently trace every single one with my fingertip.

Despite the night air, my entire body flushed. My pulse echoed between my legs. I had to squeeze them together and shut my eyes in a vain attempt to push him from my dreams.

Thoughts of Jude morphed into thoughts of Hazel. Could

she truly have murdered someone? There had to be some explanation. There had to be a reason Hazel would go to such lengths to hurt someone like that. The sister I knew growing up didn't have a violent bone in her body, but shit if I knew. I didn't even know whether or not she had been dating someone.

"What did you do, Hazel?" I whispered to myself over and over again. Trying desperately to wrap my mind around this.

I was deep in my thoughts—spiraling—while the sky lightened and birds began to chirp.

A rap came at the window and I jolted up to see who it was.

I froze.

Just like last night.

Jude stood outside, his hands on his hips. Even in joggers, last night's hoodie, and headphones around his neck, he looked sexy as hell. He wasn't wearing his baseball cap. Instead, his damp hair curled in waves across his forehead. I wondered what it would feel like to run my fingers through it. He had always worn it short or buzzed in high school. But longer looked good on him. *Really* good.

He also looked pissed.

I took my time, stalling the inevitable explanation he'd demand, swiping the sleep and smeared mascara away from my eyes. I peered in the rearview mirror. My hair was a rat's nest from sleeping in the car. The humidity from the rain didn't help. I ran my fingers through it, hoping I didn't look too crazy. Shrugging on my jacket, I looked back at him.

He was scowling now. With a deep sigh, I opened the car door. Jude stepped back to let me out.

"This doesn't look like Frank's house," he chastised. A deep furrow split his brow.

"It was late, and I didn't want to disturb him." Truth was, I had no desire to see, or speak, to my father. Especially not right now. "What are you doing here?" I turned it on him, pretending as though finding me sleeping in the car wasn't totally embarrassing.

"You're parked on Larsen land," he said matter-of-factly.

"I am?"

I thought I was just picking a convenient spot off the road, but close enough to head to the ranch in the morning. I needed to pack up Hazel's stuff and get back before work on Monday.

His head was tipped in confusion, like I should know I was. Maybe subconsciously I ended up here, not realizing it in the dark.

"So you're checking the fence line or something?" I asked stupidly. After twelve years of not seeing each other, he made me nervous.

"I was out for a jog. Or at least trying to." His shoulders sagged. Stepping closer, he slammed my door shut. "Come on, I'll make you breakfast."

"Oh, you don't have to do that. I should head over to the bunkhouse and start packing up Hazel's stuff."

He didn't turn around, just started walking, assuming I'd follow. There was a slight hitch in his step while his shoes crunched in the gravel. His ass looked phenomenal in those black joggers. I couldn't help but stare before lengthening my strides to catch up.

"You'll need to eat, and I'll find you some boxes. I was going to make myself some eggs anyway."

"Wait! What about my car?" I asked, husting after him.

"I'll come back and get it for you later."

We walked in silence that was anything but comfortable. His presence beside me was like standing on asphalt in direct sunlight on a ninety-degree day—*blistering*.

I tried my best to ignore him as he gave me sidelong glances loaded with unspoken words. I knew he must have some old, harbored grudge against me for how I left things.

We walked down the road as it wound along barbed-wire fencing. Cows and calves grazed in the nearby pasture. So many days growing up, I would come out here just to watch the cattle. I found it soothing while they lumbered along and chewed their cud.

Evergreens shaded the edge of wild grasses and sagebrush. Between the pines, I could see the rock cliffs that corralled the Deschutes, and beyond. Hills and valleys rolled toward the Cascade Range.

A feeling of homesickness I never felt while I was gone soured my gut. For all the times I wanted to escape this place, I forgot how breathtaking Oregon was.

The rain had stopped during the night, leaving the grass damp and seeping through my Converse. Puffy, white clouds floated across the blue sky, promising sunshine.

Jude turned right, the gravel road becoming mud where it needed to be regraded. His hand reached out to my elbow, guiding me to walk the edge of the road.

Our eyes connected then, and he sniffed a sharp inhale through his nose, releasing me as if I burned him.

"Walk on the side or you'll get those white shoes dirty.

Didn't really pack for the ranch, huh?" He turned his head to look straight ahead, and I did the same.

I knew things would be different between us—awkward even—but I didn't expect the ache in my heart seeing the hurt in his eyes.

"I'm only here for the day. My flight takes off early tomorrow morning."

"You sure that's enough time?" he asked.

No, I wasn't sure, but I needed to get this done and leave. "It will have to be," I said.

We passed the large, whitewash sign. The letter T brand, which curved into bull horns, topped the green lettering and date:

THORNBRUSH RANCH, EST. 1934

Home of Willows Rodeo Champions

Home. The ranch had always felt more like home than my own. Hazel spent more time at Thornbrush than anywhere else, and because she was here, so was I.

Then it became, since Jude was here, I didn't want to be anywhere else. Memories of us racing our horses through the fields and along the bluffs overlooking the river. The power of my horse beneath me while the wind rushed through my hair. I felt free. I hadn't felt that way since—

My feet stalled. The double-wide Jude had moved into his junior year when Chuck had moved into the big house to help Lloyd stood surrounded by uncut grass and a grove of pine trees. It looked nothing like I remembered. It was now painted white with a covered porch running the length of it. Fern baskets hung from the cedar awnings. It looked surprisingly cute. It was hard to imagine Jude as the one living in this charming, little house—at least not the Jude I used to know.

I followed him up the porch steps to the front door. The door was now matte black with a brushed-bronze door handle.

I paused on the steps. It looked different, more modern, but I still remembered running out that door feeling like a fool for sleeping with my best friend. I never thought I'd be back here.

Jude pushed open the door and peered over his shoulder.

"You coming?" he prompted.

Was he remembering the same thing I was? Did he ever think about that night? It scared me shitless to still obsess over it, even more so to think he didn't think of it at all.

I still recalled how we crashed together, hurrying to strip each other of our clothes. We couldn't seem to get them off fast enough. His firm hands on my hips as he lifted me and threw me on his bed. How he crawled up my body, the brush of his skin against mine sending shivers in his wake. How his lips made me moan as his mouth trailed along the inside of my thigh. We started out just touching each other and kissing. It wasn't until that moment that I knew my body could feel that way.

I hadn't planned for it to go farther than that. I kept telling myself I shouldn't be doing this. We were friends. I was leaving and this was horrible timing … like most things in my life. I couldn't deny him anymore, though. He was driving me crazy with his tongue and fingers. Any doubt I had in that moment was buried with heated want. As he lowered kisses down my stomach and spread my wetness over my clit, I thought I might fly off the bed. I remember him hesitating, asking me if I was sure. And for the first time ever, I had decided I wasn't going to be indecisive and took what I wanted. And like a fucking, stupid, eighteen-year-old, I rolled him over, found a condom in his bedside drawer, and climbed right on top of him.

And like the coward I was, while he slept, I had snuck out and ghosted him.

Now I bolstered my courage and nodded, following Jude into the house.

"Oh, wow," I commented, looking around.

It did not appear to be the same double-wide at all. The floors were now gray plank with colorful, Southwestern-style rugs. Walls had come down to create an open-concept kitchen and living room. The kitchen had white cabinets and quartz countertops. The same brushed-bronze hardware on the front door was also on the drawers and cabinets, even the faucet over the farmhouse sink. A brown, leather sectional faced a large, flat-screen TV. Steer skulls and canvas prints of cows and horses decorated the walls. Jude had done some work. From where I stood, I could see the short hallway off the entry leading to two bedrooms, one made into an office, and a full bathroom.

"Yeah, I hired some guys to fix it up thinking Lina might move in here, but she still prefers her room in the big house."

I remembered little Lina Larsen, Jude's cousin. She was fourteen when I saw her last and seemed to be following in Hazel's footsteps as a barrel racer. She was funny, bright, and always up for fun. Always pushing her big cousin, Jude, into doing stupid shit. Like riding one of the older colts bareback until he was bucked off. She would be sitting on the fence posting of the round pen, crying with laughter, while Jude lay on the ground, sputtering. I'd be right there keeping time with a stopwatch. As soon as he caught his breath, he would call out, "Time." I'd tell him how many seconds he stayed on, and the idiot who never backed down from a challenge would be right back on that son of a gun, attempting to beat his record. Pretty sure Chuck yelled at all of us and made us muck stalls for a week after that.

"What's Lina up to now?" I asked conversationally, anything to help break the awkwardness.

"She's on the circuit—barrel racing. She's at a rodeo in Indiana this weekend."

I nodded, following Jude into the kitchen. He set his headphones on the counter and began rummaging through the cabinets.

"Do you come home often?" I asked. He seemed unfamiliar with the layout of the kitchen.

"This is my first time back in twelve years." He found a pan and straightened to look at me. Pointedly.

Yep, because of me.

That's what that look told me.

I gulped. "Jude, look …" I began.

"Romy, I knew you were leaving. I was leaving, too, but you didn't respond to any of my calls. You ignored my texts. We never went a day without talking to each other, and then that just stopped completely." He set the pan down on the gas range. "You vanished on me—on everyone—except, apparently, Uncle Chuck. Why would you ask him to keep that from me? We were best friends. We were …" He ran a hand through his hair in frustration. "I've been worried for years, wondering if you were okay."

His last words were like a shot to the heart. He was worried about me? I felt guilty asking Chuck not to tell him we talked. Honestly, I assumed, at some point, he would have said something to Jude.

I'd been selfish, confused, and ashamed. Now being back here, facing him, all those old feelings rushed to the surface. "I was just messed up in my head back then. After my mom died, my dad and I were not getting along, and kids at school … I just felt like I needed to leave, start fresh and find myself, you know?"

He scoffed. "Fucking *find yourself*? That's your explanation? I had to wait twelve years for you to tell me that. You couldn't say that to me then? You were my best friend, Romy. What was I to you if you felt like you had to fucking cut me out of your life so you could fucking *find yourself*?"

He turned to wash his hands in the sink, as if he couldn't stand to look at me. I slumped down on the stool at the counter. I wanted to wash the shame away and watch it circle down the drain.

He didn't know that the other reason I never returned was because of him.

"That's the last of them." Jude grimaced as he stomped on the stack of cardboard boxes in the truck bed.

"Is your knee okay?" I was hesitant to ask, but I had noticed he favored his right leg as he climbed the ladder to pull down broken-down boxes from the garage loft.

The garage in the big house was larger than my apartment in California. The four-car garage held Chuck's and Lloyd's trucks, and an old vintage Chevy. The fourth bay was set up as a home gym, complete with treadmill, weight bench, pull-up bar, rowing machine, a rack of weights and exercise bands, a heavy bag, and the mat where Jude used to wrestle Rob and Christian.

"Tore my ACL and meniscus. I had surgery four months ago." His words were short. Clipped. They had been since chewing me out before breakfast. I suppose I deserved it after my bullshit excuse for leaving him.

My temper flared. I was tired of the ice out, and I didn't need to explain myself to him. "What the hell, Jude? Then you shouldn't be doing all this for me."

"I'm fine." He waved me off.

"Shouldn't you be wearing a knee brace at least?"

"I depended on it too much and it weakened my muscles. I just wear a sleeve now when I work out."

"Are you training to get back in the cage?" Despite my frustration, watching him struggle caused my heart to ache. He couldn't possibly think about returning to MMA. I saw how much punishment those athletes experienced during a fight.

"Don't know."

He shuffled out of the truck bed, gingerly climbing down to protect his joint. I couldn't help but wince with sympathy.

Horse hooves clopped up the paved driveway, and I turned to see Chuck's signature salt and pepper mustache shaded beneath his Stetson. I'm not surprised he was still wearing the same ol' hat.

"He better retire after a third knee injury," he grumbled as he approached.

"Chuck!" I waved, smiling brightly, happy to see the old man who was more like a father.

"Hi, darlin'," he drawled. His warm, brown eyes caught mine, giving me another gut twist of homesickness. "Is it possible this one got even prettier?" he asked, raising his eyebrows at Jude.

My cheeks flamed.

Jude just scoffed behind me. I ignored him. Did he think I was prettier, too?

I shook my head. "Three knee surgeries! You have to know when to quit." I knew I was goading him. But I wanted something—anything—from him, even if it was a return of his anger.

"You know Jude. That's why they call him 'The Bull' now. He charges his opponent and screw the circumstances."

That sounded exactly like Jude. Just like that stallion he rode, he never backed down from a challenge.

"Plus, he has that mean mug of his. Not the most approachable, if you ask me. Probably why he's still single, too." He winked at me.

My heart leaped just an inch with that little tidbit of information.

"Laying it on thick, huh, Uncle? I'm *right* here," Jude complained.

Chuck shrugged, then swung his leg over the saddle to dismount. "Do you need help with anything?"

"Just need some packing tape and the key to the bunkhouse," Jude replied.

Chuck handed me the reins as if twelve years was only a blip in time. "Hold on to Gus. I'll be right back."

The horse was beautiful. A red bay with a white blaze down his nose.

"Gus?" I asked Jude after Chuck disappeared into the house.

All the horses were named after Disney characters. Lina had started it after she came to live with the Larsen men when she was ten. Her mom and Chuck were never together, only dated when he was on the rodeo circuit, and Lina had been a surprise. She bounced back and forth between her mom's Portland home and the ranch, but her love of horses eventually kept her here.

"Yeah, after Gus-Gus, the mouse from *Cinderella*."

"Ah." I nodded, reaching out to stroke Gus's nose. He smelled like hay, dust, and horse sweat, and that feeling of longing washed over me again.

The house door shut behind us, as Chuck came out through the garage.

"Got it," he said, tossing the tape to Jude. "Follow me."

I handed the reins back to Chuck, and he effortlessly hoisted himself back into the saddle. Jude slammed up the tailgate, causing me to flinch. I was not looking forward to this. I followed him, hoisting myself into the passenger seat.

Closing my eyes, I took a deep breath. It must have been more audible than I thought because before I could open my eyes again, Jude had grabbed my hand and squeezed it. His eyes found mine, and they were softer now, full of sympathy and what I hoped was forgiveness.

"I'll be there with you, honey."

My breath caught. *Honey.* He used to call me that.

It was an olive branch, and it helped center me for what I was about to face.

Chapter 7
Jude

She pulled her hair back in a messy ponytail at the nape of her neck, diving into yet another drawer of Hazel's clothes.

Fuck. I wanted to wrap my hand around that ponytail, give it a good tug until her lips lined up with mine. The thought made my jeans grow tight.

"This box is done," she announced, pushing it toward me with her foot.

Settle down, you! I told my dick. This was neither the time nor the place, and if it didn't get the memo, this was about to get *real* uncomfortable.

Even in the bunkhouse, knowing a man was killed here, I couldn't help but stare at her. She was heartbreakingly beautiful. The memories of her, the feelings that came surging back at her proximity, were like a punch in the gut. The need to take her into my arms or pin her against the nearest wall was almost overwhelming, as if I was walking through quicksand, my muscles straining to break free. The frustration and anger I felt earlier was slowly dissipating, replaced by a need to comfort her. I just knew, though, my brand of comfort would only cause her to retreat.

Instead, I watched her, feeling that if I looked at her long enough, I could memorize her for the next time she disappeared. Recall all the facial expressions that gave away each emotion. If I could read her like I used to, I could dive in to help fix the problem before she even knew to ask, just as I had done when we were young.

"Earth to Jude!" Romy snapped her fingers. "Going to tape that box or just stare at me all day?" She smirked, teasing me like she used to.

It was exactly the refocus I needed.

With each box she packed, she was searching, looking between shirts, through shoeboxes.

"What are you looking for?" I asked her. "Maybe I can help look, too."

She tucked a loose lock behind her ear. "I don't know. Hazel just said she had something for me. She was pretty vague, so I don't know if she meant here in the bunkhouse or just on the ranch. I guess it is possible the cops confiscated it, whatever it was."

"Did you look in the bunks?" I asked her, gesturing to the beds where the ranch hands and trainers slept.

She shook her head. "Not yet."

She hadn't wanted to go toward the bunks. I didn't blame her.

Bullet holes scarred the wooden bed frames. The drywall was patched in the ceiling directly above one bunk and in two places on the wall. How many shots were fired before Jesse was killed? Did Hazel fire all those rounds?

Uncle Chuck, or one of the other ranch hands, must have attempted to clean up. Whatever mess was created by the police search was put back into place, except for the kitchenette where pots and pans, empty, glass beer bottles, and old mail still littered the counters. The place smelled like Lysol and spackle. Dark-brown spots stained the antique wood floors. Grandpa would grimace if he saw the state of the original homestead that belonged to his grandparents, pioneers of the Oregon Trail.

Now the bunkhouse, it was never full during the cold months. It was only full during the summer when it filled up with hired hands. Spring and summer were the busiest seasons, and now with all of this, the bunkhouse was empty. Uncle Chuck needed to hire help, and I'd do what I could to fill in so he could focus on Grandpa and other areas of the ranch, like training.

"This is going to take longer than I thought." Romy put her hands on her hips and surveyed the room. "I have to leave by midnight if I'm going to make my flight."

"Can you take a later flight?" I offered.

Romy stood silent, thinking. Biting her bottom lip. My own tongue darted out to lick my upper lip, wishing I could taste hers instead.

I jerked my eyes back to the bunks, and she followed my gaze to the patched bullet holes.

"Fuck it!"

"What?" My head jerked back to her in surprise.

"I can't leave tonight." She shook her head, punctuating her words. "I can't just go back to San Jose as if nothing happened, like my sister isn't in jail. I'm getting laid off anyway ..." Her voice dwindled as though she was processing her thoughts aloud.

"What? You're getting laid off? Why?" My brows shot up. I didn't even know what she did for a living.

"Yeah, more school budget cuts." She shrugged.

Ah, so a teacher. I bet she made a great teacher. How could they let her go? If given a choice, I would never let her go.

"What do you want to do?" I asked, willing to help her in any way I could.

All she did was take her cell phone out of her back pocket and say, "I need to make a call" before walking out.

Who did she have to call? A boyfriend? Just the thought of it pissed me off. It irritated me to think he'd let her come here alone to deal with all this bullshit. *Fuck no.* I shook my head to break my line of thought.

She must be calling the airline or her boss.

I watched her pace in front of the window, the phone to her ear while she talked.

She wasn't running away this time. She was staying, even if it was only for a bit longer.

I closed the tailgate with the last of the loaded boxes and turned back to see Romy studying the bunkhouse.

Like all of the buildings—besides the big house—the siding was white. It stood next to the horse stables. The farrier was here today, and we could hear Uncle Chuck talking with him in between the clamoring of filing hooves, hammering, and the sizzle of new horseshoes being fitted. We spent all day sorting through Hazel's things, but whatever Romy was looking for still hadn't revealed itself.

"Do you want to grab a burger?" I asked before I could think too long about it.

Her eyes, the color of a dusk sky, brightened. "The Burger Shack?"

"Best burgers and shakes in Willows," I proclaimed, the corners of my mouth lifting.

"You read my mind." She smiled, heading toward the passenger-side door.

Unlike when she saw Uncle Chuck come up the drive, this smile was directed toward me. I'd do anything to earn that smile. She could have all the burgers and shakes she wanted if it meant seeing her face light up like that.

We drove the boxes back to the garage, storing them between the cars—at least until Romy could secure a storage unit. Uncle Chuck insisted she didn't have to pay for one, but she turned down the offer. Always one to stand on her own two feet, her stubborn independence apparently extended to taking care of her sister, too. Dr. Deborah would refer to that as being anti-dependent, rejecting help even when it was needed.

After we unloaded the boxes, we headed into town.

Sunday night was quiet in Willows. It was still early for the busy tourist season, and most visitors went home on Sundays. A short line stood in front of the walk-up Burger Shack. While we waited in line, she picked at her nails and kept her eyes down, avoiding the looks of the customers. I wanted to wrap a protective arm around her, but I kept my hands stuffed in my pockets. As soon as we ordered our food and shakes, and she took that first sip of cookies-and-cream milkshake, her face softened.

I could feel eyes on us as we sat and ate. I didn't know if they were looking at me—I was often recognized when I was out in public—or if they were scrutinizing Romy, Frank Miller's daughter and Hazel's sister. I made eye contact with a few looky-loos until they uncomfortably shifted away.

One of the waitresses came up to our table to deposit a fresh ketchup bottle, banging it against the table and making our glasses rattle.

"Hope your fucking sister gets what's coming to her." The woman who appeared to be about Uncle Chuck's age, her graying hair pulled back in a bun, glared at Romy.

"Excuse me?" Romy snapped, her eyes as sharp as steel as she turned toward the woman.

There's her fire. I knew she still had it in her.

"My boy never should have gone to work for you Larsens." The woman's narrowed gaze shifted to me. "You think you own this town, but I'll tell you what. Justice will be served, and karma's a bitch."

With her last words, she stormed away, disappearing into the kitchen behind the counter.

I turned to Romy. Her face was flushed with anger, and all I wanted to do was shield her from the sting. An old feeling of my hackles rising in defense of my best friend caused my own blood to boil. I should have done something to stop that woman before she got a word in edgewise.

"Hey." I reached out, my hand encompassing hers, which was still wrapped around her shake. "Ignore what that woman said. She's obviously upset, but it's not about either of us."

"I think she might be Jesse's mom," she whispered, her eyes darting around us.

People had turned to watch. I'm sure by tomorrow morning, the gossip from the Burger Shack would be all around town.

"Do you want to get out of here?"

A feeling of déjà vu washed over me, a vivid memory from high school when we played hooky. I found her hiding under the bleachers after PE, dwelling over some girl drama. I had asked her the exact same question. She had taken my hand and we snuck off campus, spending the day at the river instead, drinking warm beer I stole from the ranch hands.

She nodded, packing up her burger and shoving the last of her fries in her mouth.

I stuffed our burgers back into the paper bag and stood from the booth.

I'd decided she wasn't going anywhere tonight. "You're staying with me."

Romy nearly choked on her french fries. "Wha-what?"

"I know you're not going to stay with Frank." I handed her purse to her. "You haven't even let him know you're in town, and hell if I'll let you sleep in that car again."

"Jude." She said it like a scolding.

It made my toes curl in my boots. But I'd behave myself.

"I'll sleep on the couch. Besides, this way, you'll be close to the bunkhouse and can keep looking tomorrow."

I turned on my heels, walking out to the parking lot.

58

"I can't kick you out of your own bed." She trailed behind me.

"Sure you can."

We piled into the truck. I took a pull on my shake before setting it into the cup holder and handed Romy the burger bag.

She held the bag in her lap. "I'll call around and see if there's a cabin or room available."

"It's not a problem, Romy, seriously. Save yourself the trouble."

"I can't—" She stopped herself midsentence, and I waited for her to finish. Just like last night when she considered getting in the truck with me, I watched the gears roll around while she pondered it.

Her lips pursed in thought, and I couldn't help but ogle her mouth. Er … maybe this was a bad idea. Would I be able to stay away from her while she was sleeping in the next room? Just having her alone in the cab of the truck made the blood go straight to my cock, like my skin was on fire if I didn't touch her.

"Okay," she finally agreed.

"Okay?" I asked, surprised.

"Just to be close to the bunkhouse. I only have a sub until Wednesday, so I'll have to leave before then."

I nodded, pressing my lips together to keep from smiling, and turned on the ignition.

Three more days? I could do three more days with Romy.

But would three days be enough?

Something told me it would never be enough.

CHAPTER 8
Romy

Here comes what I can only assume will be another restless night. This time in a room I never thought I'd return to.

The bedroom was different than it was twelve years ago. The king-size bed rearranged to face the window with a view into the dark trees. The plank floors carried into the bedroom. Beneath the white, down-covered bed was a blue, orange, and cream-colored Southwestern-style shag rug. My bare toes sunk into the plushness, and I just about groaned with pleasure. Throw pillows that matched the rug were the only other color in the room. Another set of steer horns hung over the bed; otherwise, the dove-gray walls were bare. The only things unchanged were a seven-drawer antique dresser and a round, lasso-framed mirror … and Jude's scent.

It hit me like a cloud as I plunged into the comforter. Laundry soap, hay, and something fresh—like mint—enveloped me. It was comforting and disconcerting all in one breath. Never mind that the man it belonged to was sleeping in the other room.

He had been a complete gentleman, allowing me space to shower and get ready for bed. He gave me a quiet "Good night," then went around to turn off the lights. I shut the door and stood against it, my palms flat against the wood, my heart pounding, wondering what would happen if I walked back out and straddled his lap on the couch. I melted to the floor, drawing my knees to my chest, and squeezed my eyes shut.

Twelve years, and memories of him beneath me still haunted me. It was nearly painful being in his presence now. It made me long for my best friend, but even after all these years, now knowing what it felt like to be with him, there was so much regret and grief. I suppose I never stopped wanting him, missing him, needing him. I just pushed it as far back into my heart as I could until I no longer ached for him.

I just needed to get through this and back to California.

Pulling myself off the floor, I curled up beneath the covers and it almost made it worse. It felt like I was wrapped up in *him*. Entangled in him. As if I were trapped in a tidal wave, spinning and suffocating if I didn't break the surface.

I spun in my dreams, surrounded by his kisses, his fingers tracing every inch before digging into my hips. I felt as if I was begging for him, craving his touch, seeking a way to relieve the tension, wanting desperately to feel him against me.

But all I got was an open ocean of nothingness.

I awoke in the morning, tangled in the bedsheets, the early light breaking through the pine boughs. I still felt the thrumming pulse in my core. My nose was filled with his scent, my heartbeat pulsing between my thighs. It was a dream, but I was left wanting. Craving. Aching if I didn't get relief. If I couldn't let him touch me, at least I could pretend, even if only for a moment.

My hand skimmed the hem of my shirt, lifting it, my fingers gliding over my stomach, then up, cupping my breast until I felt the peak of my nipple. I pinched it hard, recalling how Jude pulled it between his teeth years ago. My fingertip made soft circles around the hardened tip, while my other hand slid down my stomach, past the waistband of my sleep shorts to slide through my slit.

I was soaked.

Jude.

He did this to me, and he hadn't even touched me. It had only been a dream.

My finger dipped in, dragging the wetness up to my clit, and I nearly bucked off the bed when I touched the sensitive spot. While one hand rubbed slow circles around my nipple, my other hand caressed my clit. Light circles. My hips rocked with each pass, chasing my building arousal.

But it wasn't enough. It just made me want something to fill me. To feel that added pressure, to touch that place deep inside me that made me explode.

Knowing Jude may be in the next room, imagining him hearing me while I masturbated to his memory, heightened my pleasure. Would he have to go to the shower so he could stroke his cock to my moaning?

I needed more.

My fingers pinched my nipple while one finger plunged inside, pumping, then gliding back up to circle my clit. Pump, glide, circle. Pump, glide, circle. My hips continued to rock. I could feel my orgasm reaching its precipice.

More.

"Jude." His name came out on a breath. I bit my lip to keep from moaning it aloud.

Two fingers pushed in, pumping. I pinched my nipple again while I thrust my fingers as deep as I could go. My walls tightened. Blood rushed to my ears.

My mouth fell open on a pant, my hips continuing to roll while aftershocks racked my body. I squeezed my eyes shut, sliding my fingers out, giving my clit one last pass over. My body jerked.

I pulled my hand from my shorts, lying still while I caught my breath.

The house was silent. Did Jude hear me?

It had been a while since I brought myself to climax. I had always needed a toy to help get me there. Apparently, all I needed was a Jude sex dream, my fingers, and the risk of him hearing me come.

Then came a knock at the front door, and I just about flew off the bed.

I climbed up the driveway to the big house. Clinking weights and man grunts echoed from the garage.

Chuck came to the double-wide looking for me. My face was still hot when I greeted him at the door.

The blanket and pillow were stacked on the couch in the living room, and Jude was already gone. Chuck needed our help moving cattle from the north to the east pasture. Thinking all

I would be doing was packing Hazel's belongings and heading back to California, I hadn't planned for riding. A year apart, Hazel and I had always shared clothes, so I proceeded to the garage to rummage through her boxes for boots and chaps.

The fourth bay garage door was up, allowing the morning sun to stream in. Jude was shirtless, his back muscles glistening and rolling as he repped out pull-ups.

He hadn't seen me yet. I couldn't move, mesmerized. His back muscles bulged and rippled. His bull tattoo came alive with each repetition.

How many was he going to do?

I stood there for what seemed like an eternity before he gracefully dropped back to his feet. He scooped up a towel hanging on the weight bench, drying his brow. Sweat dripped from the tips of his hair.

Oh, my God! Of course he has a perfectly chiseled six-pack. Or is that an eight-pack?

I could picture myself running my tongue down those sculpted abs right to that decadent *V* cutting toward the waistband of his workout shorts.

And then his glacial eyes collided with mine.

My cheeks burned crimson.

"Morning." His voice sounded rough from sleep and breathless from exertion. It was damn sexy.

"Morning," I called back, remembering to move. "Just getting some boots and chaps from Hazel's things." I threw a thumb over my shoulder. He was too sexy for his own good without his shirt on. An echo of a pulse from my early morning activity caused me to hurry over to the boxes. "Chuck asked for our help to move the cattle to the east pasture."

The air shifted with his approaching footsteps. "Yeah, he told me. He left bacon and bagels in the kitchen. Feel free to help yourself. I'm just finishing up here, then I'll go clean up and meet you at the stables."

"Uh-huh." *Don't look at him.*

He stepped behind me, and I could feel the heat radiating off his body. I leaned down to dig through a box of boots, and my ass brushed his leg.

Shit.

His hand went to my hip, and I straightened. It was like a heat wave washing over me. He was so close that his chest grazed my back when he breathed.

"You all right?" His words brushed hot and moist across the shell of my ear.

No, of course not, and your touch isn't helping, I wanted to say.

"Yeah." A lie.

I stepped away from his grasp and turned to him.

A big mistake because he was wearing that lopsided smirk. He knew I was full of shit.

"It's okay to talk to me, Romy. This is a fucked-up situation. I wouldn't wish it on my worst enemy, and we're all dealing with the repercussions. You don't have to face this alone."

I exhaled, drawing myself away from my extremely inappropriate thoughts. "I know, I'm just still processing it." I shook my head. Still dumbfounded. "It still doesn't seem real, and none of it makes sense. I have no idea what Hazel wants me to find or what really happened."

"Maybe a ride and some fresh mountain air will do us both

some good."

I nodded, then brightened. "Does Chuck still have Winnie?" I asked, remembering my favorite quarter horse. The mare was as sweet as honey.

Jude's half smile turned into a real grin, and I couldn't help but beam back at him. "I think he does."

"This will be great, Jude. You're right. Just what I need." I swooped up the chaps with the boots and hustled into the big house to grab breakfast.

As I opened the door to the house, I looked over my shoulder to catch Jude still watching me. This time, his eyes had lowered to my ass, and that flush flashed hot again.

CHAPTER 9
Jude

God, I missed this. The fresh country air laced with cattle and manure, the sun on my face making me grin from ear to ear. The strong gelding beneath me. Guiding the herd from one pasture to the next. How did I let over a decade go by without getting on a horse? Yet it felt as though no time had passed.

"Round up that heifer!" I called across the herd to where Romy sat atop Winnie.

She had said she hadn't ridden a horse since high school, but she still looked as if she belonged in this world. She was one with the mare, effortlessly turning Winnie's head to guide her as we rounded up the cattle. With each flick of the reins, kick of her heels, or click of her tongue, Winnie responded to her just as she had twelve years ago. Horses could remember people for years, and despite their separation, Winnie *knew* Romy.

And she was stunning.

Her blonde hair was tied back again, tempting me as it did yesterday. One of the Thornbrush caps with the T-horned brand shaded her eyes, and those jeans fit her like a glove. The chaps only accentuated the flare of her hips.

The hips I couldn't help but grab when her ass was mere inches away from my dick.

Her scent was still in my nostrils. More coconut this time, her hair still fresh from her shower last night. It was addicting.

"Haw! Haw!" Romy yelled, bringing the stray heifer back to the herd.

Uncle Chuck's dogs bayed around us, closing in on the herd to lead them through the east pasture gate. It was still cool for May, but the sun was strong and I tipped my cowboy hat to wipe my brow.

"Bring 'em in!" I hollered. Romy came up the rear, heading to where I rode Chip. She sidled Winnie up beside me. "It appears we got them all."

"That was fun." She was breathless and smiling.

We followed the cattle through the gate before I hopped off to close it behind them.

Romy dismounted, and we led our horses to the fence, leaning against it to gaze out at the relocated cattle.

"So, a teacher, huh?" I asked.

Years might have separated us, but she never left my thoughts after all that time. I wanted to learn everything there was to know, even if it meant her telling me why she really left. Even if it hurts.

"Yeah. Seventh grade humanities."

"Middle school is rough."

I hated my middle school years. Awkward and long-limbed, I mostly kept to myself. Only finding camaraderie with wrestling and horses … and Romy. Always Romy.

"Tell me about it. I thought I could make a difference. I know my teachers did. I wanted to be that safe space for my students. To help make someone else's horrid school experience just a little bit easier. Even thinking back to all the bitchy girls I constantly dealt with, I still considered school my safe place, you know? Well, that and the ranch." She gave me a side-eyed glance.

A loaded glance that if I read too much into, she was telling me that I had also been her safe place. At least I'd hoped so. There were so many times Romy and Hazel "lived" at the ranch instead of their own home.

"I'm not sure how much more I can take, though," she continued. "I can't even seem to get my feet underneath me, let alone inspire a bunch of preteens. Not sure I'm cut out for it."

If anyone was cut out for it, Romy was. She didn't put up with shit—never had—and it was obvious she was passionate about it.

"I don't believe that. I have no doubt you've helped more kids than you realize."

"Perhaps." But her voice sounded far away, distant. As if she was already resigned to her failure as a teacher.

Not wanting to push her, I asked, "What would you do instead?"

She shrugged. "What about you? If you're done fighting, what's next?"

I mimicked her shrug. "Looks like we're a couple of unemployed drifters," I joked.

Romy hip-checked me and laughed. "Why, aren't we quite

the pair?"

We sounded good.

I could sense her walls slipping. We used to be so comfortable with each other—affectionate even—even when we were supposed to be just friends, when she was dating someone else. Chase was always jealous of our relationship, and it stroked my ego each time he lashed out at me. She was mine, whether he or Romy realized it.

And I thought she had that night. She and Chase had broken up, going their separate ways for college.

She had waited for *me* that last day. Sexy in cutoff shorts and a tight top that tied around her neck while she leaned against the railing in the arena, watching her sister circle barrels. I drew her away from there, bringing her into the shadows of the tack room, and before either of us could speak a word, she fisted my shirt, pulling me against her in a crushing kiss. We were desperate for each other. It felt like a goodbye, but it also felt urgent. Like if we didn't consume each other right in that moment, the world would end.

My cock painfully hard, I had grabbed Romy's hand and we hurried to the double-wide, barely waiting for me to kick the door closed before I scooped her up in my arms and threw her onto my bed. In our haste, we fumbled with our clothes, our teeth clashing, tongues stroking, fingers exploring. It was as if our bodies belonged to each other before we ever collided. We were completely consumed with each other and connected in a way that made me feel as though Romy was truly *mine*.

Except she wasn't. Not back then, at least.

But damn, now that she was here … what I wouldn't do to

have her. Have her in my arms, my bed, and in my life. Forever.

The sun beat down on her, gleaming off her hair. Romy looked as if she belonged here—her feet in boots, her legs in chaps, and wearing a red, Vexil hoodie with the classic horns logo spread across her perfectly round tits. What I wouldn't give to slowly peel her out of it.

She inched closer, this time leaning into me, her head tentatively resting on my shoulder. Just like she had so many times before. I didn't dare move.

Don't fuck this up, I repeated over and over in my head.

We looked out at the herd. The calves and heifers reuniting. The mothers bowed their heads to nose their young.

She relaxed, and I could feel the tension ease from her body. The weight of her head comforting on my shoulder.

I released a breath, allowing my own tension to lift, and rested my cheek against her hair. Her coconut scent now mingled with grass, horse, and sunshine. She felt like home. It made me smile to know that some things hadn't changed.

Maybe she wouldn't run this time.

We walked the horses back to the stable, the bray of horses greeting us. We talked the whole way back. She shared stories of her students, and I shared stories of opponents I had faced in the cage. Neither one of us mentioned other relationships. I still didn't know if she was single; I was scared to know the answer. What if she had someone back in California? What then? Could I convince her to stay for me, that she was always meant to be mine?

I knew she had to leave to finish out the school year, but it was almost summer break. She could come back, couldn't she? She'd want to be here for her sister.

After today, I'd have two more days left with her, and I needed to know. Did she feel what I felt? Those feelings never went away for me. And now seeing her, being in her presence, it felt like more. As if all these years, the universe was just biding its time, our orbits never quite lining up ... until this moment.

Her cell phone rang in her back pocket.

"Hazel," she said, glancing at the screen. "I don't have my wallet on me."

I didn't hesitate to pull out my wallet from my back pocket.

"Here." I handed her my credit card.

"You don't have to."

"You better hurry before she runs out of time."

Romy bit her lip, taking a moment to decide.

I shook my head, shoving the card into her hand. She could be so stubborn.

Romy punched in the numbers, then listened to the automated message before I heard a muffled hello.

"Hello? Hazel? Are you doing okay?" Romy's face slacked and her rosy cheeks dimmed.

Giving her conversation privacy, I took the reins of our horses and walked them to their stalls to untack.

Worry laced her voice from across the stable. I wanted so fucking badly to return to her side, to rub her shoulders, to hold her hand—anything to give her comfort while she talked to Hazel. I busied myself unsaddling the horses, checking their hooves, brushing them down, and giving them a big scoop of oats before leaving them to rest in their stalls.

"Okay, I'll see you tomorrow then." Romy was finishing her call by the time I returned to where she stood in the threshold. "Okay. Bye, sis."

Romy hung up, turning to look at me. Color had still not returned to her face.

"I'm going to the jail tomorrow to visit her." Her jaw was set firm, and her eyes were molten metal. There she was. My determined girl.

I nodded. "I'll drive you."

"Jude." She said it like a warning, but really, all it did was spread heat through my veins and give the wrong idea to my cock.

"Romy. You're not going to the jail by yourself. I'll drive you." I reached out to grip her elbow, wanting to draw her near me. To show her I was here for her.

"Fine." She took a hesitant step closer. "But I'm going in alone. She only put *me* on her visitor list."

My eyebrows rose. "Not Frank?"

She lifted her hand, pushing my hat back from my forehead. Her fingers hovered at my brim, and I felt the air thicken between us. Our eyes, now unobscured by my hat, connected. "No. Frank would only create a scene. It's best if I go alone."

Uncle Chuck came marching into the stables with two shovels in his hands.

"All moved?" he asked.

We stepped apart.

"Yep. All settled in the east pasture," I told him, taking off my hat to wipe my brow and attempt to shake off the elevated beating in my chest caused by Romy's nearness.

"Good, I appreciate it. I need the stalls mucked. We'll have more help tomorrow," he said, handing us both a shovel. "I hired a guy who just moved here from eastern Oregon, looking for work. He'll be here tomorrow. And it sounds like Lina should be rolling in tomorrow afternoon, too."

"Will that be enough help, or will you need to hire out?" I asked him.

"I'll probably have to borrow ranch hands as needed, but it will have to do for now. I know you both have to get back to your lives."

I didn't say anything. I didn't know if there was a life to get back to anymore. I'd forgotten the soreness in my knee while I was out riding with Romy, until now.

"Well ..." Romy pondered.

My head shot in her direction. "Well, what?"

"Without a job after next week, I may need to think about coming back for the summer."

My eyes went wide. She risked a lowered glance at me through her lashes, and a surge of hope shot through my chest.

"Really?" My voice came out like an excited little boy. I cleared my throat.

A slight smile curled her lips, but she averted her gaze to Uncle Chuck.

He was beaming at us. "You know, they say the more hands we have on a ranch, the lighter the work."

Come on! I rolled my eyes and chuckled. "Who's 'they'?"

Uncle Chuck shrugged. "I have no clue, but they're right.

Best get crackin'. The stalls won't shovel themselves."

Uncle Chuck winked at me over Romy's head as she headed to the nearest stall.

I flipped him off.

His booming laughter carried out the stable as he climbed the hill back up to the big house.

CHAPTER 10
Romy

The waiting room for visitors at Arnold County Jail smelled like sweat and dusty, vintage fabric. My legs scratched against the rough, rust-colored threads of the chair—chairs that had probably been here since the '80s. Two other visitors waited, staring into their hands, brows tense, and … bored. Cell phones, wallets, and purses were stashed in lockers at the last checkpoint, leaving us all to occupy ourselves with nothing but our thoughts. For me, it was the swirling realization that I was about to meet with an inmate. The room was windowless, as small as the pantry in the big house. Cinder block walls were caked with beige industrial paint, sucking out every bit of vibrancy.

How was this my life now?

The heavy fire door across the room gave a few clicks, the mechanical lock deactivating, followed by a loud beep. A female guard stepped through.

"Romy Miller!" she bellowed as if I were standing amid a crowd of hundreds instead of sitting in an airtight room of three.

"That's me." I got to my feet.

"Follow me." Lines bracketed her mouth as though she never smiled.

I followed her past the door.

The door closed behind me, automatically locking in my wake. I flinched, hearing the finality of that click. It was settling in now that my sister was confined here.

I followed the guard down a long hallway, and small, thick, glass windows punctuated the hall, giving a glimpse of trees outside. The jail was in the middle of nowhere, surrounded by woods.

We walked through another door into a room where cubicles divided by glass separated visitors from the inmates.

"Number six," she barked at me, stalling in her steps to guard the door.

I nodded, walking past her.

I don't know what I was expecting, but it wasn't this.

Hazel sat behind the glass, dressed in orange, her wrists shackled. Her blonde hair was dry and stringy around her slouched shoulders. Dark circles shadowed her grayish-green eyes, tears tracking down her pale cheeks at the sight of me. My rodeo darling sister, who always had her hair perfectly curled and her makeup flawless, looked broken and older than her thirty-two years.

I hustled into the metal chair, grabbing the red phone off the partitioned wall. Hazel hesitantly picked up hers.

All I heard was my name through muffled sobs.

"Hi, sis," I said in greeting, my nose stinging while I struggled to hold back my own tears.

She slammed her hand against her mouth, her face crumpling at my voice.

"It's okay. It's okay," I told her. We both knew it wasn't okay.

I didn't know what else to say, so I waited, letting her breathe, trying to regain control of her emotions. Allowing the time I needed to gather my own.

"I didn't think I'd ever see you again." Her voice was stained with tears.

I nearly lost it, swallowing down the burning knot. "I'm here now."

"We don't have much time. They could take me back to my cell at any moment, but I need you to know ..." Her voice waned as she took in a shuddering inhale.

"Anything," I encouraged. Though I knew she wouldn't be able to tell me everything. They were listening. She had to be careful what she said.

"I love you, and I did what I needed to do."

I gulped. *She did what she needed to do?* "Don't say anything you shouldn't," I warned, looking around at the guards who were stationed at the doors.

The room had the same cinder block walls as the waiting room with beige industrial paint, but behind Hazel, even on the glass, graffitied greetings, curses, names, and numbers adorned the surface.

"Did you get everything packed up?" she asked.

"Yes. Chuck said he can store the boxes in the garage for you if you'd rather do that. I haven't rented out a storage unit yet."

"He doesn't have to do that, but I know those Larsen men are stubborn pains in the asses." She snorted a small laugh.

"That they are." I cracked a smile at her laugh and at the said Larsen men. "Jude helped me pack everything up, but we didn't find what you had for me."

"So Jude's back?" Her brows raised and her lips curved. "How's that going?"

"What's that supposed to mean?" I narrowed my eyes. Sister-teasing picking up right where it left off over a decade ago.

She shrugged. "Pretty sure there was a reason why you cut everyone off—and it wasn't just because of Dad, shitty kids at school, and you being sick of small-town livin'."

Chuck was dropping hints as if he needed to play matchmaker, and now my sister. I had to redirect this conversation. It wasn't why I was here.

I had spent another restless night, super aware of Jude's presence in the next room. The attraction was still there, maybe even more so—I mean, the man had only become sexier—but I wasn't ready to process my feelings for him. Part of me was still that confused, eighteen-year-old girl. The old feelings were there, but some new feelings, too. It almost felt as though I couldn't breathe around him ... like my heart squeezed every time I saw that cute, lopsided grin of his. Over a decade might have passed, but that grin was still the same one that was imprinted in my memory.

"Something like that," I dismissed, releasing the air from my lungs. Just thinking about him made my chest tight. "Anyway, I couldn't find what you wanted me to look for."

She nodded. "Figured as much." Her eyes shifted to the guards around the room. "How's Bronte?"

Really? She's going to change the subject and ask about her horse?

Her eyes grew wide with a knowing look, and she nodded.

Oh. I think I was picking up what she was putting down.

"You need me to check on Bronte for you?" I asked for confirmation.

She nodded again and loosened a deep breath. "Thank you, sis."

A guard marched over to Hazel. "Time to go." The guard leaned down to the chair leg with a key to unlock Hazel's ankle shackles from the cubicle.

"I know you'll find what you're looking for," Hazel said. "I love you."

And she hung up the phone.

I kept the phone pressed to my ear, listening to the dead air as I watched her close herself back off.

She gave me a forlorn smile, while the guard grabbed her elbow and ushered her away.

"Visiting hours are over," the guard behind me announced.

I returned the phone to the receiver on the wall.

Whatever she needed me to find was in Bronte's stall. She had to know then. She had to know that someone would find whatever it was in the bunkhouse, so she hid it.

Did she do it then? Was this planned?

Was my perfect, responsible big sister a murderer?

CHAPTER 11
Jude

I t was coming on two hours, and Romy was still in there. It chaffed my skin to watch her walk into the jailhouse without me. I knew I couldn't go with her, and I was typically a patient man, but *fuck*, it was hard not to march into the jail demanding to know when she'd return. I felt helpless. I couldn't protect her while she was in there alone. So I'd wait. It dawned on me then that I'd always be willing to wait for her.

I did my best to occupy myself with the truck radio, walking around the nearly empty parking lot and playing on my phone.

I had several ignored texts from Alex Torres, my coach. The last one came in this morning.

COACH

How's the knee?

Bored, I went ahead and texted him back.

ME

Getting better all the time.

My cell started ringing in my hand. *Coach.*

Shit!

"Hello?" I answered tentatively.

"Now you answer!" Alex yelled into the phone.

I grimaced. I was exceptional at avoiding the things I didn't want to deal with. Coach was one of them because I knew he would ask me to shit or get off the pot.

"There's a lot going on right now," I excused.

"No shit! But the least you could do is text me back so I know you're alive."

"My bad."

Alex exhaled into the phone. He was exasperated with me. "Look, I know you're still rehabbing your knee, but I have some news. The guy who was going to fight Mike Reyes dropped out, so Reyes named you. He wants your belt."

"Fuck! I hate that guy." Mike Reyes was the newest, up-and-coming light-heavyweight. He was young, twenty-two, and cocky. And the worst part, he was good. *Really* good.

"Yeah, me too, but here's the thing. He wants to win it in the cage—against you. He's been talking shit online all week, saying you're broken and he could beat you on the ground."

Mike Reyes was a Muay Thai and jujitsu guy with a damaging kick who could wrap you up like a python. There was a reason he was so cocky. But his wrestling and boxing were nowhere near what they could be. He couldn't beat me on the ground and pound, not when I've knocked out more experienced Muay Thai guys than him in the past. They throw that leg out, I grab it, take them down, and grind my fists into their face until the ref stops it.

I laughed. "He can dream."

"I know you've been talking about retirement, but the fight organization wants to see this matchup. I've been getting pressure from Venture. He wants you to take the fight. Be the top headliner for the August card."

I scratched the back of my neck, then flipped my baseball cap around. I leaned against the truck, feeling the wind woosh out of me.

Venture—Mr. Kevin Venture—owner of the organization. I still had a contract. He signed my paychecks. Not sure how easily I could get out of this one.

"I don't know, man." I stuffed my free hand into my pocket, fiddling with my keys.

Alex cleared his throat. "I know it would be a short training camp. We can talk about it. Can you come to the gym?"

Shit. I didn't tell anyone, other than my therapist, I was going home.

I clenched my jaw. "See, the thing is ... I'm not in Nevada right now."

"What?" He practically yelled into the phone. "Where are you?"

"I'm dealing with some shit at the ranch and helping my uncle." I said it through my teeth, apprehensive of his reaction.

"You never go home."

I trifled with my hat. "I know, but I figured I could recover anywhere, so I'm here."

"You're doing physical therapy on a ranch? Are you insane? How can you strengthen a knee while riding a horse?"

"I'm getting it done."

"I'm booking a flight."

Oh, God! He couldn't come here.

"You really don't have to do that."

"We're talking about this in person, and if we're fighting in August, we need to start training—now!"

I didn't think I was ready to retire, but I didn't know if I was ready to get back in the cage, either. Thinking about it made my gut clench and a zing shoot straight to my knee, like I needed to protect it. Timing couldn't be worse with what was going on at the ranch … and with Romy.

"I can't convince you not to come, can I?" But I already knew the answer. I scratched the scruff on my jaw.

"Nope. Thornbrush Ranch, right? I'm googling it right now. Yep, found you. I'll be there tomorrow."

Tomorrow? The day Romy was supposed to head back to California. I was running out of time with her, and now this.

The building door swung open, and Romy walked out, spotting me leaning against the truck.

"I gotta go," I announced.

"All right, man. I'll catch you later. I'll text you the time you can expect me."

Great.

"Later," I said, hurrying to hang up as Romy approached me.

I studied her face, searching for any sign of distress. Instead, she looked pissed.

"Who was that?" she asked. It came out as a command, but I don't think her anger was directed at me. Something had happened in there.

"No one."

I didn't think I wanted to tell her. I didn't even know if there was anything to tell. I had a feeling she'd tell me I shouldn't, just like I knew Uncle Chuck would insist I retire, and then ask what the fuck I'm even doing considering it. And damn it, I cared what she thought.

"We have to check on Hazel's horse, Bronte," she reported, ignoring my response.

I opened the passenger door for her and moved with quick, long strides around the hood to hop in.

She clasped her hands in her lap, staring straight out the windshield. I could practically feel the heat radiating off her.

"What happened in there? Did she say something?" My voice came out more demanding than I intended.

I gripped the steering wheel. Damn it, Hazel. What did you do? She pissed off my girl—no, not *mine*, but fuck, I wanted her to be mine, and that fucking pissed me off even more.

Romy was seething. She turned to me, her eyes like flint. My entire body tensed, just like it did right before a fight, and I had to remind myself to breathe and stay calm.

"Do you think she killed him?" Romy asked through clenched teeth.

"I—"

She didn't even let me answer before she charged in with hers. "I think my sister fucking killed him."

That was the last thing I thought she would say. I shuddered a breath. I wanted to reach out and grasp her hand, to lend her comfort, but knowing Romy—at least I felt like I still knew her—she never wanted to be touched when she was upset.

"Really? Did she say something?" I asked. My brows

pinched.

"My sister may have been the sugary sweet, effervescent rodeo queen we all loved, but if there is anything I know of my sister, she took care of shit. Especially if backed into a corner. Something isn't sitting right with me, and I think it may be because this was planned. Every bit of it. She knew the bunkhouse would be searched by cops after this. Whatever she has for me she hid in Bronte's stall. She didn't want it found in the bunkhouse."

"There has to be an explanation ..."

I couldn't wrap my mind around Hazel hurting someone, let alone killing them. I remembered her being so vibrant, full of energy, her smile contagious. Always gentle with horses and humans alike. But she was right. Hazel always took the helm when the ship needed to be righted. And this ship was fucking rocky.

"Well," she said, crossing her arms over her chest. "I think we're about to find out."

We pulled up to the stables just as Uncle Chuck came out to greet us. Raised voices could be heard before we even got out of the truck.

Another truck and horse trailer were parked in front of the stables, and directly behind that one was my little cousin, Lina, hanging out of her truck window, her own horse trailer hooked behind, yelling at the man who was glaring at her.

"That's my fucking spot! It has been for years!"

Romy and I barreled out of the truck, reaching Uncle

Chuck.

"Lina," Uncle Chuck called, "just park there, and we'll unload Mushu. Then you can park up by the house."

She threw a glare at her dad before turning back to the man who stood firm by his truck.

"Fine!" She cut the engine and jumped out, slamming the door before joining us by the stables. "Why did you hire this fucking asshat?"

The question was directed at Uncle Chuck. He ignored her, and as soon as Lina noticed Romy and me standing beside him, she squealed, did a little skip, and ran to throw herself into my arms.

"Jude!" She wrapped her arms around my neck. "Oh, my God, Romy!" She leaned toward Romy, wrapping her up into a big group hug.

My arm pressed against the side of Romy's breast, and I just about jumped out of my skin. Those hot tingles sending my hair on end.

Lina Larsen was still the spitfire I remembered, charging into every situation with a sailor's mouth, either ready to start a fight or throw a party. She and I had stayed in touch over the years, and Uncle Chuck was constantly bragging about his baby girl. She was a champion barrel racer at eighteen, and she currently held the record for fastest time at the Willows Rodeo.

Now twenty-six years old, she'd grown into a beautiful, young woman. She looked just like early photos of her mother during her buckle bunny days. Her brown hair was pulled back in a braid, nearly reaching her waist. She looked tan and healthy, and she had big, smoky-brown eyes that sparkled when she laughed.

Apparently, grown men saw it as well.

Over Lina's shoulder, I studied the "asshat." He leaned against his truck with his arms crossed, his biceps huge beneath his canvas coat, and his eyes were fixed on Lina. His cowboy hat shadowed most of his face, but he appeared to be well into his thirties. His jaw was covered with a tight, brown beard, his mouth set firm in a scowl.

"That's our new hire," Uncle Chuck explained. "Hey, Reed! Come on over!"

Lina released Romy and me and stepped away to stand by her dad, her arms automatically crossed, a smug look on her face.

Reed pushed off the truck and walked over to us, his eyes now hidden beneath the brim of his hat, avoiding the judgment of two Larsens. The man was large, a couple inches taller than me, and looked as if he was raised on good ol' farm grain and beef. He'd fit in with the hands no problem.

"Reed Ownstead, this is my nephew, Jude, and our dear friend, Romy Miller. And it appears you already met my daughter, Lina." Uncle Chuck made the introductions.

I pushed up my sleeves, revealing my corded, tattooed arms. I put out my hand, gripping Reed's big mit firmly to let him know who was in charge, and if he so much as looked at my cousin the wrong way, he'd have to answer to me.

"Nice to meet you," he drawled. At least someone taught him some manners.

The man didn't smile, his eyes scanning Romy, and I had to consciously keep my body still to refrain from looking like a

Paleolithic asshole while Romy shook his hand.

Romy's eyes flicked to mine before I even realized I released a small growl. I cleared my throat to try and cover it up.

"Lina," Reed greeted, tipping his hat like a gentleman. He said her name as though he was more familiar with her than he was, and I didn't like it one bit.

Lina huffed, refusing to shake the man's hand.

"Reed just moved here from Joseph. His daughter and her mother live here. He wanted to be close by, so we may have a little one on the ranch from time to time," Uncle Chuck explained, ignoring the obvious tension between his daughter and the new guy.

"Mushu's been in the trailer for hours, so I need to get him out and rinsed down, especially if I'm going to have to park up at the big house." Lina shot a pointed look at her dad before walking long strides to her trailer.

"Follow me to the bunkhouse so you can unpack," Uncle Chuck directed Reed, heading past the stable.

"Nice meeting you both," Reed volleyed over his shoulder, following Uncle Chuck.

"I don't think Lina likes him very much," Romy commented when they were all out of earshot.

"No, I don't think she does." I wasn't sure about him, either.

CHAPTER 12
Romy

"What do you think we're looking for?" Jude asked me. He tied Bronte up outside the stall and was brushing him.

"I'm not sure," I replied, shoveling out the hay.

Perhaps there was a loose board somewhere.

The anger was slowly dissipating with each scoop of the shovel, allowing me to let off some steam. I didn't want to say too much, knowing Lina was on the other side of the stable taking care of her horse and tack.

In the far corner, the shovel caught on a board that was slightly raised. I set the shovel against the wall and crouched down to take a better look at the board. It was a shorter board, cut to fit into the corner, and it looked like it was missing its fastenings.

"Did you find something?" Jude entered the stall and hunkered down beside me.

I wedged my fingers between the boards, and it lifted with ease.

"Shit!"

A shoebox lay in the shadows beneath the floor.

"Holy fuck!" Jude said in a loud whisper, close enough I could feel his breath on my cheek.

I hoisted up the shoebox and lifted the lid.

Wads of money wrapped in rubber bands were stuffed in there, as well as a cell phone and a piece of yellow-lined paper that looked as though it had been ripped from a notepad.

My hands shook.

"What the fuck?" I whispered, searching for confirmation from Jude.

His eyes were wide.

I unfolded the paper, scrutinizing Hazel's blocky letters. She used to dot her eyes with hearts, but not anymore.

> If you find this, I'm either already dead or I've disappeared. I believe in karma, and Jesse will get his, if he hasn't already.
> Tell Dad and Romy, I did what I had to do, and I love them.

I couldn't speak. My mouth went dry, my stomach went sour. I handed the note over to Jude to read for himself.

"Damn. She did it," Jude said.

Yeah, but it still didn't sit right with me. Did she snap? I couldn't imagine the sister I knew and loved doing something to this extreme, even if she felt there was no other choice. This was evidence of premeditation. Was she planning to get rid of Jesse before taking off? Did she think Jesse was going to kill her? Was she suicidal? I couldn't wrap my head around any of it.

"What do I do, Jude? Do I give this note to her lawyer? Do you think it would help her case?"

"I don't know. This is evidence. Maybe it would prove that she needed help and was running out of options. It may be advantageous."

"Or it might not. I think premeditated murder is far worse. Maybe it was self-defense? Maybe Jesse was abusive?"

I thought discovering this box would answer my questions, but instead, all it did was create more.

I dropped on my ass, putting my head between my knees. Exhaustion and emotional fatigue dumped on me like a load of dirt and gravel.

Jude returned the note and box to Hazel's hiding place. The air shifted as he sat down beside me, his arm wrapping around my shoulders.

I leaned into him, welcoming his strength and warmth. Inhaling what I was now recognizing as the fragrance of *home*—Jude's scent of fresh soap and spearmint and the stable's smell of horse and hay. It was comfort and it was peace.

And all I wanted was to sit here and feel both until I could find the motivation to return to my feet.

Lina walked over to us while we returned Bronte to a clean stall and a bag of oats.

"How are you holding up?" she asked, giving me a sympathetic smile.

I'm sure it was painted all over my face. I was barely holding on. I shrugged. "Hanging in there."

"This is so fucking surreal," Lina said, shaking her head. "Definitely not on my bingo card. Especially with Hazel. I feel as though we're all living in an episode of *Law and Order*."

"Tell me about it."

"You know what we need?" Lina smiled, looping her arm around mine and exchanging glances with Jude and me. "We need a bonfire night."

"I don't know, Lina. Romy heads back tomorrow, and from what I hear, your bonfires can get kind of wild," Jude said, closing Bronte's stall.

"Your last night?" she proclaimed. "Well then, all the more reason to do it! We'll invite some friends, and I'll bring the booze. We'll make a real shindig of it." Her eyes sparkled.

"You already invited people over, didn't you?" Jude gave his baby cousin a knowing smirk.

"Well, sure. I told Kale Pardy that when I was back in town, he and his sister had to come out to the ranch. We had nights out while we were on the circuit, but I told him it was nothing compared to bonfires at Thornbrush."

"Did you ask Uncle Chuck?" Jude questioned.

"Fuck no! What, do you think I'm a child? He'll be fine. Shit, he'll probably want to send us with a truckload of food anyway," Lina brushed off.

A drink, or two or three, did sound good. Anything to get my mind off this shitstorm.

CHAPTER 13
Jude

I forgot how beautiful sunsets were on the ranch. The twilight sky was putting on a show. Brilliant shades of pink, orange, and purples faded to the dark-blue expanse as the sun disappeared over the rocky horizon.

The burn pile was in a wide-open area, where the property sloped down to the craggy ledge overlooking the river. The location was absent of long grasses and trees. Hot as hell during the summer months, but as soon as that sun dipped, you could feel the breeze drift over the bluff. Nothing obstructed the view or muffled the sound of rushing water against rapids.

A shed stood nearby, offering a place to tie up our horses. It stored the necessary firewood and folding chairs.

Romy, Lina, and Sage—the bartender from the Rooster who turned out to be Kale's sister—were approaching slowly, laughing and talking as they passed a bottle of Rosé from one saddle to the other.

"Do you think there'll still be enough booze for us once they get here?" Christian asked as we dismounted to tie up our horses.

"If I know Lina, those saddlebags are packed," Kale said, taking his hat off to hang on the saddle horn and running a hand through his curly, dark hair.

Christian and Kale were both bull riders and, most recently, roommates. Christian had stayed back for the last stretch of rodeos, recovering from a fall last month, but he was gearing up to return to the circuit. The next rodeo was Willows's very own, in July.

"You keep sucking that down, and there'll be no more for us!" Christian called.

"Shut the fuck up, Christian!" Sage yelled back.

My brows arched, giving Christian a look. "Doesn't appear that she likes you very much."

Christian shrugged and rolled his eyes. "She just doesn't know she's in love with me yet."

"You both just enjoy annoying each other," Kale dismissed. "You don't want that pink shit anyway. I got the beer in my saddlebags."

"Good man," Christian said, slapping his back.

The guys started to set out the chairs, while I picked up a load of wood and kindling for the fire.

"You'll need more than that if we're having a real bonfire," Lina hollered as they approached, leading the horses to where ours were tied up.

"Then you better get your ass over here and help me," I told her, arranging the logs on the pile of ash and charcoal.

"Here, bro." Christian handed me a beer.

I stood, cracked the can, and looked over at Romy, leaving the rest of the wood to Lina.

The evening light made her blonde hair gleam. It was down tonight in soft waves, reaching her waist. One of Lina's black cowboy hats on her head. Romy wore a tight, long-sleeved, black, ribbed shirt and a black belt cinching her waist. And those curves! *Damn!* I wanted to trace them, grip her thighs, and hoist her legs around my waist. She was gorgeous.

Her eyes sparkled as she laughed at something Sage said while she dismounted. Sage handed the bottle to Romy. She took a couple gulps. I watched her slender neck swallow before returning it, wiping the back of her hand across her mouth. That rosy mouth that I was constantly drawn to, that I couldn't help imagining around my cock while I fisted her hair. Those dark lashes fluttering up to glance at me.

My cock twitched, and I downed that beer as if I was parched.

"You should have seen him! He couldn't get any words out other than 'kaw kaw,' like a damn seagull, his arms and legs twitching. I told him to turn it down, but he insisted he wanted the TENS unit higher," Kale said.

We were all dying with laughter while Kale shared the story of Christian getting electrode therapy for his back.

"I didn't mean for you to turn it all the way up," Christian complained.

"I would have paid money to see that." Sage wiped away tears.

Romy was hunched over in her seat, laughing, and I couldn't help but smile. She had a quick laugh that when she really got going sounded more like hiccups. I forgot how much I missed her giggles.

She noticed me staring at her, and her face softened into a sweet grin, her laughter slowly dissipating. If not for the heat of the fire, I'd swear she was blushing. If she was, she quickly hid it behind her plastic cup of wine, taking a sip but never diverting her eyes from mine.

Fuck, she was beautiful.

Tomorrow she was going to leave. She said she'd return, but what if she changed her mind? Despite everything, she looked happy here. I wanted to encapsulate it. I wanted to give her a reason to return, to share more moments like this.

Romy shivered under my gaze and my jeans tightened.

I went and sat in the open seat beside her. "Are you cold?"

"A little," she replied.

I didn't hesitate to shrug out of my Carhartt jacket and drape it around her shoulders.

"Thank you." She pulled her arms through the sleeves.

My chest swelled seeing her in my jacket. She didn't think I noticed, but I saw her lean toward the collar to sniff it.

I didn't want it back. I wanted her to wallow in it until all she smelled was me on her.

"I almost forgot!" Lina declared, rushing over to her saddlebag. "I brought a speaker!" She pulled out a Bluetooth speaker, then rushed back over to the fire. "There is no such thing as a Thornbrush bonfire without music." She handed Sage her phone. "Here, pick a playlist."

Sage scrolled through Lina's phone until she landed on a playlist, and Morgan Wallen started streaming through the speaker.

"This is my shit!" Lina announced, pulling Romy up from her seat.

"I may need more wine for this," Romy complained, but her eyes were bright in the firelight.

Sage set the phone down, clutching the bottle of wine.

The three women danced to the beat and sang "Cowgirls" as loudly as they could, while Sage poured the bottle into Lina's open mouth and then Romy's.

My girl was getting tipsy.

Not. My. Girl. I had to remind myself.

The way she was moving her hips right now, though. *Fuck.* I wanted that ass in my hands. Even better, I wanted that ass in my lap, rubbing against my dick until she made me explode.

The sound of clopping hooves signaled a rider approaching. Thinking it was Uncle Chuck, I got up to greet him but stopped when I noticed it was the new hire, Reed.

His eyes were hard, dark orbs when he glanced toward Lina.

"Chuck wanted me to bring out some hot dogs for you all," Reed announced, dismounting and opening his saddlebags.

"Probably the nicest thing you've ever done," Lina snarked while she continued to dance with Romy and Sage, her eyes narrowed on Reed as if she didn't trust him out of her sight.

"Not the *nicest*, Lina," he replied, a spark of recognition in his eyes. I definitely did not like that. Did they know each other?

"Oh, fuck off, Reed! You're killing our vibe," Lina huffed, dropping back into her seat.

"I'll take those dogs," I said bluntly.

Reed handed me the package of hot dogs and buns.

"Make sure it burns out before you call it a night," Reed threw out as he remounted his horse.

Lina rolled her eyes, leaning back to gaze at the stars. She released a breath as if she was exasperated.

Everyone was quiet while we waited for Reed to ride away.

"What the hell was that?" Kale asked, once Reed was out of earshot. He was staring straight at Lina. "Is that the guy?"

"What guy?" I demanded, looking between Kale and Lina.

She lounged in her chair, grabbing the bottle from Sage and taking another gulp.

"No one," Lina grumbled.

"Not *no one*. She had him give her a tattoo when we were at the Saddle Room in Joseph. In fact, if I recall correctly, you proclaimed you were in love with him," Kale explained.

"Shut the fuck up, Kale! I was drunk. I say stupid shit when I'm drunk. And he's a fucking asshole. Not someone I want to waste my time talking about."

Kale lifted his hands in surrender. "Whatever. We won't speak another word about it."

"Yeah, what happens on the circuit, stays on the circuit," Christian chimed in. "Right, Sage?"

"You wish," Sage snarked.

"I do wish." Christian winked at her.

"Can you guys just fuck already and put us out of our misery?" Lina moaned.

"That's what I've been saying!" Kale added with amusement.

"*Great.*" Sage shook her head. "Now I need to deal with

both of you. It's never going to happen." She turned to Romy. "Kale is just tired of hearing Christian whine about his big, fat crush on me. You all have to get over it. Christian annoys the hell out of me, and the last thing I need is him crowing once he gets some."

"Baby, are you sure you're not going to be the one crowing?" Christian's eyes softened, and he gave her a sexy wink.

"Ugh! You're impossible!" Sage hollered, throwing an empty beer can at his head.

Christian dodged it, chuckling.

"She wants me, bro," he whispered to me.

I chuckled. There was some obvious tension there, but it did seem mostly one-sided.

Romy gave a loud, audible yawn beside me. She was looking so cozy in my jacket before the fire. It had been a long couple days for her.

"Do you want to head back?" I asked.

She nodded, setting her cup down on the dirt. "If that's all right."

"I'm going to ride back with Romy," I announced.

"Romy!" Lina jumped from her seat, falling into Romy's embrace. "You have to come back! We've missed you too much."

I smiled, my heart full, seeing my little cousin hold on to Romy—to make her feel wanted and missed, like part of the family.

I wanted to make sure Romy knew that.

"I'll be back," Romy declared, giving Lina one last squeeze.

"Good," Sage said, getting up to give Romy a side hug. "I can show you some of my work."

"I'd love to see your art studio," Romy promised.

After we said our goodbyes, we mounted our horses. Without a word, we both smirked, and before I could give Chip the command, she was racing across the field of sagebrush, making me chase after her.

We finished putting up the horses for the night, and I met her at the open stable doors. Stars punctuated the night. The earth was still. Quiet. I had gotten so used to the high intensity of Vegas, I forgot what real peace felt like.

It felt damn good. And seeing this woman standing on the threshold, in my jacket, waiting for me to join her in the dark, felt …

Damn good.

"Tonight was fun." Her lips tipped in a smile.

"Yeah, it was. Reminds me of everything I've missed." *Like you.*

I inched toward her, my boots bumping into hers. I could feel a prickle of electricity along my skin. It was like a tether, reeling me in.

Her eyes sparked in the dim light of the stable, and her lips parted on a deep exhale.

That fucking mouth.

I wanted to taste her, to feel those lips on mine, to have that tongue trace down my chest to my throbbing cock. I always knew that I wanted Romy, but now I realized I needed her, too.

Women had a habit of walking out of my life. It scared the shit out of me that I might lose her again, that it may be another twelve years before I saw her. Now, having her back, I didn't think I could survive it.

"Jude, I ... I'm sorry how I left." She struggled to find the words, but I knew. It was what I wanted to hear her say that morning I found her in her car.

"I know, honey."

"Do you ... do you ever think about that night? Before I left?" she asked.

I turned my ball cap around. I didn't know what I expected from her, but it wasn't that. Relief washed over me. She wouldn't have asked if she didn't think about it, too. She had no idea how often I'd thought about her, how I regretted not working harder to track her down, how she ruined other relationships for me.

"Romy." Her name came out like a prayer. "I don't think without thinking about you. It's always been that way for me. Like breathing. I don't know how to live without it."

Her face crumpled as if she was in pain, her eyes glistening. "Jude—"

I didn't wait for her to finish what she was about to say. I slid my hand into her hair, tugging at her roots, knocking her hat off. She sucked in a breath. I held mine. Our eyes bounced between each other until my gaze fell on her parted lips. Pink and pouty. I needed to taste her. To be reminded how her mouth felt against mine all those years ago.

Her tongue darted across her bottom lip before pulling it in between her teeth. It was utterly distracting. I barely noticed she had leaned into my grip, closing the distance, before I realized she brushed a quick and tentative kiss against my mouth.

"I—I'm sorry," she stammered again. I released her, and she shuffled back until she bumped into the stable door.

But I followed her, drawing her chin up to look at me. "I'm not. Fuck, Romy. I've dreamed of this for twelve years." A sheen glazed over her silver eyes, and I couldn't bear to see her shed a tear. I wanted nothing more than to show her exactly what I had dreamed. And just as her kiss was the key to unlocking my heart, I flew open that door and crushed my mouth to hers.

Desperate, her lips molded to mine. Romy's body bowed toward me, her arms reaching to wrap around my neck, drawing me closer.

Her chest rose with panting breaths, her breasts pressed against me.

She tilted her head, angling her mouth to deepen the kiss. I slid my tongue along the seam of her lips, and she parted for me. Her mouth was as sweet as the wine she drank, and I vowed I'd kiss her until I was drunk. I caressed my tongue along hers, sucking it into my mouth. Showing her exactly what I could do with it. I'd learned a few things since I last had her in my arms.

I wanted to feel every inch of her against my body. I walked her backward until she leaned against the rolled-back door. Pressing against her, my cock was so hard, I was afraid I'd blow a load in my pants like a damn teenager. Fuck, I had to have her.

Romy bit my lower lip and I groaned, grinding against her. She pulled back and came up for a breath. But I wasn't about to breathe. I wanted to devour her. I leaned into her smoky, coconut-scented hair, kissing her jaw and tracing the curve of her neck, gently sucking the sensitive spot below her ear.

Her knees buckled, but I didn't let her fall. I'd never let her fall. Pressing my leg between hers, I kept her upright while I tasted her skin. My hand trailed her side, beneath the open jacket, finding her breast. Gently squeezing. Her nipple hardened through her shirt at my touch. I swiped my thumb across and was rewarded with the buck of her hips. A delicious sound emanated from her, and I drew slow circles over the stiffened peak as she ground against my leg. I could feel the inner seam of her jeans shift as she moved against me.

"That's it, honey, use me. Grind that pretty pussy on me. Do those tight jeans rub you just right?"

"Oh my God, yes," she breathed, her hand wrapping around my neck to pull me back. "Kiss me, Jude."

This time, it was a tender, sensual kiss. Slow and smoldering. My thumb continued to stroke, and my girl responded with increased rhythm as she rocked against me. Fuck, I wanted to feel how wet she was. I wanted to taste her. Remind myself how sweet she tasted on my tongue. I wanted to sink inside her and never come out. But if this was what she wanted, I'd give it to her. I'd give her anything she wanted.

Because she was *mine*.

This time, I'd make her mine. She wasn't running away from me again.

I could feel the heat and pulsing of her pussy on my thigh.

Her hand trailed down the front of my shirt, landing on my belt buckle before finding my rock-hard dick. I leaned into her touch, wanting her to feel exactly what she did to me. The pressure of her hand shot an electric current into my lower belly. She hummed while she rubbed me through my pants, gently squeezing until I twitched in her grasp.

"You're driving me fucking crazy," I whispered into her mouth.

"More." She said it as if it was all she could get out through her panting.

I wanted more, too, but this would have to suffice—for now.

"What do you want, honey? Do you want to come? Do you want to rub your hot, little cunt on my leg until you scream?"

She fisted my shirt, drawing me closer, almost to the point of slamming herself against my leg. "More, Jude. I need more."

"We'll have to get in my truck and drive back to my place." Fuck, we hadn't made it out of the stable, and I wasn't sure I could wait, either.

She was breathless as we stared into each other's eyes. Her eyes were bright, silver galaxies that held more beauty than anything else in this universe.

God, she was breathtaking.

"Then take me to the truck," she demanded.

Her wish was my command.

I straightened, hoisting her up into my arms, gripping her perfect, tight ass, her legs wrapping around my waist. I leaned down and picked up Lina's discarded hat before walking us out of the stables. She trailed kisses along my jaw while I carried her. It took everything in me not to sprint to the truck.

I set her down, unlocking the driver's-side door.

"Get in," I ordered, flinging the hat onto the dashboard.

She never took her eyes off me, lifting herself into the cab and sliding back across the bench seat. I stalked her like a hunter, ready to devour her, shutting us in the cab, following her across the seat until her head rested against the passenger-side door. I parted her legs, settling my hips between them, until I could reach her lips again.

"Um … shit! I don't have a condom," I said breathlessly, continuing to kiss down her neck. "Tell me what you want, Romy. I'd gladly eat you right here. Do you want me to fuck you with my tongue?"

Romy nodded against the door. Her eyes hooded with desire. Desire for *me*. I'd dreamed of this so many times. I was ready to burn every moment into my memory, especially those beautiful eyes. I didn't move, waiting for her to say the words. I wouldn't do this if she didn't say it.

"Please, Jude. I've been tested. I'm clean."

My dick twitched. I liked the sound of her begging.

"Good. Me too." I inched back down her body, running my hands over her breasts. She arched into my palms before I continued my journey to her waist. Reaching the button of her jeans, I slowly pulled down the zipper.

She helped me shimmy her jeans down over her knees, and I parted her legs. The tattoo I'd only glimpsed through ripped denim was a vibrant phoenix, curving around her thigh and traveling up her hip. I knew Romy well enough to know why she would choose it. She had started a new life after leaving Willows, broken free of the ashes. And she blazed just as bright. Just as fucking brilliant.

Romy's pink, lace underwear was already dark along her

slit.

I beamed with pride, knowing I did this to her. "You're already wet for me, aren't you?"

She nodded, biting the corner of her lip. Even in the moonlight, I could see her blush.

My tongue darted out between my teeth, craving her, and she groaned, seeing my tongue so close to where she wanted it, pushing her hips toward me. Eager.

"Now you're going to have to be a good girl and stay still for me if you want me to eat this pussy and make you come."

I parted her knees wider.

CHAPTER 14
Romy

"Jude, please, seriously! You're killing me." I was quickly unraveling. Unable to think about anything but this growing *need*.

His eyes were like twin pilot lights, blazing in the dark as he peered up at me from between my legs. I stroked the scruff of his cheek, twinning my fingers through his hair until I could grip his soft, dark locks.

That damn crooked grin of his made me rock my hips forward, seeking the friction I desperately wanted. God, I needed him to touch me.

He threaded his thumbs beneath the sides of my panties. Painfully slowly, he inched them down, never taking his eyes off mine.

My heart did a funny, little flutter, making me want to cough to return it to its natural rhythm.

Please, stop looking at me like that.

I didn't want to think about the warmth now spreading from my chest, his eyes still holding mine.

So I gripped his hair harder, urging him on.

"Stay still, honey," he practically growled this time.

He lowered his head, his eyes still watching me beneath dark lashes.

Then he flattened his tongue.

My mouth fell open on a moan as he ran it through my pussy up to my clit, circling that little bundle of nerves with the tip of his tongue, then gently nipped it between his teeth.

I moaned, closing my eyes. My hips rolled toward him. His fingers dug in, holding me in place as he sucked my clit into his mouth, then plunged his tongue inside of me.

"Jude!" I cried.

I ground my hips as he moved from sucking to flicking his tongue before swirling along my opening and plunging into my soaked center. His tongue rolled back up, lavishing me, and before I could demand more, his finger stroked my entrance and slid in. He continued to torture me with his tongue while his finger sank deeper, curling to hit the spot that made me feel as if I was going to fly off the seat.

God, he knew exactly what I needed. No one had ever read my body like he could.

I ground against his finger, wishing it was his cock—that I was filled with *him*.

"Fuck, Romy, my memory doesn't do this justice." His voice was low and rumbly, reverberating through my core while his lips brushed me.

"Play with your nipples while I fuck you with my finger and eat this beautiful pussy," he told me.

My eyes cracked open to see his mouth glistening with me, and I wanted his lips. I wanted to taste myself on him.

"Kiss me, Jude."

He cocked his head and gave me a little smirk. "I thought I told you to play with yourself, honey. Push up your shirt and take out your tits. I want to see you rub and pinch those perfect, hard nipples while you watch me fuck you. I'll let you taste yourself when I'm good and done."

A thrill went through me. This was a side of him I never saw when we were eighteen. I liked him bossy, especially if he was going to call me *honey* and talk dirty.

I pushed up my shirt, bringing my hands to my chest, feeling the hardened peaks through my bra. I released my breasts from their cups, squeezing them gently, brushing my thumbs across my nipples, sending an extra zing of intensity straight to my clit.

"Good girl." He smiled. "Now you can taste how fucking good we are together." He hovered over me, pressing his lips to mine.

I moaned, my mouth opening for him. As his tongue stroked across mine, he plunged two fingers into me.

Yes!

He swallowed my gasp.

"Do you taste yourself on my lips? Don't you taste fucking good?"

I hummed, no longer capable of words, as he thrust his fingers in and out, curling them to stroke against that secret spot not even I could reach. My toes curled in my boots. He pressed his hardened cock against the inside of my thigh, continuing to thrust, stroke, and curl those damn fingers.

Was it this good before? As his body pressed against mine,

I could barely remember before, this moment taking up space and expanding in every molecule of my body.

"That's it, honey, ride my hand. Come for me."

His lips pressed back against mine. My hand dove into his hair, holding him to me. I was on the brink, climbing that tidal wave, knowing I was so close to crashing, to finding that surge of pleasure.

I gripped him harder, feeling the pleasure skyrocket. The heel of his hand pressed against my clit, his fingers stroked my inner wall, and I rode it as if we were climbing altitude, my breath coming in jagged pants with the thinning air.

My climax hit me with such intensity, my mouth went numb. I gripped Jude to me, my hands clamping in his hair and shirt while my body curled in on him. His hand stilled, and he let me ride it until he milked every shudder out of me, my walls locking him in.

I held him to me, panting against his neck, while he slowly extricated his fingers, stroking up through my heat, drawing out an aftershock.

"*Jude*," I gasped. "That was—" I could barely form words. My lips tingled. My body felt boneless. I hadn't come like that since … well, since him.

He raised his head, his eyes hooded. "Incredible. If I could watch you come beneath me every night for the rest of my life, I'd die a happy man."

His thumbs brushed across my cheeks almost reverently.

My heart did that silly, little leap again, and I quickly tamped it down.

Shut up, heart!

Voices and laughter pierced through the sound of our heaving breaths. We stilled, hearing the clops of horses nearing the stables.

"Let's go to the house," Jude said, shifting to help me pull up my panties and jeans.

He gave me that gut-crushing tilt of his lips before tucking a loose tendril of hair behind my ear, lightly kissing me again.

I was still buttoning my pants when Jude started the truck and wrapped his arm around my shoulders. He drew me against his side, and I let him, feeling completely Jell-O-fied.

Pulling away from the stables, the headlights hit the group of returning horses, giving us a flash of their knowing smirks.

Shit. They're all going to know what we were doing.

I was too comfortable with the weight of Jude's arm to shrug it off.

Did I just step into quicksand? Again? This time, I wasn't sure it would be so easy to escape.

Thank God I was leaving tomorrow.

As we entered the double-wide, Jude flicked on lights, illuminating the living room. The pressure of his hand on my lower back followed me in, as if he wasn't ready to let me go.

What was he expecting now? I wanted to invite him to bed with me. I didn't feel half as satiated as I had hoped. Instead, I felt as though he was burrowing into my system, making me crave more of him. I wanted to taste him just like he tasted me. I wanted to slide my hands down his abs. I wanted to run my fingers along his tattoos. I wanted his cum on my lips. My mouth salivated with the thought.

But now, for some reason, my stomach cramped with nerves. He just gave me the most remarkable orgasm in his truck, and *now* I was nervous? What was wrong with me?

I knew this feeling well. Too well. And last time, I ran.

He grasped my hand, turning me to look at him.

Heat still radiated off him, his blue eyes soft and loving.

I was freaking weak in the knees. Who knew it was a real thing? I didn't know if it was from the intense release my body just experienced that caused all the blood to rush out of my legs or if it was the way he was looking at me now.

He stepped into me, lowering his forehead to mine, and spoke softly, "Don't think I don't want you right now. *Fuck*." He closed his eyes briefly. "I'd love nothing more. But if I follow you to that bed, I don't think I'll be able to control myself, and I know I won't want to let you go in the morning."

My body did a little twitch, an echo of his fingers inside me. It now felt empty without him. It felt *wrong*.

"Are you sure?" I asked. I know I wasn't.

Jude nodded, kissing my forehead. "Go get in bed. You need rest. Good night, Romy."

The warm press of his lips was so sweet and gentle. Contrasting from the fevered kisses a moment ago.

"Night, Jude," I said tentatively, taking off his jacket and handing it to him to hang up.

I walked away from him in the living room, down the hall to the bedroom. I wanted him to follow me. I held my breath and willed him to follow me. My center tightened with every step away from him.

But he didn't follow me.

Waking up my last morning at Thornbrush, knowing I was leaving, felt as if I was being skinned alive. Each step I took, packing my bag, felt like I was being flayed.

I didn't remember feeling this way before. Last time I left, it felt as though fire was licking at my heels and I needed to run before it consumed me.

Now, all I felt was anxiety. Leaving my sister to deal with this bullshit she got herself into, leaving the ranch that felt more like home than any place I'd ever lived, and leaving Jude … all to go back to a thankless career that was pushing me out the door. To the chance of running into my ex and his new girlfriend. None of it felt right.

It didn't help that Travis texted me again this morning, asking me when I was going to come get my stuff out of the apartment. It was the last thing I wanted to deal with.

What was I doing? My life seemed more up in the air than it ever had.

I could stay here …

It was only a whisper of a thought. Too flimsy to grab ahold of before it drifted away.

Taking my bag out to the quiet living room, I heard Jude's muffled voice. He was standing outside on the back porch, the sliding door closed. His bare back and tattoos on full display.

How did this man become so fucking hot?

I wanted to run my hand down those ridged back muscles, feel the warmth of his skin, but something stopped me from going to him.

Wearing his damn hat backward, his cell phone was pressed to his ear.

I strained to listen.

"Shit. An eight-week camp? I know, I know … we'll talk about it when you get here. Did he really say that? Fuck Reyes! He makes it really easy to want to say yes to this fight just so I can pound his face in. Okay … watch the curves on the Pass. Truckers scream down the mountain. No." He chuckled. "You're not in Vegas anymore. Wait until you get to the ranch …"

Who was coming here from Vegas? Jude hadn't told me anyone else was coming to the ranch. Did he need to tell me? It almost sounded like he was planning on getting back in the cage. The fucker hadn't even fully recovered from his surgery.

A surge of frustration and irrational anger gripped my throat. I was in the dark, and for whatever reason, I felt as though he was hiding something from me. Just like Travis. I hated feeling that I was being shielded from the truth, that others knew something I didn't when I walked into a room. There was obviously still a lot I didn't know about Jude now. He had established a whole life and career without me over the past decade.

He doesn't even live here, I had to remind myself. The ranch isn't his life anymore. My life was a mess right now, and I wasn't ready to put my heart on the line anyway.

Maybe it was my fucking trust issues or my habit of avoiding conflict, but it was exactly the swift ass-kicking I needed.

Dodge this while you still can, Romy.

My bag in hand, I turned and walked out the door.

Just like the coward I was before, once again, I was leaving without saying goodbye.

I shook my head, disappointed in myself. But not enough to make me turn back.

The rental car was parked next to Jude's truck. I pressed the button to unlock the doors. Throwing my purse and carry-on into the passenger seat, I didn't waste time turning it on and reversing out of the driveway. But I wasn't leaving.

Not yet.

CHAPTER 15
Romy

Chuck was still in the kitchen of the big house sipping his morning coffee when I walked in. The room smelled like bacon and freshly brewed French roast. He stood at the large center island, his hat on the counter waiting to be donned for the day.

"Taking off?" he asked, his bushy, brown brows raised.

"I have to get back for work," I said, setting my purse on the counter.

"Want a cup before you hit the road?"

Caffeine was exactly what I needed. After Jude said good night, I thought my body would succumb to the sheets, exhausted from the foreplay, but instead, all I felt was Jude's heavy presence around me ... and his absence.

I realized I hadn't slept well in a while. I was exhausted.

Chuck pushed a large, terracotta mug across the counter, setting cream and sugar before me with a spoon.

I made up my coffee, stirring in the sugar.

"Should we expect you back?" he asked.

I shrugged. I had planned on returning, but now I didn't

know. Everything just seemed so hard right now. Finding answers wasn't coming easily.

"Does Jude know?"

I took a sip of coffee, avoiding Chuck's gaze.

"He will soon enough," I told him.

"You know that won't sit well with him."

I chanced a glance at him. He was frowning at me, and the last thing I wanted was Chuck disappointed in me. If I was honest, he'd been more of a father figure than my own dad ever was. Always including me in ranch activities while Hazel ran loops around barrels. He knew I hid out here when Mom was sick, and he never once asked me how I was doing—just knew that I needed something to occupy my aching heart.

Guilt lashed through me. Not just because I wasn't saying goodbye to Jude, but because I was leaving Chuck and the ranch when they needed the help. This was my chance to repay him for all the years he took me under his wing. And what was I doing? Abandoning him.

But this time, I wouldn't disappear.

"Can you give my number to the investigator or lawyers if they ask for it? I want to be able to help where I can."

I didn't know if I should tell him—or anyone—about the box in Bronte's stall. It may be best if Jude and I kept that to ourselves for now. I had a feeling it would only hurt my sister's case, and I was still wrestling with the need to protect her, even though I was pissed at her.

"Of course. Can I share it with Jude, too?" There was a mischievous glint to his eyes.

I scoffed, despite the pang of sadness. "If he asks for it."

But I didn't want to talk about Jude; there was something I still needed to know. "Can I ask you a question?"

"Shoot."

"It's just that I've been out of Hazel's life for so long, I feel as if I don't know my sister anymore. I need to know about her and Jesse."

Chuck gave me a sympathetic tilt to his lips. "You know they were together, right?"

"I mean, I kind of figured."

Chuck nodded. "I hired Jesse to help with the cattle and break in some horses. He was great with the animals—a hard worker and energy for days. And you know Hazel and her big, type A personality." He let out a short laugh.

"Yeah, Willows's own shining star," I agreed.

"Our pride and joy. I suppose they matched each other in intensity and work ethic. I knew they would either hit it off or clash. From the very beginning, they made this ranch operate like a well-oiled machine—Hazel oversaw training and the stables, and Jesse managed the cattle and the hired hands. I don't know what I would have done without them while I helped my dad transition to assisted living. Did you know that applying for Medicaid is like a second job?" He chuckled, but there was no humor in it.

I smiled hearing him laugh.

"I relied heavily on them. I suppose I should have checked in more, but I was absorbed in my dad's shit. Pardon my language."

I shook my head, excusing his curse, waiting for him to continue.

He took a big gulp of his coffee. "I'll tell you what I told the investigators. They had one of those intense relationships where they were either near inseparable or yelling at each other. Some of my ranch hands complained, and I did talk to them about it. But Jesse kind of just brushed me off. Hazel, on the other hand, since she knew how much I relied on her—I mean, I see her like another daughter—she took it seriously. I know she tried to set boundaries between her relationship and her job, but when you live on a ranch, that makes it kind of difficult."

"Did it get better?" I wet my lips with my mug.

"For a time, but … I think it was a couple months before all this happened. Hazel just didn't seem like herself. She was quiet and reserved, still doing her job with the same grit, but just letting Jesse boss her around. Whatever boundaries she had set, she just allowed him to walk all over them."

"That doesn't sound like Hazel," I commented.

"No, it doesn't. I tried to talk to Jesse again. I asked him if she was okay. He just dismissed me and said, 'Yeah, she's fine.' I should have talked to Hazel about it. That's my one regret. I guess I thought whatever it was would just blow over. I didn't want to get in the middle of their business. I'm sorry, Romy. If I had, maybe I could have stopped this." His deep frown pulled down the sides of his mustache.

"I know, Chuck. None of this was your fault." I heaved a deep sigh.

I was more convinced now that Hazel had done this. But something must have forced her hand. I still had so many questions. I thought I knew my sister well enough. Had she hit her breaking point and thought killing Jesse was her only means of escape? How bad did it have to get before someone snapped like that?

Part of my anger dissipated at the thought of her having no other choice.

"I know you want answers, Romy. I think we all do."

I nodded. "It's still just so surreal. I'm still processing everything. You'll call me if you hear anything, right?"

"Of course. Here, let's get that to go for you." Chuck reached for my coffee.

"Thank you."

He pulled a thermos from one of the cupboards, pouring it over the sink. "I should probably tell you … Jude may be returning to Vegas."

My heart plummeted, my lungs constricting. "What? Is he thinking about fighting again?"

That call this morning.

Chuck grunted, handing me the thermos. "Seems our boy isn't quite ready to hang up the gloves."

What the fuck, Jude? That selfish bastard. He's going to leave his uncle to tend the ranch on his own? Not to mention, there apparently needed to be a buffer between Lina and the new guy.

What was he thinking? Apparently, winning belts and making money with blood on his fists was a bigger priority than sticking around to help his family. Who gives a fuck that his uncle needed him? Or risking more than just a busted-up knee?

"Bullheaded jackass," I muttered, throwing my purse

across my shoulder.

"They don't call him 'The Bull' for no reason." Chuck followed me out to the car.

"Well, good luck to him." And good riddance.

I suppose having his tongue inside me didn't equate to him sharing his plans.

Chuck sighed, opening my car door for me. "Unfortunately, he comes by it honestly."

I turned to give Chuck a soft smile. "You at least know when to ask for help."

"Took years to swallow that pill. He'll figure it out."

The crunch of tires rolling across the gravel drive made my throat clench. Shit! Here we go. Didn't think I was getting away that easily for a second.

I turned toward the driveway as an old, blue Jeep Wagoneer pulled up. I knew that SUV. My pulse ratcheted up. Spent many rodeo circuits in the back seat following my sister around.

"Shit! Thought I could come and leave before word got to him," I muttered.

"You didn't call him?" Chuck asked, stepping away from my car, giving me easy access to hop in and take off before my father cut the engine.

"Nope."

"He must have heard you were in town."

"Hazel." Shit, sis. You couldn't not tell him?

I crossed my arms, shielding myself, preparing for whatever emotionally manipulative bullshit he was about to spout.

I would much rather face Jude right now than Frank Miller.

He slammed the car into park, hopping out as soon as the

engine shut off.

"So you weren't going to answer any of your old man's calls?" he demanded before his boots even hit the driveway.

Frank Miller looked as though he had aged thirty years since I last saw him. Where his hair was once blond like mine, it was now gray. No longer the clean-shaven, impeccably dressed man I once knew, he now had a bushy, peppered beard, jeans that looked two sizes too big on him, and an old Harley shirt hanging off his shoulders. According to Frank Miller, life did this to him, not his own poor choices or the empty beer cans that most likely littered his kitchen counter. Oh no, of course Frank was never to blame. He was always the victim.

"I'm just leaving," I told him, leaning in to put my purse and the thermos in the car.

"You're going to leave me and your sister alone to deal with all this shit? I raised you better than that, Romy May."

"No, Dad," I scoffed. "Mom raised me. You were too busy being a rodeo dad to Hazel to take notice of me."

"Oh, don't give me that old bullshit. That's not fair, and you know it."

"If I learned anything from you, it was that the only person I can rely on is myself. So you can do what you've always done … wallow in Hazel's drama. How *could* she do this to you?" I rolled my eyes.

His already ruddy face—he more than likely drank his breakfast—turned beet red. "Don't you dare speak to me like that."

"Oh, I dare. Do me a favor, Frank. Lose my number this time? And don't try to track me down again."

Frank stumbled slightly as he stepped forward. "What the fuck is this 'Frank' shit? I'm your father, and you'll show me some respect."

With a calm and steady voice, I stared directly at him to make sure he heard my words. "Both how I refer to you and the respect you think you deserve are earned, not freely given."

I turned to Chuck, whose face had drained of color, his lips pinched firmly as if in restraint. "Bye, Chuck. I'll talk to you soon."

"Take care, darlin'," he said, holding the door again as I got in the car.

"You ungrateful, little bitch," I heard Frank say, right as Chuck closed my door.

Oh, no, he *didn't*. Nothing ever changed with him.

I was just about ready to get back out when Chuck gave the roof of the Hyundai a firm pat, as if to assure me he was taking care of it.

I needed to get out of here before Willows sucked me dry.

Turning on the car and shifting in reverse, I started backing out of the driveway just as I saw Jude's truck fly around the corner. His eyes were wide and wild—desperate—as he watched my car roll away. Then he glanced back at Frank, who was still red-faced and spitting his words, while Chuck tried to direct him back to his car.

My eyes connected with Jude's through the car window. Hurt etched his brow, and his jaw was clenched. He gave me a quick nod before heading over to where Frank and Chuck were going at it.

He would put an end to this.

Now it truly was time for me to leave. I told myself I'd feel some relief once I was headed back down the Pass and returning to San Jose.

Then why did it feel like I was being gutted? Like my heart was being cleaved from my chest with each passing mile marker?

CHAPTER 16
Jude

I came on too strong. I pushed too hard. Too fast. What the hell was wrong with me?

So I let her go.

I could have very well chased her down the mountain, all the way to her gate. Fuck the airline security. I'd make this a damn '90s rom-com for her if I could.

But I chose not to.

My therapist said it was because I thought I deserved abandonment, that I wasn't worth sticking around for. Not even my own mother thought I had been worth it. Romy seemed to just confirm that belief.

"You know you could just call her?" Alex suggested as I hit mile four on the rowing machine.

"Yeah, I know," I grunted out.

Uncle Chuck offered me Romy's number as soon as we escorted Frank off the property. But I simply shook my head without saying a word and retreated. Once again, I had scared her off. She chose to leave without saying goodbye, and I didn't think I could handle the rejection right now.

Show your cards and you get burned.

Maybe one of these days, I'd learn.

It had been a week since she left. Uncle Chuck and Coach were getting tired of watching me mope around. I threw all of my pent-up frustration into working out, cleaning stalls, and repairing fences.

I made Alex do it with me. He committed all his gusto into helping me, just like any task he took on. And he was fucking cheerful doing it! I was going to knock that perfect, little smirk off his face if he kept this up.

It was *obnoxious*.

"Afraid she won't pick up?" Alex sat on the bench press, his arms resting on his knees, watching the mileage on the console.

Alex Torres looked like the happiest guy in the world when he stepped out of his black, rental Expedition, his Versace duffel bag draped across his chest. His perfectly white smile gleamed brighter when he took in a big whiff of high desert air, bragging about renting the most quintessential mountain cabin. I don't think he'd ever been in a place that wasn't sunny and hot 24/7, evidenced by his perma-tan. He absolutely did not know how to pack for an Oregon spring. The man brought shorts and T-shirts.

Even now, as he oversaw my workout in the garage, he was wearing a pair of my sweats, the hoodie pulled up tight over his face. He may have to grow a beard if he wanted to keep his face warm, too.

"This is classic Romy," I told him between reps. "I *know* she won't fuckin' pick up."

Apparently, this was classic Jude, too. Me wanting something so badly I go balls to the walls, only to be left feeling rejected.

"You don't seem okay with it. Won't even talk to me about this fight."

"No, I'm not fucking okay," I asserted.

At least I could be honest that I wasn't okay. That's growth, right?

"Venture's expecting my call. What do I tell him? We have eight weeks. It's already going to be a short camp."

"You don't have to remind me," I whined. Mile five was the worst!

Alex shoved off his knees, coming to stand beside me. "You should go to her since we're obviously not getting anything done. Sort out your shit with her, and as soon as you're back, we'll hit Vegas for your eight-week training camp."

"I'm not going to Vegas."

The ranch needed me. Uncle Chuck needed me. And someone had to keep Lina and Reed from biting each other's heads off. And, what if she came back …

"Figured as much." Alex released a deep exhale. "What if I propose we do our training here—at the ranch?"

Mile five. Done.

I stopped to look at him. "What?"

Sweat dripped in my eyes. My muscles were on fire.

He was giving me that straight, white smile of his, dimples popping.

"But you need to push this to the side for now. Just temporarily until after the fight. No distractions. Having this

Romy shit hanging over your head … Your mental game needs to be on point, 100 percent."

"The 'Romy shit' isn't hanging over my head," I seethed. I didn't like what he implied or the sound of Romy's name coming out of his mouth.

"Don't start lying to yourself, too," Alex said. "I need you to be 'The Bull' right now, or a shortened camp isn't going to work."

"You're an annoying asshole, you know that?"

"I've been told that a time or two. So here's the thing—I'd like to think I'm a pretty good sleuth when it comes to internet stalking. Like, do you remember that one time, when we found out that girl you were talking to was totally catfishing you?"

I rolled my eyes and groaned. "Don't remind me. Another reason why I stay off social media now. I was an idiot."

"That you were. But that's beside the point. The point is, I'm a damn good detective when it comes to finding someone on the internet."

I huffed. The man didn't need any detective skills to find women. They came to him.

"Well," he continued, "I figured out where she teaches."

My breath caught in my throat. "I don't know whether I should pummel you or thank you."

Alex brushed me off. "You can thank me later. If she's not going to answer your calls, you might as well just show up."

"At the school where she teaches? Are you insane? I don't think so." Hell, no. I wasn't about to waltz into a middle school and demand that the girl I was hung up on talk to me. At her place of work, mind you.

"Figured out the school schedule, too. It's posted on their website. The last day of school is on Thursday, and teachers have a workday on Friday to pack up for the summer. You can show up after she gets off, meet her in the parking lot—let's say three o'clock, right after your 1:45 plane lands in San Jose—"

"Fuck! You didn't!" I grabbed the towel off the barbell rack, scrubbing the sweat off my face.

"You can thank me by accepting this fight." He was grinning as if he already knew he'd won.

"You're not giving me much choice, are you?"

Alex shrugged. "It was a matter of time. I was just speeding up the process. We need to start training now if you're going to beat Reyes in August."

I sighed, waving my white towel in surrender. She wasn't going to come back with me, but maybe it would give me the closure I needed all these years.

"When does the flight take off?"

"Eleven thirty boarding time Friday morning." He retrieved his phone from his pocket, immediately going into his email to forward the boarding pass to me.

"Fine. I guess you better call Mr. Venture."

Chapter 17
Romy

I piled my hair into a messy bun on top of my head, sweating from packing up my classroom. The final box was everything from my desk. The curriculum materials, supplies, furniture, and posters were all going to the next teacher who inherited the classroom. I had already loaded my car with three boxes and was coming back for the last one. But I needed to leave room in my Civic for everything I was getting from my apartment.

I shot Travis a text.

ME

I'll be there around 3:30 if you want to NOT be there. I'll leave my keys on the counter.

Thankfully, Brit had some room in her small apartment garage to store my boxes while I hunted for a new apartment. Now that school was out, I could dedicate some time to that. Especially before I headed back to Willows. Hazel's lawyer had gotten ahold of me, asking for a character witness at her hearing. I still hadn't confirmed whether or not I'd be there, but I knew I should.

I taped up the final box, looking around at my classroom. I hadn't grown an attachment to it knowing how temporary every position had been over the last few years. I didn't feel any sort of way about leaving—just a sense of exhaustion and relief, ready to move on.

Over the last week, I threw myself into every end-of-school-year volunteer position. Staying busy was exactly what I needed to get my mind off Jude. When Chuck called to check up on me, I had to bite the inside of my cheek until I tasted blood so I wouldn't ask about Jude.

Part of me thought if I just kissed him, maybe fooled around a bit, I could get this out of my system, but instead, it created this insatiable need that I didn't know existed. Like all these years, this need was left dormant, just waiting to be stoked.

And stoked it was.

I blew a long exhale, whisking a loose tendril out of my eyes. I hit the lights, heading to the main office to turn in my keys and my checkout paperwork.

"Hope you have a good summer, Sandra," I told our head secretary, handing her the keys and paperwork.

"You, too! Looks like your summer break is already starting off in the parking lot." She winked, her glossy lips smirking.

My brows pinched. "What do you mean?" I shifted the box in my arms, swinging my head toward the office windows overlooking the staff parking lot.

A tall guy with bulky, tattooed arms leaned against a car, his baseball-capped head bowed, his hands shoved into his pockets.

Oh, fuck. I heaved a breath.

"I offered to call down to your classroom for him, but he insisted on waiting outside."

I didn't know if Jude cornering me in my classroom was any better than at my car.

I gave Sandra a weak smile. "Thanks."

I was a mess in cutoff shorts, a baggy T-shirt, no makeup, and my hair in an updo. I didn't even bother to look in a mirror this morning. I was sweaty and tired, about to head to my apartment—now my ex-boyfriend's apartment.

Jude lifted his head, his eyes shadowed beneath his hat, when I walked out. God, could he quit it with that lopsided smile of his! It did things to a girl. He straightened, turning his ball cap around.

I could ask him what he was doing here, but I already knew. He wasn't going to let me go as easily as he had before. He blatantly checked me out from head to toe and back again, heat traveling with his eyes. His chiseled, scruffy jaw flexed.

What I wouldn't do to feel that scruff burn between my legs again.

I shook my head. *Nope!* Don't need to go there right now.

"This isn't a great time," I told him.

He stepped toward me, his fingers skimming mine as he took the box, sending shivers down my arms. His blue eyes bored into mine.

"I could make this a great time." He winked. His lips tipped in a cocky grin.

Oh, God. Heat shot straight to my center. My toes curled

in my Converse.

I let him take the box, fishing for the car keys in my pocket, trying my best to hide the flush scalding my cheeks.

"No, really, Jude," I said, avoiding his gaze. I opened the car door and popped the trunk so he could load the box. "This isn't a great time. I have to get my stuff out of my apartment."

"Moving?" he asked, closing the trunk.

I looked at him then, his brows raised in question, waiting for my reply.

"Eventually. I'm staying with a friend right now."

"I can come with you and help." He looked so eager, his eyes so warm and … loving?

"No, I can't let you do that." I shook my head adamantly.

His eyes narrowed, scanning my face. "Why do you have to get your stuff out of *your* apartment?" It came out in nearly a growl.

I sighed. I suppose I had to let him know now. My eyes shuddered on the nearly painful words I had to say to him. I had this sinking feeling he wasn't going to like to hear what I had to say.

"It was my place with my boyfriend—ex now. He cheated, so I left him." I said it so matter-of-factly, even though I was still pissed at Travis.

Jude swallowed, his Adam's apple bobbing. His knuckles cracked when he closed his fists. "I'm fucking going with you."

I scoffed. "He's not going to be there, so you don't have anything to worry about."

"Fuck that. I'm going with you." He headed around the hood of my car, opened the passenger-side door, and got in.

Great. I looked up to the heavens. The cloudless, blue California sky made the sun feel ten times hotter—or maybe it was Jude sitting in my passenger seat.

I opened my door and slid in.

"Were you still with him when you came to Willows?" he asked as soon as I buckled.

"Wow, you're not going to beat around the bush, are you?" I snorted.

"Well, were you?" he asked again, turning in his seat to face me.

"I'm not the cheater." I was smiling at him, not because this was funny, but because this was ridiculous. "I would think you'd know me better than that."

"I don't know, Romy. I think when someone disappears on someone, after twelve years, they might not know each other anymore. So, no, I don't think I know you well enough not to assume."

I threw up my hands. "Thanks, Jude. Thanks for throwing that in my face. That's so nice of you. Can we get past this? And to answer your question very clearly, no—no, I was not with him when I let you go down on me in your truck."

His teeth ground together. Breaths heaved in his chest. I didn't know if he was going to yell at me or pounce on me. I'd much prefer the latter.

I squeezed my knees together. Goddammit. Even angry, he made me hot.

"Thank you very much for clarifying that," he groused. "I'm still going with you."

I groaned, tipping my head back before putting the keys in

the ignition. "You're being a stubborn asshole."

"You're welcome. I'll happily give you stubborn asshole if it means you don't have to walk into your ex's place by yourself."

Despite his anger irritating me, a knot grew in my throat. No one was ever protective of me. Only him.

"You thought you were going to fit all of this in your Civic?" Jude asked. "You'll have to take me back to the school to get my rental."

"It will fit. I mean, you may have to hold a couple in your lap, but it will fit," I told him. If he wasn't taking up my passenger seat, there'd be no question.

"Where are you putting it all?"

"At my friend Brit's place."

"No," he threw over his shoulder.

"What do you mean, 'no'?"

I was following Jude's perfect ass out to the apartment parking lot, where we were loading up my car.

"I'll have it shipped to Willows."

"Jude."

"Romy."

"Oh, hey! Romy—" Travis came around the corner right then. A gorgeous, auburn-haired woman in leggings and a bright-pink sports bra holding his hand.

"Shit!" I exclaimed, startled, nearly dropping the box on my toe. As soon as the surprise washed away, it was replaced with frustration. "Travis, I texted you so you'd know when I was here."

"Yeah, I thought you'd be gone by now," he said sheepishly.

The air shifted at my side, Jude retracing his steps to stand beside me.

"You could have texted," I told him.

Why didn't he text? Did he want to rub this in my face?

Jude grabbed my box to put on top of his. "You could have fucking texted her, man, to see if she was done." His voice was calm and deep, demanding that Travis look at him, not me.

Travis shot a look at Jude. Then a double take. "Who—wait, holy shit! Jude 'The Bull' Larsen?"

Of course Travis would recognize the cage fighter beside me.

"Yes, Travis, yes, he is." I smirked at him, wrapping a hand around Jude's bulging bicep, ready to take advantage of this.

Travis's eyes grew huge, star-struck. "Are you"—he gestured between us—"seeing each other?"

"It's not …" Jude began.

"Yes, yes we are," I butted in. I hoped Travis saw the fucking glow Jude gave me. I could feel Jude's eyes boring into the side of my face, but I ignored him.

"Wow, you didn't waste any time," Travis sneered.

Asshole.

"You're right. There's no time to waste when the man you *just* wasted an entire year on never could satisfy you. Now that I know how fulfilled—or should I say 'filled'—I can feel, I'm desperate to make up for lost time." I turned to Christina, or whatever her name was. Her eyes flicked over Jude's physique appreciatively before connecting with mine. "I hope you have better luck with him."

Travis's ears grew two shades redder.

Jude cleared his throat, forcing me to look up at him. His brow was pinched, studying me to discern the truth through my snarky remarks. I gave him a brief pleading look to play along.

"You know what?" Jude turned to consider Travis, shifting the boxes in his strong arms. "I'm so glad you fucked up. I'm not about to waste Romy's time or leave her unsatisfied. That last box in there," he said, jerking his head toward the apartment, "you can have it shipped to Thornbrush Ranch, Willows, Oregon."

"I … I don't know where that is," Travis stumbled, the red spreading from his ears to his face.

"I *know* you know how to use your phone, Travis," I jeered. "Look it up."

Jude and I turned on our heels, heading to my car, ignoring his new girlfriend whispering how hot "The Bull" was. That's right, missy. I just got a major upgrade.

Jude stuffed the last two boxes in the back seat, and I reached for my purse.

"There's one more thing I have to do," I told him, pulling out my vibrator and hustling back over to where they were heading to the apartment.

Travis looked up, surprise on his face.

"Here, you can have *my precious* lovebug. She's going to need it." I switched my gaze to Christina, her mouth hanging ajar. "Trust me, you'll thank me."

Without letting them get a word in edgewise, I jogged back to the car.

Jude had a smug look on his face. "Not going to need that?"

We both slid into the car, closing the doors and shutting out this chapter of my life.

"Nope." I popped the P. "I think I'm good." My lips tipped in a knowing look.

"Is this your way of apologizing for taking off without saying goodbye?"

"Maybe." I tightened my jaw, hoping he'd see it that way.

"Then you're coming home with me," Jude declared, his aquamarine eyes penetrating.

I don't think he saw my attempt to apologize as cute. His face was serious. He wasn't playing.

Where was home for him now? That call he was on before I left … Chuck saying he would return to Vegas.

"Jude, I can't go to Vegas with you."

"No, not Vegas. The ranch."

Oh. So he didn't intend to fight again?

He leaned forward, tipping my chin until my mouth was inches from his.

"You're coming *home* with me, honey," he repeated, his breath skittering across my lips.

I gasped.

"We have a flight tomorrow. I'll pick you up at eight in the morning. We're going home, Romy."

"Bossy much?" I chided, but my words came out breathy and needy.

I wanted him to kiss me.

"Romy, honey." His lips tipped. "I think I know you well enough to know you would debate for hours on whether to get on that plane, and I'm not about to miss our flight. So if I need to be demanding, I will be. If I have to throw you over my shoulder and show you just how in control I can be, just say the word." The last words came out a raspy whisper, but I'd never heard him more clearly.

My stomach flipped. I liked this version of Jude, confident and assertive.

"Okay," was all I managed to say.

I shifted in my seat, wanting to close the distance.

He chucked my chin. "That's my girl."

I groaned when he leaned back in his seat, buckling the seat belt.

Jerk. He wasn't going to kiss me?

The tip of his lips turned into a genuine grin, smile lines bracketing his gorgeous smile. His sky-blue eyes twinkled.

I was in trouble, and we both knew it.

CHAPTER 18
Jude

Knowing she needed time to process going home with me and running into her ex and his new girlfriend—what a fucking tool—I left her at Brit's house while I checked into my hotel. I gave her a night to ponder. A night for me to cool my jets. After that encounter with the guy who cheated on her, I wanted to punch some shit, throw her over my shoulder, take her to my preverbal cave like a fuckin' Neanderthal, and claim her as mine all night long.

Hell, yes, I worried she'd back out, but I needed to trust her and whatever was between us. I needed to give her room to breathe, to come to the realization on her own that going home to the ranch was *right*.

I showed back up at eight the next morning to help her pack a couple bags before I gripped her hand and walked her to my rental car. She didn't waffle or hum indecisively like I thought she might. No. Romy pumped my hand as it held hers, as if to assure herself this was all real.

I could barely keep my eyes off her, let alone my hands, as we boarded the plane. I couldn't help it. I had to touch her.

I tucked a tendril of hair behind her ear, grasped her hand, pressed my palm against the small of her back, and tucked her into my side.

She didn't pull away from me, either. She leaned into my touch. Resting her head on my shoulder like she'd done all those years ago.

Contentment washed over me as she took a nap on my shoulder midair while my hand never left her thigh. I barely paid attention to my in-flight movie, too distracted by the way her dark lashes fanned across her pink cheeks, how her rosy lips parted in soft, shallow breaths.

Once we touched down in Portland and hit the road in my truck, she seemed relaxed, kicking off her Converse and propping her feet up on the dash while we talked all the way home.

The four-hour drive to Willows turned into a chance to talk uninterrupted. We laughed at old memories and new jokes, played our favorite songs for each other, even shared moments from our lives the other had missed. When she started to get hangry, I went through the drive-thru for burgers and soft-serves. I didn't press for updates on Hazel, ask her about her last relationship, or mention my impending fight. There would be time for all that.

Instead, I learned that she loved trashy reality TV and read romantasy books with dragons, that she preferred her chocolate dark with sea salt caramel, and she had a huge celebrity girl crush on Zendaya.

I shared with her that I loved the HGTV channel. She laughed, unable to picture me getting down with some *House*

Hunters or reruns of *Fixer Upper*. Not only had I updated the double-wide, but I had done my own home renovation projects on my Vegas house—laying new floors, grouting tile. I considered flipping houses as a hobby, but I had yet to see that idea to fruition.

Even when I saw Romy's shoulders bunch toward her ears with worry as we wound up the Pass toward Willows, I kept it light. I ran my hand along her knee to soothe her. And when we turned off Highway 20 to the gravel road toward Thornbrush, I continued stroking her knee until I saw her posture loosen.

I breathed in the fresh country air as soon as we exited my truck, pulling Romy into my side. Relief. Pure, sheer relief in knowing I had Romy home with me.

We stepped out in front of the double-wide, bags in hand. It was a warm day, promising a hot summer, but a cool breeze blew through the pines off the Deschutes. In the distance, I could hear the cattle grazing out in the pasture.

Home.

It felt more like home than it ever had, especially with this girl tucked at my side.

"Go ahead." I nudged her forward, taking her bags. "Let's get you settled in. I already made up the bedroom for you."

She shot me a look. "A little cocky, don't you think?"

I gave her a wink. "Determined."

She giggled. Really fucking giggled. And it was the cutest thing I'd ever heard.

"Don't worry, though, I'll sleep on the couch," I assured her, noticing her hesitation in ascending the steps.

I'd step carefully, take this slow—anything to make us last

this time.

"Jude, I'm not going to kick you out of your own bed." Her cheeks flamed, and I knew exactly what she was picturing.

Believe me, it was seared into my mind. I wanted to see her writhe beneath me. In my bed, while screaming my name. It was *all* I pictured.

"Honey, there'll be time for that." I hovered over her, leaning down to drop a peck on the tip of her nose.

She scoffed a laugh. "You're such a gentleman."

"Only for you."

I watched Romy through the front windows. Her cell phone pressed to her ear as she paced back and forth on the porch. I couldn't make out her words, but her mouth was tight—firm—while she spoke to Hazel. She kept pushing her hand through her hair. Whatever was being said, Romy was furious. I couldn't see her eyes, shielded beneath aviator sunglasses. But I could imagine those silver orbs ablaze.

"She needs a break," Lina commented from her seat on the kitchen stool.

I took a gulp of my after-workout protein shake. I had given Romy space and time once we got back. I didn't want to push too hard. Too fast. I was like an excited, little boy having her here ... in my house, in my bed. I had to be patient. I wasn't going to fuck this up. So instead, I channeled all my pent-up energy—and sexual frustration—into helping Uncle Chuck around the ranch and adding an extra workout to my daily regimen. Not to mention the extra-long showers to rub one out.

My cell phone buzzed in my pocket. Setting down my shake, I pulled it out.

COACH

Have you told her yet?

I had texted Alex last night to let him know we were back, and we had training scheduled for Monday.

ME

No.

COACH

You're going to have to. The press release just went live.

ME

Shit!

My cell vibrated again with the corresponding link. I clicked on it.

SUMMER FIGHT NIGHT: LARSEN VS. REYES

MMA action returns August 20th in Venture Fight Organization's Summer Fight Night: Larsen vs. Reyes at MGM Arena in Las Vegas. The main event begins at 10 p.m. with prelims at 7 p.m.

Four-time light-heavyweight champion Jude Larsen (20–3–1) goes head-to-head with undefeated Mike Reyes (11–0). Current title holder Larsen gets back in the cage after his third knee surgery in five years. Reyes looks to make his winning streak 12–0 and take the belt.

Oh, God. I ran a hand down my face.

I needed to tell Romy.

I wasn't sure how she was going to take it, and I felt that I had to be gentle with her right now. Anything could trigger her to take off again. If I was being honest with myself, like my therapist was helping me to be, I'd say I was scared shitless to lose her.

"She's going to create a hole in that porch," Lina commented. "The girl is stressed. You need to help her *de-stress*."

I shot Lina a look, shaking my head.

"What?" she asked innocently. Her youthful appearance—cheeks still rosy from her trail ride, and her brown, wind-blown braids—made her look innocent. But I knew my cousin. She was far from it. "If you're not going to, then it's up to me. Let's go out tonight."

"It's Sunday night," I told her matter-of-factly.

"So." She drew out the word. "No one works tomorrow. Come on! It'll be fun! We can go to the Rooster. They have a live band there tonight, and the patio's open."

"It's Memorial Day Weekend. It will be crawling with tourists."

"Ugh!" She groaned. "Don't be a fucking loser. If you're worried about someone noticing you, the lighting there isn't that great, and you're not as big as you think you are."

"Ouch! Little brat."

She shrugged. "Someone has to keep your ego in check."

"The last time I went there, Christian announced my entrance to the entire bar."

"And how did that work out for you?"

God, she was extra annoying today.

But she wasn't wrong.

I found Romy. That's how it worked out for me. But I hadn't been there long enough for someone to bother me. The idea of a crowded bar gave me anxiety.

Deep inhale. Count to ten. Deep exhale.

"That's what I thought." Lina took my breathing to mean I was relenting. "If the champ ends up having too many fans fawning over him, then we just go sit outside on the patio." She leaned over the counter to give me a condescending pat on the cheek. "You'll be fine."

"I'm the drama queen? Are you fucking kidding me!" Romy yelled, her voice cutting through the glass.

Our heads swung to the front windows. Romy threw up a hand in disbelief.

I tightened my jaw. My knuckles whitened, gripping my protein shake. *Fucking Hazel.*

"Okay, she may need a drink after that call," I conceded.

"Yes!" Lina did a little wiggly dance on the stool.

Romy hung up the phone and stormed through the front door, pushing her sunglasses atop her head. She tossed her cell phone onto the kitchen island. "She's fucking lying, and I know it. The most frustrating thing is that I think she has convinced herself it's the truth. She's pleading self-defense, but the investigators didn't find any evidence of a fight. She's going to lose, and they are going to find her guilty."

"I'm so sorry, honey." I sidled up to her, close enough for her to know I was right here if she needed me, but far enough away to give her space.

"Jesse and Hazel would get into some pretty heated arguments," Lina offered.

"That's what Chuck said." Romy nodded.

"Maybe the jury will recognize the signs of abuse." Lina popped a shoulder.

Romy's eyes connected with mine.

"Was that what was going on?" she asked Lina.

"I don't know." She shook her head. "But she sure wasn't herself leading up to everything. It makes me wonder …"

We waited for Lina to finish her thought, but like me, she noticed that Romy's eyes drooped and her mouth tightened. If I still knew her like I thought I did, she was now feeling guilty for losing her temper with Hazel.

"You need a drink," Lina advised.

Romy gave a humorless laugh. "Yeah, probably a few strong ones."

Lina's eyes sparkled, clapping her hands together. "Perfect because we're going out tonight. And don't even think there is any other answer than 'Hell, yes!'"

"Sure, but I didn't bring any going-out clothes," Romy said.

Lina waved her off. "It's just the Rooster, nothing fancy. There'll be live music, and I already told this champ"—Lina gave me a wink—"that if it's too much for anyone, we can hang out on the patio. We'll have a few drinks and shoot the shit, unwind. It's exactly what we all need. I know I need to get away from the ranch. Fucking Reed is on my last nerve," she grumbled. "If I have to hear his smug voice one more time, I'm going to scream."

The last thing I wanted was some douchebag giving my

baby cousin a hard time, even if she was a pain in my ass sometimes. I knew she could take care of herself, but I still couldn't help being protective of her.

"Do I need to talk to him?" I offered.

"Nah, I got it handled. He might be a thorn in my fucking side, but I can dish it out just as well as he can. He'll be looking for another job by the end of the year."

"Lina," I warned. "Your dad needs the help. Reed seems to know what he's doing."

She waved it off, hopping down from her stool. "I'll make him be our designated driver tonight, then. He'll *love* that."

"I thought you just said you needed to get away from him, little cuz," I said, staring at her with a raised brow.

With evil intent in her eyes and a swish of her hips, she walked out without a word. I think she was right; she didn't need my help. Reed was in trouble if he thought Lina was going to let him get comfortable here.

CHAPTER 19
Romy

"Thanks for that," Lina said, patting Reed's solid chest as she and I slid out the back seat of his four-door Dodge Ram.

Reed's jaw ticked, but he didn't say a word while Lina breezed past him, his eyes following her ass in her Daisy Dukes. He shut the door behind us, quickly returning to his usual glower.

Jude waited for us, taking my hand as if it was the most normal thing in the world. I smiled up at him. He looked good tonight in his tight, black T-shirt, showing off his sleeve tats and delicious muscles, with dark-wash jeans that hugged his sculpted ass. He wasn't wearing his hat tonight, his dark hair tousled in a careless way, curling around his ears and falling across his forehead. Jesus, I wanted to run my fingers through those locks. Where was the nearest secluded wall I could get pushed up against?

It was a warm night, so I opted for a yellow, floral sundress with a pair of cowboy boots. No bra. I felt bold and wanted to dress up, like I needed a "power suit" to help brush off

Hazel's call, so I chose something that made me feel sexy. Jude confirmed it was the right choice with the way his eyes appraised every inch of me. It made me feel formidable.

He leaned down to whisper in my ear, his lips brushing the outer shell. "You look fucking incredible. I'm dying to know what's under that dress." I felt my pulse pick up, knowing he'd find nothing.

We followed Lina into the loud bar.

I gave Jude my sexiest smirk. "I guess you'll have to find out for yourself."

His already-blazing blues heated, and his hand didn't leave mine, pulling me behind him as we weaved through the crowd toward the bustling bar.

The billiard table was abandoned tonight for other entertainment. The cover band was loud in the small bar, sending the rumble of the bass through the soles of my boots. People were dancing and singing under the glow of the neon cowboy and beer signs.

Sage and two other bartenders were slinging drinks for the tourists and regulars who packed the only bar in town.

"Can you go bother someone else?" Sage was saying to Christian when we joined him at the bar.

"Baby, you know you bother me, too." He wagged his brows, leaning across the bar to snag an olive from the prep board and pop it in his mouth.

"Get your grubby hands away from here," she scolded, pushing his hand away.

"Ooh, do that again." He exaggerated a full-body shudder before reaching his hand out to her.

"Oh, thank God you're all here," Sage said to us, giving Christian a side-eye. "What can I get ya'll?"

Jude exchanged fist bumps with Christian.

"Whiskey sours for Romy and me and the pilsner on tap for Jude," Lina ordered. "Oh, and a soda for that one," she said dismissively, pointing out Reed who found a seat at the bar.

Sage glanced at Reed.

"A coke, please. I'll take it here," he ordered in his gruff voice.

"You got it!" Sage went right to work.

"You sure, bro?" Christian asked Reed, but Reed only grunted.

"Ordering for me now?" Jude turned to his cousin.

"I invited you all, so I'm in charge of our outing. Gotta ensure we have fun, and if it means making sure you're not a grumpy ass, then yes, yes, I will order for you," Lina said, putting her hands on her hips.

Jude chuckled. "At least you know my order."

"Besides, I'm here to make sure Romy has a good time, and you're a vital part of that."

"Fair enough," he said, giving my hand a squeeze. I squeezed back.

Lina pulled me away from Jude. "Come on, let's go grab a table. You got the drinks?" She threw the last phrase over her shoulder. It was more of a command than a request.

"I got the drinks," he confirmed.

I followed Lina over to a high-top table with four chairs. It was far enough in the corner that we would be able to talk over the thrum of the electric guitars and chatter, but it was close enough to the band that we could still enjoy the music.

The band was playing a Zac Brown Band cover when Jude and Christian came over with our drinks.

Jude sat beside me, his hand immediately going to the leg of my chair, grabbing it to draw me closer. He sat sideways, his legs bracketing me while his arm rested across the back of my chair. He was so close, I could feel the heat emanating from him.

I took a gulp of my cold drink.

He set his beer down, his hand going to my bare knee. The chilly condensation left from his glass imprinted on my thigh, causing my flesh to pebble. His thumb stroked back and forth where the hem of my dress fluttered, nearly driving me to distraction.

I tilted my head to look up at him, his eyes heated as he took me in. His lips tipped in a knowing, adoring way. That delicious scruff begging me to scratch my nails along his jaw.

This man!

He didn't know that I nearly called this off. I might still be in California if Brit hadn't told me to get my head out of my ass … that I would never learn if I could trust anyone if I didn't give them a chance. And if anyone deserved a chance, wasn't the man who flew all the way to San Jose to fetch me worth entrusting with my heart?

"You won't know if you don't try," Brit soothed, handing me a big bowl of ice cream. "You can't keep running."

She was right. I knew she was right. But getting over years of engrained trust issues was easier said than done, especially with Travis's cheating still relatively fresh. All I knew how to do was protect my heart, to run before I got burned. Not how to give my trust and my heart freely.

I wanted to learn, though, for Jude. He deserved that.

So I decided to do something that scared the shit out of me—to trust.

When Jude showed up this morning, he didn't even bat an eye when I slowly started packing, mentally debating to take this leap, dragging my feet. Thinking that if I stalled, he'd say or do something that warranted me telling him to fuck off, and then I could sit my ass right back down on Brit's couch. Instead, he grabbed a suitcase and helped me pack, even folding my underwear into neat piles. I had no excuse.

Despite the years apart, he was still the only one who truly knew me. Knowing the right things to say to distract me from my own mental spiraling, to lend a comforting touch when I was feeling anxious, or to make me laugh when I became too serious. He even knew when I was pissed and just needed space to cool down. He had been my best friend, and I didn't realize until now just how much I'd missed him. How I had been homesick for him.

"Drink that down," Lina told me, nudging me out of my thoughts. "Then we'll get you another one before we hit the dance floor."

I was in my head. Rolling around my feelings for Jude and trying to wash away my frustration and guilt about Hazel made me withdraw.

The phone call still didn't sit right with me. She was telling investigators, and me, it was self-defense, but could it also be premeditated? She had a note and money stashed away. Was she planning an escape? Was she thinking Jesse was going to kill her? Was she plotting to kill him before he could kill her? There were so many questions milling around in my brain, I just couldn't see the truth through the trees. At least, not yet.

I needed to brush it off. For tonight anyway. I needed a break from my mental roller coaster.

I pounded back the whiskey cocktail.

"Damn, girl," Lina sing-songed. "Let me get us another one."

She hopped off her chair and headed back to the bar.

"You doing okay?" Jude asked.

Not wanting Christian to hear my business, I shrugged. I wasn't in the mood to talk about it anyway.

"Sage is brilliant. She already had two more ready for us," Lina said, quickly returning to her seat and handing me another whiskey sour.

"That's why she's my future wife." Christian sighed, hearts in his eyes.

Jude scoffed a laugh. "Does she know that?"

"I tell her every chance I get. She just doesn't believe me yet." Christian took a big swallow of his beer.

Lina rolled her eyes, ignoring Christian. "She offered to fill a pitcher for you guys, too." Her eyebrows quirked over the rim of her glass as she took a sip.

"I'm good," Jude returned, nursing his beer. "I have a workout tomorrow."

"When do you *not* have a workout?" Lina inquired.

"Bro needs to keep that impeccable bod in shape," Christian teased. "I mean, look at him. He's hot!" He licked his pointer finger, pretending to touch Jude's shoulder, and made a sizzling sound.

Lina grumbled while Jude laughed, and I couldn't help but do my own scan of his body. I pressed my knee against his, wanting to feel more of him. He answered it with his own knee press.

The band started the first notes of Blanco Brown's "The Git Up," and Lina just about screamed.

"Romy Miller! Come on! Get that ass up and shake it with me!"

She flew off her seat, taking my hand and pulling me off my seat.

"Hold on." I laughed, then took another gulp of my drink before shooting Jude a wink and a smile and joining her on the dance floor.

CHAPTER 20
Jude

"Y ou're a goner, bro," Christian commented, nudging his shoulder with mine as I watched Romy smile and laugh while she danced.

Her long, wavy hair swayed as she and Lina joined the crowd in a line dance. Her creamy skin was glowing tonight, that yellow dress swishing midthigh. A peek of that phoenix flashing every time she turned was driving me wild.

"Yeah." I didn't say much more. It's a fact. It's been a fact since we were teenagers. The truth—she was my endgame.

I couldn't take my eyes off her. Her smile is radiant, her eyes glitter when she laughs. She's gorgeous inside and out, and it's like a sucker punch to the gut.

"Have you told her about your fight yet?" Christian asked.

I took another sip of my beer and straightened out in my seat, resting my elbows on the table. The question made me uneasy because I was nervous to tell her. "Not yet."

"I saw the press release. You're going to have to tell her."

"I know. I'm just waiting for the right moment, but with this shit with her sister, I haven't wanted to add anything else to what she has going on."

I couldn't resist glancing back at Romy and Lina to make sure they were having a good time. She was magnetic. Both of them were, really. And apparently, I wasn't the only one who saw it. Reed had turned in his barstool, pretending to be interested in the band but repeatedly flitting his eyes to Lina.

"What's the worst that could happen?" Christian asked.

I scanned the room, landing on another high-top table diagonal from ours. Two guys in cowboy hats had their fists around the necks of their beer bottles while staring at the girls. An unsettling feeling filled my gut.

One of them, sandy-colored hair falling across his forehead beneath his hat, had his eyes narrowed on Romy.

"She'll leave," I said absently. "Hey, who's that?" I nodded toward the other table.

In all my years facing opponents in the cage, I could tell when someone was unhinged. This man gripped his beer hard enough that I wouldn't be surprised if it shattered. His friend beside him was trying to speak to him, but he ignored him, his jaw ticking while his eyes zeroed in on Romy.

I didn't fucking like it.

"Shit," Christian said. "That's Junior Matheus, Jesse's brother."

Jesse's brother? Oh, fuck. I needed to get Romy out of here. First Jesse's mom, now his brother.

As soon as Junior pushed himself away from the table and started charging toward Romy, I was out of my seat.

Fuck that!

Three long strides in my six-foot-three frame, and I was

stepping in between Junior and Romy before he could even reach her. I pushed her behind me.

His face scrunched in a crimson fury, his eyes flaming at Romy behind my shoulder. He didn't even register that I was in front of him, he was in such a rage. Most likely drunk, too, he could only see one thing. He stepped forward, intent on getting to Romy. But I wasn't about to let that happen. He'd have to go through me first.

"Your sister's a fucking, murderous cunt!" he roared. "Just you wait! I'm going to do everything in my power to make sure she rots in that fucking jail cell for what she did to my brother."

Romy's hand went to my back, and I could feel her pulse through her palm.

There was no way this guy was going to intimidate my girl.

"You better back the fuck up," I told him, hoping he'd swing his attention to me.

But he didn't. He raised his arm, pointing at her shielded behind me, inches away from my face. I felt my blood boil at his audacity to invade my space.

"Don't believe a word that comes out of that bitch's mouth. Hazel's bat-shit crazy," he ground out, his words slicing through the din of the bar.

"Get out of here, Junior!" Lina called from behind us.

Junior ignored her, his anger still directed toward Romy.

"Get your hand out of my face," I demanded. I itched to push it out of my air space.

He still ignored me, even though I towered over him.

Junior's focus was solely on Romy, and I was two seconds from laying this guy out.

"All you Millers are fucking crazy!" Junior yelled. "You should all be locked up."

This guy needed to get out of my face, or it wasn't going to end well for him.

"Back. Up." I punctuated each word, my voice raising, while I pushed him back a step.

That finally caused his attention to swing toward me. "Don't touch me."

"Don't talk to my fucking girl like that." I was just about to erupt.

"I'll talk to her any way I want!" Junior hollered.

This fucking guy was asking for it. I was seething.

"You need to leave, or I'll take you out myself. *Now*." I balled my fists, my knuckles cracking. My muscles tightened and twitched. I was so close to unleashing on this asshole.

"Leave it to a Larsen to protect the sister of a murderous cunt," he spat.

What the fuck was that supposed to mean?

My ears roared, drowning out the silence of the bar and every thought but the need to end this guy.

I could feel my blood boiling in my veins, my muscles contracting, my jaw tightening, as I drew my arm back.

Like any other practiced movement, I let out a whoosh of breath from my lungs as my arm flew forward, landing right where I needed to end this.

Right on the button. My fist connected with his jaw. I could feel it click beneath my knuckles.

I watched in pure satisfaction as Junior locked up, his eyes rolling back as he collapsed like a damn tree.

I didn't even hear the thud as he hit the bar floor, only the gasps all around me as if someone was sucking the air right out of the Rooster.

It sure as hell felt like air was being sucked out of me.

"Jude!" Romy yelled, grabbing my arm, tugging me away. Bringing me back to the present.

The bar erupted. Commotion ensued, people rushing toward us. One of the male bartenders hopped the bar to intervene.

"We gotta go, bro." Christian rushed to our side, pulling on my other arm.

Romy? All I thought was *Romy*.

She was gripping my arm, looking up at me with a furrowed brow, concern in her pretty eyes. I drew her to my side, tucking her beneath my arm, leaning in to bury a kiss in her hair.

Coconuts.

Somehow, the smell centered me.

"Are you all right, honey?" I asked into her tropical-scented hair.

She nodded against my lips, but I could tell how her body tensed against mine. She was far from okay.

The volume of the bar amplified as the crowd rushed toward us and Junior, who was still laid out on the floor.

Reed hustled over, pushing back some of the crowd to lead us through to the exit.

We were just stepping outside when Christian gasped. "Shit, there were people with their phones out."

Fuck!

"Fuck!" I yelled into the night.

This was going to be all over the news by morning. How could I have fucked up so badly? I never once unleashed like that unless it was in the cage.

Alex was going to kill me.

"I need to make a call." Not having a hat to fiddle with, I pushed a hand through my hair.

"What's wrong?" Romy asked at my side.

This was not how I wanted to tell her.

My eyes flicked to her, my anger quickly replaced with fear.

"What is it?" she asked again, her eyes bouncing back and forth between mine.

I swallowed. "I just broke a rule in my contract."

Her brows pinched, her lips turned down in a frown. "But aren't you retiring?"

My eyes shuddered. Resigned.

Breathe in. Count to ten. Breathe out.

I opened my eyes again to peer into hers. "I accepted a fight in August."

Romy said nothing, only took a step back. The color drained from her face.

"Romy—" I needed to explain more, but I didn't know what to say.

She pushed past me, a hand covering her mouth as she ran to the side of the bar. Lina rushed after her, grabbing her hair, while Romy vomited in the bushes.

CHAPTER 21
Jude

"I really fucked up," I told Alex as we slowed to a walk on the dirt road.

"No kidding," he agreed. "I'm not sure it will be easy to get out of this one."

I rested my hands on my hips, pulling in cool breaths of air while I walked out my burning muscles. We were slowly adding jogging to my cardio sessions, and my knee was holding up better than anticipated.

"I told Mr. Venture I'd go ahead and announce my retirement," I said through panting breaths, "but he said no, that I wasn't getting out of it. I'm fighting and I'm being fined."

I wiped the sweat from my eyes with the back of my hand.

"I figured as much," Alex said. "Thanks to your trigger fist there, the organization is getting more publicity than they have in months. Reyes is digging it, too. You should see the shit he's posting online. Do you want me to make a call to Jessica?"

I shook my head, disappointed in myself. I kept off social media just for that reason. I didn't want to know what Reyes was spouting, and I didn't want to get Jessica involved, either.

She might be my ex, but as a publicist, she knew how to pull some strings to kill a story. We had ended things on fairly good terms, even though I was miserable at the time of our breakup—but that was mostly on me, not her. She would do it if I asked her to, but I really didn't want to pull anyone else into this. It was my fuck up. I needed to fix it myself, even if I didn't regret knocking out Junior. I'd do it again if it meant protecting Romy.

"Have you talked to Romy?" Alex asked.

I stalled in my steps, heading over to the split rail fence along the road. Alex followed, propping a foot up on the rail to lean into a hamstring stretch.

I shook my head. "I'm giving her space."

It had been nearly a week since the Rooster. As soon as we got home, Lina helped Romy wash up and get to bed.

"You fucked up, cuz," Lina said as she left that night.

I was well aware.

Thank goodness there was plenty to keep us busy on the ranch, and Coach and I were doing daily doubles. Eight weeks was not nearly enough time to prepare for this fight.

"She's been helping lead trail rides with Lina, so she's gone most of the day. I'm usually up helping Uncle Chuck before she wakes up. And she's been eating meals up at the big house. Last night, she came in and just stopped to look at me. I didn't even know what to say, so I just stared at her," I told him.

Alex shook his head. "Well, that's awkward. She's probably waiting for you to say something. Most likely, she thinks you're avoiding her."

"Avoiding her?" I scoffed. "If I push too hard, she'll retreat, she'll leave. So I'm giving her time."

"Is that what you're afraid of? Her leaving?"

Alex and I switched legs, leaning into the stretch. My hip flexors were tight. I needed to roll them out once we got back to the garage.

"That's what she does. She leaves when shit gets hard."

"Jude, she's still here. From what you told me, she's dealing with some pretty tough shit. She came back with you, *and* she's still here."

I shrugged. "It's only a matter of time before she realizes I'm not worth it and decides to leave."

Alex huffed a laugh. "Damn, Bull. Is that what you think? You're not worth sticking around for? Wow, your mom did a number on you, didn't she?"

"You sound like my therapist," I quipped.

"Maybe you should pay me like I have a PhD in psychology, too," he said with a sly smile. "Seriously though, man, you need to stop selling yourself short. You charge into things—fuck the risks—because you've always thought you weren't good enough unless you're winning."

"Jesus, stop psychoanalyzing me," I huffed.

He hit the nail on the head.

Alex's smirk turned into a sympathetic smile that told me he felt for me, but we both knew he was right.

"Sometimes you have to lose to win," he said matter-of-factly.

In the indoor arena, Lina jogged beside a filly. The gray horse, tacked only with a bridle and reins, cantered at her side, following her to a step stool. Clicking her tongue in encouragement, she called the horse to a stop beside her. She was a natural with horses. Just like her father. Maybe even more so.

She spotted me resting against the gate and leaned into the horse, giving it a generous pet before hopping from the stool.

"Have your ears been burning?" she asked, smiling, while she and the horse approached me.

"What?" Were my ears burning? Now they might be.

"Romy was just in here. We were talking about you." She gave me a pointed look.

Ah, shit. I was still in the doghouse.

"All good things, I hope?" I joked, trying to lighten the load on my chest.

"No, we hate your guts."

It was wishful thinking.

"You're both pissed at me then?"

"Jude, you're a fucking idiot."

I groaned. "So I've been told."

Lina's lips tipped in a frown. "You're not getting any younger, you've had three knee surgeries, and you're going to fight again? For what? Prove some macho desire that you're the best, fuck the circumstances?"

"Is that what Romy thinks?"

"That's what we all think. Dad just believes you need to figure it out on your own. I'm wondering, though, how many times you have to put yourself in harm's way before you learn enough is enough?"

I nod. "It's all I know, Lina. It's the only thing I'm good

at." *And if I lose fighting, I don't know who'd I be.*

"That's not true. I saw what you did with the ranch and that piece-of-shit tin can you turned into a home. I've seen the projects you've completed in your Vegas house."

"With money that I earned from fighting," I stated.

"Sure, but it all came from you—the designs, managing the projects, not just updating your place but also the stables. Dad showed me what you want to do with this," she said, waving at the arena. "And I think it looks amazing. He just doesn't like taking your money." She huffed a laugh.

"It's the least I can do to help pay back for all the years Uncle Chuck took care of me," I mumbled, afraid to get too deep.

She shook her head. "We're family, Jude. We don't pay each other back for caring for each other. I love you, cuz, but you need to swallow your fucking pride and go talk to Romy. She thinks you're leaving, abandoning the ranch when we need you the most. All to go put your body at risk in a cage. You hurt her when you didn't tell her, and now she's wondering if she can trust you. All she wants is for you to talk to her."

Talk about a gut punch. I fucked up big time. While I'm afraid she's going to run and leave me again, here I am basically doing the same to her. I needed to make this right.

"Actually, that's what I wanted to talk to you about. I need your help."

CHAPTER 22
Romy

"Fucking Reed," Lina mumbled as she swung a leg up into the saddle.

"What now?" I asked from my perch on Winnie.

"That man can't help but overstep. He has no fucking boundaries."

I frowned because I barely heard more than grunts come out of him.

"He feels the need to point out everything, or my stirrups are too long. He literally stopped me mid-trail ride to come up and adjust my stirrups because he said it was bugging the hell out of him. Like what the actual fuck? It's not like I can't adjust it myself!" She seemed frazzled.

I pinched my lips together to keep from laughing. "I can't believe him."

Lina shot me a glare before pressing her heels in. I followed her up the dirt road toward the stables. We had just finished leading a group of tourists on a trail ride. Reed and another hired hand were returning the rest of the mounts to the stable, leaving Lina and me to ride together.

"I'm ready for a burger and a cold beer," Lina practically groaned.

"Oh God, that sounds good." My stomach grumbled at the thought.

Chuck was hosting a barbeque for employees, rodeo riders, and their families before the busy season. Next week, everyone would be either harvesting and baling hay, branding cattle, or preparing for the Fourth of July rodeo. On top of all that, Chuck wanted to run two trail rides a day for tourists, which I volunteered to lead since Lina was heading back out on the circuit. Still not accustomed to riding every day, my legs were feeling it this afternoon. I was ready to relax with some grilled grub and a drink with a proof.

Lina and I rubbed down the horses and put them up for the night, scooping extra feed in their troughs before washing our hands and heading over to the big house.

The scent of the smoke from the grill made my mouth water. Voices and laughter filtered from the back of the house. Walking up the driveway, we headed around the house to the large deck and lawn that expanded to the back of the property.

The back of the house had one of the best views of the Deschutes. It was on a hill, the lawn spilling down toward a rough outcropping that overlooked the river. The sun was already dipping in the sky, casting a golden glow.

Kids ran across the lawn, bubble wands trailing bubbles in their wake, giggles floating with them. A couple of ranch hands sat on a bench strumming guitars, one of them singing as they played.

Releasing a breath, a feeling of contentment washed over

me. This felt good. Comfortable. Happy. Like home.

I scanned the crowd. Reed chased a little, blonde girl in overalls down the lawn toward the river, scooping her up and tossing her in his arms. She let out a shrill giggle, Reed beaming down at her. I didn't even know the man knew how to smile.

"Humph," Lina huffed beside me, stomping toward the deck.

I followed her toward Chuck, who manned the grill.

Chuck shifted to the side, revealing Jude leaning against the railing beside him. My heart squeezed seeing him. Dark hair escaping from the front of his backward cap, his tight, navy T-shirt showing off his tatted muscles. Our eyes connected before his quickly trailed down my body. I still had on my dusty jeans and boots. I had shed my hoodie when we finished our trail ride, leaving me in a basic, white tank top. His lips tipped in his signature grin, and I felt my cheeks heat.

We had both been avoiding each other this week. I felt embarrassed not being able to hold my liquor after all the excitement with Junior, worried about Jude and what would happen with his contract, and so beyond livid that he didn't tell me he was taking a fight in Vegas. That he didn't plan to stay.

I didn't want to talk to him right now. I needed time to sort it all out in my head.

Junior had scared me, and it also made me wonder more about what happened between Jesse and Hazel. I knew Hazel was lying, but what part was she lying about? And why? What was she hiding? Did Junior know something I didn't?

Then the look on Jude's face. His want to take care of me

even when I'd been so angry at him made me second-guess why I was even mad at him in the first place.

I was so confused.

I was giving myself whiplash. I was going from being pissed that he would abandon his uncle when Chuck needed him most, to being angry he would put himself in harm's way for a payout and not even tell me about it. Then convincing myself I had no right to be mad at him. I didn't deserve a say. He wasn't obligated to tell me his plans. Not after I ran out on him—not once, but twice. We weren't in a relationship. There was no commitment. Right?

Lowering my gaze, I went to grab a Coors Light from the icy cooler.

The deck stairs creaked, and I raised my head to see Jude. He stooped and leaned in to grab a beer.

We popped the tops, letting the hiss of the carbonation break our awkward silence.

"Hi," he rasped.

God, I missed his voice.

I took a swig from the can.

"Hi."

He lifted his can to his lips. Those perfect, pillowy lips surrounded by delicious scruff. I missed those even more.

"Do you want a burger?"

I couldn't help but smile. "Yes, I'm *starving*."

I could see the veins in his neck as he swallowed slowly. His eyes flitted to my mouth before returning to my eyes. "Come with me," he said, gesturing for me to follow him up the stairs to the deck.

My lips trembled around my grin. "Yes, *sir*."

He threw a smoldering glance over his shoulder, the side of his mouth quirked. "I guess you can be polite when you want to be," he teased.

I followed him to the grill where Chuck stood with a metal spatula, wearing a chef's apron that read: I'm the Secret Ingredient.

"Hey, darlin'. Trail ride go all right?" he asked, flipping a burger.

Jude offered me a plate, the bun laid out, ready to accept a patty.

"Everyone seemed satisfied. Everyone except Lina, that is. She was not thrilled that Reed tagged along," I reported, taking my plate from Jude.

Chuck guffawed. "She needs to get over whatever problem she has with him. I need him to learn the ropes in case he has to take a group out while Lina's back on circuit." He shoveled burgers on our buns. "Condiments are on the table."

"Thanks," we both said, heading over to the picnic table to load up our burgers.

I ate my burger with everything on it—cheese, tomatoes, lettuce, pickles, ketchup, mustard, even mayonnaise. Jude layered his with tomatoes, lettuce, pickles, and mustard.

"Counting calories?" I asked, my brows raised.

Jude pressed his lips together. "Always."

Okay ... sensitive topic right now.

"Follow me," he said, picking up his plate and beer.

I followed him, tracking our way through the yard, saying hello as we went.

"Where are we going?" I asked, stepping over rocks.

Voices dimmed, the rush of the river growing. The faint scents of grass and pine filtered through the breeze. Jude led us along the craggy cliff edge overlooking the river until we stepped into one of the open pastures.

"Jude, what is this?"

In the middle of the pasture stood his truck. A white screen was pulled flat across two poles on either end of the tailgate. An inflatable mattress with blankets and pillows was laid out in the truck bed.

He turned to me, his eyes twinkling in the twilight. "Would you go to the movies with me?"

"What—" I looked back and forth between him and the truck. Was he asking me out on a date? "Jude, we haven't spoken to each other all week."

"I know, Romy. I fucked up. I want to make it up to you."

"Jude, I—"

"Can we just eat and talk? Then you can decide if you want to stay and watch a movie with me."

We sat in the truck bed, eating our burgers and sipping our beers. Jude's long legs were stretched out, my own curled beneath me as we leaned against the pillows. The sun continued to dip below the horizon. Any chill I would have felt was kept at bay by the heat radiating off Jude's body, his shoulder inches from mine.

"I thought if I found just the right moment to tell you and explain, you might understand," he said.

"Aren't you worried about getting hurt again?" I asked.

"Yeah, but … I don't know. Ever since the doctor told me I should consider retiring, I've been depressed. Fighting is the one thing I excel at. I've always been good at it. If I don't have fighting, then what good am I?"

"Jude, you can't believe that." It hurt my heart to hear him say that. "You have the ranch." *You have me*, I wanted to say. "Look what you've created. You turned that old double-wide into a home."

Jude released a short laugh. "Lina said the same thing. She seems to think I have a future in flipping houses."

"Well, is that something you'd like to do?"

"Maybe. I have some ideas to update the arena. I showed Uncle Chuck the plans I had an architect buddy of mine draw up. I'm just waiting for him to tell me to pull the trigger, but now with everything going on, it isn't really a priority." Jude took another bite of his burger.

I took a swig of my beer. "So when do you leave?" I was afraid to know.

Jude set his burger down, his eyes scanning my face. "I'm not leaving."

"But don't you have to prepare for your fight?"

"I told my coach the only way I was taking this fight was if I could train right here on the ranch. I'm not going anywhere, honey."

I inhaled a shuddering breath, my eyes fluttering closed in relief. He was staying. My heart rate slowed to a steady rhythm. "I'm sorry I was mad at you. I'm not really sure I even had a right to be mad. I just …" I didn't know what else to say.

He didn't deserve this.

"Sure, you do. I should have told you as soon as I knew. I told you I was in this with you, and that takes honesty and openness. I was just afraid that if I told you, you would have refused to come home with me, and it scared me," he confided. "Would you have?"

I considered his question for a moment. Perhaps. I released the tension from my shoulders. "Maybe. Honestly, I was waiting for any little reason to back out. For you to say something stupid," I teased. He gave me a wry smile, and I chuckled. "Or do something that would warrant me backing out. I want to be able to trust you, to trust these feelings—"

"You have feelings?" He beamed.

Shaking my head, of course that's all he heard.

I laughed. "Yes, Jude, I have feelings."

"Thank God, honey." He set his plate down, his hands cupping my face.

I let my face rest against his palms. "You're just going to have to be patient with me."

"I'd wait an eternity for you." His thumbs stroked my cheeks.

I leaned into his touch. "But I need you to be honest with me. Don't keep things from me, thinking you need to hold back to protect me. I'm not as delicate as you seem to think. I don't want gentle."

"Fuck," he muttered. "You don't want gentle? You're making it hard for me to take this slow."

"Making what hard?" I taunted.

"Jesus, you're going to be the death of me. You know that

I'm crazy about you. I've been crazy about you since I was sixteen."

"Sixteen! I thought it was only when we were eighteen."

"Honey." He dipped his head, his lips lightly brushing over mine. "I had the worst crush on you. You had to know by the way I followed you around like a lost pup."

"I thought you were doing it just to annoy Chase."

He chuckled. "That too."

I giggled. "And now?"

"I'm still crushing on you and following you like a lost pup."

His bottom lip nestled into the seam of mine, gently pressing his mouth to mine. His lips moved slightly, softly caressing. His tongue slid along my upper lip. I parted on a breath, opening for him, our tongues gliding over each other. It was tender and sweet. Unlike the kiss we shared in the stables.

Jude's hands did not leave my face, his fingers threading through my hair, angling my head to give him more access. He sucked my tongue into his mouth, and I let out a moan.

I needed more. I always seemed to need more with him. It was never enough.

I pressed my hand against his chest. His heart thumped beneath my palm, while his mouth moved to the corner of my mouth, trailing along my jaw to that sensitive spot beneath my ear. I tipped my head, earning a pleased hum from Jude as his jaw scraped along my neck. My eyes fluttered closed, feeling him nip my earlobe before his tongue brought it to his lips to suck into his mouth.

"Jude." I sighed, trailing my hand down his firm chest,

along the hard ridges of his abs, until I reached his belt buckle.

His hand left my hair to stall my hand.

"What about our movie date?" he inquired against the skin of my neck.

"Do you want to watch a movie?" I asked him, my words coming out seductive and slightly breathless.

"I'm trying to be patient ... take this slow."

I bit my lip. "And I said I didn't want gentle."

Jude groaned at that, but he lifted his head to look at me, his eyes scanning my face.

"I have *How to Lose a Guy in 10 Days* queued up. We are definitely going to need some background noise for what I'm about to do to you. Those sweet moans are for my ears only." His hands slid to my hips and lifted me to straddle his lap.

"Mmm, Matthew McConaughey," I purred.

"On second thought, fuck the movie."

I grinned. My hands rested on his chest. The ridge of his arousal hit between my legs. I couldn't help but rock my hips, and liquid heat shot straight to my pussy.

"Not a McConaughey fan?" I quipped.

"He's all right," he said, emphasizing the *all right* with a McConaughey accent. "I'm more of a Glen Powell kinda guy," he noted, unable to keep a straight face.

I busted up laughing. His smile grew at my laughter before turning serious.

"More like not wanting to share my girl with the rest of the ranch fan." His hand dove back into my hair, pulling it away from my face, drawing me closer to him.

My laughter faded.

"I'm not that loud," I said against his lips.

Jude pulled back again to look at me. "Honey, everyone heard what we were doing in my truck the other night. It's not a secret."

I scoffed in insult, playfully hitting his shoulder. "You try to be quiet with someone between your legs doing whatever that trick was you did with your tongue."

Jude chuckled, his teeth bright in the twilight, smile lines creasing his cheeks. As much as I adored his lopsided smiles, his big, genuine grins gutted me. "Is that a challenge? You know I thrive on challenges."

I rolled my hips again just to punish him for that one. "You're on."

We could play. We didn't need to dive into anything. Just do what felt good. And this felt good.

"I've been thinking about you all week," I said coyly, slowly rolling my hips again, his cock growing harder as it rubbed against me, adding friction right where I needed it.

"Oh, really? And what were you doing when you thought of me?"

I pressed my breasts against his chest and dipped a soft kiss on his lips. My hips shifted with my movement, my clit rubbing against his hardened cock. My core pulsed.

"Did you touch yourself?" he whispered against my mouth.

His question shot a jolt of electricity to my center. "Every night since being in your bed," I confided. "I imagined you were there with me, that it was your fingers touching me, caressing me right where I needed it."

He growled and flipped us so I was on my back and he was

hovering above me, his knee between my legs. He sucked my bottom lip into his mouth, his teeth scraping against it, while he thrust his cock against my thigh. I shuddered.

He released my lip to whisper in my mouth, "Show me."

CHAPTER 23
Jude

Pump the breaks. Patience is a virtue. Cool your fucking jets.

All things I was telling myself, while Romy gazed up at me with those gorgeous, smoky eyes. All things I silenced as her hand wrapped around her throat.

Loose strands from her braid fanned across the pillows I had laid out in the back of the truck. The sunset cast a golden glow on everything it touched, and Romy was no exception. After being outside over the past week, her creamy skin had bronzed.

Her lips parted on an exhale while her hand trailed from her neck, down between her breasts. Her chest rose. The hardened pebbles of her nipples cut through her thin tank top. My eyes followed her hand skimming gently down past her stomach until it reached the hem of her top. Her fingers dipping beneath the hem.

My lungs froze.

She fluttered her nails along her stomach, her top lifting to give me a glimpse of her toned stomach.

Fuck, she was incredible.

Romy unbuttoned her jeans, her eyes not leaving my face while she slowly unzipped her pants. Her fingertips brushed against the top of her lace underwear. Pink again. She looked so good in pink.

She released a shuddering breath as her hand lowered into her panties, her hips lifting to reach her touch.

I swallowed, wishing my view was unimpeded. But there was something about leaving it veiled, watching her hand stroke beneath the lace.

"Are you wet, honey?" I asked, my voice hoarse in my ears.

"So wet."

"Show me."

Like the good, obedient girl she was, she withdrew her hand, holding it up for me to inspect. Her cum glistened on her fingertips, and I could almost smell how sweet she was. I grabbed her wrist, bringing her hand to my mouth, sucking her wetness. It was like salted honey. The best fucking thing I ever tasted. I leaned over her to lay a soft kiss on her lips, our tongues slowly caressing while she tasted herself.

"Tell me how you use your fingers," I murmured against her mouth. "Do you start with your perfect, wet pussy or circle that sensitive, little clit?"

"Both," she whispered as I hummed in approval, watching again as her hand disappeared beneath her waistband.

Her hips bucked, her breaths starting to quicken as I observed her curling her hand, picturing a finger dipping inside.

"Are you going to come for me? Show me what you've been

doing every night while I'm feet away from you in the next room?" It was killing me not to touch her, but it was so hot just watching her.

"*Jude*," she panted. "Touch me."

Anything. I'd do anything for this girl.

"Where do you want me to touch you?" I asked, lowering my head to nip at her perfect nipples through her tank top, making her yelp with pleasure.

"Anywhere. Everywhere," she said breathlessly.

I turned her face to mine, kissing her slowly, my tongue stroking hers while she rocked against her hand. She moaned in my mouth.

I ran my fingers down her throat, feathering across her collarbone, caressing the curve of her breast. She arched into my hand.

I remembered how she responded to my thumb scraping across her nipple, so I traced the stiffened peak. She hissed between her teeth. My girl had sensitive tits.

"Don't stop," she whispered.

Watching down the slope of her breasts, over the dip of her belly, where her hand continued to circle her clit, I mirrored how she circled her hand with my forefinger on her nipple. It hardened beneath my fingertip, allowing me to pinch and roll it through the fabric with my fingers.

Her breathing continued to quicken as she increased the stroke of her hand, going from dipping inside to coasting back up to her clit, then back into her center.

"Tell me how close you are. Let me hear you."

"Touch me," she begged again. "I need more of you, Jude."

"Tell me where to touch you, honey."

She pulled her hand out of her panties, grabbing my hand away from her breast to replace hers with mine between her legs. "Here."

She was soaked and slippery.

Feeling how wet she made herself, hearing her continue to moan while I started to circle her clit, made my cock leak.

"I'm so close," she breathed, but her lips were tilted in a cute smile. "But I want more, Jude."

"So much for going slow."

She had a devilish glint in her eyes. "Not gentle, remember? I want to touch you. I want your cock in my mouth while I ride your hand."

Fuck.

"Please, Jude."

I groaned. "How can I say no when you ask so nicely."

I withdrew my hand, getting up on my knees to unbuckle my belt. My cock was aching, straining to break free. Pulling down my pants and boxers, the evening air hit my already burning skin, the sensation causing my dick to twitch.

Romy's breath hitched. "God, it's bigger than I remember."

I leaned down, brushing my lips across hers while I took my dick in my hand, giving it a couple long strokes. The muscles in my lower belly tightened and pulsed. I wasn't going to last long.

She reached out a hand, replacing mine. Her thumb slipped over the tip, spreading my precum. With a mischievous grin, she sucked it off her finger. I just about lost it watching her puffy lips wrap around her thumb before she seized my cock. Her grip tightened as she ran her fist up and down my shaft, her thumb running along the tip to catch my cum. Her creamy skin looked so good contrasted against my tan skin.

"Fuck, Romy."

"Shh," she hushed, her hand still stroking. "If I'm going to put your cock in my mouth, *you're* going to have to be quiet."

I pinched my lips together, biting the inside of my cheeks. Fire was in her eyes, challenging me as she raised herself up on her elbow, bringing my dick to her mouth. She watched me while her tongue darted out, swirling around the head, running over the tip to swipe up the moisture.

I sucked in air through my teeth, determined not to groan aloud. Her hand tightened around the base while she ran her tongue down the underside of my cock until her lips surrounded the head, sucking it. I couldn't wait any longer. I thrust into her mouth, her teeth lightly scraping across my tender flesh. Her cheeks hollowed out while her tongue continued to torture me, running up and down, again, again, and again.

"Keep looking at me, honey," I demanded, her lashes fluttering up. I weaved my fingers through her hair, steadying her head.

I ran my hand along the inside of her thigh, skimming along the crevice where her hip joint met her pelvis, edging along the inside of her lacy underwear. She shuddered at the delicate sweep of my fingertips. Shifting the fabric to the side, the lace scraped against her sensitive skin, causing her to release a throaty moan against my cock. The vibration caused an unbidden groan to escape my lips.

I wasn't about to let her win this one.

With the lace of her underwear pushed to the side, I could

feel how wet she was. I swirled a fingertip at her entrance, spreading the moisture. I added another finger, continuing to swirl until I dipped both fingers in—just an inch. She widened her legs for me, granting me permission, and when she thrust her hips against my fingers, she was begging for it.

"Patience, honey. Remember?"

I churned my fingers at her entrance again, inching them inside her moist heat. Her hips bucked eagerly.

I slowly backed out of her mouth, allowing us both to take a deep breath, before I plunged my fingers into her at the same moment I thrust to the back of her throat.

Her brows pinched and she whined, gripping the back side of my thigh to hold me still. She felt incredible. So warm. So wet. So tight.

"Greedy girl, your pussy is sucking my finger inside."

My heart pounded in my chest and in my cock. The walls of her pussy fluttered against my fingers, tightening as I curved them perfectly to touch the spot I knew she couldn't reach, while I thrust my dick into her pretty mouth.

"You like being stuffed at both ends?" I asked her. She looked so sexy taking my cock while she rocked against my fingers.

She groaned in confirmation, the vibration sending another jolt through my groin. Tightening my balls. I was going to come.

I could tell she was close, too, by the way her hips moved frantically, her walls constricting against my fingers.

"Come with me, honey. Soak my hand while I coat the back of your throat."

She nodded against my shaft; her brows furrowed.

"I'm going to fill your pretty mouth, but next time, I'm covering those beautiful tits. Do you want me to mark all of you, honey? Do you want me to come in your mouth? I need to pull out now if you don't want that," I told her, barely able to get the words out.

Her lips only tightened around me, sucking me back to her throat. Her hand squeezed at the base. Her knees pinched together while I curled my fingers deeper inside, pressing into her G-spot.

Romy's muffled cries while her core pulsed against my fingers sent me over the threshold. My thrusts became jolting until my orgasm rocked through, sending wave after wave down my abdomen. My balls tightened all the way through the end of my cock until I released myself into her mouth. Her throat gulped on reflex. It was so fucking sexy watching her swallow me down.

I gently stroked her, swiping her cum through her sensitive folds while I backed out of her mouth. She twitched beneath my touch, still riding the waves, trying to catch her breath after her own climax.

I tenderly brushed hair out of her face, running my thumb along her swollen bottom lip, my other hand still unable to stop wringing out every ounce of pleasure from her.

I dipped my fingers in one last time, wanting this connection to last a little longer. She twitched under me.

"Jude!" she cried out, pressing her thighs together, trapping my hand against her.

I smiled to myself as I took her wetness, coating her lips,

before bringing her mouth to mine. Tasting us mixed together. *Victorious.*

"*Jude*," she whispered now, her hand going out to my arm. Lovingly running her nails along my skin.

Tucking myself back into my pants, I lowered myself on my elbow beside her.

"That … that was amazing," she said between pants.

Her chest rose and fell with her heavy breaths. Her cheeks were flushed. Her eyes still hooded with desire. Air vacated my lungs while I consumed her beauty.

"You're so beautiful, Romy. I could watch you unravel beneath me forever." I grinned, leaning in to press my lips to the side of her mouth.

She smiled up at me, running her fingers through the hair at the nape of my neck.

"Especially if it means the *whole* ranch can hear what I do to you." I winked.

Her mouth hung open in disbelief, and I couldn't help but wrap my arms around her, holding her to me while I laughed into her coconut-scented locks.

CHAPTER 24
Romy

"How was your movie date?" Lina asked, wagging her brows when I entered the stables the next morning to tack up Winnie.

My heartbeat shot to my core at the memory. There was just something about watching how I made Jude lose control while he pleasured me. This large, tattooed man, who quietly commanded any room he walked into, falling apart by my touch. No wonder I didn't last long when he had his fingers inside me.

I gave Lina a wry smile.

"Ha! I knew it!" She clapped, a little skip in her step as she ran to wrap her arms around me. "Please tell me ya'll fucked!"

"Lina!" I gasped. "He's your cousin. And no, we had a very nice evening talking."

"Talking?" She looked aghast. "I thought Jude had better game than that."

I wasn't about to kiss and tell.

I laughed. "It was good for us to get on the same page."

After our "movie date" in the truck, Jude and I drove back

to the house, his arm around me, softly stroking my shoulder. We had been quiet, exchanging awed smiles with each other. I wanted him to come to bed with me. In fact, I had pulled his hand toward his room. I wasn't nearly done with him. But he had insisted we hit the brakes; he'd sleep on the couch.

I didn't want to part from him, so I washed up, put on my pajamas, and crawled onto the couch with him. We shared all the highlights and lowlights of the past twelve years. He told me how he struggled with depression, but he was going to therapy and taking medication. Being back on the ranch, he was slowly feeling as though he was regaining his equilibrium. He hadn't recognized how much he had lost of himself being away from his family and Thornbrush.

I shared with him that I didn't know if I wanted to continue teaching, that it was draining all my energy and joy. It felt rewarding at first, but now it just felt as if I was taken for granted and unappreciated. I didn't know what I wanted to do, but I didn't know if I could continue giving of myself when there was no one to fill my tank.

Although I had avoided returning to Willows, it wasn't until now that I sensed my homesickness. Could you feel homesick when you know you are home?

I didn't know. But the chest-tightening longing I felt whenever I stepped out the front door—taking in the sweeping high desert and mountains, breathing in the scent of grass and pine, and listening to the distant rush of the river with the bellows of cattle—made me yearn to stay still. To settle my feet in the dirt of this place.

Of course, I didn't tell that part to Jude. Even talking into the wee hours of the morning, we tiptoed around the questions of "what now?" and "are you going to leave?" I didn't want to ask him if he was returning to Vegas after this fight. I didn't want to consider further than the here and now. I needed to figure out what was going to happen with Hazel first before I made any life-changing decisions. Thinking beyond that was too overwhelming.

At some point in our conversation, I fell asleep on the couch, only to wake up alone in his bed. I had never slept so hard. I didn't even notice him carrying me to the bed.

But for the first time, I woke up rested and with a smile on my face. I hurried out of bed to wish him good morning, but he had already left for the day. My smile nearly faltered, if not for the coffee and note on the kitchen counter—with his phone number on it. Like we were high school kids again exchanging numbers. I felt like a teenager, too, excited about my crush.

I quickly pulled out my phone, typed in his number, and texted him.

ME

Hi.

JUDE

Who's this?

ME

It's me.

JUDE

Who's me?

I rolled my eyes at that.

ME

Do you give your number
out to other girls?

JUDE

Only the gorgeous blonde ones
who scream my name.

My scoff was followed by a soft giggle. I watched three
dots pop up on the screen while he texted.

JUDE

JK. I hope you slept well in
my bed. 😏

I loved this part of our friendship. I always had. We could
banter and laugh all day back in high school. I never tired of
our conversations. But I didn't remember Jude being such a flirt
or having such a filthy mouth. Then again, I hadn't known he
had liked me since we were sixteen. It made my belly flutter.

Now as I tacked up Winnie, preparing to lead another trail
ride with Lina, my back pocket buzzed. I swiped my phone
from my jeans and read the text.

JUDE

Since I won last night, does that
mean I get a prize?

I laughed under my breath.

"What?" Lina asked.

"Nothing," I told her, while my fingers flew over the phone
screen, texting him back.

ME

Who said there was a prize?

JUDE

Honey, I don't think you can dodge this one. I play for keeps. I'm pretty sure I have you beat. You're going to break the rural noise ordinance.

"Oh, you got it bad," Lina tittered as she hoisted herself into the saddle.

I must have had the silliest smile on my face because she was looking at me with a knowing smirk.

Just then, Reed walked into the stable.

"People are already arriving for the trail ride," he barked.

Lina didn't look up, only adjusted Mushu's reins. "Thanks for the announcement."

"They're waiting. It's supposed to be a two-hour ride, and it's already ten o'clock."

It was the most I'd ever heard from Reed.

Lina shot him a glare. "And? Why don't you go use those stellar social skills and keep them occupied until we're ready."

Reed turned on his spurs, grumbling as he retreated to the outdoor arena.

"Can he get any more fucking bossy?" Lina asked. "I'll go make sure he's not killing our TripAdvisor rating while you saddle up."

While Lina rode out of the stable, I shook my head at their antics. Thank goodness Lina was leaving for the circuit tomorrow. They could use a break from each other. I also thought Lina could be a little oblivious to her feelings, like I was.

Before I grabbed Winnie's tack, I shot back a text.

ME

I don't know, babe. Pretty sure you're going to cause a stampede with all the "fucks" you'll be yelling when I ride you. We'll see who earns the prize. 🏆

I pocketed my phone with a satisfied grin on my face, threw the blanket and saddle over my arm, and headed over to Winnie's stall.

Why were we taking things slow, again?

CHAPTER 25
Romy

I sat in front of the computer in Jude's office, staring at a blank document screen.

Exhausted from being out in the fields and a night of training, he barely had enough energy to eat our dinner of grilled chicken before he collapsed on the couch. He was snoring by the time I got out of the shower.

Leaving him to rest, I decided to do what Ms. Hoya, Hazel's defense attorney, asked of me. Ignoring her calls, she had decided to show up at the ranch when I returned from the trail ride to speak with me. She said if I didn't decide to testify in court, the least I could do was write a character letter for Hazel she could provide during the hearing.

I didn't know what I could say about Hazel. I didn't feel like I knew my sister at all—at least not the one she became over the last decade. I only knew the big sister I idolized in my childhood, who held us together when Mom passed, the one who was our father's pride and joy and refused to respect my boundaries with him. At least, that's where I could start.

From the time I could walk, I wanted to be just like my big sister. She never once complained that her baby sister followed her around. In fact, she mothered me just as much as our mother did. She took care of me. She stood up for me with other kids, even with our own father at times. Frank and I never got along, and she was our buffer.

When I wanted to learn to ride a horse, she taught me everything she knew. When I wanted to learn to put on makeup, she let me use whatever she had. She listened to me. She was always patient with me, even when I was a brat and probably needed to be yelled at. She never once made me feel undeserving of her time. Some of my favorite memories were when she would cancel plans with her friends to take me horseback riding or floating down the river.

Everyone loved Hazel. She was popular at school. Even at home. I can confidently say she was my parents' favorite child. My mom might have denied it, but my father would probably confirm that today. She was the responsible one. She was happy and easygoing, always making friends. She was beautiful and generous, always giving of her time. She loved horses and barrel racing, and she loved teaching others what she was passionate about. I'm a certified teacher, but I'm certain Hazel has more patience for teaching than I ever will.

When our mother passed away from breast cancer, Hazel held us together. She was the one who made sure I got to school, had dinner on the table, and saw that the perfectly healthy parent who was still alive got out of bed. We wouldn't have gotten through that first year without Mom if it wasn't for Hazel.

I never wanted to stay in Willows like she did—or maybe she felt she had to because I didn't. She supported my dream to move to a big city, to do something rewarding with my life. I was never bitter toward her, even though I constantly felt compared. Our father always reminded me that I was the disappointment. She knew if I didn't leave, it would beat me down to the point that I might not have survived it. She didn't want that for me, and she made sure I could leave. But she stayed.

I wonder if she would have left, too, if our mom hadn't died or if I had decided to stay? I think she might have felt obligated to stay for our father and for the town that loved her and named her their rodeo queen.

I don't know what happened over the last twelve years. I'm angry at myself for not making the effort to be there for her when she probably needed me. I'm angry at her for not asking for help when she probably needed it. I'm angry at her for letting things get so bad that whatever choices were made landed her where she is now. I'm mad that no one, including myself, anticipated the costs of these choices until now.

Through my blurry vision, I reread my words. I might not be able to trust Hazel. I might be livid with her for making the choice to shoot that gun, but if I could support my sister once in my life, this was the best I could do.

Not ready to email it to the lawyer, I saved the document, shut down the computer, and went out to the living room.

A tear escaped my eye, and I wiped it away before it could course down my cheek. I sniffed it all back, gulping down the emotions.

Jude snored softly, a blanket pulled up to his bare chest, his corded arms resting behind his head. God, he was handsome.

He looked so peaceful, a lock of hair lying across his forehead, dark lashes fluttering as he dreamed. My heart ached, and I wanted him to hold me.

He didn't even open his eyes when I lifted the corner of the blanket and scooted in beside him. Jude emitted a low hum, his body shifting to his side so he could pull me back against his chest. His arm wrapped around my middle, holding me to him. His breath coasted across my ear while his legs intertwined with mine, his chest rising and falling soothingly against my back. Why did I ever think of running from him?

He laid a soft kiss to my head, his stubble catching my hair, before tucking my head beneath his chin.

"*Romy*," he breathed, before settling back into sleep.

For as long as I could remember, I'd been running. I didn't want to run anymore. Because for the first time ever, in Jude's arms, I knew I was home and I could finally breathe.

CHAPTER 26
Romy

Well, hello there.

Waking up to Jude's warm body wrapped around me, his knee pressed between my legs and his morning wood poking my ass, negated the fact that I was sore from riding all day every day and then sleeping on the couch.

The couch seemed deceivingly comfortable. Jude hadn't once complained, but he had to be hurting from sleeping on the stiff, leather couch the last couple weeks. He was going to have to fight me because tonight he was sleeping in the bed with me.

The thought made me giddy. My libido was screaming at me. I wiggled my butt into his boner.

Jude groaned. "You're evil in the morning," he rasped. His voice sounded so sexy waking up. Gritty.

I thrust my ass back into him. Jude's fingers pressed into my hip, digging into my sides to keep me in place.

He peppered kisses along the curve of my neck, sending shivers down my body and making me giggle. I turned in his arms, putting a hand to his face, and scraped my fingers along his unshaved jaw.

"Morning," I greeted, smiling up at him.

"Morning," he returned, leaning down to give me a light kiss.

His blue eyes were still heavy from sleep and what I knew must be desire. He put a hand between us to adjust himself.

"This couch sucks," I stated.

Jude released a throaty chuckle. "It's not that bad."

"You've got to be kidding me. Your back must be killing you. You're sleeping in your bed tonight."

"Romy," he warned.

"Jude." I reached between us, gripping the bulge in his boxer briefs.

Jude hissed through his teeth. "Evil, evil woman."

I tightened my grasp, and he bucked into my hand. I nuzzled my nose into his neck, inhaling his delicious, spicy scent. Pumping my grasp, I nipped at his black-and-gray neck tattoo before soothing it with my tongue.

Jude twitched as I gripped harder. "You're sleeping in the bed tonight," I ordered.

"What about you? We're supposed to take things slow."

Putting a hand to his shoulder, I pushed him onto his back and straddled him. My sleep shorts rode up my thighs. His hardened cock now pressed right where I needed it. I rolled my hips.

"I thought we addressed this. Patient, not gentle." I leaned down, taking his bottom lip between my teeth. "But if it's slow you want, I can show you how *slowly* I can torture you." I rolled my hips again, Jude thrusting against my core.

His fingers skimmed the inside of my thighs while I continued to rock my hips, this time sucking his tongue into my mouth. His fingertips explored the hem of my shorts, achingly close to where I wanted him.

"Are you not wearing any underwear?"

"I never wear underwear to bed."

He groaned, swiping his fingers along the crease of my hips.

"Sleep in the bed tonight," I told him, still rocking against him. I could feel the dampness growing between us.

"Okay," he breathed.

"Say it."

"I'll sleep in the bed tonight."

Smiling against his lips, I gave him a quick peck and jumped off the couch.

"*Romy*," he growled, reaching for me. I took a step back. His brow furrowed; his mouth pinched in frustration.

Quickly turning on my heels, I swayed my hips as I headed to the bathroom.

Feeling rather smug, I threw over my shoulder, "I win. I'll collect my prize tonight."

"Fuck!" I heard him yell from the living room.

That's right, baby. I play for keeps, too.

It was my fourth time leading the trail ride. Reed accompanied me this afternoon, taking up the rear as we led the riders past Thomas Rock.

It was a deep river canyon with sheer, basalt cliffs. Thousands of people visited the area each year for rock climbing, hiking, mountain biking, and horseback riding. Other than the Willows Rodeo, this was the major attraction for vacationers traveling to central Oregon. Twisted Creek ran along the trail we traveled. It was the most popular trail ride Thornbrush Ranch offered, and it was almost always full, just like today.

Without Lina around, I didn't mind Reed's company on the trail. He was quiet and serious, and he made sure we didn't end up with any wayward tourists.

We were nearing the place where we forded the creek when Winnie stumbled, practically tossing me.

"Ho," I cued, pulling up on the reins.

The other horses behind me slowed to a stop.

Dismounting, I ran a hand down Winnie's forelegs finding she threw a shoe. Nails were left protruding.

"Shit." It was my own damn fault. I hadn't checked her hooves like I usually do, distracted by the lawyer's call.

Reed rode up beside me.

"Threw a shoe?" he asked, seeing me with the horse's hoof perched on my thigh.

I picked a rock from the tender hoof before setting it back down.

"You didn't happen to bring any tools with you?" I asked him.

He shook his head. "No."

Shit. I blew out a breath.

Looking back at the waiting riders, some of them pulling

out their phones to snap photos of the creek and canyon, I knew I had to think of something. These people were expecting their four-hour trail ride to end on time. They weren't expecting to just sit on horses and wait until I could fix Winnie up enough to ride out of here. Most of them probably had dinner reservations in town.

I turned back to Reed. "You're going to have to lead them back and get the kit and a boot."

Unless I had a boot or duct tape, I shouldn't try to move an unshod horse. Otherwise, I could lame her with a bruised hoof.

They had at least an hour left of the ride before they circled back to the ranch. It would take Reed probably another hour to return with the farrier kit. I pulled my phone out of my pocket. It was nearly four o'clock. There was no service where we were in the canyon, so I couldn't call Jude or Chuck to help.

"Do you want to take the group back and I stay with Winnie?" Reed offered.

It was a nice offer. I had a feeling Reed wasn't as bad as Lina claimed him to be.

I shook my head, wanting to stay with Winnie to make sure she was okay. "It's all right. I'll just pull Winnie off the trail, and we'll wait in the shade."

Reed nodded. "I'll be back as soon as I can."

"Thanks, Reed."

"We're going to ford the creek here," Reed instructed, taking command of the riders. I hadn't seen him take charge like that before, and it eased any concerns I had about him leading the rest of the trail ride. "Romy's horse threw a shoe, so I'm going to lead us the rest of the way. Make sure you keep your feet in the stirrups and two hands on the reins. Otherwise, you might end up wet."

Some of the riders snickered at the possibility of landing in the creek, while others shot me concerned looks.

I gave them all reassuring smiles, waving as they passed. "You're all in good hands. Enjoy the rest of the ride!"

I waited, watching them cross the creek, return to the trail, and disappear out of sight. Knowing we needed to make room for possible hikers, I gently led Winnie off the trail. She hobbled slightly, huffing.

"I know, girl. It can't feel great."

Ponderosa pines shaded grassy areas along the water, and I found a flat spot to sit. It was a nice afternoon, sunny but not too hot. A cool breeze blew off the water, lifting loose hair from my sweaty neck. I removed my cowboy hat, setting it in the grass beside me.

"This isn't too bad." I sighed, resting my arms on my knees.

Winnie shifted a little, bending down to grab a mouthful of grass before sniffing my hair. I stroked her nose to reassure her and myself while we waited.

CHAPTER 27
Jude

"I should insist all my fighters spend at least part of their training camp working a ranch," Alex said, dusting off his lucky jeans as we hopped out of the truck in front of the stables. "I'm exhausted."

I nodded in agreement. "Mind if we skip the workout this evening? I think my body forgot it isn't eighteen anymore."

We had just spent the majority of the day raking and baling hay with Uncle Chuck and a few borrowed ranch hands. Now there were about two hundred square hay bales lying in the west and south fields.

"Make sure you take an ice bath tonight. We'll go hard tomorrow morning to make up for missing tonight."

"Sure thing, Coach." Romy would be back soon from the trail ride, and I wanted to get cleaned up before she returned. Flashes of her this morning straddling my lap while she rolled her hips tightened my pants.

I quickly adjusted myself before following Alex to his parked rental car.

We exchanged knucks, and Alex slid into his driver's seat.

I raised a hand in farewell while he turned the car around and headed away from the stables.

I wanted to make this evening special for Romy. She'd be tired from her trail ride, and while she showered, I'd grill some steaks and pour us some wine. Maybe put on some music while we talked about our day and ate. I wanted that with her. But not just tonight. I wanted it every evening. I think that's what she meant by being patient with her because if she really looked, she would know I was already all in. I had been in love with Romy since we were kids, and I don't think it ever went away, like a banked fire waiting to be fed and grow.

I was the one pulling back on the reins, trying to slow us to a trot, while Romy was rearing to charge forward into our physical relationship. I wanted that with her, I did, but I also wanted more.

Years of living on her memory, the fooling around … I was dying with anticipation. She had no idea how badly I wanted her. And I knew it was going to be good. If the foreplay was any indication of just how good it would be, hell, I knew this would far surpass our teenage hookup.

But I didn't just want sex from her. I wanted the mornings, the weekends, the holidays, the little moments in between. I worried that if she knew that's what I wanted from her—that I wanted *all* of her—she wouldn't want the same. She may be staying, but that nagging feeling that I wasn't worth someone giving their all twisted my gut. So I would do my best to be patient with her while silently loving her.

The clop of riders coming up the road to the stable steadied my heart. She was back sooner than I had expected, thinking I had at least a half hour before they returned.

Reed was leading the group, and he directed the riders to pull up at the paddock fence before dismounting.

But no Romy. My heart clenched in my chest. Where was she? I scanned the group, even though I knew she wasn't there. I looked back toward the road, but there were no lone riders.

In four long strides, I was at Reed's side. "Where's Romy?"

He tipped up his hat to look at me. His lips thinned on a swallow. "Her horse threw a shoe."

My brows shot to my hat. "And you left them on the trail?"

"We didn't pack farrier tools, so I had to bring the group back. We'll take care of the horses, and then I'll grab the kit and go get them. She was fine when we left."

Fucking Reed. I was starting to understand why Lina always said that. "Where?"

"I left her by the ford."

"When was that?"

"About an hour ago."

It was already getting late in the day.

"I'll take the tools to her. Take care of the guests and the horses."

I didn't wait for Reed's response. I just turned on my heels and stormed into the stable.

What the fuck? He was just going to leave her out there with the horse and lead the riders back himself? What was he thinking?

Pulling my phone out of my back pocket, I dialed up Romy, but it went straight to voicemail. Fuck! She was out of range.

At this rate, the sun would be setting by the time I reached her. Did either of us know the trail well enough to follow it in the dark?

I grabbed the farrier kit and a boot, along with Bronte's tack.

All the horses were either out on the ranch or exhausted from the trail ride, so I saddled up Hazel's horse, Bronte. He hadn't been ridden since Hazel, but I knew Hazel took countless trail rides with him. If any horse knew that trail, it was Bronte.

CHAPTER 28
Romy

Lying beneath the shade of a large pine with the river's cool breeze wafting over me was my kind of peace. I knew Reed would be nearly two hours, so I covered my face with my hat and settled in for a nap while Winnie snuffled grass nearby.

Nearing the hour mark, I was drifting off to sleep when I heard the crunch and shuffle of hiking boots treading down the trail. I sat up, resituating the hat back on my head. The hiker's head was lowered beneath his cap, watching his feet as he chose his steps carefully. Dusting off the butt of my jeans, I pulled Winnie toward me to make sure she was off the trail to allow the hiker to pass.

I stayed to the side, a smile ready for the hiker when he passed. The hiker seemed familiar, but most people seemed familiar in the place I grew up.

Winnie brayed, causing the hiker to look up.

My stomach plummeted.

The hiker's face broke out in a sneer beneath the shadow of his bill.

Junior.

My smile faded into a glare.

"I thought I might run into you here this week," he said. His voice was a lot calmer than it had been at the Rooster, his face more serene. It was far more unsettling than him cursing at me. A purple-and-yellow bruise still marred his jaw where Jude hit him.

"What do you want?" I demanded. I wasn't about to put up with this guy's bullshit again. And it wasn't lost on me that we were both alone on this trail.

Reed was probably just heading back my way. It was going to be another hour out here.

"Hazel's hearing is coming up," he commented.

"Yeah, and?"

"It's in your best interest not to testify."

His light-gray eyes were unnervingly pale, and his pupils were blown out, making them appear beady. Winnie shifted her weight beside me, sensing my unease. I stretched out a hand to rest on her shoulder, hoping to steady her.

I wasn't planning on testifying, but that letter was still saved on the computer. I hadn't decided whether I was going to send it or not.

"We'll see," is all I said, before something snapped in him and he moved off the trail to get in my face.

Winnie winced, nervous by his sudden movements, and stepped back on the trail.

Junior towered over me, his chest rising and falling. He stopped inches from me. I backed away, but with the trees behind me, there was no room to retreat. I could step to the side, but there was nothing but ankle-twisting rock.

"Your fucking bitch of a sister needs to spend the rest of her days in jail, and I swear to God, I'll make sure that happens." He glared down at me.

"What do you care what happens to her? The DA is already trying her for murder." I repeated what the lawyer told me.

"She's claiming self-defense, that she's the victim here. But she stole from my brother, then killed him. She deserves to be in there for life. I intend to make sure that happens."

My eyes narrowed. She stole from him? Was that Jesse's money I found? Junior didn't know about the note or the box of money. I needed to make sure he—or anyone—couldn't find it.

"Fuck you," I fumed.

And that was the wrong thing to say because before I realized what was happening, Junior kicked out his leg, wrapping it around one of mine. I lost my balance, and my hat fell off my head. Putting my hands out to catch myself, I toppled, hitting my hip on the rocky ground. He gripped my arm, wrenching it behind me until I could do nothing but flip onto my stomach to keep him from breaking my arm. My cheek hit a jutting rock. Hard. Stinging pain shooting through my skull.

I ground my teeth in pain as he wrenched harder on my arm, twisting my shoulder behind me. His knee landed on my back, pinning me down.

"Motherfucker! Get off me!" I bucked my hips and kicked my legs, hoping to connect with some bodily limb of his.

"Shut the fuck up," he growled in my ear. He was closer than I thought. I could feel his hot, moist breath against my neck, and cold, clammy fear washed over me.

I screamed again, hoping someone on the trail would hear. I kicked my legs as hard as I could, but it only made Junior's grip tighten and my arm twist more. My scream changed from anger and fear to pain. He lifted my shoulders off the ground, only to slam me down, my head bouncing off that rock again, and this time I felt something wet run down my cheek.

"Listen! I know who your boyfriend is. I've been wanting to talk to you before I go to the cops and press charges for assault. That would ruin his career and could land him time. So we're going to talk. Well, you're just going to listen, but we're going to come to an agreement."

Oh God, Jude. I couldn't let that happen to him. He loved the sport. It made him whole. It fed his soul. Without MMA, he'd crumble. He'd just confided in me about his depression since he couldn't fight while he recovered from knee surgery. This would break him. I couldn't let Junior do that to him.

"Are you going to listen?"

I nodded into the dirt.

"Good. Now you're going to refuse to testify at the hearing. In fact, maybe even consider not attending. Let the justice system handle this for what it is—murder—and I'll leave you and Jude 'The big bad Bull' Larsen alone," he said in a mocking tone. "If I hear otherwise, I'm going right to the cops to press charges. Agreed?"

I nodded again.

"Say it."

"Okay. Agreed," I spat.

Junior released my arm, hoisting himself off my back,

which only dug me into the ground once more while he stepped away. Relief and pain radiated through my shoulder. I cradled it against my stomach.

"Shit," he said, looking down at me. "If anyone asks, you fell off your horse. Understand? I don't want to have to make another visit."

I sat up, gingerly touching my cheek. My fingertips came away slippery with blood.

"Understand?"

"I understand." I didn't want another visit by him, either.

"Good." He chuckled to himself as if he'd just thought of some deranged joke. "See you around, Romy Miller."

I glared a fare-fucking-well to him.

I saw him before he saw me. And it wasn't Reed coming down the trail on the other side of the creek—it was Jude.

"Shit," I whispered, rolling my shoulder one more time.

Jude was going to freak out.

I did my best to wipe the blood off my cheek with the hem of my shirt, but now my shirt was stained and I probably looked worse than I thought. My shoulder was sore. I couldn't lift it more than ninety degrees, but it would heal.

"I was expecting Reed!" I called over the water.

Jude looked up from the water where he was fording, spotting me on the trail with Winnie.

"Fucking Reed," Jude said. Just like Lina.

My short laugh ended in a hiss, grabbing my shoulder to keep it still.

"What happened?" Concern laced his voice as he neared. He zeroed in on where I held my arm. When he saw my face, his eyes grew wide. "Fuck, Romy! What happened?"

He dug his heels into the horse as it splashed through the creek, trying to urge it on to get to me. Splashing up the bank, the horse trotted a few feet to the trail. He barely stopped the horse before hopping down and rushing to me.

"I'm all right. I just fell."

I had never fallen from a horse in my life. Pretty sure Jude knew that, too. I averted my eyes, not wanting to see Jude's worry or reveal the lie.

"You fell off Winnie? Reed said you were fine when he—"

"It was after he left," I interrupted.

"What the hell, Romy? You know you shouldn't ride if she threw a shoe."

Yes, I did know that, but he couldn't know I had a visitor while I waited. He didn't need to know that Junior touched me and threatened me, threatened him. Knowing what Jude did while sober in a crowded bar, I worried what he would do away from it. I wasn't about to visit two people in jail.

"It was stupid. Let's just get her booted and get back to the ranch." I grabbed Winnie's rein, still avoiding direct eye contact.

"Okay. Let's get this done so we can get you home and clean up that cut."

He reached out to lend a comforting touch to my arm, but it caused me to flinch and hiss in pain.

"Shit, Romy. Is your arm that bad?"

"Just sore. It's not broken." The ligaments in my shoulder

may be strained, but I knew Junior hadn't gone so far as breaking it.

"Maybe we should take you to urgent care."

"No." I shrugged with my good shoulder. "I'll just ice it when we get back."

I looked up at him then.

His brow furrowed in concern, his eyes searching mine, scanning my face, every inch of me, to try and detect other injuries. I cupped his jaw with my right hand and gave him what I hoped was a reassuring smile.

"Come on, let's take care of Winnie so we can get out of here."

Jude nodded before turning to the saddlebag to pull out the farrier kit and boot. It was then that I noticed he rode Hazel's horse.

"You brought Bronte?"

"I figured if we get out of here late, Bronte may know the trails better than either of us." He gave me a tender smile.

My chest warmed. Tears pricked at the back of my eyes, stinging my nose. I took a shuddering breath to tamp down the emotions. He'd thought to bring Bronte, not knowing what state we would be in but wanting to ensure we returned safely. No one had ever considered my safety before. For some reason, bringing my sister's horse made me feel ... loved. Bronte was not my horse, but it made me feel like I did as a child when my mom would bring me my bear. Any tears or hurts would quickly be soothed away by snuggling Bear.

So I gripped Bronte's reins, stroking his shoulder, soothing my hurts, while Jude got out the tools and boot. And I kept petting him while I watched Jude work on Winnie's hoof, removing the nail heads and filing. Petting until I felt centered and calm.

He couldn't know what happened today. It would hurt him. I wasn't about to let anything hurt him.

Once booted, I added a leadrope to Winnie's bridle, tying her to Bronte's saddle.

"We'll have to ride in the saddle together." I fluttered my eyelashes at him. Teasing him also helped settle the lump in my throat. "The one-horse trope is my favorite romance trope."

"Oh, is it?" Jude gave me his lopsided grin.

I stepped in his space, my boots bumping into his. "Hmm-hmm," I hummed. "My arm is hurt, so you may need to help me up into the saddle." I peered at him with my most demure expression.

He stepped toward me, his voice darkening. "I think I can manage that, my lady." Jude grabbed my hips and sent a thrill through me.

With my good hand gripping the saddle horn and Jude's strong grasp, I was able to hoist myself into the saddle. I sat forward, allowing room for Jude to mount behind the cantle and reach for the reins.

"Tight fit," he remarked while holding in a breath.

His thighs bracketed mine, and his buckle dug into my lower back.

"That's what she said," I joked. Anything to brush the emotions under the rug … to disperse the residual fear.

Jude scoffed. "You better be good, or we might never get out of here." He pinched my side, making me release a shortened squeal before taking up the reins.

With one hand spread across my belly and the other holding the reins, he clicked his tongue and flicked the reins. Bronte started with a lurch before fording the creek. Settling into the saddle, I relaxed against his chest. Even when a jostle sent a twinge through my shoulder, I didn't complain because I was safe, but my thoughts about Hazel's situation were bothering me more now than ever.

CHAPTER 29
Romy

Let's just say those romantasy books make sharing a horse seem so much more erotic because that was the most uncomfortable ride I'd ever been on. It couldn't have been enjoyable for Bronte either.

By the time we reached the ranch, the sun was barely hovering over the Cascade Range. Jude urged me to go inside so we could get a better look at my injuries, but I insisted he take care of the horses first. I watched as he untacked and examined Winnie's hoof, rebooting it and shooting a text to Chuck that we were back.

"The farrier will be here tomorrow," he told me, repocketing his phone.

I nodded.

Jude kept stealing concerned glances. I didn't blame him. I was unusually quiet, but I was drained. I hadn't realized how much adrenaline I used until it evaporated, leaving me feeling heavy and droopy.

We climbed into his truck and drove the short distance around the property to Jude's. Relief flooded me when I saw the timed porch lights illuminating the little house. Home. That's what it felt like, and my heart squeezed. I wanted it to be my home. With Jude.

"Let me get those," Jude offered, crouching down in front of me when we entered the front door.

I lifted my foot, letting Jude pry off one boot then the other, his fingers lingering at each ankle, skimming over my arches as if checking for unseen injury.

I was fine. I had to be.

"Doing okay, honey?"

I smiled softly down at him, stepping in between his knees. Crouched in front of me—his hands gripping the back of my thighs—his chin was at sternum level.

"I'm doing okay." I ran my palm along his rugged jaw, the scrape of his scruff sending tingles up my arm.

He rested his head on my breasts, breathing me in, holding me to him.

I took off his hat, reaching over to hang it on the coat-tree before running my fingers through his dark locks.

I was safe.

He was safe.

I wouldn't do anything to jeopardize this. And if it meant staying silent for now, that's what I'd do. At least until I figured something else out.

"Let's take care of you." His voice rumbled through my rib cage, spreading warmth through my chest and into my belly.

When was the last time I let someone take care of me? Maybe Hazel when I was a child? I'd gotten used to taking care of myself. Because I felt as though I could only depend on myself.

But I could let Jude care for me. Isn't that part of trusting? Trusting someone enough that you could lean on them?

Jude's hands and eyes never left me as he stood. "Come on."

He kicked off his own boots and led me into the bathroom. Flicking on the light, he hit the dial to heat up the shower. Washcloth in hand, he ran it under the sink faucet. He gently started to blot the blood away from my cheek, and I glimpsed my reflection in the mirror. It didn't look as bad as I thought it would. The shallow scrape was red and puffy and stung when he touched it, but it would probably just leave a bruise.

"Sorry," he whispered when I let out a hiss between my teeth.

"It's all right. I'll clean it up in the shower."

"Okay." Jude reached into the medicine cabinet, pulling out the antibiotic ointment. "I'll leave this out for after the shower. Steaks all right for dinner?"

"Sounds delicious. Jude …"

He stalled at the door. His eyes were soft, but his brows were pinched.

I wanted him to stay. I didn't want him to leave me alone in the bathroom. I wasn't ready to be left alone.

"Can you help me with my shirt?"

His jaw flexed. Pausing. Considering. He gave a jerky nod.

Stepping back to me, I raised my one good arm, his fingertips grazing my stomach as he wrapped them around the hem of my shirt. He lifted it to help me pull my arm out, then over my head until he could slip it off my sore shoulder.

We stood there looking at each other, the air thickening

with steam. The way he was staring at me felt as though every pore was opening, my bronchial tubes expanding with each breath.

I wanted to touch him. I wanted his hands on me. I needed him to ground me. I needed everything to be okay, to wash away the feeling that things were far from it.

I reached out to him, running my hand down his chest, feeling every dip, plane, and ridge of his pecs and abdominals under his T-shirt. I wanted the firmness and weight of him on me. Anything to pull me back down to earth and tether me here. My fingers grazed his belt buckle. I gripped it, drawing him to me.

"*Romy.*" His voice almost sounded pained, as if he was warring with himself. His fingers flexed at his side.

"I need you." I would beg for him if I had to, anything to soothe this ache that was blooming.

He was so close, I could feel how hard he was. How much he wanted me pressed into my lower stomach. But he still hadn't touched me. Our heavy breaths and the stream of water hitting the tub made my ears ring.

"Touch me. *Please.*"

As if he had never touched me before, he tentatively reached out to brush a loose strand of hair away from my temple. He ran his hand down my braid until he reached the band, pulling it out. He dropped it on the ground, and I didn't care. Not once did his eyes leave mine while his fingers ran through the plait until my hair hung loose around my shoulders.

"You're so beautiful." He said it in a whisper, but it was louder than the water and our panting combined.

The growing need between us. All the patience. The years we missed. The hesitancy to trust someone with my heart. It didn't matter in this moment.

Moisture coated us. The back of his hand trailed down my bare arms, causing me to shiver.

"Cold?"

I shook my head. I was far from it. I was on fire.

Leaning down, he rested his forehead on mine. I closed my eyes, zeroing in on his scent, the need I couldn't resist, the desire coiling between us, the feeling that my heart would burst from my chest. His nose nudged mine. I tilted my face up to his. His fingers laced with mine, and I wanted to hold on to him forever. Our breaths mingled, coasting across our lips. I parted my mouth, silently urging him to kiss me. But he didn't.

He stepped into me, and there was nowhere to go but the counter. As if I weighed nothing, he threw his arm around my waist and hoisted me up onto it. I wrapped my legs around him, hooking my heels behind him to press him to me. He thrust gently, his erection rubbing against my core.

I pushed up his shirt hem, and he reached a hand behind him, gripping his collar to pull it over his head. I bit my lip seeing him half bare. His rigid lats. His firm pecs and his defined eight-pack. The man was a chiseled god. I couldn't help but run my fingers over him. Marveling. His groan came out a near purr.

Reaching my good hand behind me, I popped the clasps on my bra, letting the straps slip down my arms. Jude's gaze felt like a caress, stroking down my throat to my collarbone, to my breasts as my bra slid down my arms. My nipples hardened as if he were touching them.

It was his turn to suck in his lip. I wanted not just his eyes and his hands; I wanted his mouth.

I threaded my fingers through his hair, bringing his head toward me. Wanting his mouth on me so badly. Tasting every part of me until I let go. Until I let my heart fall.

Jude tossed my bra to the floor. He bent down, leaning me back until my head rested against the foggy mirror. His soft, pillowy lips pressed against my chest. The moisture of his mouth left a shivering trail across my skin as he traveled down between my breasts. I arched toward him.

"What do you want, honey?" he asked, his lips brushing across the inside curve of my breast.

"Your mouth." I could barely voice more than those two words.

"Want me to suck your stiff, little nipple into my mouth?"

"Yes."

Jude's tongue darted out, tracing the areola of one nipple before turning to the other to do the same. It wasn't enough. It was a tease. I wanted him to draw me into his mouth. He did it again, each time his tongue nearing the peak.

"Jude, please."

He didn't wait for me to beg more, his mouth now covering over the hard tip. His tongue flicking it just as he did my clit when he went down on me in his truck. Electric pulses zinged right to that bundle of nerves with each swirl of his tongue. His teeth lightly clutched the stiffened bud, pulling it and making me gasp. I held his head to me, my body arching into him. He thrust against my core. And I wanted more. I needed more.

He must have recognized my silent plea because he left my breasts, trailing his mouth down my sternum, down the dip of my stomach until he reached the button of my jeans.

"These have to fucking go." He peeked up at me from where he hovered over my waistband.

I nodded my head against the mirror. Desperate for him. I was rewarded with his lopsided grin. He made my stomach flutter every time he gave me that look, and I could feel myself falling.

Jude straightened, assisting me off the counter, then helping me out of my pants, taking my panties with them, sliding them down. He never stopped touching me, as if he needed the contact as much as I did. His fingertips feathered along the back of my thighs while he helped me step out of my jeans, causing my flesh to pucker. Straightening, his heated gaze strummed up my body.

Licking my bottom lip, I bit down to keep from moaning. I reached for him, taking the time to unbuckle his belt, popping the button and unzipping his jeans. His bulge strained against his boxers. My fingers hooked into his boxer briefs, and I bent down, slowly pulling them down his thick, muscular legs. His hardened cock sprung free, jutting out, begging me to touch it. A bead of precum gleamed at the head, inviting me to lap it up. My tongue darted out, but he tipped my chin up to look at him.

"Not yet, greedy girl. There will be time for that," he said gruffly. "Right now, I want to take care of you."

The warmth of his words spread like lava, pooling in my center.

He took my hand, helping me to stand. He walked

backward, never taking his eyes off me, drawing us toward the shower. He pulled back the curtain, more steam billowing around us, beading on our naked bodies. He didn't let me go, making sure we both stepped into the tub safely.

The warm stream hit us, drenched us. Rivulets of water ran down our chests.

And he did exactly as he said. He took care of me.

His hands never left me. Running them through my hair to wet it before lathering it with shampoo and conditioner. Argan oil and coconut saturating the room. He pumped body wash into a washcloth before running it over my body, paying special attention to my breasts. They felt so heavy and tender. My nipples stiffened with each pass of the terry cloth. He rubbed the washcloth between my legs, causing me to twitch and buck my hips. I wanted him to stay there, but he didn't, turning me under the showerhead to rinse.

"Your turn, honey." He handed me the washcloth. Desire ran over me like the stream of water. Gripping the washcloth over his cock, I slowly twisted and pulled while he jerked in my grasp. I liked watching this man unravel for me.

"*Romy*," he growled.

His hand paused my ministrations, and I smiled up at him, pleased that I could make his control slip.

We were running low on hot water, but my skin was burning.

"Jude, I want you."

"You have me."

I wrapped my hand around his neck, drawing him down to me. He still hadn't kissed me. I could barely stand it. I understood his hesitancy. It was like if he did, it would make this all too real for him, and I had already broken his heart once. But it was real for me, too, and I wanted to show him just how real it was. I didn't want to break his heart again.

I pressed up on my tiptoes, darting my tongue out to trace his bottom lip. It was the switch I was needing—he was needing. He gathered me in his arms, pressing our wet bodies together, his lips crushing into mine. His cock slipped closer to where I needed it. His tongue licked along the seam of my mouth. I opened for him, and our tongues stroked and explored. I hitched my leg up, putting my foot on the shower shelf. I gripped his length, notching it at my entrance.

He stopped, breaking our kiss. "Not yet. The water is getting cold. Let's get out."

"*Jude*," I whined. We were so close.

He chuckled, turning off the shower. "Come on."

He pulled the towels off the rack, draping me in one before opening the curtain. We dried ourselves off and rehung the towels.

"Come here." He gripped my waist and lifted me into his arms, wrapping my legs around his middle.

I kissed him every step he took on the way to the bedroom. My hair was still wet and dripping down my back, but I didn't care as his eyes burned into me while he carefully and deliberately laid me down on the bed.

CHAPTER 30
Romy

Falling into the plush duvet lifted a cloud of what I came to recognize as the smell of home. Laundry soap, spearmint, and spice. Jude's scent. And now my own, sweet and tropical.

Jude crawled up from the bottom of the bed, his corded muscles rolling and flexing as he stalked toward me like an apex predator. But I had never felt safer in his sight. I could let him prowl after me forever.

His cock was rock hard and protruding between his legs, inching toward me. I bent my knees, letting them fall apart, opening for him.

"So needy," he quipped.

"Always," I whispered.

He hovered over me now, his cock inches away from my entrance. He dipped his head, brushing his lips across mine. I ran my hands up his back until I could bury my fingers into his hair, holding him to me. Wanting to devour him.

He put a hand between us, gripping his dick to run the tip through me, letting it glide over my clit. I bucked each time.

My pussy pulsed.

"You're so wet," he whispered, breathing against my mouth.

He did it again and again until I was writhing, trying to suck him in.

"I need you," I whined.

"You want me inside you?" he asked, peering into my eyes. His eyes were blazing blue now. Burning the hottest flame.

"Please, Jude. I need you to fuck me. Now."

He sucked in a breath. I could feel his heart pounding through his chest.

"God, I love hearing you say that."

He reached past me, his body pressing me into the mattress momentarily, to open the top drawer of the nightstand. He pulled out a condom, breaking it open. I watched with rapt attention as he slid it over his cock. His arms flexing deliciously as he sheathed himself.

"I want you so badly, honey, I'm not sure I can take this slow."

A thrill went through me. "I trust you."

I wet my lips, hoping he saw just how much I wanted him, too. Needed him.

"Fuck. Me." I arched into him again, pushing my hips toward him, begging for him.

Jude groaned. "*Fuck.* How did I get so lucky?"

My giggle was cut short when Jude's fingers swiped through my slick slit. He circled around my swollen bud before swiping through, pushing one finger into my pussy, stroking it, loosening it, before adding a second finger.

"You sure you can handle me right now?"

I knew I could take him. I had only once before, but somehow, he was larger, thicker, harder than he was then.

"Uh-huh," I quietly panted.

He removed his fingers, and I moaned at the vacancy. But that emptiness was brief because then Jude's cock was notched at my entrance.

"Take a breath."

I took a shuddering breath, too amped up, buzzing. I felt ready to burst, as if someone had turned the tuning pegs on a guitar so tightly, the strings were about to pop.

He pushed in just an inch.

"So tight. God, I missed this. Missed you. Breathe, honey."

I tried to steady my heart, drawing air through my nose. Slowly, he inched forward, his eyes never leaving mine. I arched into him, my mouth falling open on a silent cry as he deeply buried himself.

"Look at you. We fit so perfectly. You should see yourself. How beautiful you are."

He stayed still for just a moment, waiting for me to relax around him.

I rocked my hips, wanting him to move. I dug my fingers into his firm ass, pressing him into me, needing him to advance.

"Please, Jude. *Move.*" I raised my head, bringing my lips to his, nipping, urging him on.

Jude drew out a couple inches before thrusting back in. I gasped. He took my hands off him, circling my wrists in his hands so he could hold them at my sides, against the bed, to give himself more leverage to thrust. His thrusts were starting to pack a punch, each time hitting just in the right spot, the friction building.

He pulled out, this time barely inside me, the root of his cock rubbing against my clit. And he stayed there, let me grind against him. Sliding in just enough while he put pressure on my hips. It felt so good. Too good.

"Jude!" I cried out.

He chuckled into the crook of my neck. "There's my loud girl."

I could feel the pressure building. "I'm going to come."

"Not yet." He released me, sitting up on his heels, but still deep inside. "Get on your knees."

I moaned while he slowly, torturously pulled out. Feeling immediately empty, I scrambled onto my knees so I wouldn't have to wait long for him to fill me again.

He rubbed and kneaded my ass. "You're perfect. Lie all the way down and stick your ass in the air."

I did as he instructed, resting all the way down on the mattress, taking the pressure off my shoulder while I propped myself up on my knees, giving him the perfect view of my ass.

Gripping my hips, he thrust back inside. The new position brought him deeper, hitting walls that had never been touched. It drove me wild, and I pushed against him. Jude slapped a sharp spank on my ass. I rocked my hips against him, moaning. The sting of his spank sent a spark straight to where his cock was buried inside. Another spank on the other ass cheek, and I felt as though I was about ready to crumble. No one had ever spanked me before, and I loved it.

"I'm so close, Jude."

"Honey, I'm so close, too. Come with me?" He said each

word between pants, his thrusts becoming erratic.

I reached between my legs, feeling where he was deep inside me. I spread the wetness through my slit and over my clit, circling while he continued to pound into me.

He groaned. "My naughty girl, touching herself while I fuck her from behind?"

I hummed a reply.

He gently pushed down on my lower back until I was flat on my belly, my hand trapped between my legs, still circling. He straddled me, pushing my legs together, tightening my pussy around him and adding more friction. I couldn't move as he thrust inside me over and over again.

I wanted to wriggle and writhe beneath him, but his weight made me take it. Take it all. The pleasure was climbing. Blood was pounding in my ears. I couldn't stand it. It was too intense.

My cries came out a jagged laugh. "Oh God! I can't take it! I'm going to come!"

"Take it, honey. Come for me!"

Jude's encouragement and a swipe of my finger across my clit one last time was all I needed to explode.

Jude jerked and grunted. My walls fluttered against his pulsating cock. His thrusts slowed as he came, draping his body across my back.

We lie there, panting, my damp hair plastered beneath my cheek pressed to the bed. Jude was still buried deep. He twitched inside me, shooting aftershocks through my core. My hips involuntarily rocked against him. My heart pounded in my ears.

The weight of him on top of me brought me back down.

Grounded me. Centered me.

His lips brushed my cheek beneath the tender scrape.

"That was incredible." My voice was raspy from screaming. My lips tingled around the words.

"So good." He was still breathing heavily, trying to catch his breath. "Did I hurt you?" he asked.

"No. It made me forget about the pain."

"Good. I'm so sorry you were in pain to begin with. I'll be right back."

He gently pulled out and I groaned. Feeling him leave me made me want to put him right back in. It was a vacant feeling I didn't particularly like. I wanted him to stay buried inside and never leave. I felt whole being with Jude, our flesh as one.

Jude padded across the hall to the bathroom, where I figured he was disposing of the condom. Water ran for a second. Then he was back. Too spent, I hadn't even moved. He had a washcloth in his hand and the tube of antibiotic ointment.

"Don't move," he ordered.

"I'm not sure I can yet."

I spied that sexy tip of his lip as he went to work, tenderly wiping between my legs. I pulsed as he swiped over me. A promise for more later. He discarded the washcloth and then squeezed ointment onto his fingertip. The mattress dipped under his knees. With a featherlight touch, he patted it across the cut. It was such a juxtaposition from how he just played with my body.

"Does it hurt?"

"No."

A lump formed in my throat. *Oh, don't cry after sex.* Never once in my life had I cried after sex. And it wasn't even the earth-shattering orgasm he just drew out of me, but the way he now tenderly took care of me.

I swallowed it down and closed my eyes tightly.

The bed rose with Jude's body weight. I kept my eyes closed, listening to him rummage through drawers before returning to the bed.

"Sit up, honey."

Finally feeling that my emotions had settled, I pushed myself up. Jude already had a pair of boxer briefs on, and he was holding out one of my shirts and sweatpants. Could this guy get any sweeter?

"Here." He helped me pull on the sweatpants, remembering that I didn't sleep with underwear, and then slid the shirt over my head, gently helping me shrug my bad arm into the sleeve.

"Thank you." I drew my hair out from the collar. My damp hair was left in tangles, but I didn't care. Because this man was slowly melting my walls.

Jude leaned down, pressing a kiss to my lips.

"You're so good to me," I whispered, my hands cupping his face.

"Always," he murmured.

My heart galloped like a band of wild horses.

I wrapped my arms around his shoulders. His eyes were so soft and warm, but hesitant, as if he was waiting for me to run. And I couldn't blame him.

This feeling of home with him was one thing I was not ready to part with.

He pulled me toward him, wrapping my legs around his

middle. "Come on. I'll get you some ice for that shoulder. You can ice it while I make you dinner."

He lifted me, carrying me to the kitchen.

This man was making it impossible for me to ever say goodbye to him. Not that I was. He just didn't believe it quite yet.

CHAPTER 31
Jude

Waking up to Romy snuggled against me made it nearly unbearable to leave the bed at four every morning. But I forced myself to do it, knowing that when I returned, we would pick up right where we left off.

For the first time ever, I didn't feel like I had to question whether or not I was worthy of her. She would prove it with breakfast on the table after my morning training session before she and I went to our respective ranch jobs. When we spotted each other across the outdoor arena or the field, we traded smiles that meant something—a secret that only she and I knew. And every night, she proved it with her mouth, her hands, her body.

I was crazy for this woman, and my pride was at an all-time high knowing she was mine. No one or nothing could ruin it for us. While she was proving to me that I was worthy, I was proving to her that she could trust me. I shared everything about the upcoming fight, how the training was going, and what to expect. Coach was going to fly out one of my teammates who trained in Muay Thai and jujitsu. It wasn't hard for me to keep her in the loop. Now that we had given in to each other, it felt as though we were free and in this together.

The only thing that I wasn't ready to share was that I was in love with her. Shit, I was scared. Just admitting it to myself had taken years. I worried that confessing would frighten her, and I was too afraid of losing her to bare that truth. So I would be patient and let my actions speak for themselves.

Over the next few weeks leading up to the Willows Rodeo, it was all hands on deck. Uncle Chuck and Christian took over the training for the rodeo contestants. Lina was still out on circuit, breaking records and preparing for her own entry into the rodeo and would return by the fourth. I insisted Romy carry tools on all her trail rides and have Reed with her. If he wasn't going to go, then I sure as hell would, but Uncle Chuck needed me on the cattle.

The cows required branding, vaccinations, and castrations, while the yearlings were transported for slaughter. We borrowed ranch hands, and Uncle Chuck let me hire a couple temporary cowboys to help while I oversaw the operation. I even wrangled Alex into getting his hands dirty. Always eager, he jumped in happily with the vaccine gun, and per usual—like most things—was a quick learner.

After dinner, I would meet Alex and my teammate Troy at our garage gym for a sparring session. I was exhausted by the end of every day, but I'd never been happier because my girl was at home, waiting for me.

Romy would already be in bed by the time I returned. I would shower and snuggle in beside her while trying not to wake her. But every time, she would wake with an adorable, sleepy smile, her hands finding me in the dark. We would collide, drawing out each other's pleasure until we had to catch our breaths. Until our hearts settled. Falling asleep in each other's arms.

"I couldn't see her," Romy grumbled, pulling herself up into the truck.

Hazel's hearing was supposed to be this week, right after the Fourth of July holiday. Romy hadn't heard from her in weeks, and her lawyer kept calling to ask Romy to testify. She tensed every time she looked at the caller ID, hitting ignore.

I couldn't totally blame her. After what we found in the stables, and her last visit with Hazel, I knew Romy well enough to know this was her favorite defense mechanism.

Avoid. Or run.

At least she wasn't running. Just avoiding. Baby steps.

Until today, that is. With the hearing a couple days away, Romy, my indecisive girl, hadn't decided whether she would testify or send in a character letter. She said she needed more clarity and hoped Hazel could give it to her.

Not wanting her to go by herself, I volunteered to drive.

"What do you mean you couldn't see her?" I asked.

Romy buckled up, pushing a breath out her nose before answering, "She's under suicide watch."

That was not what I was expecting to hear.

"What?"

"Yep. I need to call her lawyer."

"All right." I nodded.

I turned the key in the ignition and pulled out of the jail's parking lot, heading toward Highway 20, while Romy dialed the lawyer.

"Hi, Angela, it's Romy Miller. I just tried to visit Hazel, but they said she's under suicide watch … yeah …"

Romy was silent while she listened. Ms. Hoya's voice was muffled as I tried my best to listen in.

"So what does that mean for the hearing? Okay, I see." Romy rubbed the space between her brows, her lashes fluttering closed. "I just don't know. I understand how it could help, but I'm just not sure … Okay. I'll call you as soon as I decide. All right. Thank you. Bye."

Romy hung up her cell, returning it to her purse. "Apparently, she tried to slit her wrists with a broken spoon."

"Oh God, Romy." My stomach dropped. "I'm so sorry."

I reached across the bench seat, squeezing her fingers.

"Yeah …" She released a deep breath. "So they're postponing her hearing for a couple weeks."

"That should give you more time to decide whether or not you want to be there," I suggested.

In my periphery, she shook her head. "I don't need more time. I mean, this is just so fucked up."

"I know, honey. I'm sorry." I didn't know what else to say other than to agree with her.

"I'm not going to the hearing."

She couldn't mean that. She needed to be there for her sister. She'd regret it if she didn't. "Well, you have time to decide."

Slowly, she turned in her seat. "Jude, I just said I wasn't

going. Did you hear me?" She pulled her hand away. I chanced a glance away from the road to look at her. Her face was scrunched in anger, her mouth tight around the edges. "I don't need any more time to decide. I'm not going. Hazel chose to do this; she can deal with the consequences. My being there isn't going to change the justice system or make any of this better."

"Romy, I—"

"I just need you to listen to what I'm saying. And I'm not going. End of story."

She sat back in the seat, her arms crossing over her chest like a shield.

"Okay," was all I could say. Any more and she'd be even more pissed.

The rest of the ride to the ranch was in silence. The tension was so thick, you'd need a cleaver to hack it. But in our silence, she fumed. Her anger boiling to the point that as soon as we pulled up to the ranch, she flung open the door, slammed it, and stormed into the house.

I was left in the truck. I didn't know how to help her. To make this better for her.

I sat there, leaving her to cool down while I searched for the right words to comfort her. Because she hadn't realized yet that she was grieving the loss of the sister she knew and all the time she had lost in between.

A rap came on my window, and I turned to see Lina standing in the dirt driveway.

I got out of the truck, shoving my hands into my pockets.

"Trouble in paradise?" Her brows were raised pointedly.

"Things aren't going well with Hazel."

"Ah. Well, I was just coming by to say hi since I just got in, but maybe this isn't the best time."

I snorted. It was far from the best time, but I was glad to see Lina. "Want to go raid the fridge in the big house?" I asked, slapping my stomach.

"Don't you have training or weight cutting or something?" she queried.

Not knowing how long Romy and I would be visiting the jail, I had canceled my sparring session for tonight. I'd make up for it tomorrow before the rodeo.

"Nah, I have the night off, and Coach says I need to bulk up more."

"Perfect. Let's go eat junk food and drink beer."

"I don't know if she's pissed at me because she thought I wasn't listening, or if she's just lashing out because I'm the nearest punching bag."

I stuffed the last of my burrito into my mouth before washing it down with the rest of my beer.

Lina wiped her mouth. "Both. Sounds as though you were being dismissive."

"How? All I do is consider her feelings."

Romy was a tough girl, but she was also sensitive. She tried to show that things didn't bother her. But I knew when they did. She often covered it up with anger, but she also wasn't talking to me about it or trusting me. Not really, anyway. If I was being honest, it made me feel pretty shitty and insecure. As if I was unworthy to push back the curtain and see what was actually in her head—or worse, her heart.

"Have you asked her how she's feeling?" Lina probed, digging into the chips and salsa.

"Yeah. The last time I asked her, she said 'fine.'"

Lina nearly spit out the dip. "You know that's girl code for 'not fine,' right?"

"I've been around the block, Lina. I know what that means. But I also know Romy well enough that it also means 'I don't want to talk about it.' That's why I'm here and not there right now."

"Huh. Okay." Lina leaned back in the rickety, old chair. "Maybe you need to get her to talk about it or fight about it. It can't be healthy bottling it all up like that. I know I always feel better after I have a good vent sesh."

"I know you do. You feel better about Reed now?"

While we dug through the kitchen for burrito ingredients, the fattest burritos with all the fixings, which included Fritos—don't knock it till you try it—I heard my share of how annoying and terrible Reed was. Apparently, being away from the ranch and Reed the last couple weeks was not enough to douse her hatred of the man.

"Hell no! But this is making me feel better." She raised her beer can, tipping it to mine.

"Me too." I tapped her can.

"Maybe that's what you need. Alcohol and a distraction. The rodeo could serve both for you," Lina suggested with a mischievous smirk.

"Are you implying I get Romy drunk?"

"Fuck yes, and the Willows Rodeo offers plenty of

distractions." She winked.

"Lina, I don't want her ogling the cowboys."

"Why not? She'll see how good she has it. I don't know about you, but watching the broncs gets me horny." She fanned herself as if she was already hot just thinking about it.

"Gross. And don't say *horny* in front of me again. If I knew it would do any good, I'd lock you in your room until you're eighty."

"Would you prefer I say hot and bothered or extremely turned on?" she asked.

I rolled my eyes.

Lina scoffed. "You and Dad." She shook her head in disappointment. "But in all seriousness, just help Romy have fun tomorrow. And if she gets drunk in the process, so be it. Maybe she will feel up to sharing some shit. Or maybe she's wanting you to fight. I don't think anyone has ever fought for her. Fighting and fucking can be real cathartic."

I rubbed my brows. "Lina, I swear to God, I don't want to know that."

"What?" she asked, with a shoulder shrug, feigning innocence.

It made me wonder, though. Maybe Romy was waiting for me to put up a fight? Lina wasn't wrong that no one had ever fought for her. Fighting was in my blood, but facing an opponent in the cage was very different. Fighting *for* Romy required mental sparring, but the strategy must be similar. Catch your opponent off guard, and you can wrap them up in a D'Arce choke and make them tap. That's what I needed to do. I needed to demonstrate to Romy I was willing to challenge her and, if necessary, make her submit or, in this case, trust me.

"All right. We'll ensure Romy has fun at the rodeo. But don't convince her to do shots with you at the barn dance. I don't want any cowboys sniffing around. I know how those turn out."

Lina rolled her eyes. "No promises. Just have her wear your hat, and she'll be fine."

I shook my head, laughing, and pushed in my chair.

"Well, this was just what I needed," I said, placing my plate in the sink. "Thanks, cuz. I better get some rest before my morning workout."

"Same. Tomorrow is going to be a long day."

Lina and I had trekked all the way to the big house, and it was nice to have the time to walk home in the peace of night. Stars littered the dark expanse as if a child spilled a jar of glitter across it. There was no breeze tonight, promising tomorrow would be a scorcher. Dangerous because heat meant a lot of drinking at the rodeo.

By the time I reached the front door, the house was silent. Lights inside were turned off. Lysol and Pine-Sol lingered in the air. I checked my phone, wondering if I missed a text from Romy, but there was nothing. Her steady breathing sounded from the bedroom, and I knew she was already asleep. I got ready for bed and then climbed in beside her, but for the first time, she didn't turn into me. She remained curled on her side, her back facing me, asleep.

I didn't want to hyperanalyze it, but my damn mind couldn't help but question whether or not she was pulling away. Did she feel the same way? Did she want this? It couldn't be just sex for her, could it? I wouldn't fault her if sex was a major factor for sticking around. Because the sex was *incredible*. The best I've ever had. The girl was fucking feral. A beast in the sack. I was here for it. I thought it was the same for her, but maybe it wasn't. Was I enough for her? Because if it turned out I wasn't, it would destroy me.

I ruminated most of the night. It was definitely the shittiest sleep I had since I left the couch. And it didn't help that when I woke up the next morning, her side of the bed was already cold.

Chapter 32
Romy

I was already upset about Hazel's suicide attempt and the delayed hearing, but then Jude had to insist I wait and decide whether or not I wanted to testify after I'd *told* him I wouldn't. Not respecting my boundaries, just like Hazel with Frank. It triggered me, and I couldn't slam that truck door hard enough.

I waited for him to chase after me, but when he didn't, I decided to rage-clean. I ended up disinfecting every surface, trapping every dust bunny and conditioning every wood surface while I continued to spin in angry circles in my head about needing Jude to just respect my choice, and whether or not to tell him about Junior. I felt like this was such a clusterfuck! I just knew if I told Jude, he'd *murder* Junior. I wasn't about to visit two people in jail!

Then when Jude didn't come home, I decided to remain quiet—at least until after his fight. I couldn't be what distracted him from this.

When he finally snuck into bed last night smelling like beer, I was pissed all over again. Did he seriously go drinking instead of facing me?

Coward.

Did he not consider such behavior would hurt my already fragile trust? Especially after what my ex did?

I was furious. I couldn't decide if I wanted to push him out of the bed or climb him like a tree. And just like I rage-cleaned, I would have rage-fucked him.

Feigning sleep while I weighed my options, Jude started snoring, and I knew my window of opportunity had closed.

My phone read two forty-five in the morning. *Fuck!* So much for sleep.

I tiptoed around the room, blindly finding leggings and a sports bra before escaping to the bathroom to change.

Pulling on a pair of tennis shoes, I bypassed the truck in front of the double-wide and headed to the dirt road.

The early morning was still quiet, except for the chirps of crickets and the sleepy bellows of cattle. I shoved earbuds into my ears and found a power playlist, slipping my cell phone into the small, hidden pocket on my waistband to jog across the property to the big house.

It had been over a month since I exercised. The last time was in my apartment gym in California, and I needed this.

Rolling up the garage door, I hit the switch, casting fluorescent light across the equipment.

My lungs were already on fire from my run across the ranch. Shit. I was out of shape.

My muscles already warm, I hopped onto the rowing machine. I was going to row out my aggression with female rage music blaring, fueling me across this tumultuous sea, until I burned out. My shoulder protested at first, but I ignored the twinge. I was willing to power through it if it meant vanquishing Junior's attack and threat from my thoughts and dousing my anger at Jude.

Lost in a Miranda Lambert tune and the tick of the time on the machine console, I didn't notice someone approaching until his shadow cast over me. Looking up, Jude stood in the garage door wearing workout shorts and a hoodie, that damn hat on backward, and his lips pinched in worry. He pointed at his ear, gesturing I take out my earbud.

Slowing my movements to a stop, I set my feet down and released the handles to reach up and remove it.

"You going to tell me what's going on?" Jude's voice had a hard edge to it.

I kind of liked it. Not sure what that said about me. But I was still pissed, and I wasn't about to tell him what was going on.

"Nope," I said, starting to return my earbud to my ear.

"I've never once seen you in the gym, and now you're rowing that thing like a fucking shield maiden. You're angry—I get it—but you need to talk to me."

I got up off the rower. "Vikings row. Shield maidens fight."

"That's beside the point."

I scoffed. "You don't get it."

"Then help me understand." He shuffled his hat around, his one tell that gave away his discomfort.

"There's nothing to understand, Jude. I just need some space."

I regretted my last words as soon as they left my mouth.

Honestly, the last thing I wanted was space from him.

Jude's face fell, his arms dropping to his side as if the wind was knocked from his sails.

But I couldn't tell him. I just needed time to let my anger fizzle out. And then things could return to the way they were. Happy. Fun. Having the most earth-shattering orgasms. While we got through this bullshit.

"Okay," he said. His nose pinched with a deep inhale that he held in his lungs before pushing air out his mouth.

His *okay* could have easily been *I'm giving up on you* the way it hit me in the gut.

My mouth went dry. I didn't even think to bring a water bottle.

Not wanting to stay there a moment longer, I shoved my earbud back in, turning up the volume as loud as I could before walking the three miles back to the house.

Thank goodness Jude was busy all day helping Chuck load up tack, horses, and bulls for the rodeo because it kept me from seeing that look of resignation on his face. The ranch didn't offer trail rides today since it was a holiday and the rodeo was taking precedence, which was unfortunate for me because I needed to keep myself busy.

Physically exhausted from not sleeping, the impromptu early morning workout, and emotionally drained on top of that, I did manage a nap before spending the afternoon on the computer searching for teaching jobs.

Staying on the ranch was not part of my plan, and I

needed an income. I just had my California teaching license, so that's where I was looking. There were very few positions open, but I was able to find two positions teaching humanities that I applied to. Both in different districts—one being in the toughest district in LA and another one in San Diego. If I ended up getting a call to interview, then I'd have to leave.

My cell phone buzzed on the desktop.

JUDE

Hitching a ride with Uncle Chuck at 2. You coming with us?

That meant I had about forty-five minutes to get ready. I wasn't sure I wanted to be sandwiched between Jude and Chuck while we drove into town.

ME

I'll hit Sage up for a ride.

Sage had given me her number when she joined us for the bonfire.

JUDE

Ok, see you there.

I gripped my phone in my hand, letting the edges dig into my palm. I was about two seconds away from throwing it across the office. Why was he being so fucking complacent? I wanted him to fight. Demand I come with him. Not lie down and take it.

With angry jabs of my fingers, I texted Sage.

ME

Can I ride with you to the rodeo?

SAGE

Sure! I can be there by three.

ME

Perfect. See you then!

Taking a quick shower, I then blew out my hair and curled it into soft waves down my back. I hadn't worn makeup in weeks, and it felt so good to layer mascara on my lashes, bronzer on my cheeks, and red lipstick on my lips.

Determined to wear something that made me feel hot as a temptress, I pulled out a denim minidress from the closet. The bodice was fitted and would show off my ample cleavage, and the skirt flared at the hips, hitting me just above midthigh. The straps were adjustable, allowing me to show off my back. I wrapped a hair tie around my wrist in case I got sweaty and wanted to give Jude more than a glimpse of my skin.

A honk beeped from outside, and I threw my purse over my shoulder and stepped into boots before meeting Sage.

"Look at you! Are we trying to make someone jealous tonight?" Sage called from where she stood at her open Jeep door.

She was dressed in Daisy Dukes and a tight, white tank. As always, her hair was piled on her head in a messy bun, and her lips were bright crimson, making her smile seem the brightest white. This time, she also had a red bandanna tied like a headband around her head. Oversize sunglasses shielded her eyes.

I laughed. "Something like that. Should I ask you the same thing? Or are we trying to grab the attention of a certain cowboy?"

Sage scoffed. "Christian *thinks* he has a chance, but he knows I don't do cowboys."

"No?"

"Been there, done that. It's not worth the trouble. I'm just going to be a supportive sister and drink beer. It's my patriotic duty every year."

I briefly saluted her before piling into the passenger seat.

CHAPTER 33
Jude

As soon as we got out of the truck in the packed, open-field parking lot, the sun was already beating down on us. Music, the bells and lowing of cattle, the crowd cheering, and the booming voice of the announcer echoed through the stadium speakers.

A wave of nostalgia hit me as Uncle Chuck and I funneled in with the rest of the Fourth of July crowd. Everyone was decked out in cowboy hats and boots … red, white, and blue, and a few Support the Troops army-green tees. The air was fragrant with dirt, hay, fried food, manure, and horse. So many Independence Days were spent in those grandstands, eating hot dogs while watching Uncle Chuck lasso a calf or Hazel Miller run the quickest loops around barrels, then being treated to the biggest fireworks show in Oregon. Pretty sure there were a handful of years I fell asleep in the back of the truck with a sticky smile on my face.

This time was special, though, because it would be the first time seeing Lina barrel race, and she was currently holding the fastest record of the season.

With a beer and dog in hand, I settled into a seat, my eyes scrutinizing the entrance for Romy and Sage. Uncle Chuck headed down to the corrals. I pulled my cowboy hat down low, hoping no one would recognize me. I hated being noticed on days like today. My fists clenched every time I heard someone yell, "Hey, look, it's Jude 'The Bull' Larsen!"

After a show led by Warm Springs dancers in full regalia and the "National Anthem," the ladies of the rodeo court galloped in a loop around the arena. The announcer proclaimed each princess, and this year's queen, before welcoming the men and ladies of today's competitions. All competing for ten thousand dollars and a Willows Rodeo belt buckle.

Lina, Christian, and Kale were among them. Unable to clap with my hands full, I yelled as loudly as I could. Lina spotted me, giving me the biggest grin and the tiniest wave.

The first competition was the bucking broncos. I scanned the crowd, spotting Romy walking in. She was sexy as hell, dressed for revenge. Her tan legs looked so long. I yearned to wrap them around me. My cock twitched, seeing how perky her tits appeared in that denim dress. God, and that mouth! Ruby lipstick that I wanted to see smudged on my dick.

Under the shade of my cowboy hat, I watched her like a fucking creep. She hadn't seen me yet, but I could tell she was casually looking while talking to Sage on their way to find a seat.

If it was space she wanted, she would get it, but only for a time because I was gearing up for a fight, and this one wasn't in a cage.

Lina was on deck, and I could see her sidestepping Mushu toward the arena entrance, holding him back even though he was raring to go. The announcer boomed her name, and the crowd cheered and whistled. Apparently, there was only one hometown champion here today, and it wasn't me.

Capturing my own performance jitters for my baby cousin, I couldn't help but yell, "Go, Lina!"

Romy spun in her seat when she heard me holler. She gave me a look that said more than she'd said in the last two days, then spun back around to sip her beer.

Then Lina and her horse were off. Her seat barely in the saddle, her legs flapping in the stirrups like wings as they made the quickest, sharpest loops around the barrels in the arena. I watched the timer tick down on the scoreboard.

One barrel. It remained still.

I held my breath as she charged toward the second. Mushu dragged his butt around the barrel, his hind quarter muscles working hard. Dirt kicked up so thick, I could barely see Mushu's feet. Lina pushed down her heels and held her hands low, effortlessly guiding him to change direction.

She rounded the final barrel, kicking as hard as she could while Mushu scattered dust. Then she gave him his head, plowing back to the gate.

The timer stopped.

Clocking her at … 18.3 seconds!

The crowd went wild. Up on my feet, I jumped up and down, cheering with the rest of them. She did it!

Romy turned again, our eyes instantly connecting. This time, she smiled. I gave her the most charming cowboy tip of the hat I could, making her laugh before she shifted back in her seat.

Got ya, honey.

"That was incredible, Lina!" Romy wrapped her arms around Lina's shoulders.

"I'm so proud of you, darlin'," Uncle Chuck beamed, getting his own hug from his daughter.

I took in the shiny, new belt buckle around her waist. "You earned it, cuz." She gave me knucks.

Christian, Kale, and Sage all took their turns congratulating Lina as we headed to the Willows Trading Post, otherwise known as the barn dance or the beer garden. Nightfall wasn't for another hour, so we had time to celebrate before the fireworks.

Lina looped her arm through Romy's. "We're getting drunk tonight!"

Romy snickered. Lina shot me a wink over her shoulder.

"I guess I'm buying," Uncle Chuck grumbled.

"You're a good man, Chuck." Christian patted Uncle Chuck's shoulder.

"Not for you, dipshit." Uncle Chuck shrugged him off.

"Aw, man!" Christian complained.

A live band was playing classic country underneath the hundreds of strung lights that lined the old, converted barn's rafters. Attempting to compete with the volume of the music, rodeo-goers already deep in their cups shouted their conversations and boomed their laughs. A dozen couples line-danced in front of the stage, the heels of their boots clicking against the worn, wood floor.

Our group headed over to the bar, while Uncle Chuck ordered everyone whiskey and a beer back.

"You're the best, Daddy," Lina said, leaning in to kiss her dad on the cheek.

"Only for my baby girl."

We all toasted the rodeo competitors before slamming back our shots.

"More!" Lina yelled, lifting her shot glass.

Seeing the rodeo star in our midst, the bartender came around to refill our shot glasses. We all slung them back, chasing them down with the frothy, light beer. Four refills later, and we were just as loud as the rest of the Trading Post crowd.

The band was starting to get really good. Kale and Christian were pretending they knew the words to every song, singing into their beer bottles like microphones. Romy looked as though she was having fun, finally letting go, laughing and talking with Sage, Lina, and Uncle Chuck. She still hadn't said more than two words to me.

"Sage, will you dance with me?" Christian asked, his hand outstretched. The poor guy was always shooting his shot.

"Not a chance. I don't do cowboys."

"Would you do *this* cowboy?"

"In your dreams."

"Every night, baby."

Sage turned away, putting her back to him. "Should I go

order us some curly fries?"

"Yes, please! I'm starved!" Lina exclaimed.

Christian's shoulders slumped watching Sage walk away.

I gave him a thump on the back. "I'm sure there are plenty of other girls who would dance with you."

"Buckle bunnies are wearing on me and not in the good way." He pouted.

"I'll dance with you," Romy piped up.

My eyes shot to her. A spike of jealousy carving through my chest. He was one of my oldest friends, and I knew he wouldn't slide in like that. But the alcohol coursing through my system wasn't rational. I sucked in air through my nose.

"Yeah?" Christian's eyes lit up.

"Sure." She threw back her shot, washing it down with a gulp of beer before hopping off her barstool.

"Is that all right, bro?" Christian asked me.

Romy gripped his arm, pulling him away. "He's not my keeper. Come on."

Christian must have felt my eyes driving daggers into him because he mouthed "sorry" before shrugging and following her to the dance floor.

I could feel heat building in my gut watching Christian hold her hand while she followed him in a two-step. Any closer and her body would be pressed against him. I took a sip of my beer, hoping that it would cool my insides, but it stung like the whiskey going down my throat. Romy moved his hand to her lower back.

Lina shuffled over to me, her back leaning against the high-top table while she looked at me. "Seems she means war.

Are you going to stand for that?"

Taking my gaze away from the dance floor, I glanced at Lina. Her brows raised expectantly, waiting for me. She was right. This was my moment.

"Fuck it." I chugged the rest of my beer, slamming it down on the table.

Romy was still spinning in Christian's arms to the rhythm of the music. She was laughing. But all I heard was my heart pounding in my ears.

Barely slowing down, I dropped my hat on Romy's head, then threw her over my shoulder.

CHAPTER 34
Jude

"What the hell, Jude?"

I didn't stop as I left the beer garden and rounded the back of the building. The building butted up to a cluster of ponderosa pines. Other than the dumpster being back here, there was no reason for someone to interrupt. It was dusk, and I stepped into the shadow of the barn before setting her down.

"You fucking caveman!" She smacked my chest while trying to keep my hat from falling off her head.

"I had to get your damn attention somehow!" My chest was heaving in anger.

This time, she shoved me. "Oh, and you think you can act all jealous and possessive right now? You didn't even chase after me or fight for us." Her words slurred a little at the end.

"What are you talking about?" She was drunk and not making sense, and my own buzz and frustration was blurring my comprehension. "All I've ever done is chase after you. I have to … because you *run*."

"Fuck you! One time, Jude. You chased after me *one time*."

She held up a finger in my face. "You think that's all I need for me to trust you? I want someone who will *always* chase after me no matter how shitty things get, and if you can't be that someone, then I need to leave."

She pivoted on her boots, but I gripped her arm, spinning her back to me. "Is that what you want, honey? For me to be the hunter and you the prey? You want me to fucking chase you?"

Romy released a heady breath from her throat. She glared at me from beneath her thick, dark lashes. "What if it was what I wanted?"

I stepped into her, my toes knocking hers. Our chests rose out of anger and desire. My hand stilled on her arm, scorching me. Her eyes darkened in the gray light, panting breaths feathered across my face through her perfect, pouty lips.

"I'd track you down." I took a step forward, forcing her to take a step back. "I'd hunt you." Another step. "You'd run, but then I'd follow your scent." I leaned in, taking a whiff of her hair. She smelled extra tropical today with her addition of sunscreen. I'd know her scent anywhere. "Then when I find you …"

I pushed her against the wall. She let out a gasp. Placing my forearms on either side of her head, I ground my hips against her, letting her feel what she did to me. She tipped her face up in defiance yet begged me to kiss her.

"I'd capture you. Pin you to the wall."

"Then what?" she asked in a breathless whisper.

"I'd make you come. Make you scream till this whole fucking rodeo knew you're mine."

"Oh, you think so? How?" Her words were breathless, but

her eyes were blazing, challenging me.

"First with my fingers. One, then two."

I ran the back of my fingers over her arms, lightly caressing her collarbone, then down the curves of her breasts. She shivered against me. My hands ran over her hips, and then her thighs, until I found the hem of her dress. I skimmed my fingers up her bare legs, pushing up the denim. Her ass filled my palms. Gripping those perfect globes, I pulled her against me, grinding into her.

"Then when you're right there, right on the edge, thinking you couldn't take any more, begging me for more, I'd run my tongue through your pussy, lapping up every ounce of you."

I dipped my head to her neck, my lips coasting over her skin. I could feel it prickle under my touch. She tipped her head, allowing me access until I could nip and suck on her ear.

"And then I'd suck that perfect, little clit into my mouth until you're soaking my face."

"*Jude*," she breathed, her hips reflexively rocking into mine, seeking the friction I knew she wanted.

"Just when you think you can't stand another one"—I hoisted her up, my hands still gripping her ass, while she wrapped her legs around me—"I'd thrust into you."

I shoved my hardened cock against her, my zipper and her lace panties adding friction. I thrust again, and Romy almost lost my hat, holding it to her head. Her hips bucked, searching for more. I gave it to her again.

"I'd fuck you against the wall until your pussy was milking my cock, begging me to coat you inside with my cum. Brand you. Make you mine."

Romy moaned, looping her arms around my neck, pulling me as close as she could. Any closer and I'd be climbing into her skin. And *fuck*. I wanted that.

I continued thrusting against her, and she returned with her own hip rolls.

"Please, Jude. I want you inside me."

Neither one of us seemed to care that a rodeo was going on around us or that fireworks were starting to go off. Music and the cheers of the crowd did not compare to my name on her lips.

"You want to fuck in public, my dirty girl?" I asked.

She nodded against my neck, her hips seeking.

"You need to say it," I demanded.

"*Please.* I want you to fuck me right here. I don't give a fuck that we're in public. Right now, it feels like I might stop breathing if I don't have you filling me. I need it."

"Not that, honey. Though that's fucking hot. I need you to say that you're mine. I need to hear you say it."

She raised her face from my neck to gaze into my eyes. "I'm yours, Jude. I always have been."

Maybe because we were both tipsy, but neither one of us seemed to care that I didn't have a condom on me.

"Fuck yes, you are."

"Please, Jude. I'm on birth control. I want to feel you inside me. All of you."

It was the least of my concerns because I'd gladly put a baby in her right now if she'd let me. She was it for me. Romy was *mine*. My forever.

I shifted the silk of her panties, swiping my fingers through her center. So warm and soft. She was already wet and ready for me. One arm still holding her tightly against me, I unbuckled and unzipped my pants, releasing my throbbing cock.

Explosions echoed off the high desert, and colored light flickered across her face while I pushed into her with one powerful thrust. Her lips parted on my name.

I clapped a hand over her mouth.

"You're going to have to be quiet, honey," I whispered into her ear.

She whimpered under my hand, rolling her hips to get me to move. She felt so fucking good bare. So tight and wet. I could feel every pulse and flutter.

"I'll move if you promise to be quiet."

She nodded; her eyes pained, hungry for it.

"Good girl."

I pulled out a couple inches, my balls tightening. I wasn't going to last long. This was going to be a quick fuck. We ran the risk of someone stumbling across us behind the barn, but I had a feeling my girl liked the possibility of someone finding us here, that it added to her arousal.

Then I slammed into her, pushing her against the wall.

A muffled whine rumbled her chest.

"Shh," I told her, pounding into her again.

Her teeth clamped down on the fleshy part of my palm by my thumb. I hissed from the sting, but it shot right to my cock.

"Fuck, honey," I whispered into her ear. My own teeth scraping against the shell.

I could feel the pressure building in my lower spine, my blood pumping violently into my cock. The wall of her pussy fluttered around me, and I could tell she was close, too.

Her legs were like a vise around me. I reached between us to feel where my bare cock disappeared into her. I wish I could see it, but in the dark and in this position, it was impossible. Next time, I'd have to have her ride me with the lights on. Just the thought made my balls contract.

I spread her wetness through her slit, pushing her panties farther to the side. The lace scraped against her, causing her to shudder.

"You like that?"

She nodded against my hand.

Pulling the lace tightly over her clit, the elastic edges parted her. I could feel the back of her underwear wedged between her ass, snagging on the rough wood of the barn. I thrust again, loosening my hold, the lace scraping back down her clit as the wall tugged. She writhed in my arms. I withdrew a few inches, pulling again on her panties, allowing the lace to scrape back up that sensitive bundle of nerves. She bit down harder on my hand to keep from screaming. Blood rushed through my veins. The pressure in my balls was near unbearable. Each time I thrust, I'd let the wall snag her panties so the lace would rasp down her clit, and then when I retreated, I'd pull it so tight, the lace would rake back up.

Romy squirmed.

"Fuck, honey," I muttered.

She was panting through her nose, her eyes fluttering closed as her core flexed around me, squeezing me as firmly as she could. Her pussy tightened around my cock, milking me for all I was worth while we came together. My orgasm rocked through my body. Holding her to me, her legs and arms shaking while I shot ropes of cum into her. She curled into me, gripping me tightly while she rode the waves of her climax.

Nearly collapsing against the wall, her teeth retracted from my palm. She kissed it before brushing her lips tenderly against my hand. Her lipstick smeared, stamping my skin in red and teethmarks. My chest swelled with pride, seeing the evidence of what we did to each other.

"We missed the fireworks," she whispered once my hand left her mouth.

"No, we didn't. They were right here."

She gave me the softest, most loving look, her lips tipping up.

I set her back on her feet, helping her adjust her panties and dress before tucking myself back in.

"Jude?" She glanced up at me under the shadow of my hat, a flirty smile now on her lips.

"Hmm?" I was suddenly feeling loose and sleepy.

"Does this mean you captured me?"

I brought her hand to my lips. I was so in love with this girl. "It means, I'm yours, honey."

CHAPTER 35
Romy

I was vibrating like a live wire while the crowd milled around me. A warm breeze flitted across my skin, lifting the hair from my neck. The beads of sweat cooled at its touch.

I tipped my face, holding Jude's hat to my head, and closed my eyes. Even though my body hummed, I felt light and airy. And hot! It wasn't just from the evening temperature or the stadium lights.

Still descending from the unbelievable orgasm Jude gave me, the high of knowing he was mine, and the liquor coursing through my veins, I was floating like a feather on the wind while I buzzed like a bee. Jude's release still leaked from me, and I squeezed my legs together, feeling a primal need to keep it there.

I lifted a hand to my cheek. It ached; I was smiling so big. People were probably thinking, "Let's go around the drunk girl."

I giggled to myself.

Yep, crazy in love and very drunk.

I felt the air shift around me as people brushed past to the exit.

"Romy Miller."

Warm, moist, sour breath whiffed across my nose. My eyes popped open.

Junior. I cringed.

Where was Jude? I hadn't noticed him exit the restrooms yet.

I scanned the crowd before returning my glare to Junior, who stood in front of me. Dirty-blond whiskers coated his jaw, and his cowboy hat shadowed his pale eyes.

Acrid heat washed over me. Bitter saliva filled the back of my throat.

I stepped back, clenching my fists. Readying myself to knee him in the balls if I had to.

"You're a moron to approach me here, Junior."

He gave me a smile that he probably thought was cute, but it said more like *creep*. "Just saying a friendly hello to the local girl."

"You better leave before Jude gets here."

"Nah. I'm not worried about him."

"Then you are more insane than I thought."

"Not as insane as your sister, it seems."

My jaw clenched and my eyes narrowed. "Did you have anything to do with her being put on suicide watch?"

Junior shrugged. "I might've paid her a visit."

"What? How? There was no way in hell she would ever put you on her visitor's list." I was getting the spins.

"She did."

"Why the hell would she do that?"

"Maybe because I knew what she was planning, and she wanted to make sure I wouldn't talk."

I took a steadying breath, trying to refocus. Attempting to halt the sway of intoxication.

"What was she planning?"

"Oh, I think you already have your suspicions. Probably why you agreed to stay quiet, not just because of Jude Larsen."

"You're a fucking asshole," I seethed.

Junior looked over my shoulder, his face going suddenly stoic before turning away. "Nice talking with ya."

I turned. Jude was marching toward us, his face stormy.

"What the *fuck* did he want?" Jude's voice sounded as though it had gravel in it.

He gritted his teeth, his jaw popping on a swallow while he clenched his fists.

The alcohol started to evaporate, rolling in my stomach. I wasn't about to see another fight, and I wasn't about to lose it in the bushes again, either. Jude's biceps were like cement under my hands. I cast a glance over my shoulder where Jude's eyes narrowed, but Junior was already lost in the crowd.

Rubbing my hands down his coiled muscles, I attempted to soothe him. It was as much for him as it was for me. Junior terrified me, but there was no way I would admit it. I skimmed over his balled fists until they relaxed enough for me to intertwine my fingers. His breath slowed and his tension lifted.

"Nothing." I pushed on my tiptoes to kiss his jaw. "Let's just go home."

He leaned down, nudging my nose with his. Releasing one

of my hands, he threaded his fingers through my hair. "Yeah, okay, but I can tell it's not nothing. This conversation is far from over, but we can discuss it at home."

"I'm tired, Jude. Can we just go home and go to bed? We can talk tomorrow."

He pulled me into him, my chest pressing against his.

"Honey." He tipped back the hat to catch my eyes peering beneath the brim. He waited for my lashes to flutter up, capturing my gaze. "This is me chasing after you. I need you to trust me, but you need to give me a chance first. You know you can tell me anything."

I grimaced. Not *anything*. I still couldn't tell him about what happened with Junior. It killed me not to tell him, but it would hurt more if he knew the truth.

He dropped a soft peck on my nose, followed by a defeated inhale. "All right. We're both tipsy anyway. But we *are* talking tomorrow."

I reluctantly nodded. "Tomorrow, I promise."

My mouth felt like cotton, and the light was so bright it shined through my eyelids. I groaned, reaching for the other side of the bed, but Jude was already gone for the morning. A dull ache between my legs and a sting at my lower back told me that we might have been a little too rough last night.

A smile flickered across my lips remembering how Jude overpowered me—owned me—while a whole damn rodeo was happening. I giggled to myself. That was the hottest moment of my life. I had a feeling this was the start of many moments like that with Jude around.

"What's so funny?" came a husky voice as he walked into the bedroom.

I think I'm in love. My mouth watered at the sight of him. And it was not just because he looked sexy as hell, all sweaty from his morning workout, double-fisting a steaming mug of coffee and iced water, but because this man knew just how to take care of me. He was right. I really needed to start trusting him.

Even if I had to push him past his breaking point. Even if my own fears and triggers tried to sabotage what was obviously growing between us. I told him I needed him to fight for me—for us—and he more than proved he could last night.

I propped myself on my elbows, biting my lip, and attempted to give him the sexiest look. Even though I probably appeared a little rough this morning. I'm pretty sure mascara was smudged under my eyes and lipstick smeared across my face. After another round when we got home, we passed out.

"Just thinking about how you plowed me against the barn last night."

The bed dipped when Jude sat down on the edge beside me.

"Oh, yeah?" His lopsided grin came out to play this morning. "Like it a little rough, do you? The risk of being caught?"

I lowered my lashes, feeling my cheeks heat. "I think it may be my kink."

He leaned down, dragging his tongue across my lower lip. I opened for him, but he didn't connect. Instead, his lips fluttered over mine while he said, "I like my girl a little wild and untamed."

I bit his lower lip, sucking it into my mouth. His breath hitched. I liked him calling me *his girl*.

"Kiss me and give me that coffee, Jude."

"Bossy as well." He chuckled, dropping a quick peck before placing the mug in my hands and setting the water down on the bedside table.

I breathed in the aroma. *Sweet nectar of the gods!*

I eyed him suspiciously over the rim of the coffee. "You're wanting to talk now, aren't you?"

He gave me a soft smile. "Hydrate and let yourself wake up. We'll talk after my shower."

Jude popped a kiss on my head before heading to the bathroom.

I could follow him in there, but then I'd just be delaying the inevitable. I took a big gulp of coffee. Some of the things we said were a little fuzzy, but Junior's creepy face and Jude claiming me were very vivid in my mind. If we belonged to each other now, he needed to know what was going on.

By the time I emptied my mug and drained my water, Jude walked back in, a towel slung low around his hips. The man was delectable. He had to know it. That sexy V showing me right where to look.

"I'm going to put some clothes on. Otherwise, you're going to be way too distracted, and I've been known to give you what you want." He winked.

"Ah, you're no fun."

He chuckled, pulling on a pair of Wranglers and a

charcoal-gray T-shirt. He ruffled his wet hair, giving it a sexy, messy look.

"One second." He grabbed my empty water glass, padded back down the hall, and returned with it refilled.

"I'm not going to get out of this, am I?"

"Nope. No excuses."

"What if I have to go to the bathroom?"

He rolled his eyes. "Better go now."

I slowly heaved out of bed, stretching like a cat so my tits were in his face.

"Better put some clothes on, too." Jude fell back on the bed, rubbing his closed eyes.

"Like I said, no fun."

"Go."

I screeched when a hand smacked me on the ass cheek.

I left him laughing into the pillow. I took my time using the bathroom—washing my face, running a brush through my hair—before returning to the bedroom to grab a pair of jeans and a tank top.

"Okay." I heaved a sigh, settling cross-legged on the mattress beside him. "Where should I start?"

"If you want, we can start with how you feel after what I said last night?"

I lifted an eyebrow. "What part? When you told me to be quiet so you could fuck me in public, or when you asked me if I liked being fucked against the wall while my panties rubbed against my clit?"

"*Jesus*, Romy." Jude ran a hand down his face.

"For the record, I liked it very much."

"I gathered as much." He guffawed. "I meant when I said I wanted you to be mine."

I pressed my lips together, nodding. "I liked that, too."

His eyes shuddered, searching for patience. I knew I had to be exasperating. "Maybe I'll start." He sat up and took my hands in his. The rough pads of his thumbs scraping across my knuckles. "I want us to be together. To make a real go at this. I want to date you and tell everyone that this incredibly gorgeous woman belongs to me. I want you to be mine and no one else's."

My heart pounded. It felt as if it may fly right out of my rib cage. "I don't want anyone else, Jude. Only you. When I asked you to be patient with me, I meant that I needed time to figure out what I really wanted and if it was even possible to have it. And I've decided. I want you. I'd love nothing more than to go on dates with you and call you mine."

Jude tipped his gaze to the ceiling, as if peering into the heavens, and gave an audible sigh of relief. "Thank, fuck!"

"But …"

"But what?" His gaze shot to mine.

"What about your life in Vegas? What about your career? What about my job in California? I don't think I can do long distance."

"Wait. Did you get a new job?"

"No, but I applied for a couple," I said sheepishly.

I watched the color drain from his cheeks. He didn't like that answer, but he didn't chastise me for it. Instead, he asked, "Did you hear back?"

"Not yet."

"I thought you were burned out from teaching."

He wasn't wrong. It didn't feel as rewarding as it once did, and I wasn't sure if it was totally worth all the energy I put into it. Why did I have to choose the most underappreciated profession for myself? Doing it for *the kids* just wasn't enough anymore.

"I am, but if you're going back to Vegas, I can't stay here. My teaching license is in California. I'd have to make a living somehow."

"You do realize I make enough money that you wouldn't have to work."

"I can't take your money, Jude. And I don't think I want to move to Vegas."

"I'm selling my house anyway."

That was news. I wondered when he'd made that decision. Apparently, we both had made decisions without each other.

"What? Why?"

He shrugged. "Didn't feel like home anymore. I guess it hasn't for a while. My real estate agent said I will make a nice profit on it after all the renovations I've done."

"Then where do you plan on moving?"

"Truthfully?" he asked.

I nodded.

"I was hoping you and I could decide that together."

My breath caught, and I could feel a blush creeping up my cheeks. He wanted a future together. Here I was, just doing my best to stop pushing him away and running, and he was making plans to include me. He had way more faith in me than I ever had in myself. It made me fall in love with him just a little bit more.

"I think I'd like that. Would you consider California?"

"If that's where you needed to be, then I'm there."

He couldn't give up everything for me. I might have asked the question, but I couldn't let him do that just for me. It had to be for him, too.

"*Jude*. I don't want you to drop everything for me. That wouldn't be fair. I don't think you'd really be happy doing that. You love fighting."

"I love"—his teeth clicked on the word—"spending time with you more. I'm realizing I love this ranch. This is where I feel at home."

"The ranch?"

That came as a surprise, given that we both ran away from here when we were eighteen and never looked back. But after the last few weeks, maybe it wasn't a complete surprise. I was falling in love with the ranch again, too.

"Uncle Chuck needs the help, and maybe it's been the years away and growing up, but I've come to appreciate the quiet life and physical labor that works you so hard, you fall fast asleep as soon as your head hits the pillow. It's rewarding working with the land and the animals. Besides, you can't get sunsets in Vegas like you can here."

I knew what he meant. Of any place in the world, this place felt most like home to me. It spiked my happy endorphins every time I stepped outside. "I wouldn't blame you if you chose to stay."

"Would you consider staying?"

"I don't know, Jude. I'd need a job—"

"You have a job here. You've become as much a part of the

ranch as I have this summer."

I did feel as though I was part of the ranch now. Maybe I always had been, but I didn't realize that as a confused and resentful kid. I was too self-absorbed to see what was right in front of me. I think I had to leave to discover that for myself. Thornbrush was home.

Would Jude give up everything for me? For the ranch? Could I join him?

"But wouldn't you have to travel a lot for your fights and be gone for weeks at a time with training?"

Jude scratched the back of his neck. "Coach jokes that he should send everyone to train on a ranch." He chuckled. "I feel stronger than I have in years, but I think everyone is right. This may be my last fight."

This was the time to tell him, then. He might not even get to fight if Junior followed through with his threat.

"I have to tell you something." I grimaced as soon as the words left my mouth. "But I need you to promise not to fly off the handle."

"Okay ... this can't be good."

I peered down at his hands holding mine. Strong and rough. Hands that could be so gentle yet pound someone's face in without breaking a sweat. But he needed to know. I needed to trust him with this. He was a man of integrity. He was dependable. He was goodness. He was trustworthy. I just had to show him that I could put my faith in him. That it all started with me being honest.

I took a deep breath and exhaled. "I didn't fall off the horse the other day." I clenched my jaw, waiting for his response.

His brow pinched with confusion. "What do you mean?"

I nervously rolled my lips together. "Well, what happened was …"

"Romy."

"So while I was waiting for Reed, Junior found me on the trail …"

His eyes darkened like a sea in a hurricane.

"He threatened to press charges against you if I testified."

Jude's hands tightened on mine. His nostrils flared. "He fucking did *what*?"

CHAPTER 36
Jude

A wave of blistering heat and nausea hit me like a freight train.

Junior found her on the trail. He threatened her. He touched her. He fucking *hurt* her.

"He doesn't want me testifying on Hazel's behalf. He said he'd press assault charges against you if I did." Her words sounded distant over the roaring in my ears, as though she was speaking through one of those playground phones that allowed you to speak from one side of a play structure to the other.

I could feel my vision narrow, my body temperature spike.

"He. Put. His. Fucking. Hands. On. You." Each word was punctuated and came out like acid on my tongue. My jaw was so tight, I could barely unlock it to speak, as if I were grinding gravel in between my teeth.

Romy flinched, and I loosened my grip when I realized I was squeezing her hands.

He was the one who hurt her. He was the one who put that fucking flinch in her. He was the one who made my girl feel scared and vulnerable. I saw how she trembled last night after he approached her. She wanted to appear tough and unbothered, but she was the one who was left bruised and bleeding.

Sucking in air that felt too thick, I tried to slow the blood rushing in my ears, but my mind spun on a reel—*Junior hurt her. Made her bleed.*

And then she lied to me about it. I hate that she felt she couldn't put all of her trust in me.

"I'm fine, Jude. It's nothing permanent."

"Bullshit!"

I couldn't sit here any longer. I jumped to my feet, pacing the room, running my hand through my hair.

"I'm going to fucking kill him."

"You just promised you wouldn't fly off the handle!"

She was right. I did. Otherwise, she might never have told me. But that fucking piece of shit touched her … hurt her.

I continued to walk, my fingers laced behind my head, breathing to the count of ten, closing my eyes to focus on my lungs contracting and expanding. Just like therapy had taught me. Just like I needed to do before facing my opponents. I had to have a level head. Prove to her she could trust me, that I could stay calm for her when she needed me to.

"What was he doing last night? What did he want?"

Romy shrugged. She seemed so calm despite the seriousness of this. Almost nonchalant, and it didn't help the fury I was battling.

"I don't know. Probably just reminding me not to talk. He wasn't going to do anything, not in front of so many people."

"He did something in front of an entire bar," I reminded

her, still pacing.

"The man's determined and angry, Jude. He says he knows Hazel planned this."

I stopped in my tracks. "What do you mean he knows Hazel planned this? Does he know about the note? Does he know something we don't?"

Romy sat up on her knees, facing me at the end of the bed. "I don't know. He said he was on Hazel's visitor's list, and he had just paid her a visit before her so-called suicide attempt. Whatever they talked about, I think it may have prompted her to threaten her life."

"Okay …" I tried to wrap my head around this. "So he believes Hazel planned to murder his brother? Is he planning to testify against her?"

"I'm not sure, but I think I need to find out. I don't know if he actually has anything, but it's enough to scare Hazel."

She had to do it. She had to testify. To talk to the lawyer. It could protect her from whatever fallout Junior's threats caused.

"You need to call Ms. Hoya and tell her everything."

"But he'll go to the cops. He could send you to jail."

I shook my head. "He's all talk. After what he pulled with you, he's not saying shit. You could press charges against *him*."

Her brows pinched. "I don't have proof. It would be my word against his. There's video evidence of you punching him in the face, though."

"Shit." She was right.

"What would that accomplish anyway? We'd just trade jail time and drag this out forever. Not to mention ruin your career."

"My career's done anyway." This was just giving me more reason to retire.

Romy huffed through her nose. "If your career is done, then you should choose to retire because *you* want to, not because of some low life."

She wasn't wrong, but she was far more important. "I still think you need to talk to Hazel's lawyer. Maybe at least tell her about the note. If Junior gets wind of you helping Hazel, then we face that together. Okay?"

I gathered her in my arms at the edge of the bed.

"Okay." Her voice was quiet against my shoulder. "Together."

Smoothing her hair down her back, I caressed her silky strands, comforting us both.

"Honey, you need to talk to me. No more thinking you can do this alone. We both have to be able to trust each other, and that means we're fully transparent. I made a mistake not telling you about my fight, and I don't want to make that mistake again. I'm willing to put it all on the line if you are."

She nodded. "I can do that. Full transparency."

I buried my nose in her hair, breathing in her sweet scent. "If you don't, expect me to go full caveman. I'm not going to accept *fine* or *nothing*. Unless you want me to fuck it out of you."

Her muffled laughter rumbled through my chest. "Is that a promise?"

"Cross my heart, hope to die, stick a finger in my eye."

She bopped a finger in my eye.

Grabbing her hand, I pulled her across my lap. "Better watch out. Naughty girls get spanked."

I gave her ass a firm smack, causing her to squeal.

I needed her to know that I loved her. That I would do anything for her. But this didn't feel like the right time. Instead, I told myself we had talked enough about feelings today. This was progress, after all. She was willing to put her trust in me.

I pulled her to her feet and gave her another pat on the butt for good measure as we walked out the bedroom door.

"Now let's go get some breakfast so I can beat my aggression out on some new fence posts," I said.

When really, I was just chickenshit because I was still worried I wasn't enough to keep her here.

CHAPTER 37
Romy

"**D**oes this look okay?" It was the fourth outfit I'd tried on.

"You look delicious." His bottom lip disappeared between his teeth.

Jude lay across the bed watching me change. He had cleaned up the stubble along his jaw and effortlessly applied styling gel through his dark locks.

Could he get any sexier? Seriously.

But instead of stroking his ego, I rolled my eyes. "I'm not trying to look edible. I'm trying to look professional."

I smoothed my hands over the black, cotton jersey dress that hit right above my knees. It was the nicest dress I owned. Most of my clothes were meant for the classroom, or these days, for ranch work. None of them said "courtroom drama."

After a two-week delay, Hazel was finally going before the judge to receive her charges. Ms. Hoya was not surprised by the note I found or the stowed-away cash and cell phone. She said that we'll keep that knowledge to ourselves for now; otherwise, we'd have to turn it in as evidence, and the prosecution could use it against her. Hazel was still adamant she acted in self-defense, and it sounded as though Ms. Hoya was going with it. She told me the investigator took photos of Hazel the day of her arrest. Her arms and torso were littered with bruises, some deep purple and others yellowed with age. More evidence Hazel and Jesse's relationship was abusive. However, they may need to swallow the unlawful possession and evading arrest charges.

I decided not to submit a character letter to the judge—at least for now. Jude supported my decision to hold off on testifying. Neither one of us were aware of what Junior knew or what he intended to do. But we both surmised that he was bound to fuck up somewhere. We would wait for him to play his hand before we decided. It was nice to think as *we* now, knowing Jude and I were in this together.

Jude pushed off the mattress, wrapping me in his arms, his face automatically burrowing into my hair. This was his new way of soothing himself—and me. He never hugged me now without his nose buried in my locks. He said it was like "taking a hit of a piña colada and happiness." His therapist told him the sense of smell carried the most powerful trigger to our memories, and he wanted to have my scent burned into his brain. He wanted to be able to ride on the high all day while he trained and worked, until his next fix when we collided in the evenings.

I loved it! It comforted me just as much as it did him and made me feel cherished. Wanted. Needed. Like we belonged to each other.

I couldn't get enough of his scent, either. And if we were

comparing it to shooting back a cocktail, Jude was like a spicy mint julep.

Did I just invent a cocktail? Because there definitely should be one, and I'd call it "The Horny Bull." I snickered at my own cleverness.

My arms tightened around his waist, and I pressed my cheek to his broad chest. "You know you don't have to go with me. I know Chuck said he didn't need you, but he can't rely on just the seasonal help to move the herd. Plus, with your fight in less than four weeks, you should be training nonstop."

Jude cupped my face, tipping it up to look at him, my chin resting on his sternum. His aqua eyes shone with warmth and tenderness, causing my heart to skip a beat.

I was falling, hard and fast, and I had a feeling he'd catch me if I asked him to. With how attentive he'd been since the rodeo, I could tell he was just biding his time until he told me how he really felt. But I could tell he was scared, nervous even, wondering if he would spook me if he peeled back the curtain to reveal he was falling, too.

But I wasn't scared. Not anymore.

We had been tiptoeing around it for days. Showing each other, often two times a day—morning and night, sometimes even with a quickie in his truck or tack room—how much we craved one another. We couldn't get enough. We were head over heels, half embarrassing Chuck, when we'd spot each other across the stable yard or open field, running toward each other as if it had been months instead of mere hours. I couldn't resist jumping into Jude's arms, wrapping my legs around his waist and peppering his face with kisses. I held on to him like a freaking koala until Chuck cleared his throat and we'd break apart, exchanging looks that promised off-the-chart orgasms later.

I was totally obsessed with him, and I died every time he flipped that baseball hat backward. He thought it was so cute and teased me relentlessly. Now he flipped his hat on purpose just to hear me release an involuntary moan.

There were so many times he caught those three little words on the way out of his mouth. It made me secretly giggle, release an inner-girl squeal, and kick my legs in excitement. I just needed to give him a little push.

And it needed to be soon.

Jude was leaving in two weeks for Vegas. He had a series of promotional events he had to attend before the big fight. He tried to get out of them, but his boss, Mr. Venture, reminded him he was in no position to break contractual obligations after the "bar fight." It was hardly a bar fight when one punch ended in a knockout. Alex also advised Jude to finish the last of his training at their home gym.

He didn't want to go, not when Chuck needed his help and I was in the middle of Hazel's legal shit. But I insisted he do it. I promised we'd FaceTime every night, and I planned on flying to Vegas for his fight. I hadn't told him yet that I'd received calls to interview for those teaching positions I applied for, but I would … soon.

"Nothing is more important than you." His thumbs swept my cheeks. "I won't be able to be here for you in a couple of weeks, so you need to give me this one. You have to let me be here for you now while I still can."

We leaned into each other, our noses brushing. Our lips connected on a soft, sweet kiss. A kiss that said it all without speaking the words. Heat flooded my belly and bloomed between my legs. If he just opened his mouth for me to taste him, I'd be pushing him down on the mattress.

"Mmm. Delicious."

"Hey, that's my word!"

I giggled. "We should probably go before you make me late."

"*I* make you late?" He did a whole show of checking me out from head to toe, as if I was wearing this casual sheath dress to tempt him.

I patted him on his chest. *Damn!* His pecs had gotten harder and more defined over the last few weeks. *Wrong move, Romy.* I wanted to peel that blue-collared dress shirt right off him.

"Okay, you're right."

"What did you say?" His eyes were wide in wonder.

I grabbed my one pair of heels. Nude sandals with a four-inch chunky heel.

"Nothing." I shrugged, then headed out of the room.

"*Romy.* You said I was right!" he said in amusement, following me out to the living room.

I stopped to pull on one shoe.

"Don't get used to it, buddy."

I leaned down to pull on the other, giving Jude a perfect view of my ass while he shoved his feet into his boots.

"You're just asking for it, aren't you?" He gave me a sound smack on the butt.

My breath hitched on the impact, liquid heat returning. Promising fun later.

Honestly, I was anxious about today. I had no idea what to expect. I couldn't think of anything other than the imminent fact I was about to see my sister escorted before a judge, while Junior sat behind the prosecution, that creepy, smug look on his face.

Jude noticed my change in demeanor as soon as I straightened and shrugged on my purse.

"Hey." He drew me back into him. "It's okay to worry."

"I just don't know what to expect."

"I know, honey, but I'll be there with you. You're not doing this alone. Remember? Whatever you face, we face together. Junior won't get within ten feet of you. I'll make sure of it. I promise."

He kissed my head, and I took one more pull of his cologne before nodding into his shoulder.

"Together."

I didn't say a word while I gripped Jude's hand on our way back to the truck, still processing what the judge ordered. Hazel was denied bail to await her trial for first-degree murder, unlawful carry, and evading arrest.

"Thanks for keeping your mouth shut, Romy Miller!" Junior cupped his hands around his mouth to holler across the courthouse parking lot.

Jude stiffened, swinging around to face him where he stood beside his beat-up 4x4.

"Jude. Don't." I pulled him back to me. "It's not worth it."

"Good. Keep your dog in check!" Junior wailed.

Oh, wow! He didn't just say that. He was trying to goad Jude into swinging at him. That would be just what he wanted, Jude hitting him in front of the courthouse.

"Fuck you, Junior!" I yelled back, tugging Jude with me. "Ignore him."

"He makes it pretty hard to," Jude admitted. "You should file a restraining order."

"If he comes near me again, I will." I led him the remaining way to the truck.

"You need to. I don't want him deciding to come near you as soon as I leave town. I want to make sure you're safe."

I understood Jude's concern. Even more so now. I felt as if my heart still hadn't kick-started since hearing the charges, seeing my big sister staring numbly into space, looking so broken, and the announcement that the next court date was August 20th— the day of Jude's fight. Of course, my father didn't show up today, but I wouldn't be surprised if he showed up if it went to trial. Knowing Frank, he only made an appearance when it benefited him, when he could swing the attention to himself.

"I'm serious, Romy. I won't feel as though I can leave you otherwise. As it is, I don't feel good about going into this fight knowing you can't be there with me, and I can't be here with you."

That's why, twenty-five minutes later, we were entering the Willows Police Department.

"Well, I'll be damned," one of the deputies declared when we walked in.

I would have noticed him anywhere. In fact, I was surprised I had yet to run into him, considering he was the only restaurant owner in town, and, apparently, worked on the police force. If not for the thinning hair on top and the fact that he looked a little broader through the chest, his neck thickened with muscles, Chase Houghton looked exactly the same.

"Chase," Jude greeted, going in for a handshake.

Chase tried to hide the flinch, but I saw it as soon as Jude gripped the hell out of his hand with his large mitts.

"Good to see you, Romy," Chase said, giving me a side hug. "You look great!"

I swore I heard a growl escape Jude.

"You, too, Chase." I returned the brief side hug.

"What can I do ya for?" he asked, looping his thumbs through his gun belt.

"We need to file a restraining order." Jude's voice was low and serious, very reminiscent of Jude "The Mood."

I wondered if Chase recognized it as well because his eyebrows rose. "This doesn't happen to be about you coldcocking Junior Matheus at the Rooster, does it?"

Jude only pressed his lips together in response.

"We all know. The whole department follows MMA, and we're big Jude 'The Bull' fans. Not to mention, I know everything that happens in this town way before it comes across my desk. Benefits of owning one of the only restaurants in town where the local book club meets. They're more like a bunch of Karens who drink their lunch and troll the Nextdoor app," Chase said conversationally, but it came across like gloating. He rubbed his jaw, sizing up Jude, trying to see if he was impressed at all.

It was interesting to watch. Chase was always puffing up his chest around Jude as if he were in competition, and it didn't feel much different now. Only these men weren't in high school anymore.

I turned to Jude, threading my fingers through his and giving his palm a squeeze. His eyes flicked to me for just a moment, and it was all the reassurance he needed to know I chose him, that we were here together.

"Come to my office," Chase gestured, bringing us over to his desk hidden behind a cubicle in the bullpen.

He shoved some file boxes out of the way and pushed an extra chair in front of the desk for Jude and me to sit down.

"It's for me, Chase … the restraining order," I explained, not wanting Jude to feel as if he had to do this for me, even though I knew he would. I was a big girl. I could handle this. I also wanted Jude to feel confident that he didn't need to worry while he was away.

"Ah, I see. It has to do with Hazel then?" he asked, steepling his fingers beneath his clean-shaven chin.

I nodded. "Junior's angry and wants justice for his brother. But he's taken it a bit too far." I exchanged looks with Jude, hoping he understood why I wasn't going to tell Chase about Junior attacking me. "On more than one occasion, he has approached me, made me feel unsafe—in public, too."

"He approached her at the rodeo," Jude supplied.

"He doesn't want me to speak on Hazel's behalf."

Chase's dark brows rose even higher than they did earlier. "He's trying to obstruct justice?"

I held up a hand to stop him there. "I don't want to press any charges against him. I just want to make sure he stays away from me, so I can feel safe in Willows and not worry that I'm going to face retaliation from him should I decide to testify."

Chase nodded, listening. "We can do that. Let me go grab the paperwork you need to fill out. Once it's completed, you just have to take it to the courthouse to file."

"Thank you, Chase."

Chase got up and walked away, leaving Jude and me at his desk.

"I'm so proud of you, honey," Jude said, leaning in to wrap his arm around me and pucker kisses into my hair.

"Thanks, babe. You're right. This is the correct thing to do."

"Did you just tell me I'm right for the second time today?" He pulled away, beaming at me.

I giggled. "Don't get used to it. This is unprecedented and probably will never happen again," I teased.

"I better get this in writing, then, to commemorate the day."

Chase cleared his throat, interrupting our flirting. I was getting quite used to people clearing their phlegm around us.

"It shouldn't take too long to file if you get it to the courthouse today. We can have it served on Junior by tomorrow morning," he informed, handing me the form and a pen.

"So you and Romy, then?" Chase asked, gesturing to me as if I wasn't sitting right in front of him.

"Yep," Jude said, crossing his arms over his chest and leaning back in the chair. Making his biceps bulge. I bit back a laugh.

"I always figured there was something between you two. Thought that's why Romy dropped off the face of the earth."

I shook my head, signing my name with a flourish, digging the tip of the pen into the paper while I dated it. "Pretty sure it's none of your business, Chase."

"Just making small talk, Rom."

The nickname grated on my nerves. As though he still knew me as he did when we were kids. Other than my sister, he'd been the only other one to call me that. I never liked it coming out of his mouth then, and I certainly didn't like it now. Especially in front of Jude.

I handed him the form and gave him my most syrupy smile. "Uh-huh. Surprised you even noticed, considering the whole time we were dating, you were hoping to date my sister instead." Reminding him of his parting words. "At least he chose me for me, not because of Hazel. Hate to break it to ya, but Hazel would have never chosen you. We Miller girls like our dicks big."

Chase's face went beet red, and Jude let out a choked laugh before slapping a hand over his mouth.

I pushed out of my seat, pulling Jude with me.

"*He* is also the reason why I came back and why I intend to stay." This really wasn't about Chase. This was all for Jude. I was so in love with the man, and I wanted him to see I was willing to stand up for him and our relationship. Words would never hold the same weight as actions. He needed to believe he was enough for me. That he was more than worthy.

I started to turn around but then swung back around to see

Chase looking dumbfounded. "Oh, here's your pen. Thanks so much, Chase. I really appreciate you helping me out. See you around town."

I wiggled my fingers at him before intertwining my fingers through Jude's and marching out of there as if I owned the place. Jude wasn't the only one proud of me.

CHAPTER 38
Jude

We were barely out of the police department before I was swinging Romy in my arms, laughing.

"My feisty girl! I loved that so much! Did you see Chase's face? You just told him his dick was small! I forgot how much I enjoyed irritating him! And did I hear that right? You're really staying?"

Romy was giggling, her breath hot in my ear as she held on to my neck.

"I'm staying, Jude."

I set her down on her feet, crushing my mouth to hers. She pushed against my chest, causing me to pull back and look down at her.

"But we should probably talk."

My stomach plummeted at that *but*.

"Come on, let's go for a ride," she said, leading me to the stables.

After dropping off the paperwork at the courthouse, she was quiet on the drive home, snuggling into my side on the bench seat. My heart was thrashing around like a caged bird. Doubt swirled around in my mind. She had just defended me in front of the dude I was jealous of all through high school. Then she drops that bomb on me? *We should probably talk.* Four words no one ever wants to hear.

She was staying. However, that *but* hung over me like a storm cloud. It was still hard to believe she could possibly want me. That's where my toxic thoughts went. My brain was so programmed to think I would never be enough for someone to ever want me. I knew it wasn't true, but I was still working on changing that narrative.

I could tell she was trying to ease my tension, rubbing her hand along my thigh and flitting soft smiles my way whenever I glanced away from the road.

When we turned into Thornbrush, she finally said, "Let's change, then head to the stables."

I thought she might want to pull out the box Hazel hid, but instead, she guided me toward Chip's stall.

After saddling Chip and Winnie, I followed her through the open fields. We would have to bale again soon. The hay field was already long enough to brush grass tips beneath my stirrups. Nervous, I flipped the Thornbrush Ranch cap I was now wearing, even though the setting sun caused me to squint.

Romy sat tall in the saddle, her wavy, blonde hair flowing behind her. The sun glowed off her crown like a halo, washing her in gold. After several summer weeks working the ranch, her creamy skin was brown beneath her white, cropped tee. Peeks of her belly and thighs from those high-waisted, ripped jeans she always wore made me want to stop my horse and pull her down so I could touch every hidden inch of her. She was stunning. It was a wonder my lungs still functioned when I looked at her.

No matter where she was leading me, I knew I would follow. If it was to the ends of the earth, I would gladly trail behind her. I'd known it for a long time now. I might have regretted never doing more to find her all those years ago, but it wouldn't have led us here. Maybe we needed to lose each other for a while to be ready to find each other again.

We rode on through the prickly sagebrush—how the ranch got its name. The land opened to the view of the river beyond.

Before I realized it, she had led us to the burn pile. It was the best place on the ranch to watch the sunset, but instead of sitting around the pit of ashes, we tied our horses to the hitching post and walked past it to where the craggy edge overlooked the Deschutes River. Facing west, there was nothing but the snowcapped, volcanic rock mountains of the Cascade Range and forested hills. Facing east lie arid desert studded with more sagebrush and tumbleweed, shaded by ponderosa pines.

"This is my favorite place on the ranch," I told her, standing there on the cliff.

She smiled up at me. "I know."

"You do?" I tried to remember if I'd told her.

She nodded. "I notice things. Teacher, you know."

I looked at her and released a huffing laugh. "I need to remember that. You must have eyes in the back of your head. Won't get anything past you."

Her smile faded. "I got calls to interview for a couple of teaching positions."

"Romy! That's great!" I was genuinely happy for her. I wanted her to find every success in life. I would be her biggest cheerleader if she'd let me. But I couldn't ignore the sting of disappointment beneath it.

"They're in California, of course. I'm going to thank them but decline the interviews."

"You shouldn't do that."

"I'm staying, Jude. I want to follow my heart for once, and my heart is here."

"We'll figure it out. I could go with you."

She shook her head. "I don't want that."

My heart dropped.

"It's painful to even think about leaving this place, leaving you. I was homesick for so long, I think I became accustomed to the feeling. Like it was my norm. I don't want to feel that way anymore, and I couldn't let you feel that way, either. Being here these last couple months, being with you, being a part of the ranch. Seeing *you* be a part of the ranch. I understand how you feel about this place—"

"But *you're* my home." She truly was. I could be at home anywhere she was.

She held up a hand to stop me. "I saw how you took *this* all in the last time we were here." Romy gestured to the amazing view. "You had a smile on your face that lit you from the inside out, and you were breathing it in as though you were either trying to memorize it or absorb it into your very being. That's how I feel every time I look at you."

My chest tightened, and I couldn't wait a moment more to touch her. I stepped into her, one hand digging into her hip, the other cupping her jaw. My fingers buried beneath the hair at her temple while my thumb stroked her cheek. She leaned her head into my hand, as if she could mold it to her skin, her eyes gleaming, gazing at me with such love and tenderness.

She was incredible. Beautiful. I had fallen hard for this fiery, independent woman. I loved that she wasn't willing to put up with shit, to challenge me, to put her trust in me despite the number of people who'd let her down—including me. I felt so honored that she was choosing me. I loved that she saw me … maybe she always had. Maybe I was just too consumed with convincing myself that I was the only one who felt that way.

"I didn't know you were watching. I thought you were too busy laughing with the girls while you passed wine back and forth in your saddles." My voice came out breathless. I almost cringed at how trivial it sounded after she basically just told me I was her sunset. My damn self-doubt needed to fuck off.

I thought back to her standing in the dim light of the stable after the bonfire. Looking so luscious, lust blazing in her eyes. The night she'd asked me if I ever thought of that night all those years ago. I had known she was leaving again, and I couldn't help but take the chance to kiss her. She drove me wild when she'd told me to take her to the truck. She saw me even then.

"It's hard not to look at you, Jude. People are drawn to you. It's always been that way. I think it's endearing that *you've* never noticed. I know you don't realize it because you can be hard on yourself and you often doubt yourself, but you are such an incredible, selfless, and generous man. Your successful fighting career would have made a lesser man an arrogant ass, but that's not you. Instead, you give to the people who matter to you. You'd give the skin off your own back. Just look at what you've done for the ranch—improving the facilities, investing funds where Chuck lets you."

I chuckled at that. Yeah, where he *lets* me. One of these days, Uncle Chuck may let me buy him new equipment and renovate the arena.

She smiled, turning her face just enough to brush a kiss across my palm. "What you've done for me. Being there for me, even when I've tried to push you away. Making me breakfast every morning and making sure I have your support, no matter what.

"I see you, Jude. I know we've both been scared. Scared of getting hurt. Scared of losing each other. But I don't feel afraid anymore. You know why?"

"Why?" I asked in a whisper.

"Because I trust how I feel about you, and the strength of that feeling is strong enough to lift me up. To keep me from stumbling. Strong enough to hold all my pieces together, even when I feel like I'm falling apart. I'm crazy about you, Jude Larsen, and I want to quit dodging these feelings. I want you to catch me because I'm falling for you."

My lungs froze up just for a moment, before the peace of relief rolled over me, breathing life back into me.

"Honey," I said on my first exhale. "I feel as if I've been plummeting, just waiting for you to fall with me."

She giggled. I loved her fucking giggle so much, it made my chest hurt.

"We can catch each other." She was so close now, I could feel her breath brush my lips.

I smiled, repeating her words. "We can catch each other."

She reached up, taking the hat from my head and placing it on her own. She turned it backward with a smirk. I leaned down, pressing my lips to hers. Tender and gentle. My lips molded around the bow of her lip, nestling my bottom lip between hers.

"I'll love on each and every piece of you," I said, dropping a kiss to either corner of her mouth. "Every single piece." My mouth traced her jaw along her throat to the sensitive spot beneath her ear. She shuddered beneath my hands as they dug into her hip, pressing her to me. "I never needed to hold you together, though," I whispered against her ear. "You've done that all on your own. You show your strength with fury and claws, but it's your quiet inner strength that shows your fortitude. We are more alike than we both realize. Protective of our hearts because we've had to be—no one else was willing to do it for us—but we don't have to anymore. Because I know mine is in good hands. You have to know I would die a happy man just knowing you trusted me enough to protect yours."

Salty wetness moistened my lips, and I lifted my head to see tears silently slipping down her face.

"Oh, Romy, honey." It killed me to see her cry. "What is it?"

"I didn't know how much I needed to hear that. I've been so guarded."

Emotion stung behind my nose. "I know, honey."

She never had to tell me because I *knew* her. Every piece of her. Even back then when she felt as if she had no choice but to build walls, to shield herself from her father's emotional abuse all through high school. I had built walls, too, but brick by brick, we tore them down for each other.

"You have my heart," she mumbled while I swiped tears from beneath her beautiful eyes.

I leaned in, brushing my lips across her cheeks to kiss her tears away. "You've always had mine, and I trust you to keep it. I don't think I ever really got it back after you left."

"I'll keep it forever." Her lashes fluttered closed. The last of her tears escaped for me to vanquish. She tipped back her head as though she were sunning her face beneath the sunbeam of our love.

"Good because I intend to keep yours forever, too."

I gathered her in my arms, letting her hop up to wrap her legs around my waist. She hugged my neck, burrowing her face while I gripped her ass. I let her cry silently there, dampening the hair at my nape, her lips coasting softly along the curve of my neck.

"Love me, babe?" She murmured it as if she needed reassurance.

I was such a fool for her; I never wanted her to question it. She should only demand it because that was what she deserved.

"I'll always love you," I confirmed, desire rocking through me.

I wanted to show her how much I loved her. How much I craved her every moment of every day.

"Let's ride back so I can love you properly," I told her.

Her legs tightened around me. I could almost feel the pulse in her center.

"No," she whispered in my ear. Her breath sent shivers down my spine. "I want you to fuck me in the dirt until I feel that I'm as much a part of this place as the sagebrush roots."

CHAPTER 39
Romy

"As stubborn as the sagebrush, too." Jude's voice had grown husky, saturated with need.

"Fuck me, babe," I demanded.

The love in my heart felt crushing, bursting, all-consuming. So intense I could barely stand it. The joy in knowing Jude felt the same way made it near impossible to hold it inside without it going somewhere. I was overflowing, and if Jude wasn't inside me soon, I felt as though I would detonate.

I nipped his ear before sucking it into my mouth. His arms trembled ever so slightly where they held me. I dove my fingers into the soft hair at the nape of his neck, massaging, wanting to coax the need from him. I could tell he was debating whether he should really lay me down on the ground, out here in the open.

Always thinking of me.

And again, it made me fall more in love with him.

Unwrapping my legs from around him, I slid down his body, feeling him hard against me. I knew all he needed was a push, and he would be right there with me. His eyes glistened like the ocean, and I wanted to dive into them and never leave. I'd become a mermaid if it meant staying in those eyes forever.

His dark brows furrowed as if he, too, could barely contain his emotions. Like it pained him to hold it back. Words were not enough for him. I knew that about him. He needed to see it, feel it, to be assured I trusted him with my heart.

I ran my hands down his broad chest, down the dips and swells of his stomach until they landed on his belt. Pressing up on my tiptoes, I met him where he leaned over me, our lips catching the heat growing between us. Tasting each other, feeling our teeth clash before our tongues could glide. The sensation shot right to my core, and my need grew.

"*Jude*," I pleaded into his mouth.

"Me too, honey."

He captured my mouth again, his hands deep in my hair while he held me there. He didn't stop me when I unbuckled his belt or undid his pants. I wanted to feel him. To feel what our love did to him. His lower abs clenched when he felt my fingertips against his skin. My hand dove down past his waistband, gripping his velvety length. I stroked him from root to tip, urging that precum to leak until I could swipe it with my thumb.

"Greedy girl," he growled.

"Always when it comes to you," I whispered into the golden evening.

I continued stroking while his hands explored my curves until he found the button of my jeans. My breath hitched when he discovered I was soaked. His middle finger glided through my slit and over that bud of nerves.

I pulled my hand away, pushing him back.

He released me with a whine, but understanding my intention, he lowered himself to the ground, pulling me into his lap.

Now leveled face-to-face while I straddled him, his eyes bore into me as if he could see my soul, and all I saw was love illuminating the space around us. Moisture pricked in my eyes again. I wasn't someone who typically cried, and I wasn't about to become a sap, but this man drew it out of me.

Staring into each other's eyes, we ground against one another. My panties were drenched. Jude wrapped his fingers around my breast, his thumb drawing little circles around the stiffened peak that cut through my top.

In a maneuver Jude showed me—some jujitsu move—I had him in my guard on the ground, pulling him on top of me.

"Oh, is that how this is going to go?" he asked, that sexy, lopsided grin coming out to play. "I knew I'd regret teaching that move to you."

"I've got a deadly judo chop, too," I quipped.

"I'm a dead man." But his voice came out muffled as his lips disappeared in the crook of my neck.

His large hands squeezed my breasts, and I arched into him.

"Fuck me." I didn't think I could wait any longer.

I watched him as he dropped kisses down my chest, between my breasts, down my sternum, and at the dip of my bare stomach. The whole time his hands never left mine.

Kneeling between my thighs, he hitched one leg over his

shoulder, his mouth still leaving a damp trail down my belly. Hooking his fingers in the waistband of my jeans and panties, he drew them down. The grit of the dirt and the sharpness of the rocks dug into my backside, but not for long because as soon as he had my pants down around my boots, his hands encompassed my ass, lifting me slightly until he was inches from where I needed him.

"You're so unbelievably beautiful, Romy. I don't know how I got so lucky."

His words made my chest ache. "I'm the lucky one." I brushed a lock of hair that had fallen across his forehead. "To have a man look at me the way you do."

"You take my breath away."

He pressed his lips to the inside of my knee. I didn't want him to take his time anymore. I didn't need him to be gentle. Not tonight.

I gripped his shirt, dragging him back up to me until I could pull his mouth down on mine. He braced his arms on either side of my head. His lips fit perfectly around mine. Our bodies, too. As though we were made for each other.

I pawed at his denim, needing him out of them. One hand left my side to help me pull his pants and boxers down. I gripped his cock; it pulsed in my palm, echoing my heartbeat.

"I don't think I can be gentle," he breathed against my lips.

"I've never wanted you to be. I just need you to love me."

And with a single thrust, he plunged into me. I released a loud gasp.

"Love me, Jude. Hard."

He retreated slightly until he could thrust again. This time going deeper, bottoming out. I cried out. We moaned in unison at the sensation of him stretching me, taking me so deeply.

"I'll love you hard," he whispered into my mouth. "And this time, I don't care if the whole ranch hears it."

He withdrew some, nearly all the way out. All I could do was dig my nails into his shoulders and hold on.

"Scream as loud as you want, honey. I want everyone to know what my cock does to you, what you sound like with me buried so deep, what my love sounds like coming from your lips."

My pussy fluttered around him, my mouth panting against his, and I wanted him to dive back in. His arms were shaking, holding himself there, just penetrating me with his tip. It was driving me wild. The anticipation. I was soaked, and he was so thick and hard. I knew as soon as he buried himself, he would hit that spot. I squirmed beneath him.

"*Please*," I whimpered.

His hands returned to my ass, protecting my tender skin, lifting my hips just enough that my clit could grind against him.

"Oh God," I murmured.

His mouth was still against mine. We weren't kissing, though, too consumed with the intense connection building between us. But we couldn't take our lips away, allowing our panting and moaning to mingle.

"Don't hold back, honey."

My hips rocked reflexively, grinding into him. My nails nipped into his back, pulling him to me while he thrust. His own fingers dug into my ass. With every plunge, the root of his cock slid against my clit before hitting that sensitive spot deep inside.

"*Jude!*" I screamed.

He did it again. The angle hitting every sensation, making this more intense than any position we'd ever done. The fact that my ankles were still wrapped up in my jeans made it nearly impossible for me to widen my legs to relieve some of the pressure. Instead, it tightened my entrance, adding friction where we were connected. My nerve endings were on fire.

"That's it, honey. Come for me. Soak my cock."

The roll of his hips became fitful, yet he still managed to brush my clit each time he thrust inside. I was so close. I dug into his lower back, pressing him to me. I wanted to feel every inch of him.

My breath was stuttering. He dropped a kiss on my top lip. I rocked against him, my pleasure building, climbing.

It hit with such intensity, sending my blood rushing to my center. I clutched him to me, trying to keep him there, but he wasn't done. Not yet. He thrust one more time, and all I could do was release a loud moan. My pussy clenched around him, bursting with my orgasm. I could feel him stiffening, his muscles trembling, until he was throbbing inside. His cock pulsed, shooting continued waves of his cum against my walls.

I barely felt my mouth if not for the tingles in my lips. My breath came out stilted as I crashed through the ecstasy. Curling into him, we held each other while my heart settled.

As I came down from the high, I felt myself melting into the earth. The dirt and rocks scraped against my lower back and clung to my hair, but I didn't care. Jude still pulsed inside me, and I pressed my knees to his hips, keeping him there. I wanted him to stay there forever, nestled deep inside me. Never leave.

Jude's panting filled my ears, and I hadn't realized I'd squeezed my eyes shut until I opened them to look at him. He was washed in rose gold from the setting sun, staring down at me with the most intense gaze—it felt possessive and cherished at the same time. It was how I imagined Grecian gods looked. All golden, chiseled, powerful. I was the mortal he was claiming, and I would gladly submit. Because he was mine, and I was so in love with this man.

Finally able to move, I reached a hand up to his face, feeling the prickle of his stubble. I traced the puffiness of his lips, the ridge of his nose, the arch of his brow. I ran my fingers through his soft, brown waves, and the whole time, he was watching me. Seeing me love him.

We pressed our foreheads together, closing our eyes, breathing each other in, wanting to never sever this connection.

"I love you. I love you so much, Jude." The words felt so natural falling from my lips, as if my mouth was always meant to shape those words.

I felt Jude's chest, still midbreath, until he released a sigh.

"God, do you know how long I've craved to hear those words from you? Damn, you're incredible. I'm so fucking in love with you, Romy."

CHAPTER 40
Jude

Nothing could demolish this high. It was as if I was floating on air. Or so I thought.

"Well, what do you want to do?" Alex asked.

We had just finished a grappling session, but I really needed a heavy bag. I had to go find a hay bale to punch.

I wiped the towel down my face, mopping up the sweat.

"I have to call Jessica."

And I had to tell Romy. She wasn't going to like this. It already caused my gut to cramp just thinking of saying the words. She was either going to be pissed, or … no, she was going to be pissed. I wasn't scared of her ferocity, even when her temper got the best of her, but I realized now that was when she needed me the most. Just in the last few days, now that we bared our hearts, our communication was improving.

"Who's Jessica?"

Shit.

Worst possible timing for Romy to walk into the garage.

I buried my face into the towel before peeking out to look at her.

Yeah, I wasn't scared of her … well, maybe a little. It was a healthy fear for the woman I knew I'd one day call my wife. Because I never wanted to hurt her.

Romy stood beneath the open garage door, the evening light against her back. She was still wearing her boots, her jeans dusty and dirty from a long day of trail riding. Her hip was cocked, her hand resting on it, while her other hand flipped her braid back over her shoulder.

"I need to tell you something." I cringed.

I chanced a glance at Alex. He was looking hella uncomfortable.

"Um … good work tonight." He slapped me on the shoulder. "I'll see you in the morning. Bye, Romy."

"Bye, Alex," she said.

She didn't even look at him when he grabbed his water bottle and ducked out of the garage to his rental car.

"Do you want to sit with me?" I gestured to the weight bench.

"No, I'm good. I've been in the saddle all day."

I nodded, rubbing my neck with my towel. Maybe I'd take a seat.

Grabbing my hat off the rack, I brushed my hair back and pulled it on backward so she could see my eyes while I told her this. I sat down on the bench, resting my elbows on my knees, and glanced up at her.

She kicked off her boots before padding across the mat to stand in front of me. Her brow was arched, waiting for me to speak.

I blew out an exhale between my lips.

"This doesn't seem good," she commented.

"It's not. A story was released today on an MMA YouTube channel, and it kinda went viral. Mike Reyes reposted it on his social media, and it's spreading like wildfire. I'm going to have to release a statement and probably talk about it at a press conference once I'm in Vegas."

"What's the story, Jude?"

She was growing impatient. Her toe tapping.

I inhaled a deep breath. There was no way around this but through. "A reporter connected the dots. Everyone already knew about me decking Junior in the bar, but no one had really determined why until now. They found the story in the local paper about the murder on the ranch. They know I was defending you, but they are also saying I was defending a murderer. They're spinning the story to sound like I condone the killing of Jesse Matheus."

"But that's not true. They have no idea what happened. We still don't really know, but I'm becoming more and more convinced he was abusing her."

"You know that. I know that. That's why I have to make a statement. That's why I need to call my ex."

"Jessica?"

I nodded. "She's also my publicist. Hopefully, she can help me with damage control before the story becomes a bigger problem than it already is—before it affects you and Thornbrush."

"I don't give a fuck how it affects me. I worry how this impacts you and the ranch. You need to let Chuck and Lina know."

"Yeah, I'll tell them tonight and then give Jessica a call."

"Do you want me to be there with you when you tell them?"

That question eased some pressure in my chest. Man, I loved this girl. "Please."

"Done. We will face this together."

Uncle Chuck and Lina took it better than I thought. They were more pissed for me than anything. They wanted to help where they could, so I just told them to take care of Romy while I was gone.

When I called Jessica, I told her everything. I detailed what we knew, why I had to come home. I informed her about Hazel and what we suspected about her and Jesse. She wasn't surprised when I advised her about Romy. She always knew that I was in love with someone from my past. She recorded my statement, and she said she'd start constructing the narrative to highlight the facts and start reporting all the social media posts as disseminating information. Hopefully, by the time I reached Vegas, the story would be old news, but there would inevitably be questions during press conferences. Knowing Reyes, he wouldn't shy away from bringing it up, either. The dude was a shit talker.

"If someone asks you about it, just say you can't speak to the ongoing investigation and trial, that you trust the justice system to do their job," Jessica counseled. "Your statement should be a sufficient answer for everyone. If anything, it should paint you as hardworking, loyal to your family, compassionate to those involved, and focused on your fight. They don't need to know the sordid details."

To say this didn't distract me from focusing on my fight was an understatement. It did exactly what the YouTuber and Reyes set out to do. I spent days trying to regain my equilibrium, Alex throwing all his motivational pep talks at me, but I didn't latch on to a single one. I needed to get my head in the game, but it didn't help that Romy couldn't go with me, that I had to leave her to deal with the bullshit and walk into that courtroom without me. I wanted to care about this fight, but it was becoming clear that my heart wasn't in it.

"This is going to be my last one," I finally told Coach.

He only nodded and said, "I know, and you're going to go out swinging."

When the day came I was supposed to leave Romy, I was a nervous wreck. Alex was going to drive us to the Portland Airport, so I had to say goodbye to her at home.

The double-wide had become our home. At least I could leave knowing it was our home, knowing she would be here when I got back, that she would be waiting for me.

Washed in the sunrise, Romy still curled up in the blankets of our bed, we kissed and clung to each other until the very last second. Really until Alex came pounding on the door.

"I don't want to leave you," I mumbled against her lips.

"You need to go," she said, but she didn't push me to leave.

Another pound on the door.

I groaned, gripping Romy's hips to swing her over to straddle me. We had already gone one round this morning, but my dick didn't care that I needed to go. It strained against my Nike joggers, digging into her. *Those fucking tiny sleep shorts.*

"Come on, I'll walk you out." She slid off my lap.

I whined.

"Come on, big baby." She pulled on my arm until she was able to sit me up.

I adjusted myself in my sweats.

The pounding at the door was incessant. "Hold on, asshole!" I called.

"Dick!" Alex yelled through the door. "We're going to miss our flight."

Sitting on the edge of the bed, I drew Romy in between my legs, gripping the back of her thighs right beneath the curve of her ass. I stroked her perfect cheeks beneath the hem of her shorts with my thumbs.

"This is killing me."

"I know, babe, but the sooner you leave, the sooner you'll come back to me," she whispered against my lips. Her fingers dove into my hair, stroking, soothing, loving.

"I love you, honey." I pressed my lips to hers, wanting this to last.

"I know you do. I love you just as much."

She kissed me back, our tongues lingering just a little bit longer.

"Okay, I really need to go before Alex decides to knock down the door."

I intertwined my fingers with Romy's, leading her to the door, my other hand taking the handle of my suitcase.

"One last thing," she said.

"What's that?"

Romy grabbed my Thornbrush Ranch baseball cap from

the coat-tree. Pressing up on her tiptoes, she brushed her lips across mine while putting on my hat.

"You can't forget this," she murmured against my lips.

"Of course not."

Bang. Bang.

"All right. Don't get your panties in a bunch!" I called through the door.

I gave Romy another smack on the lips before lacing my feet up in tennis shoes and opening the front door.

"It's about fucking time," Alex called from where he now leaned against his rental car. But instead of looking annoyed, amusement painted his face, knowing exactly why I was taking my sweet time leaving.

I mean, look at her! Even in—*especially* in—that oversize sleep shirt that barely revealed her soft, cotton shorts, that phoenix tattoo up her thigh, and her thick, blonde hair piled into a messy bun. She was stunning.

"I love you, honey."

"I love you, too, babe." She held on to the doorknob while she buried her nose into my neck, wrapping her arm around me to hold me tight.

I burrowed my face into her hair, taking one last pull of her coconut scent, hoping it would at least last me until I got on the airplane.

"FaceTime tonight?" I asked her.

She nodded. "Text me when you take off and land."

"I will." I kissed her one last time before I willed myself to pull away. It was painful leaving her here, making myself go when I wanted nothing more than to stay.

"Bye, babe!" she called, giving me a small wave as I walked toward Alex.

He grabbed my suitcase to throw it into the trunk.

I couldn't stand it. I turned back around and ran right back up those steps, causing her to laugh as I lifted her into my arms. I melded my lips to hers, my tongue darting out to urge her to open for me one last time. She released a soft whimper into my mouth, and I ate it up. Holding her to me, feeling the press of her breasts against my chest, her lips against mine, her tongue dancing across mine, the scent of her like a cloud. I wanted to memorize it all so it would last me until I came home.

"Okay, lovebirds. If we don't get this show on the road, then we're never getting there."

Romy's lips tipped up in a smile. "I love you. Now go win a fucking fight for me," she said.

We couldn't get enough of saying those words to each other.

"I love you, honey. Always and forever. Be safe while I'm gone."

"You, too. Don't do anything I wouldn't do." She winked at me when I set her down.

I chuckled. "I'll be good, I promise."

I jogged back down the steps to the car, turning to look at her one last time. To burn the image of her standing at the threshold of our home until I could see that image again.

"Love you!" she yelled.

I blew her a kiss, then got into the car.

Alex was smiling like a fool when he got behind the wheel. "You got it bad, Bull."

"Badder than bad. It kills me to leave her."

She stood in the doorway watching us back out of the drive, and I never took my eyes off her until we were turning down the dirt road, away from the ranch.

CHAPTER 41
Jude

ME

I miss you already 🙁

HONEY

I miss you, too, babe. Thanks for siccing Lina and Sage on me. 🙂 They haven't left me alone since you left.

ME

🐷

HONEY

Oh, please. Like you didn't have anything to do with it. I've had a wine hangover almost every morning because of those two descending on me every night. Christian even invited himself over last night.

ME

I bet Sage loved that.

HONEY

Pretty sure that's why she drank a whole bottle herself. They all ended up passed out in our living room. I had to step over bodies this morning just to get to the coffeepot.

ME

I bet Christian loved that. 💀

HONEY

Ha! Sage was at least aware enough to put a whole wall of pillows between her and Christian.

ME

Lol. You trail riding today?

HONEY

Yes, and then it's bath night for the whole stable. It's been so hot, it will feel good to get a little wet.

ME

I'll get you wet.

HONEY

Another reason why I wish Lina and Sage would leave me alone for at least one night. Don't you want to see me touch myself the next time we FaceTime?

ME

Fuck! I'll text Lina.

HONEY

Thank you 😊

ME

Don't touch yourself until tonight. I want you dripping just thinking about it until then. I gotta go. Coach is waiting for me. We are going to watch a tape, and then I have back-to-back sparring sessions in the gym. Press conference is tonight, too. I'll call you when it's done.

HONEY

Ok. I'll be thinking about you all day. Love you, babe!

ME

Love you, honey! 😘

My least favorite part about being a professional fighter was the spotlight, the public life. I fucking hated it. Another reason why I never felt like Vegas was home and wasn't on social media.

Knowing that about me, it didn't surprise me to see Jessica leaning beside the conference room door. She was wearing her press badge, her head bowed over her tablet—probably keeping up with the latest reports.

She was an attractive woman, tall and curvy. Her tight, royal-blue pencil dress accentuated her hips and breasts and complemented her bronze skin. The heels she wore made her legs appear impossibly long. She knew this, though, and she knew how to use it. She brushed her long, curly, dark hair over her shoulder before raising her eyes from her screen.

Seeing me approach, her dark lashes fluttered, her brown eyes assessing. They were always scrutinizing me. I always felt as if they were passing silent judgment about what I was wearing or how I was walking or simply standing. I didn't think she meant to make me feel that way. She was a compassionate and understanding person who just gave that look. It didn't help that her lips pursed when she examined me from head to toe. I called her out on it once, and she just told me that she liked to look at me. I never truly bought it. Possibly one reason why I never let my walls down with her.

"Knew you'd need the support," she said, coming off the wall to meet Alex and me in the hall.

I could already hear the commotion of the pressroom. The click of camera shutters, the chatter of the reporters, Mr. Venture cracking some crude joke to make everyone laugh while they waited for their headliners. Mike Reyes would be meeting me in there. Our first time face-to-face.

"Appreciate it, Jess." I leaned in to give her a quick hug.

"Hey, Alex," she greeted Coach.

"Hey, Jessica. Thanks for doing this. We know it hasn't been easy keeping on top of the social media posts."

Jessica had been busy, reporting each new post as fake news or harassment. Some of them had been removed in the last twenty-four hours, but it wasn't going to stop reporters from asking about it or for Mike Reyes to make some snide comment.

"Of course. Remember what we talked about, Jude? What to say if someone asks about the court case?"

"Yeah, I got this."

She patted my shoulder. "If not, I'll be right there to back you up. Just keep bringing it back to the fight, and you should be fine."

I nodded.

Right then, the door swung open. Flashes framed a man in a suit—Mr. Venture's assistant.

"You're up," he said, opening the door wider for us to pass.

More lights flashed. A platform was raised at the front of the room, backdropped by a black banner with the Venture Fight Organization logo and sponsors. Mr. Venture sat in the middle of a large, black-clothed table, a mic positioned in front of him and one on either side of him, waiting for Reyes and me.

I sucked in a deep inhale. Counted to ten. Released an exhale.

Here goes nothing.

I stepped into the lion's den, blinded by the strobing lights that wouldn't stop flashing around me. As I took a seat, I slipped into the Bull Larsen mask I'd known for years. The one that lets me feel nothing and everything all at once.

CHAPTER 42
Romy

I had just gotten out of the shower and thrown on some pajamas before flicking on the TV to the sports network channel. Running the towel through my wet hair, I watched as Jude and the other fighter came out from their respective doors to climb the podium to their seats beside a bulky, impeccably dressed bald man. Gold rings adorned each finger and were laced together in front of him on the table.

With his authoritative voice, he announced Jude "The Bull" Larsen and Mike "Savage" Reyes as they took their seats in front of the crowd. Lights flashed.

Jude looked nervous, and I watched him fidget with his hair. He wasn't wearing his hat tonight. He was dressed in an all-black suit, his hair styled. He looked so handsome, but my anxiety spiked watching his face transform. This was the face I recognized behind the screen the last twelve years. I thought he had changed into a cold, hard person, but now I knew this was the role he had to play as "The Bull."

Alex squeezed his shoulder behind him, and then a beautiful Latina woman bowed over to whisper something in his ear.

Despite my concern for Jude, a spike of jealousy lanced through me. I wondered if that was Jessica. She was gorgeous and so tall. Seeing her lean down to him like that, so close her hair was brushing his shoulder, comfortable and familiar to him, made my stomach hurt. I didn't like that she was next to him right now when I couldn't be. I gripped my towel tighter.

Whatever she said to him, though, was enough for him to sit straighter and check his facial expressions. His brow smoothed, and his lips settled into a firm line. He looked stoic and in control now, calm and collected but ready to face a fight.

Mr. Venture was talking to the reporters, but all I noticed was Jude. He took a deep, steadying breath and then leaned his arms on the table, preparing to speak.

The first question was about Jude's knee and recovery.

"It's stronger than ever," Jude said. "You try lifting hay bales and riding a four-hundred-acre ranch from sunup to sundown, not to mention doing daily doubles and grappling every day for the last eight weeks. It may have been a short camp, but I'm more than ready to enter the cage."

Great answer, Jude. I wanted to breathe easy after his first answer, but I knew the prompts were only going to get harder.

"What do you think of this matchup?" someone asked him.

"You're all in for a treat. I don't think you could have hoped for a better matchup. Reyes is undefeated and an excellent Muy Thai and jujitsu fighter, but my experience as a ground-and-pound boxer and collegiate-style wrestler will prove a challenge for him. I plan on defending my belt to the very end."

"He just doesn't know his end is coming for him in a matter

of days." Reyes laughed into the mic.

The room tittered with laughter.

"Oh, fuck him," I said out loud to my empty living room.

Jude leaned into the mic, turning to look at Reyes down the table. Mr. Venture stepped back to give the fighters an opening. "I'm just looking forward to you putting your foot where your mouth is on Friday night. All you've done is run your mouth online and spread rumors. I think I'm already in your head. While I've been focusing on this fight, you've been worried about me and what I'm doing when you really should be worried about me laying you out in the cage."

A rumble of voices shouted questions while others chuckled at Jude's response.

Reyes guffawed. "I'm not worried about you, old man."

Old man! Jude was eight years older than this kid, but he also had the experience to back him.

"You should be," Jude chimed back.

"Reyes, what made you call out 'The Bull'?" someone off camera shouted.

"I intend to remain undefeated, and my goal has always been to climb the ladder until I can claim the belt. Haven't you heard? I'm the new, best, up-and-coming fighter, and I plan on staying that way for a very long time. It's time the belt belonged to someone who isn't broken. Anyone who has gone up against Larsen in the last few years hasn't been able to beat him. Do you know what they all have in common? They aren't me. Everyone claims he's one of the greatest in the sport today, and to prove, once and for all, that I'll be the greatest of all time, I will defeat the champ. I plan on leaving Vegas with the belt around my waist."

Applause sounded from the reporters before they quieted again to ask more questions.

"Go ahead," Mr. Venture said, gesturing to another reporter.

"This is for Larsen. There has been some talk about you retiring. Is this to be your last fight?"

I held my breath. He hadn't exactly spelled it out for me, but we were under agreement that we were both staying on the ranch.

"All I can say is that announcement isn't coming tonight. I'm focused on this fight right now."

I puffed a breath out my nose.

"Reyes, your social media has blown up the last few weeks after reposting a video about Larsen and the ranch he trained on. There have been some pretty serious allegations about what goes on there, including Larsen's role in supporting a murderer. What made you decide to repost that?"

Oh, here we go. I flopped down on the couch, preparing myself for what I was about to hear.

Reyes leaned closer to the microphone. "Yeah, I don't think it's okay that we gloss over the fact that Larsen seems a bit unhinged. A wild fucking bull. Reckless. He may say he is focused on this fight, but the bar fight just shows that he's spiraling. He's not going to be facing me with a level head. I thought it was important to show everyone why the man can't hold it together right now. Someone died on his family ranch, and he went so far as beating the shit out of someone who spoke against his employee—who is in jail for murder—just because he's banging the sister. That doesn't sit right with me, and it shouldn't sit right with this organization, either."

Shit!

This kid had some serious balls to just come out and say that, while also blaming his own fighting organization with Mr. Venture right beside him. It made me want to climb into the cage and punch his face in.

My eyes shot to Jude. His eyes were burning, but he was keeping it cool. I could see his knuckles blanch, but he didn't flinch.

"What has happened on my family ranch has nothing to do with this fight. My family and the ranch were impacted greatly with what occurred this spring, and that's why I relocated my training camp there. I'm loyal to my family above all else.

"But I also trust the justice system to investigate and conduct a trial to determine the judgment. It's not our job to pass it. As for the bar fight—one punch, mind you, and I have already released a statement, which should be enough. The man was harassing my family, harassing the woman I love, and I did what I thought needed to happen in the moment. To protect those I care about. We have since gotten law enforcement involved, so the issue should not arise again.

"My answer may not sit right with everyone, but I can assure you this organization has supported me every step of the way in my career. Reyes and his camp may think I'm not mentally prepared ... that I'm distracted ... but I can tell you, anyone who knows what it feels like to love someone or something so badly that you'd do anything to protect it knows exactly what I'm about to do in that cage. I'm coming for you,

Reyes, and you better be prepared."

The room erupted. Jude pushed away from the table. Lights strobed on cameras. No one stopped him as Jude stormed out the side door, Alex and Jessica on his heels.

My eyes welled, and I didn't realize I was biting the insides of my cheeks until a metallic taste burst on my tongue. He just announced to the world that he loves me!

The sportscasters were going crazy from the news floor, announcing this as one of the most anticipated fights of all time. But I didn't hear much more as I ran to grab my cell phone from the bedroom.

I dialed Jude. It rang and rang and rang.

"You've reached Jude Larsen. I'm unable to pick up the phone right now. Please leave a message or shoot me a text, and I'll get back to you as soon as I can. Later."

I hung up and dialed again. Voicemail.

Pick up, Jude! I dialed him one more time, and when he didn't answer, I texted him.

ME

I watched the press
conference. Call me back.

I went to the kitchen, setting my phone on the counter so I could hear it if he called while I made myself a sandwich for dinner. The sandwich tasted like cardboard as I waited for his call.

My anxiety thrummed. I washed my plate and put it on the drying rack. I almost contemplated calling Lina to come over and distract me, but she would likely bring wine, and I needed a night off from drinking.

What I really needed was Jude. I needed to know he was okay. I needed to assure him that I was okay. I wanted to make sure he wasn't in his head because, knowing him, he was probably overthinking everything he just said and worrying how it would be perceived.

ME

> I'm not mad. Just worried.
> Call me back.

I couldn't help texting him one more time.

Jude

My hands were shaking and tingling as I stormed back toward the elevators. I needed to go lie down. I could feel my heart pounding, beating in my skull. Was I breathing? I couldn't tell.

"Jude! Jude! Wait up, man."

Alex was chasing me with Jessica right behind him.

I looked down at my phone, my vision blurring and fading in and out. My phone was vibrating, lighting up with incoming texts and calls.

"Hand that to me," Jessica said, slipping my cell phone out of my grasp. "You need to breathe."

I barely felt her hand rubbing my back.

"Jude, look at me." Jessica's voice hovered in my ear, but I couldn't see her. "We need to take him to his room. I think he's having a panic attack."

"Come on, man. We need to get you to your room." Alex,

at least I thought it was Alex, gripped my arm, pulling me down the hallway.

"I—I—I can't ... I can't do this." I managed to release the words from my throat.

I didn't want to be here anymore. I didn't want to do this. I wanted to go home. I wanted Romy. I think I blacked out at some point back in that pressroom because I had no idea what I'd said.

"Jude, listen to me." Alex gripped my neck, bringing us face-to-face. "What's five plus three?"

I attempted a breath, but it was like breathing through a pinched straw. My head swam. My heart pounded in my ears. Was I having a heart attack?

"I'm going to pass out," I confided.

"No, you're not." Alex pulled me a few steps before pushing me down into a chair. "What's five plus three?" he asked again.

"Five plus three?"

It was the math question Alex always asked me in the corner when I felt as if I was being pulled under.

"Yeah, five plus three."

I took a shuddering breath, squeezing my eyes shut to think. "Five plus three. Five plus three is ... eight."

Alex patted my shoulder. "Good. Now take a deep breath, count to ten, and breathe out."

"We have to get him up to his room." Jessica's voice sounded anxious beside us. "The last thing we need is anyone seeing him like this."

"I need ... I need to call Romy," I said, putting my hand out for my phone.

"It's blowing up with press calls. We're going to turn it off for a while, at least until we can assess the situation," Jessica explained, pocketing my phone.

"I'll give her a call," Alex spoke up, knowing that's what I needed. I needed Romy. "Let's just get you settled first, and then I'll call her."

"I'll put in a call to his therapist."

"No. I got this." I didn't need to talk to someone right now. I just needed Romy.

"You're in the middle of a panic attack, Jude. You need to see a doctor and talk to your therapist," Jessica urged.

"She's right." Alex helped me to my feet. "I'll get our doc in, and Jessica can call Dr. Deborah. You fight in less than forty-eight hours. We have to make sure you're okay before you head into the cage."

Jessica tucked herself into my side, her shoulder holding me up, while Alex took the other side.

"The elevator is just right here, baby. Let's get you up to your room. We'll run a shower and get you some electrolyte water while we wait for the doctor."

Hearing Jessica call me *baby* made me feel as though I was betraying Romy in some way, even though I wasn't the one saying it. It felt all kinds of *wrong*. Like how a horse must feel when someone pats it on the muzzle. I didn't like it one fucking bit.

Romy

I watched the dusk turn into dark through the blinds ... waiting.

My body was exhausted from being in the saddle most of the day and bathing over a dozen horses. I needed the rest. I wanted to try and call him one last time before I fell asleep.

I dialed his number, preparing myself to get his voicemail again.

Come on, Jude. Pick up.

"Hello?" came a sultry voice.

I pulled the phone away from my ear. Did I call the wrong number? But no, Jude's name and face flashed on the screen.

"Who's this?"

"This is Jessica. How can I help you?"

Jessica. *Shit.* Jude's ex and publicist. Why was she answering his phone?

"Um." I hated that I hesitated. "Is Jude there?"

"He's in the shower right now."

Fuck! She was in his hotel room while he took a shower? What the fuck? There must be an explanation for why she was there ... wasn't there?

I felt my heart fracture into a thousand tiny pieces.

"Do you want me to take a message?" she asked.

If he didn't have the decency to call me back, letting me worry all night, I didn't need him calling me back.

"No. It's all right. Have a good night."

I ended the call before she could say another word.

There was no way in hell I was going to sleep now. I hurled my phone across the room, letting it land with a thunk on the rug. I hoped it fucking shattered! Throwing myself against the pillows like a petulant child, I wanted to rage. Scream. I couldn't take this. I needed to know what was going on. I needed *him*.

My pulse pounded in my ears while I huffed breaths into the pillow. It progressed louder and louder until I thought my chest would burst.

But it was feet drumming up the porch steps.

Then a fist was pummeling the front door.

CHAPTER 43
Romy

"How in the hell did this happen?" I asked, shoving my feet into boots and throwing one of Jude's hoodies over my head. His scent engulfed me, souring my stomach, but I took a steadying breath, shoving it down deep. I'd deal with all that bullshit later.

"Someone had to let them all out," Lina panted.

"All twenty-eight horses?"

She shook her head, and I followed her out the double-wide into the dark. The night was still, except for the sounds of crickets. We ran, our boots pounding into the soil as we hustled toward the stables.

"Did Reed not hear anyone?" I asked.

The bunkhouse was literally right next door to the stables. If he heard something spook the horses, he would have been right there.

I thought Lina would reply with her typical *fucking Reed* comment, but instead, her face was pale in the moonlight.

"Something's not right." Lina huffed as we ran.

A horse ran past as we neared the stables. I could see the

whites of her eyes as she cantered by.

"Fuck! They're spooked. This is going to take forever to calm them down enough to round them back up," I commented.

"Go to the stables, turn on all the lights, and have all the stalls open and ready. Dad, Reed, and I will start going after the older ones—they usually won't go too far from their beds this late at night."

I nodded, jogging toward the stables.

With the clopping of hooves, I turned to see the silhouettes of horses in the dark. Some managed to jump the fence into the paddock, while others were scattering down the dirt road or adjacent fields. Chuck, Reed, and a couple of other ranch hands stretched their hands wide trying to round them up, lassos ready at their belts.

Reaching the stables, I flicked on each switch, illuminating one end to the other. Every door hung open as if someone had run through, flipping the latch of each stall.

"What the fuck?" I whispered. Who would have done this … and why?

"Where is it, Romy?"

His tired slur came from behind me, and I spun around.

My father stepped out of the shadows.

"Shit! Dad! What the hell? Did you do this?"

I hadn't seen Frank since the day he came stumbling drunk onto the ranch, yelling at me. He looked as though he'd been dragged through the mud. His hair was disheveled, and deep grooves lined his eyes. Of course he was drunk; I could smell the stench of cheap beer wafting off him.

"We need it."

"What are you talking about? Did you fucking let all the horses out? Why would you do this? *How* did you do this?"

"Bronte trusts me," he said simply.

"So you thought you could just come onto private property and do whatever the fuck you wanted?" I was pissed! Not only did I have to hear Jude's ex answer his phone, but now I had hours of rounding up horses because of Frank's drunk ass.

I could feel my blood boiling. "Chuck!" I yelled. We needed to call the police. He needed to be dropped in the drunk tank, at the very least.

Cold, hard metal pressed against my temple, followed by a loud click on my ear.

I sucked in a breath.

I knew before I even looked to my left who stood there, a gun held to my head.

"Yell again, and we'll have a bigger problem," Junior hissed.

"Not only are you trespassing, but you're also ignoring the restraining order," I blurted out, side-eyeing him. Junior's hat was pulled low over his face, shadowing his eyes, but I could see the twitch of his lip, the slight hesitation.

"We're not going to hurt you, Romy," Frank said.

"Speak for yourself, old man," quipped Junior as he spat on the ground by my boots.

Frank looked unsure, shuffling on his feet. Frank Miller was mean, a drunk, and narcissistic, but he would never raise a hand to Hazel or me.

"We just need something of Hazel's," Frank explained, holding his hands up to show he meant no harm. "She told me it was in the stables. She just didn't tell me where."

Shit! Hazel told Frank, too. I groaned. If I could move without freaking Junior out, I would have palmed my face.

"Get the gun out of my face, Junior, and maybe I can help you."

"I don't think you're in any position to make demands. Going to the cops. I told you not to talk."

"I didn't say shit. I just wanted you to stay away from me."

Does this mean he was the one who sold the story?

"Were you the one who leaked the story with that YouTube channel?" I asked.

"I wish, but the story was already in the local news. It was only a matter of time before it all came out. Good timing, though, huh?"

I scoffed.

"No. I thought your dad would be of some help. He doesn't believe his precious angel is capable of such evil, so he was willing to prove me wrong by bringing me here."

"Dad, really?" I pinned him with my best glare.

"We better hurry before they rein in the horses." Frank shuffled on his feet again, obviously uncomfortable and slightly off-balance.

The barrel of Junior's gun pushed against my face. I sucked in a breath, my heart starting to kick up. Fear finally washed over me like hot wax.

"Where is it, Romy?" Junior's voice burned against my ear.

I shuddered at his nearness.

"Bronte's stall."

I didn't think Junior would use his gun, but I wasn't about to test that theory. I just hoped someone walked in here before he decided to try it out on me.

"Slowly now," Junior ordered, shoving me forward.

I stumbled but quickly found my footing, heading over to Bronte's stall.

"It's in the corner, there. Beneath a loose board."

Junior jerked his chin, telling Frank to go for it, while he still pointed his gun at me. He knelt, brushing the dust and hay away from the corner until he could pry his fingers around the board. He huffed and heaved, but in his drunken stupor, he was mostly useless.

"I can get it, Dad," I said as calmly as I could, but I gulped at the tremble in my voice. I didn't want to be scared. Not in front of this asshole.

"Do it, then," Junior said, pushing me forward again.

I knelt beside Frank. He shifted just enough to give me room, but his eyes were pleading with me. He might have set out to do this, but now doubt was settling in as the alcohol dissipated.

Prying up the board, I pulled out the shoebox Hazel had stowed away.

I peeked over at Frank one more time, his eyes drooping with worry and sadness, before I lifted the lid. All the cash was still there. And so was the note and cell phone.

I gave Frank a subtle nod, swiping the cell phone while he pocketed the note. He took the box from my hands and passed it over to Junior.

Shoving his gun into the back of his waistband, he ran his hand over the wads of cash.

"Is this everything?"

I shrugged. "That's all there was when I found it."

"Huh," was all he said, still digging through the box as if more would appear. "This must be the money she stole from Jesse. He intended to send it to my family, but we never received it."

"That's what I told you must have happened to the money," Frank said, heaving off the floor.

Junior pursed his lips, nodding. "I knew it was either her or the Larsens who were stiffing him."

I wanted to roll my eyes, but I forced myself to hold still.

"All they've ever done is take from us. I knew it had been a mistake for Jesse to come work here. At least I'm finally getting his cut."

Horse hooves neared, and I could hear Chuck calling commands.

"You better get going, Junior," I advised.

He tucked the box beneath his arm. "It was nice doing business with you." He saluted before heading out the back of the stable.

Chuck's voice got closer, followed by Lina's and what sounded like the clopping of three horses.

I helped Frank to his feet just as they came around the corner. Chuck and Lina's eyes went wide, standing between the horses they had lassoed.

"What the hell is this?" Chuck's voice was rigid.

"We need to call 9-1-1. Junior was just here," I told them.

The whites of Lina's eyes shone brightly like the horses'. "That fucking asshole did this? I'm going to fucking kill him."

Chuck shot a look at his daughter before turning to my

father. "Frank, please tell me you didn't have something to do with this?"

Frank's shoulders slumped. "I fucked up."

I gripped his shoulder before saying to Chuck, "A drunken decision."

Chuck's jaw ticked, but he nodded before walking away with the horses in tow.

"Mocha, hazelnut latte with coconut milk, and an iced coffee for me," Sage announced, doling out the coffee orders while we sat huddled beneath blankets in the living room of the double-wide.

It took all night to get the horses back in their stalls and settled. Chuck said he'd cancel the trail rides for today. The horses needed the rest as much as we did. Even when most of the horses were back in the stable, the cops were still asking questions. Last I heard, Junior still hadn't been arrested. He was on the run with a gun and a shoebox of money. Frank turned himself in, but Chuck insisted he didn't want to press charges.

"Twenty-four hours in the drunk tank should be enough for now," Chuck said.

I didn't realize I was shivering until Lina pulled me into a hug, gripping me as hard as her little body could squeeze. She insisted on coming back to our house.

I still hadn't heard from Jude, and I wasn't sure I really wanted to talk to him. Chuck and Lina also tried calling him, but their calls went straight to voicemail. I was officially spiraling, thinking his silence meant the worst—that he was doubting our love, finding it with Jessica instead, and trying to decide an easy way to break it to me. I tried to remind myself that this was the lack of sleep and the eventful night getting to me.

Lina immediately called in backup in the form of Sage and caffeine.

I wrapped my numb fingers around the warm, paper coffee cup, staring into the wafting steam.

"Has anyone heard from him?" Sage asked.

Lina and I both shook our heads. This didn't sit right with her, either. But I wasn't about to tell her he was with Jessica.

"We need to tell him so he knows what happened." Lina rubbed my shoulder.

"No. We're not telling him shit," I grumbled, taking a tentative sip of coffee. The hot liquid was like a balm to my soul, and I almost hummed with pleasure if it wasn't for my attempt to hold the tears at bay.

"He's going to ask how the horses got out when he finds out." Lina continued to rub my shoulder blade.

"You can tell him my drunk dad is a shitty asshole. That won't be news to him. But we're not telling him about Junior. He has to focus on this fight, and with all the bullshit the press is giving him, this is the last thing he needs to worry about. At least for now."

He may have been breaking my heart at the moment, but I wasn't about to distract him from the potential fight of his career.

Lina and Sage both gave defeated sighs.

"What the hell was Junior looking for? Did he find it?" Sage asked.

I had broken down the main points of what happened with Junior on the trail and with Jude and I going to the cops to submit a restraining order, but I hadn't told them about the box.

"Hazel had a stash of cash with …" I didn't know if I should tell them about the note that was now with Frank. "With a cell phone." I shuffled my coffee to one hand to stuff my hand into my pajama pocket.

Sage's eyes went wide. "Does it work?"

I pressed the power button on the side of the iPhone. "It's dead."

"Do you have a charger?" Lina asked, jumping from her seat beside me.

"Yeah, on the bedside table," I called because Lina was already down the hall heading to the bedroom.

Without a word, Lina hustled back, finding the nearest outlet and plugging in the charger. I passed the phone to her, and she connected it.

We sat in silence, sipping our coffees, waiting for it to light back up. It seemed to take forever, but within minutes, the screen flashed on. We all huddled on the ground near the outlet, the blankets gathered around us, our coffees abandoned on the coffee table.

The passcode pad flashed on the screen.

"Shit." I tried her birthday. Nothing. I tapped in my birthday and Frank's. Still not correct. Last try. I punched in Mom's birthdate. The lock screen disappeared, revealing the home screen.

"Look at the messages," Lina suggested.

I opened the message app, but it was empty.

"Huh. She could have deleted them," she said.

"What about the call history?" Sage queried.

There was one phone number in the call history, and it was only outgoing. There didn't appear to be any incoming calls.

"Maybe call the number and see who it is?" Lina shrugged.

My fingers trembled too badly.

"Here." Lina took the phone from me, hitting the number and putting it on speaker.

The quiet living room filled with the sound of ringing while we held our breaths.

Ring.

Ring.

Ring.

Then an audible click and a woman's voice came over the line. "Sanctuary Ranch and Rescue, this is Desiree. How can I help you?"

We all exchanged looks over the phone. Lina's brow furrowed in confusion, but Sage's jaw fell open in surprise.

"Hello?" Desiree asked again over the line.

"Oh, I'm so sorry, Desiree, I think we got the wrong number," I said quickly before hitting the end button.

"What the fuck is Sanctuary Ranch?" Lina probed.

Sage's teeth clacked together when her mouth closed. She looked pale. "It's a place for rescued horses and ... battered women."

Lina and I both stared at Sage. We didn't know much about

her past relationships, other than she didn't "do cowboys."

"Where is it located?" I asked her.

"Washington. Maybe your sister was planning on leaving and going there." She picked at blue paint beneath her nails.

I leaned over the phone, gripping Sage's hand in mine. Her palm had gone cold. It could have been from her iced coffee, but based on the look on her face, I didn't think it had anything to do with the temperature of her drink.

Sage whispered, "Your sister was probably trying to leave, and he found out. He wasn't going to let her go …"

Tears stung my nose and welled in my eyes. "Knowing my sister, she wasn't about to let that stop her."

CHAPTER 44
Jude

"I'd like to think my anxiety is protecting me," I told Dr. Deborah.

After a rough night, I eventually relented to let the doctor give me Ativan and melatonin so I could rest. Dr. Deborah met me in my hotel room first thing in the morning. I was emotionally and physically wrung out, and I had to get my head on straight. The fight was tomorrow, and I wasn't about to let this wreck me.

"Our fight-or-flight response is there to protect us," Dr. Deborah confirmed, leaning over her notepad where she sat on the hotel couch. I sat across from her, shoveling my high protein plate of eggs and sausage into my mouth. I barely tasted it, only eating it because I had to fuel my body. "But we also need to remember to not let that control us, to find grounding in the heat of the moment."

"Alex was there to try and help me snap out of it, and I did my breathing technique."

"Did you do your six senses protocol?"

I shook my head. "The panic attack took over. All I could

think about was that I needed Romy and I needed to breathe. But I'm thinking more than anything, my psyche is just spent as much as my body is. This job has done more than ruin my knee."

"How do you feel about that?"

I scoffed. There she was, asking me how I felt again. I was starting to get used to it, but sometimes that simple question still got under my skin.

"I feel like I'm okay with that. I'm done fighting. I've realized there are other things worth fighting for, and this isn't it. I left home twelve years ago with a broken heart, feeling as though I had to go out and do something great, make money to prove to everyone that I was worth a shit. When really, I never needed to do that. I just needed to prove to *myself* that I was enough. Enough to be loved, to be wanted, to be needed."

"You feel like you're enough now?"

I took a bite of egg, mulling the question around while I chewed. I couldn't give an affirmative, but I was beginning to realize it.

"My mom was pretty shitty to just walk away from a three-year-old and never look back. But if she hadn't, I wouldn't have gotten the love I deserved. My uncle did it in his own way, teaching me how to work a ranch and instilling in me a strong work ethic. It might not have been the squishy, affectionate kind of love, but he always poured his time and patience into raising my cousin and me. Even caring for Romy.

"Romy … well, she has shown me a fierce, passionate kind of love that burns me to the core and raises me up. I want nothing more than to show her she is worthy of just as grand a love because that's what she has done for me. I'd do anything for her."

"Are you retiring because of her?"

I sucked the inside of my cheek, considering. "Yes and no. I'm doing this for us, and for me. I want a life with her, I want a family, and I want to start that life in the one place that feels more like home than any other."

"Oregon?"

I nodded. "I'm tired of dodging destiny. After this fight, I'm finished. I'm going home, and I'm going to make that woman my wife."

"Phone. Now." I didn't mean for it to come out a growl, but as soon as Jessica and Alex walked into my suite, I was done being coddled.

I was ready to get this show on the road and start my forever.

And it started with me calling Romy and finished with me retiring from the organization.

"It was for the best," Jessica explained. "The press was trying to get ahold of you all night. I'll warn you, it may still be ringing off the hook. If there are any numbers you don't recognize, ignore them."

"Fine. Just give me my phone." I held out my hand to her.

But Alex had it in his back pocket, and he pulled it out to hand it to me. I raised an eyebrow to him, but he only gave me a sheepish look.

Sighing, I took my phone and turned it back on. It

immediately started vibrating in my hand as notification after notification came through. Many of them were numbers I didn't recognize—press. But a half dozen of them were calls and texts from Romy.

My stomach immediately dropped.

I scrolled through my notifications. Another few were from Uncle Chuck and Lina.

Something was wrong.

"I thought you were going to call Romy," I accused Alex.

He was still wearing that look. "We were trying to make sure you were okay, and Jessica and I were attempting to detour questions. I'm sorry, man."

I ran my hand over my mouth. Romy was probably pissed at me. Why did Uncle Chuck and Lina call so many times?

"Give me a few minutes. I'll meet you in the lobby, Alex." I dismissed them both, heading over to sit on the edge of the bed.

"Um ... do you want me to stay?" Jessica asked.

I glanced at her. She stood there, biting her lip, looking a little unsure. Her eyes shone with affection and what I recognized as desire, but I didn't care what she was feeling or what she wanted from me. There was never going to be an "us." I didn't want Jessica. I wanted Romy, and it appeared, based on the number of missed texts, she wanted me, too.

I shook my head. "I'm good."

Jessica and Alex said their goodbyes and headed out. I waited to hear the electronic click of the door closing before dialing Romy.

It rang and rang and rang. When she didn't pick up, I

tapped on Lina's contact.

One ring.

"Oh my God, Jude, where the fuck have you been? We've been trying to reach you."

I grimaced. "I'm so sorry. I should have called sooner. I was getting inundated by press calls and had to shut off my phone." I didn't want to worry them more by telling her about my panic attack. There was nothing anyone could do back at the ranch. "That's my bad, though. I should have at least texted to let you know that I needed to turn it off."

"We saw the press conference."

I adjusted the bill of my hat. "That was a shit show."

"But you shut that shit down!"

"I did?" I chuckled. Maybe my answers came across differently than they had in my head.

"Yeah, you said everything perfectly. I couldn't have answered all those questions without clamming up. But you did it! I'm so proud of you, cuz. That Reyes guy is a fucking asshole. I hope you beat the living shit out of him."

I laughed, feeling the anxiety drain from my shoulders.

"Did Romy watch it?"

There was a beat of silence before she said, "I think so. She didn't say anything about it, though."

I hoped she wasn't mad at me for something I said. The panic attack hangover left everything a blur.

"Is everything okay at the ranch?" I asked, still wondering why I had missed so many calls last night.

Lina puffed a breath through the phone. Oh, God. It must be bad.

"Well, you're not going to believe what Frank Miller decided to do for fun last night. Or maybe you will."

"What did that piece of shit do?" That man was a fucking menace, and Romy didn't deserve such a shitty father. It made me all the more thankful for Uncle Chuck and how he took the Miller girls in. My uncle was truly a saint. A single dad, raising his nephew, and still making sure Romy and Hazel had a place to escape to. Not to mention raising a fucking cool daughter.

"He let the fucking horses out! We spent most of the night corralling them."

"What the fuck? Why would he do that?"

I could almost hear Lina's shrug. "A drunken temper tantrum because no one is paying attention to him. Who the fuck knows?"

"Please, tell me your dad called the cops?"

"Oh, don't worry. I'm pretty sure he's still sleeping it off in the drunk tank."

I rubbed my brow. I needed to be home helping, not sitting in this Vegas hotel room. "Horses okay?"

"Yeah, everyone is accounted for. A few shoes thrown. But we're all taking the day off while the vet and farrier get everyone right as rain. Romy, Sage, and I are having a movie day before she goes to visit her sister. After last night, we all need some serious downtime."

"She's going to go talk to Hazel?" I wasn't expecting that, not when tomorrow was the hearing. My chest hurt, knowing that Romy was having to deal with that without me.

"Yeah, but don't worry. I'm going with her."

"Who said I'm worrying?"

"I can practically hear you flipping that hat of yours from here."

I hadn't even realized it, but I had just flipped it. I adjusted the bill, settling it back on my head. "Okay, you got me there. Are you going to the hearing tomorrow, too?"

"No, I'm going to hold down the fort, but Dad and I wrote character letters. He's going to present them to the judge."

I nodded, even though she couldn't see me. "Okay. Can you ask Romy to call me after she sees her sister? I have my weigh-in this afternoon, but my phone will be on me from now on."

"Sure thing, cuz."

"Thank you. Tell Uncle Chuck that I'll give him a call, too."

"I will. Don't worry about a thing. Focus on your fight. We got it all handled here."

The thing was, I didn't think it was all handled because no matter how many texts I shot Romy, she left them all unread.

I sat on the bed, obsessively scrolling through my missed calls, landing on one answered call at 10:24 p.m. last night.

Someone answered Romy's call.

"The car's downstairs," Jessica announced, entering the suite.

I checked the time. Weigh-ins were in less than an hour.

"Did you answer Romy's call last night?" I asked, not looking up from the call log.

Silence.

I glanced up; Jessica lifted her chin. "I did. I wanted her to know you were okay so she wouldn't worry."

"What the fuck? Why didn't you say something earlier?"

"Honestly, I think it's the last thing you should be focused on. You should have your head on straight for this fight, not distracted by some girl back home."

"She's not *some girl*, Jessica. What the fuck did you say to her?"

"Nothing." Her word was clipped, pulling up our itinerary on her iPad. "Now as soon as the weigh-ins are done, I've scheduled you for a massage and ordered you a pasta dinner."

"What. Did. You. Fucking. Say to her?" I asked, slowly emphasizing each word.

"Truly, nothing. I told her you were in the shower and asked if she wanted me to take a message. She said no. That was the end of the conversation."

"Are you fucking shitting me? You told her I was in the shower like you were here in the damn room with me?" Knowing Romy, she was now spiraling, letting her temper mask her hurt and searching for an exit plan. No wonder she wasn't getting back to me.

"Yeah. What's the problem with that?" she asked, now crossing her arms in front of her chest.

"You know how that looks, Jess." I leveled her with a stern look.

"Who cares how that looks? I was doing my job last night, and that job was taking care of you. If she got the wrong impression, that's on her. You need me, Jude. So let me do my job, and let me be there for you."

I shook my head. "That was always the problem with us. We should have never mixed business with pleasure. The lines blurred, and our relationship was as much a part of your job as it was managing my promotion schedule. We wanted different things. I wanted a family, a real life outside of fighting, but your career was more important—and that's fine. We can want different things, but I hope to God you didn't purposely sabotage my relationship with the only woman I ever loved because you're now having second thoughts."

"Jude, you have to know that I will always care about you. And you're right … we were always on two different pages. But maybe seeing you yesterday, wrecked, made me doubt why we broke up. I've missed you, and I'm not sure I can still handle your public relations if it means not being with you, too."

I sucked in a breath through my nose, holding it for a count of three and then releasing. She was right. She couldn't be my publicist anymore. I nodded, agreeing. "You're right. I think after this fight, we need to go our separate ways. I'm done after this, Jessica."

"Jude—"

I held out a hand to stop her. "After this fight, I'm not sure I'm going to need a publicist anymore, and if I do, I'll find another one." I pushed myself off my knees and to my feet. "Let's get this weigh-in over with so I can go eat some fucking spaghetti."

She gave my arm a tentative squeeze as I passed her to the door, but I didn't turn to respond, only letting her follow me in my wake.

CHAPTER 45

Romy

"**D**oing all right, darlin'?" Chuck asked as we walked into the courtroom the next morning.

I smoothed my sweaty hands down my black dress.

"Doing all right. Thank you for being here with me. You've always been more of a dad to Hazel and me than anyone else."

After talking to Hazel yesterday, I knew what I needed to do. We both cried, and she finally told me her story.

She didn't want to leave Willows, but she was either going to get out of that relationship in a body bag or run as far as she could to get away from Jesse. Over the last year, she'd been hoarding small lumps of cash from her and Jesse's paychecks until the time came for her to leave. She wrote the note, knowing that she would either be taking off or she would be dead. With the cell phone, she'd called the domestic violence helpline and was pointed to resources, including the horse ranch that rehabs rescued horses and provides therapy for survivors of domestic violence.

She hadn't planned on taking Jesse's life, but she had

fought him until she could get the gun from him, turning it around on him. For a moment, after firing the handgun, she had thought of turning it on herself, but she didn't want to die. So she panicked and took off, thinking she could make it to Sanctuary Ranch. That's when the cops had caught up with her.

Junior was arrested yesterday for trespassing, vandalism, and breaking his hundred-yard restraining order. Hazel was proud of me for doing what I needed to do to keep myself safe, even after he'd threatened me, and happy that Junior was behind bars. He had been blackmailing Hazel, threatening to prove Hazel was stealing funds from Jesse, and that was what motivated her to kill his brother.

Chuck and I headed over to the bench behind the defense. Hazel turned in her seat briefly to give me a reassuring tip of her lips before turning back to the front, where the judge shuffled through papers.

I pulled the folded letter out of my purse.

"Ms. Hoya," I said quietly, getting Hazel's attorney's attention.

She turned to where Chuck and I sat.

"Ms. Miller, Mr. Larsen," she greeted with her professional coolness.

"I brought the letter." I handed the letter over the partition that divided the defense and prosecution from the audience.

Ms. Hoya reached over, taking it. "Thank you, Ms. Miller. We appreciate you doing this."

A silent tear slipped down Hazel's cheek. I gulped down the knot forming in my throat.

Ms. Hoya stood in front of the judge, presenting the character letter I had written and revised for my sister last night. My heart pounded when the judge accepted the letter, asking me to approach the bench and read it aloud.

I cleared my throat, my hands going clammy. "From the time I could walk, I wanted to be just like my big sister. She never once complained that her baby sister followed her around. In fact, she mothered me just as much as our mother did. She took care of me. She stood up for me with other kids, even with our own father at times. Our father and I never got along, and she was our buffer …"

I glanced over at Chuck, who gave me a reassuring look. I inhaled a deep, steadying breath, trying to keep the tears at bay. It didn't help that Hazel was sobbing into her hands.

"I never wanted to stay in Willows like she did, or maybe she felt that she had to because I didn't. She supported my dream to move to a big city, to do something rewarding with my life. Our father always reminded me I was the disappointment. She knew if I didn't leave, it would beat me down to the point where I may not have survived it. She didn't want that for me, and she made sure I could leave, while she stayed.

"I wonder now if she would have left, too, if our mom hadn't died, or if I had decided to stay. I think she might have felt obligated to stay for our father and for the town that loved her and named her their rodeo queen. I don't know what happened over the last twelve years. I'm angry at myself for not making the effort to be there for her when she needed me most. She had always supported me, but selfishly, I never once supported her. When things got bad, she didn't know where else to turn. She'd made the only choice she thought she could make—she prepared to leave the one place she called home. But Jesse Matheus wasn't going to let her leave. No one should ever be forced to make this choice because they are unsafe.

"Whatever happens, whatever decisions are made in response to this case, I hope it can be handled with empathy for the sister I knew and with the thought in mind that sometimes we don't know how to ask for help because we don't know how to see the forest for the trees."

I barely heard the judge thank Ms. Hoya and announce a recess to deliberate; I was focused on Hazel. Her head was buried in her hands, and her back shook. I wanted to reach out to her, to hold her hand like she had held mine so many times before.

The officers approached Hazel, guiding her to her feet to escort her out of the courtroom.

Dashing her hands against her cheeks, her eyes looked desperate for mine. When our gaze connected, she gave me a watery smile, mouthing, "Thank you."

"Love you, sis," I whispered as she was taken away.

Watching the officers lead her out, my heart fell. There was nothing left for me here. Not really.

"Am I still taking you to the airport?" Chuck asked.

When I turned to him, his caterpillar mustache was turned down. Was I doing the right thing?

"School already started this week, and they've had substitutes covering the class. They needed someone days ago."

Yesterday, I called my school district when I saw that a position in high school history had gone unfilled. They immediately contacted my former principal and by dinnertime had offered me the job.

The administrator asked, "How soon can you get here?"

So I bought a ticket last night and packed my bags. This didn't feel like the right decision, but I couldn't stay.

I nodded, too afraid to look him in the eye.

"Well, let's get you going then."

Chuck sighed, and I followed him out to his truck.

For miles, we sat in silence, cruising down the Pass.

My cell phone vibrated in my purse. I peeked inside, seeing it light up with another text notification from Jude.

"Did you tell him?" Chuck asked, glancing over at me.

I shook my head. "I didn't want to distract him from his fight."

Chuck grunted, his hand squeaking on the leather steering wheel. "You know you have a home at Thornbrush whenever you want to come back."

Tears stung my eyes and burned my throat. I stared out the windshield, the shaded road going blurry.

"Thank you, Chuck. I'm not sure what Jude wants, and maybe Jessica is it."

Chuck tapped on the breaks, slowing us around a curve, but his foot hit it a little too hard, jarring me forward before he eased back up. "Jessica? His publicist? You think he and Jessica are together?"

I chanced a glance at him now. His lips tipped up in a smirk that was so reminiscent of Jude's. My heart clenched—or what remained of it. I didn't want to be here when he returned. It would be like ripping open a wound and pouring acid onto it.

"Romy Miller, you are a smart, young woman, but one thing you unfortunately have learned is to always think the worst of people. I know your father didn't make it easy on you, neither did the kids at school—"

My mouth hung open. How did he know?

"Jude tells me everything. There is nothing that doesn't get past me. I can tell you two things—one, I've known Jude has been head over heels in love with you since he was fourteen, and two, he and Jessica would have never worked out."

"How … how …" I couldn't get the words out. Since he was fourteen? He and Jessica would have never worked out?

"Jude wants to build a life with someone, a family. He wants to be the dad he never had."

"He had you, Chuck." Those were the only words I could find. Deflecting, per usual.

"Yes, and he will always have me; we're family. But he also has you. He chose you to be his family a long time ago. He's just been hoping you'd also choose him."

I slumped into my seat, resting my elbow against the door. My head flopped, landing in my palm. He and Jessica would have never worked out? He wanted a family with me? He chose me? He wanted me to choose him?

Yet here I was, not choosing him again because my own damn heart felt that running was the only option to protect itself.

"So what's it going to be?" Uncle Chuck asked, passing beneath the airport sign as we hit the freeway.

CHAPTER 46
Jude

Inhale. Count to ten. Exhale. Count to ten. Inhale. Count to ten. Exhale.

The roar of the crowd rumbled the arena, pulsing through the locker room. Alex rubbed my arms and legs, keeping the blood flowing through my muscles while one of the organization's staff taped my hands.

My fight was next.

Charge like a bull. Fight like a bull. Stay on the ride, and don't let it buck you off.

It was the mantra I had on repeat every fight until I stepped into the cage.

"You're up, Larsen!" someone with headphones and a clipboard announced at the door of the locker room.

"This is it, man," Alex said, handing me my gloves.

I stood, adjusting my shorts one last time before pulling on the gloves.

I nodded, too busy trying to stay calm and focused to speak.

With my corner at my back, security on either side of me,

we walked down the dark hallway to the arena entrance. The din of the crowd grew, cheering for my opponent, who now waited for me in the cage.

I took one last, deep breath before the doors busted open.

The lights in the arena lowered, leaving a spotlight streaming across the crowd in anticipation of my entrance.

I waited, shifting in my shoes.

Then my walkout song, "Hooked on an 8 Second Ride" by Chris LeDoux, started to build until the electric guitar was blaring through the stadium speakers. The fans erupted. When the spotlight landed on me standing in the entrance, all I could hear was their screams.

The security in front of me started to move, and then we were walking toward the cage.

My vision tunneled, narrowing on Mike Reyes, who was jumping around in his corner, punching his fists in anticipation.

The distance to the cage felt like a mile while we followed the procession past arena seats, then around the press box where I spotted Jessica and the sportscasters. She gave me a subtle nod that said, "You got this." I returned a nod.

Fight staff and the ref met us at the steps of the cage. They checked my gloves and mouth guard before running a hand over my shoulders and arms to ensure I hadn't lathered up with Vaseline.

Alex was there, ready to shoot water into my mouth one last time and take my shoes before I jogged into the cage.

The announcer stepped into the middle, announcing Reyes as the challenger and me as the champion. The ref asked if we wanted to touch gloves, but I think we were both in the mindset that we'd rather just grind it out, so he directed us to our corners.

I continued to hop around, keeping my body warm while I focused on my breathing, dimming out the noise of the crowd to zero in on my coach in the corner.

"Stay loose. Remember your training. Focus on the ground and pound!" Alex was yelling from the other side of the cage.

I nodded, but I didn't take my eyes off Reyes. He was mean-mugging me while he hit his fist into his palm. I was ready to level that ego.

The ref stood between us, watching the clock. I brought my hands up to my fighting stance, shifting on the balls of my feet. Ready for this. Grinding my teeth into my mouth guard and breathing out through my nose, I waited like a windup toy ready to spring.

"Fight!" the ref yelled, his hand cutting down to signal the start of the round.

This was a championship fight. Five rounds. I needed to last five rounds. I wasn't going to push it in the first.

Reyes met me in the middle of the cage, his hands up. For the first few seconds, we both threw faints, testing one another. I wanted to see how far he would reach, what he intended to throw. Lowering my stance as we circled each other, knowing Reyes would take a higher stance as a Muay Thai fighter. He did just that, protecting his face while he threw a knee, thinking he could catch me beneath the chin.

Instead, I faked a shoot. Assuming I was going for a single-leg takedown, Reyes threw a knee. I grabbed it. Taking him down against the cage.

Reyes immediately threw up his guard, and I started raining down fists. I knew I didn't want to gas out with four rounds still ahead of us, but I wanted to hurt him enough to wobble his confidence. He needed to be knocked down a few notches, be reminded why I was the champ and that I had the experience to back that up.

Reyes threw up his arms to protect himself. He crunched forward as if he was trying to sit up. I threw another punch, but he wrapped his hands around my left wrist in a kimura lock.

Shit!

I could barely hear Alex yelling in my corner over the rumble of the arena.

I did as I was trained, grabbing ahold of my shorts with my left hand to battle against the lock. If he got this, he could crank my arm behind my back and rip my shoulder to shreds.

I buried my right arm beneath Reyes's head, holding on for dear life to keep him from locking up my arm. I think he realized he wasn't going to pull it because he shrimped out of position, creating distance to get us back up on our feet to face each other.

Deep breaths. Adrenaline pumped through me. I felt good. Strong.

I charged forward, throwing a flurry of one-two-one combinations. He caught one on his cheek, opening him up.

The cut seeped red.

That's when I backed him up against the cage.

Reyes covered up while I continued forward.

I barely saw it coming … Reyes was already swinging a Muay Thai round kick. It landed just above my right knee—

the knee with too many surgeries. Biting back a scream, I crumpled.

Reyes saw the opening to take me down, rushing forward to capitalize on my hurt.

The bell rang.

Saved by the fucking bell.

"Fuck." I grimaced, pushing myself up.

Hobbling to my corner, Alex pushed me down on the stool.

"My knee is dead." The knee I'd spent months recuperating.

"Ice," Alex ordered the rest of our corner.

Holding an ice pack to my knee, he knelt in front of me. Someone else in my corner pressed ice to my chest and neck.

"You caught him, Jude. Hold that ground and pound. Get off that knee and circle away from his power," Alex coached. "Circle away from those kicks."

Round two began with me shuffling forward, but I was slow.

My knee was killing me, and I really hoped I didn't just ruin the surgeon's work.

Reyes charged, throwing a teep kick, the ball of his foot jabbing me right in the solar plexus. The wind left me in a whoosh.

Fuck. Fuck. Fuck. This guy is relentless.

I allowed Reyes to back me up against the cage, buying myself time to recover. He began throwing combos, while I covered up to catch my breath. My head was down, my arms up to protect against the blows. Reyes's leg was open for the takedown.

Now was the time. Recovered enough, I went for a single-leg takedown.

With my arms wrapped around his leg, he was hopping on one foot.

It didn't stop him from punching the side of my head. Each hit reverberated pain through my skull. I had to give it to him; the kid had incredible balance. Hopping on his right leg, he was still able to knee me in the face, opening a cut above my eye.

Now I was the one seeping red.

I needed to abandon the takedown for now.

I backed away. Reyes went in for a flurry. He may have thought he had me, but the blood dripping in my eye only focused my rage. I was known for charging in, so I did just that.

I charged him, using the double-leg takedown, swooping him up in a fireman's carry over my shoulder. The years of carrying calves over my shoulders was paying off. I carried him over to my corner, right where I wanted to be, and slammed him hard to the ground. Scrambling, I threw myself on top in a side mount.

"Go in for a big elbow!" Alex yelled.

I ground into Reyes's face, throwing elbows. His nose crunched, and I knew I broke it. Reyes tried to buck out of my mount. But I kept pummeling. Cuts oozed above his eyes, and his cheeks sliced open.

But Reyes didn't stop bucking. The slippery bastard bucked until he could sneak out the back. We scrambled back to our feet, tired and bloody, right when the bell rang.

I don't know how I got back to my corner. My ears were

ringing. Alex said something. My vision was narrowing. My eye was swelling. I could taste blood but was unsure of its source.

Grabbing my face, Alex yelled at me. *What was he saying?*

He continued to yell at me until the humming started to settle.

"What's five plus three?" Alex asked.

"Eight."

"All right!" Alex grinned. *Why the hell is he grinning? Am I winning?* "Avoid knees. Avoid kicks. Stick with the ground and pound. That side mount was excellent. Keep looking for takedowns. He's hurt. I want you to capitalize on that."

I barely noticed someone icing my face and stuffing Vaseline into a cut.

"You got this, Jude!" Alex exclaimed before hurrying to the corner out of the cage.

I returned to my feet, approaching the center. I barely noticed the ref announcing the third round, my sole focus on Reyes.

I hobbled, protecting my right leg. It ached like a son of a bitch.

Reyes kicked out a few lower leg kicks, but none of them landed. They were just empty threats. But they accomplished what they intended. His kicks made me nervous enough to back away from him.

Reyes unleashed a big, sweeping leg kick, but when he swung into it, he gave me his back. My training knew this opening. I grabbed him from the back, wrapping my arms around him. And in one great, arcing motion, from my toes to my arms, I threw another slam. Reyes landed on the ground on his head and shoulders.

"He's dazed!" I heard Alex yell.

Reyes attempted to roll away from me, but I pounced, raining blows down on him.

Call it, ref. I was silently pleading as I landed punch after punch.

I wanted it to be over. I could feel my adrenaline draining. I was so damn tired. I couldn't keep this up for another two rounds. This needed to end here.

"Arm bar!" my whole corner is yelling now. At least, I think it's my corner.

I switched positions to get the arm bar, but Reyes started sitting up into guard, throwing his knee to my tailbone. I hissed in pain. The sting reverberated up my back.

Before I realized it, Reyes opened my guard and slid his left knee over my right to put me in half guard.

This wasn't good.

I was just so tired. I panted, trying to regain my breath, any remnant of strength. I could go all day rustling cattle, riding horses, and stacking hay, but that was because I loved the ranch. I loved my home. I didn't love this anymore. It wasn't worth the blood, sweat, and tears. Even if she wasn't there waiting for me. I wanted to go home.

"Get out of there, Jude!" I was so tired, I even thought I heard her voice yelling at me through the noise.

Chapter 47

Romy

"Jude!" I yelled, running down the stadium steps to get as close to the action as possible.

The crowd screamed and cried around me, but all I saw was blood dripping everywhere and Jude pinned to the ground.

"Miss, you can't go down there." Security stepped in front of me right when I reached the front row of seats. Seats left for celebrities, family, sponsors, the press. My last-minute ticket was only for general admission.

As soon as I had checked in and saw a Las Vegas flight flying out at the same time, I knew what I had to do. Instead of running away, I needed to run to him.

With a ticket to Las Vegas in hand, and a call to the school district to say I was no longer accepting the position, I chose him.

Once I landed, I told my Uber driver to take me to the MGM. When I got there, Summer Fight Night was well under way. There was no time to waste. I plowed into that arena with a mission, but now I was stuck between a security guard and the front-row spectators.

There was nothing I could do but watch him. I shuffled on my feet, itching to reach Jude. To show him that I was here. That he could win this fight.

"Alex!" I hollered, seeing him yelling through the cage. But he didn't hear me. He was solely focused on Jude.

Jude's arm was in Mike Reyes's grasp as it snaked through to grab Jude's wrist.

"Shit," I said under my breath. "Get out of there, Jude!" I was screaming now.

Jude attempted to lean forward, pushing to sit up, but instead, his arm slipped behind his back.

I covered my gasp.

There was nowhere for Jude to go; his right arm was trapped under Reyes's back.

Jude's arm was going to rip out of its socket.

"Shit. Shit. Shit," was all I could say.

And then Jude's yelling, "Tap! Tap!"

The ref rushed in. Reyes pushed away from Jude and started running around the cage, yelling in victory.

Jude could barely rise to his feet.

"Now the new light-heavyweight champion, Mike 'Savage' Reyes!" The announcer's voice echoed through the arena.

The ref held up Reyes's arm, while Mr. Venture buckled the championship belt around his waist. Reyes was bloody, veins popping in his forehead as he yelled in excitement.

The crowd lost it.

But all I could think about was getting to Jude.

"Alex!" I yelled again, hoping he could hear me. But the

crowd was deafening.

I barely even heard the sportscaster interview Reyes from the cage. Jude was being checked out in his corner, and that's all I cared about.

Then it was Jude's turn to be interviewed. He limped to the sportscaster holding the mic. The moment he submitted replayed on the jumbotron.

"What went wrong?" The sportscaster shoved the mic in Jude's face.

Jude shrugged, panting through his words. "Reyes proved he was the better fighter tonight. He earned that belt."

The arena was quiet in reverence for the longtime champ. All I could do was hold my breath.

"I want to thank my team, my coach. We worked hard, even with a short camp."

He took in a big, steadying breath, as if to hold back emotion.

"Sometimes you need to lose some to win some." He gripped Alex's shoulder, who stood beside him. "I feel like a winner tonight because I know now what I want is back home." His voice cracked with his last words.

I covered a sob with my hand.

"Does this mean you're retiring?" the sportscaster asked.

"I have no issue stepping aside and letting someone else have the spotlight, especially if they've earned it, and Reyes showed us all today that he earned this title."

Jude tore off his gloves. The arena hushed, waiting for him to say more. But he said nothing.

Only quietly set his gloves on the mat and walked out, his

corner following behind him.

The silence evaporated on a wave, cheers and hollers crescendoing against the dome of the arena.

"Jude 'The Bull' Larsen, ladies and gentlemen!" The sportscaster's voice echoed through the sound system. "Stepping down as the champ and retiring as one of the best light-heavyweights in the sport of MMA."

"Sir, please," I pleaded with the security guard. "I'm Jude's girlfriend."

"Sure, missy," he scoffed.

"Alex! Alex!" I yelled again, trying to get his attention before he took off with Jude.

Jude was already plowing his way through the crowd to exit the arena.

"Are you Romy Miller?" came a familiar female voice in front of the security guard.

I looked past him to see a beautiful, dark-haired woman dressed in a neat pantsuit and wearing a VIP badge. I recognized her from the press conference. Jessica. I hesitated for just a moment before remembering what Chuck told me.

"Yes, please, I need to get through."

She nodded, extending her arm past the security guard. "Let her through."

The security guard raised a brow to Jessica.

"She's Jude Larsen's girlfriend." Jessica had a hard, no-nonsense edge to her voice, as if she dared you to contradict her. It was all the confirmation I needed that Jude chose me. Maybe I didn't need to hate her after all.

The security guard stepped to the side, letting me pass.

"Come on. I'll take you to him." Jessica put her hand on my back, helping me navigate through the crowd.

Jude sat on an exam table in the locker room. A doctor cleaned up his cut and ran through concussion protocols. Alex held an ice pack to his knee.

"What day is it?" the doctor asked.

"Friday," Jude responded.

The doctor nodded, holding a thick swab on the gash above Jude's left eye.

I pushed forward, past staff, teammates, and other fighters mulling around the locker room.

"Jude!" I screamed, getting through the crowd.

He flinched when he turned toward my voice, his eyes going wide when they landed on me.

"Romy!" He tried to jump off the table, but the doctor and Alex pushed him back to his seat.

"Don't get up," I told him.

Alex stepped to the side so I could stand beside him. I gripped Jude's still-taped hand, red with Reyes's blood.

"What are you doing here?"

"I couldn't miss this. I had to be here for you."

"Why didn't you answer my calls? There's nothing between Jessica and me. I know she answered my phone when you called, and I can explain everything." He said it as though he knew I had to hear it.

"I know. I'm so sorry. I got in my head, and I got scared you didn't want me."

His bruised and swollen eyes sharpened. "I'll always want you."

"I know that now," I croaked through a lump in my throat.

"What about the hearing?"

"It recessed early, and Chuck made sure I could get here for you."

"I'm going to need to stitch this up," the doctor interrupted.

Jude gave him a brief nod. "Hold my hand?" he asked me.

My eyes teared. "Always."

He gave me that lopsided smirk, a little lazy with his fatigue, and despite his swollen, red eye, he was still the sexiest man I'd ever seen.

"Love you," he mouthed while the doctor started stitching him up.

"Love you," I whispered back.

My chest constricted, overwhelmed with love and the need to ease his pain.

"I'm so proud of you, babe," I told him.

"Don't move," the doctor cautioned through a smirk.

As soon as the doctor tied up the stitch and snipped it, Jude was off the table. He gripped my hands.

"I want to hug you, but I'm gross."

I tentatively raised a hand to brush a damp lock from his brow.

"I don't care. Just kiss me." I pushed up on my tiptoes. His hands, rough with tape and calluses, gently held my face as we pressed our lips together. So soft. So gentle. But so full of promises. Of forever.

"I'm ready to go home," he mumbled against my lips.

We closed our eyes, our foreheads gently resting together. The locker room faded away as we absorbed each other's touch. I gripped the waistband of his shorts. I wanted nothing more than to take him home—to Thornbrush—and take care of him.

"Me too. Let's go home."

CHAPTER 48
Romy

"I need to get ready to go," I muttered into the crook of Jude's neck.

"Not yet," Jude insisted, thrusting his sweatpants-clad boner against me.

"Jude." I giggled at the mischievous glint in his eyes. The swelling had diminished substantially around his left eye, but it was still black and blue, tape still covering his stitches.

His hands gripped my hips, holding me still on top of the kitchen counter. We had barely finished breakfast before he pushed the plates aside and lifted me up. He ran his rough fingertips up the inside of my thigh before they could skim the hem of my sleep shorts. It tickled, making me suck in a breath.

"You're lucky I'm not always jumping your bones in these tiny shorts. The fact that you don't wear panties underneath is just asking for it." His voice was still raspy with sleep. Sexy.

"Gotta let myself breath," I explained.

Jude hummed, pressing kisses along my jaw, his hand inching closer. My walls clenched in anticipation.

"Let me help you air out some more, then," he murmured

against my pulse.

My eyes flicked to the clock on the stove. "I have an hour before I need to lead a trail ride."

"Lina can lead one more without you."

For the last two days since returning to Willows, we had been holed up in the house while Jude recovered from his fight. All we'd been doing was sleeping, bathing, eating, and despite his aches and pains—fucking. Well, it was mostly me climbing on top of him and riding him until we were both satiated. I hadn't wanted him to do much of the lifting. It was a nice change of pace, being in charge in the bedroom and telling him what a good boy he was in staying still. Apparently, we're still learning things about each other because I had no idea Jude had as much of a praise kink, as he loved doling it out.

He was still limping around, his thigh blacker and bluer than his eye, but alternating ice and heat was helping his recovery, not to mention the dozens of packs of supplements the man consumed regularly.

Chuck insisted he take it easy, but I could tell Jude was restless, itching to pull his weight around the ranch. Feeling bad that he was making Jude sit out, Chuck relented to the indoor arena's renovation. Jude didn't waste any time calling his architect and contractor to get the ball rolling.

Next, he said he wanted to build us a house. He already had a place in mind on the property, but he wouldn't tell me—not until the plans were drawn up. It was worth letting him keep that secret, seeing the big grin on his face and the sparkle in his aqua eyes.

"She's going to kill Reed if she has to go on one more trail ride with him," I told him, cupping my hands on his stubbled jaw.

Jude groaned, gripping my hips to set me back down on my feet. I groaned, immediately regretting that I had to get back to work.

He rubbed his hips against me one more time. "Just so you know, you're killing me."

"Babe, I've already been on my knees for you this morning while you fucked my throat. Was that not enough for you?" I giggled, running my hand down his hardness.

He pouted. "Not nearly enough."

It was the cutest pout I'd ever seen, and it made my heart gallop. I wanted nothing more than to go back to bed with him, but there was work to be done.

"I bet it wasn't enough for you, either." His fingers bit into my waist. He rolled his hips, his hardened cock pushing into my belly. "I bet if I put a hand in your shorts, it'd come away soaked. Are you wet for me, honey?"

God, he knew exactly how to break down my resolve. "Always." My voice came out breathy with desire. *Damn it.* He got me.

His lip quirked, and his hands lifted my pajama shirt off before sliding his hand past my waistband. His fingers ran down my lower belly, causing me to inhale sharply. Achingly slow, he moved his hand. I hitched my knee, widening my stance to allow him access. Tantalizingly softly, he ran his fingers through my warm, throbbing center. I was already drenched. He spread my wetness, passing over my clit once and then twice before stroking gentle circles.

He leaned down. His mouth taking mine, his lips melding perfectly until he could suck and tug my bottom lip. I moaned into his mouth.

"That's my girl," he whispered against my lips. "You've been taking such good care of me. It's my turn to take care of you."

"Okay, but we have to make it quick." I was already close with the torturous circles he was rubbing. I just needed him inside me, and I'd explode.

"You need a fast fuck?"

He didn't wait for my answer. He pulled his hand away from between my legs. I barely had time to whine before he spun me, pushing my chest down against the counter.

"*Jude*," I breathed, grasping the cool surface and peeking over my shoulder.

He ran a possessive hand down my spine before hooking his fingers into my waistband.

"You better hold on, honey."

Jude pulled my shorts down my thighs, his hands massaging the globes of my ass as he came back up before taking himself out of his sweatpants. He was already so thick and hard, a bead of precum glistened at the head as he pumped his cock in his hand. I licked my lips, remembering just how good he tasted.

"You already tasted me this morning. It's my turn." He knelt behind me.

"Jude, your knee."

"Shh, honey. I want to taste you."

My reply was cut off when Jude parted my cheeks, burying his face in my pussy to run his tongue down my slit. My breath caught.

"Fuck, you taste so good." His voice vibrated against my core, making me want to press my thighs together, but Jude held me open with his strong grip.

His tongue thrust into me, and I bucked. It felt like a tease, a whisper of him penetrating me.

"Jude, *please*."

"What." Lick. "Do." Tongue thrust. I was getting desperate for him. "You." Lick. "Want?"

"I want you to fuck me," I pleaded, grinding against his face to ease the building tension.

"Mmm, that's my dirty girl. You want both of your holes full of me today?" His mouth left me, and he rose to his feet. The cool air against my damp flesh sent goose bumps across my skin, despite the heat coursing through me. I splayed my hands on the countertop, my aroused and sensitive nipples pressed into the chilled quartz.

"Just one thing." Jude leaned over, his dick brushing against my ass as he reached for something on the counter.

"*Jude*," I whined.

"You're already sweet, honey …" My breath caught when I felt something silky and cool drizzle across my ass and drip down between my cheeks. "But you're about to become a whole lot sweeter."

He held my hips steady, leaning down to run his tongue over my heated skin. I moaned with him when his tongue trailed down, swirling my tight hole.

"So fucking sweet." His words came out a rumble, dancing across my skin, sending shivers up my spine.

He lapped up the honey before straightening behind me.

His thumb massaged my tight, little rosebud while Jude lined up the head of his cock with my entrance.

"Take a deep breath, honey, because this will be anything but gentle."

I was so ready for him. And in one thrust, he was buried deep while his thumb filled me. I moaned against my arm. So full. So incredibly full.

Jude gripped my hip, pulling me against him with each quick thrust. The kitchen filled with the sound of slapping flesh and our heady moans as he fucked me.

At this angle, bent over on the counter, he felt impossibly deep. Every ridge and vein of his cock rubbed against the walls of my core, the addition of his thumb intensifying the sensation.

"You feel so good," I moaned.

With his other hand, he slapped my ass, sending a hot sting through my pussy. I clenched. I was so close already.

"I'm going to come, babe," I told him. "Don't fucking stop."

He didn't stop, only increasing his speed.

"Come for me. Make that pretty cunt soak my cock," he encouraged.

He pumped in and out of my pussy as if he were running a race, pushing to the finish line. I could feel myself dripping down my leg. Everything was pulsing. My grip tightened on the counter. His thrusts became erratic and stilted. He was close.

"Fuck, honey," he breathed, pumping into me. He continued to glide in and out, even while his cum filled me.

The pulse of his cock inside shot waves of pleasure through

me. I rocked against him and his thumb. Wanting it all. Needing it all.

"*Jude!* " I howled, my walls gripping him so hard on my orgasm that he could do nothing but stay embedded inside me.

He groaned, collapsing on my back. Our chests heaved. He gently removed his thumb, caressing my sides while we came down from our climax. My pussy continued to throb around him, milking him. I could feel him twitch inside me, and I reached a hand around to grip his side, wanting nothing more than to keep him right there. Buried deep inside me. Forever.

"Now I don't want to go," I complained, my cheek still pressed to the cold counter.

Jude chuckled. "That was part of my plan all along." His breath coasted through my hair.

"Jude."

"You're right. I don't think we need any more murders on the ranch."

"Jude!"

"What? Too soon?" The vibration of his laugh filtered through me.

"Yeah, too soon."

Even though, when we returned home, we received word Hazel was being released on bail to Sanctuary Ranch so she could begin healing until her next court appearance.

He wrapped his arm around my middle, helping me stand up. My legs wobbled, my blood still rushing to my core while he slowly backed out of me. I bit back a whine in protest.

"You're right. Let's clean you up so you can go save Lina from Reed." Jude went over to the sink, wetting a towel before tenderly wiping us both clean.

"I could be saving Reed from Lina."

Jude winced. "That girl sure knows how to hold a grudge."

I hummed in agreement, brushing my fingers through his soft hair.

"Ride out to our spot with me later?" he asked, pulling my shorts back up.

"I'm not sure you should be riding with your leg. Also, since when has it become *our* spot?" I smiled up at him.

"Since I made love to you in the dirt and watched you glow with the sunset." He held my face, his thumbs stroking my cheeks. I could feel my heart melt all over for him. "Please, I have something I want to show you."

His eyes pleaded with me. He looked at me with such love and affection. Damn, he was cute! It was so hard to say no to him. Not when I could so easily make him happy with one word.

"Fine." I sighed. "But you're elevating and icing that knee until then."

"Yes, ma'am." He dropped a peck on my nose and pulled me into one more embrace.

He buried his nose in my hair, and I inhaled his scent, memorizing it, hoping it would last on the trail until he could hold me again.

"You need to close your eyes," Jude directed as he helped me off Winnie.

We had ridden out to the burn pile right when the sun

was setting. The day had been blistering hot, and a forest fire burned south from us, causing the sunset to glow a vibrant orange through the haze. A warm breeze lifted the sweaty locks that had escaped my braid. I was tired from riding all day, but Jude looked so hopeful and excited—promising he'd been off his legs all day—that I easily caved.

"Don't be a brat. Close your eyes," he ordered when I hadn't done it the first time.

"Fine."

He took my hands, pulling me to walk with him. He walked backward while I stepped forward, my eyes springing open when my foot rolled on a rock.

"Don't let me fall."

"Never. Trust me. Close your eyes."

I relented, shutting them. Because I did trust him not to let me fall. To pick me up if I stumbled.

He guided me as I took careful steps past the burn pile until I knew we were getting closer to the cliff where it overlooked the Deschutes toward the hills and valleys.

"Stand right here." We paused in our steps. Jude's hands went to my shoulders, positioning me where he wanted me to stand.

"Can I open my eyes?"

Jude dropped his hands from my arms, the light shifting beneath my lids as he stepped to the side.

"Okay. You can open your eyes."

I opened them, staring at Jude. His eyes were bright and expectant, taking me in before flicking to the ground.

I lowered my gaze. There, on the ground, laid out flat, rocks holding down each corner, was a large, paper blueprint. It was an exterior drawing of a two-story house, wrapped by a covered porch and a pitched roof with large, triangular windows.

"What's this?"

"Our home," he said, his voice thick with emotion and maybe a little fear.

With a worried lip, he flipped his hat backward. He was nervous about this surprise. Unsure if it would scare me, if it would be too much, make me retreat, like I was in the habit of doing.

I didn't blame him for being afraid. I had put it there. I wanted nothing more than to drown that fear. To flood him with my love until he believed, to his very core, that he was worthy of it. To prove to him that I was no longer dodging what we had. I would never run again.

"Jude, I ... I think it's perfect," I told him, beaming up at him. My heart pounded.

"Yeah?" His face broke out in a smile.

"Yeah. Where are we going to build it?"

"Right here. Where we can watch the sunset, and I can watch you glow."

"Oh, babe, it's absolutely perfect." Tears welled up in my eyes and stung my nose.

Jude stepped into me, cupping my face.

"It's perfect," I repeated on a whisper.

"You're perfect. I just love you so much, honey."

I closed my eyes. His nose brushed along mine, inching toward my mouth. I tipped my head, offering myself to him. Letting him capture my lips with his.

And I let him catch me.

EPILOGUE

Jude

SIX MONTHS LATER

"Do you think it will be done in time?" Romy asked, rubbing gloved hands over her belly. You could barely see the swell beneath her heavy Carhartt jacket.

She looked beautiful, standing here in our spot, surrounded by dirt and snow, her hair pulled back in a braid, a bright-pink, knitted beanie poised low over her ears and sunglasses reflecting the winter sun. I didn't know she could become even more beautiful, but now she glowed like the fucking sun.

Her breath puffed into the frosty air awaiting my answer.

I studied the wooden frame of our future home, the cacophony of hammers, drills, and table saws making it difficult to believe it could get done. There was still so much to do before June. I had promised Romy we could move in before the baby was born, before the wedding we planned to have right here beneath a Thornbrush sunset.

"It will be." I would make sure of it. Even if it meant

working through every weekend until spring.

"Where am I going to have my bonfires now?" Lina grumped behind us, mourning the loss of the burn pile, now leveled by the bulldozer.

I turned to look over my shoulder to see her kicking a rock with the toe of her boot.

"Don't worry, I'm putting in a firepit. I already ordered some 'Lina proof' chairs to go around it," I said with a wink.

"What the hell does that mean?" Lina sassed back.

"Some Adirondack chairs, the kind you can't fall out of."

The sass quickly vanished, my little cousin's face brightened, running to me to throw her arms around my neck.

"You're the best, cuz! I don't care what people say about you. Thank you! But you know that means your house is going to become party central."

I laughed. I wasn't about to disappoint her, and my chest swelled with warmth. I wanted to fill this house. Even with the big house where Uncle Chuck lived, I wanted this to be the place where everyone gathered. I wanted it to always be busy, full of noise and laughter and little feet running across wood floors. All my friends on a Friday night by the fire shootin' the shit, maybe even have some fighters up here, too.

"Wouldn't want it any other way," I told her, squeezing her.

"Damn, you've been busy," Christian called, coming around the back of the house. He hadn't seen it since October, when we first laid the foundation. "In more ways than one," he teased, nodding his chin at Romy.

I pulled Romy into my side, dropping a kiss on her head.

"Busy, but happy," Romy agreed, smiling up at me.

Christian got a wistful look, pushing his cowboy hat up to scratch his brow. "I want your happy one day."

"You'll find it, bro," I consoled.

"I just need to break down her defenses," he said, his eyes flicking to Sage, who picked her way around the snow-covered rocks and sagebrush, following her new little puppy, Arlo, around.

He was a rescue. We speculated a mix—half Australian cattle dog and half Siberian husky.

"I don't know, man," I said. "You may need to hang up your hat with that one."

Sage Pardy was a tough nut to crack. She seemed as though she had walls two miles high. Rarely sharing about her personal life. Romy and Lina had grown close to her over the last few months, though, and she was always friendly. At least to me. Christian still annoyed her.

"He may be right," Romy confirmed.

Arlo's happy tail wagged, his nose skimming the ground, probably getting a good whiff of cow and horse manure. His short legs pranced through the snow. He was pretty cute. Maybe after everything slowed down, I could convince Romy to get a dog.

The pup turned, bounding toward us, straight to Christian's feet. Arlo circled, sniffing his boots, until he started jumping up on his legs.

Christian chuckled, bending down to pick up the puppy. His tail wagged faster, and he wiggled into his grasp, darting out a tongue to lick Christian's jaw.

"At least Arlo loves me," Christian bemoaned.

Sage crossed her arms. "Traitor," she huffed. "Does anyone want to puppysit tonight? I have a shift."

The engine of an ATV cut through the afternoon. Reed at the wheel, pulling a trailerful of salvaged wood from the old arena.

"You know I would," Lina said.

"Where do you want these, boss?" Reed asked.

At the same time, Lina announced, "But I have a date."

My gaze flew to her. "You have a date?"

Lina rolled her eyes. "Believe me, I already heard it from Dad. I don't need to hear it from you, too."

I could almost hear the click of Reed's jaw from where he killed the engine. His eyes bore into Lina.

"He's a really nice boy," Romy said, patting my chest, drawing my attention back to her. "I met him at the coffee shop the other day."

"He's not a *boy*, he's my age, and his name is Jones. And he's a bronc rider. You know how I feel about bronc riders." She fanned herself, her eyes flicking over to where Reed stepped off the vehicle.

"What kind of name is Jones?" My brows rose. Lina was always going after the wild ones, but if Romy said he was nice, I suppose I could be chill.

"Fucking broncs," Reed grumbled. I chuckled into Romy's shoulder at Reed's pissy attitude.

Romy elbowed me in the side.

"He goes by his last name, okay. Quit with the grilling." Lina scowled.

"I'll watch him," Christian cut in, still letting the pup

slather him with kisses.

"Like you know the first thing about dogs," Sage chastised.

"Actually, I do." His broad shoulders straightened. "My parents breed Norwegian elkhounds."

"Shit, that's right." I had almost forgotten about that. Christian's folks owned a farm closer to town. They had a few horses, but they primarily bred elkies. They'd done it for years and were successful. There were very few elkhound breeders in the Pacific Northwest, and they made excellent hunting and family dogs.

"I don't think your apartment allows dogs." Sage was trying to find every reason not to let Christian puppysit.

"Then I can come to you." Christian wasn't backing down. His eyes shone with hope.

"You're going to stay with him at my place until three in the morning?" Sage asked, her brows raised in question and surprise.

"Why not? The little guy would probably be more comfortable in his own home anyway." Christian snuggled the pup closer.

Sage shifted on her feet, and we all waited. This may be Christian's in. I wanted nothing more than to see my buddy happy.

He mimicked Arlo's cute puppy eyes.

"Fine." She threw up her hands, seeing all of us watching her. "It's your loss of sleep."

Christian's grin took up his whole face, his dimples popping and his eyes crinkling. "I already lose sleep over you, baby. What's one more night?"

"Ugh!" Sage growled. "And then he goes and says stupid shit like that. Don't make me regret this, or you'll never get puppysitting duties again."

Christian pressed his lips together, biting back his smile.

Romy and I turned into each other, trying to hide our own smiles.

"Where do you want these, boss?" Reed asked again, hoisting one of the beams as if they weighed nothing. The man was a fucking beast.

"Just in the garage would be fine." I gestured to the nearly finished three-car garage. I was planning on using the old beams to accent the vaulted ceilings.

He eyed Lina again as he walked past, a look that if I didn't know any better meant only one thing—he wanted her. But it was quickly masked with animosity. If looks could kill, her returning glare would have had him six feet under. I could feel my own protective instincts gather in my fists. I wasn't bound to a contract anymore, and if I ever needed to, I wouldn't mind putting them back to use.

Noticing me watching them, Romy gripped my hand, intertwining my fingers with hers as if to say everything was okay.

She pressed up on her toes, her mouth brushing the shell of my ear. "I bet by the end of the year, we'll be planning more than one wedding."

"Yeah, right. I'm not letting my cousin marry some dipshit named Jones."

Romy giggled, kissing me again. "Oh, babe. It's a good thing you're so hot."

Keep Reading for a Sneak Peek from Book Two of the
Thornbrush Ranch Series...
BURN THE BREEZE

PROLOGUE

Lina

H e was fucking me—*with his eyes*. Eyes that were dark and shadowed beneath a black cowboy hat. The rowdy Saddle Room bar at the Joseph Round-Up pumped classic country music over the inebriated shouts and laughter of the crowd. The bass reverberated through the soles of my boots, traveling up my bare legs, until it settled in my core. It almost felt like the cowboy who bit at his lip while he watched me was humming right into my cunt. Thick hands picked up the glass of whiskey off the bar top, bringing it to his lips. Hands that I could imagine wrapping around my throat. He sipped, his gaze locked on me. And it felt like he was sipping *me*.

"Are we getting a tattoo or what?" Viv asked, nudging my shoulder.

"You're seriously going to do that?" Kale Pardy asked, reaching over me to slam his token on the bar.

"How do ya want it?" the bartender asked.

"Neat," Kale stated matter-of-factly.

Vivian Kelly, my only barrel racing friend—because the rest were competition—was always up to get fucking trashed with me.

"Actually," I said, eyeing my cowboy on the other side of the bartop, "give that to me." I held out my hand and Viv slapped the temporary Saddle Room logo tattoo into my turned up palm.

"Oh, I see." Viv smirked, following my gaze.

Even among the bustling rodeo crowd, he seemed large. Wide set shoulders, corded arms that proved he was used to throwing calves over his shoulders—I'd let him throw me. A trim dark beard covered his square jaw. He looked older than what I typically went for, edgy and rugged. I bet he had more experience than any of the boys I've slept with. And I was tired of playing with *boys*. I needed a *man*. A man who could match me in my hidden desires, who was willing to push boundaries I had yet to explore.

His tongue darted out to lick his fuckable lips as if tasting the whiskey left there. Oh, how I'd love to taste that whiskey. Neon beer signs on the wall behind him glowed like a beacon, telling me to come hither. I felt like a moth being drawn to the fire, but I didn't care if he burned me. I'd let myself burn to ashes just to have that man touch me.

The bartender set Kale's whiskey on the bar. Before he could grab it, I swiped it up, knocking it back until every drop slid down my throat. That burn so fucking good—coursing down my throat, spreading it's warmth to my limbs, my breasts, my belly, and between my legs, until even my toes tingled in my boots.

"Hey! You fucking serious?" Kale exclaimed, looking aghast.

I shoved the glass into his chest.

"I'm in love, Kale."

Smoldering eyes, darkened by his cowboy hat, traced the curve of my breasts in my tight tank top. It felt like he was trailing a finger over my skin, dipping into my cleavage and circling my tits. His gaze traveled over my long legs as I stepped away from my friends and pushed through the crowd. I felt like I was swimming with the current, floating on a cloud, moving in slow motion toward him, while his eyes did not stop devouring me.

I stepped into his space, the shadows giving way to a handsome face, dark brown eyes that were warm and full of desire. A perfect strong nose and full lips that tipped in a lazy smile.

Cologne that smelled like sandalwood and leather hit me like a gust of wind. My breath hitched. Music pounded in my ears, but the noise of the crowd seemed to fade into the distance.

So this is what love at fucking first sight feels like?

I took a bold step closer, my toes bumping his boots, then another step until I was nearly pressing my body against his.

"You new here, cowboy?" I asked looking up at him, my hand going to his belt buckle, drawing him closer until he was pressed against me. The heat and hardness of this very large man felt so damn good against my soft skin.

"I've been around." His voice was husky and deep, a rasp to it that was fucking sexy. What I wouldn't do to hear this man tell me to "beg" and "be a good girl?"

I brushed my fingertips down the cold metal of his belt buckle, over the zipper of his jeans. I could feel the stiff bulge in his pants. Good Lord! This man was huge!

I wrapped my hand over his dick, gripping it through his jeans, just as the Saddle Room tradition demands, claiming him as mine.

He hissed through his teeth, his cock twitching in my grasp. I smirked, feeling powerful and in control. This man was going to be mine all night long.

"I was hoping you could help me with something?" I asked, holding up my other palm with the temporary tattoo.

"Yeah?" his fingertips trailed up my arms, sending shivers in their wake. "Where do you want it?"

I brushed my wavy brown hair off my shoulder and stood taller, revealing the top of my cleavage. His gaze followed my movement.

"I was thinking it should go right above my heart."

His smile grew slightly, a mischievous light flickering in his dark orbs.

"We need to get it wet first." His voice rumbled against my skin.

I pushed my tits against his chest, offering myself to him.

He set his hat on the bar beside his drink. His breath danced across my skin and I could smell the smoky sweetness of whiskey. His eyes held mine as he wrapped his large hands around my waist, holding me still while he dipped his head. I arched toward him and his lips brushed against the sensitive skin of my breast, his stubble scrapping deliciously across the swell. My lungs sucked in air to keep myself grounded. His fingers dug into my hips.

Slowly, torturously, his tongue swirled, his mouth opening to suck me in. God, I hoped this man fucking bruised me. I hope he left his mark beneath the tattoo. His mouth pulled and sucked at my skin, drawing me in. Each pull of his mouth was like a fucking tether to my clit. Each pull and pulse shot waves of pleasure to my pussy. I closed my eyes, the heady buzz of the whiskey making this feel like he was fucking me right here under the red glow of the neon. I rocked my hips against him, his cock bucking into my stomach.

I panted, my pussy pulsed. His mouth sucked. It felt like he was sucking me dry.

"I want you to fuck me," I breathed out. I don't know if I thought it or said it out loud.

But I think I said it aloud, because he answered with another thrust of his cock against my belly, his tongue darting out to soothe the skin he had most likely marked.

He pulled away. Cool air danced across my flesh where he had latched to me. His eyes held mine, now almost black with need.

Fuck, I think I did say it out loud.

He let go of my waist, but he did not step away from where we stood against each other. Peeling the plastic off the tattoo, he put pressure on it. His hand was so large it nearly covered my whole breast. I watched my chest quickly rise and fall beneath his palm. His deeply tanned skin complimenting my golden tan, his rough and calloused, mine soft and supple.

His gaze flicked back to mine, holding me there, piercing

into my very soul. All I could hear was our heaving breaths, my blood pumping in my ears, and the subtle hum of the bar disappearing into the distance.

"Come back to my place."

He didn't have to ask or demand it. I would have followed him anywhere. He could have led me into the bathroom and I would have spread my legs for him.

Author's Note

After the release of my debut *I'll Come to You*, I needed a palette cleanser. My first book was such a labor of love, peeling back every scab and helping me heal from trauma, that I needed something fun and exciting to write. However, life happens when you make plans.

Sometimes you receive a phone call you least expect, and it changes *everything*.

ACKNOWLEDGMENTS

How lucky am I to be surrounded by so many amazing cheerleaders and supporters? Just like they say "it takes a village to raise a child," it truly takes a *book nation* to create a book. The success of *Among the Willows* would have never been possible without everyone's belief in me and this book.

First and foremost, my husband, Kenny. Thank you, babe, for believing in me, for encouraging me along the way, for helping with the kids when I was in the middle of a really important writing flow, for being my research buddy, and for even reading the spicy Jude excerpts out loud to make sure it sounded sexy to my readers. This past year was hard, but we did it! We made it through to the other side. Thank you for using your MMA experience and expertise to help bring Jude's character to life and choreograph the whole fight. Not only was it fun collaborating on this project with you, but it has made this book extra special. To remind ourselves later—I'm going to conquer this bitch!

To my parents, who show up to my author events as if you're still going to my soccer games. Sorry I write smutty books, but thank you for still liking my social media posts and reminding the grandparents to steer away. I love you both! Thank you for always encouraging my brother and I to "shoot for the moon," "have faith, everything always works out," and "attitude is everything."

To my friends I've kept for close to a lifetime and new friends I have met during this journey, thank you for cheering me on, listening when I need to vent, and always being ready to grab a glass of wine. Thank you for buying my books, even when you could read them for free. It means the world to me!

To my dearest friend and PA, Tabitha Bell, thank you for believing in me and this book. You've told me from the very beginning this is going to blow up, and I'm starting to believe you. I'm so thankful the universe brought us together. Not only have we become the best of friends, but you've done so much to help me. You've helped build my confidence as a writer, helped bring ATW to life, helped organize me and inspire me. Thank you for being my beta reader and being willing to jump in as an alpha reader for book two. Shit's about to get real, girl, and we're in for a wild ride! I wouldn't want to do it with anyone else. Thank you.

To my beta readers: Crystal Gascon, Alyssa Snyder, Brookelynn Pereira, Desza Dominguez, and Tabitha Bell. Thank you for all your invaluable feedback. Without your suggestions and revisions, I truly don't think I would have been able to breath life into Jude and Romy. They were feeling a little withered when they reached you, and I was feeling a little defeated. Your enthusiasm for the story fueled my fire and made me more determined than ever to get this book into the hands of readers.

To my editors, Kathy Burge and Joyce Mochrie, thank you for your detailed inspection of the plot, characters, dialogue, word choice, grammar, and punctuation. As you both know, authors can get so caught up in telling a story, they often miss a few details or *repeated* details. Without your expertise, there would be no polished version of *Among the Willows*. Thank you for always pushing me to become a better writer.

To my Honeybees Street Team, you are all incredible! Thank you for taking a chance on this baby indie author and falling in love with our cage-fighting cowboy before you even had a chance to read the book. Your excitement and zeal for the Thornbrush Ranch series has been incredible. If not for all of you, no one would have heard of this book. Thank you so much for promoting the hell out of it and getting it noticed all over social media. You are all hardworking and talented content creators. Thank you for believing in me and going on this adventure with me!

To my readers—simply, thank you for picking up this book. I hope it was everything you hoped it would be, and a whole lot more. I hope you fell in love with Jude and Romy just as much as I did while writing them. I am beyond grateful you were intrigued enough to buy my book. Without you, I'd never be able to reach my goals and follow my dream. Thank you for making all of that possible. I hope you stick around for more …

And finally, thank you to Jude and Romy. You helped me process some shit, get out some frustration, and soothe my soul during a tough year for our family. Thank you for taking me on your ride and reminding me to *love hard* and *fight* for the things that truly matter.

About The Author

June Lark is a romance author of steamy bygone and contemporary small town love stories filled with tension and suspense, with strong heroines who save themselves and brooding heroes who fall first. After years of research and a career in teaching social studies, she is finally living her childhood dream.

She lives outside of Portland, Oregon with her husband, Kenny, two kids, K.C. and Skye Lynn, and their lovey-dovey Norwegian elkhound, Baldur. She loves spending time with her family, cooking, exploring the Pacific Northwest, retail therapy, and devouring romance novels. With a coconut milk latte in hand, you can find June Lark researching and writing in her office/kids' craft room.

www.ingramcontent.com/pod-product-compliance
Lightning Source LLC
Chambersburg PA
CBHW020414030726
47495CB00006B/1505